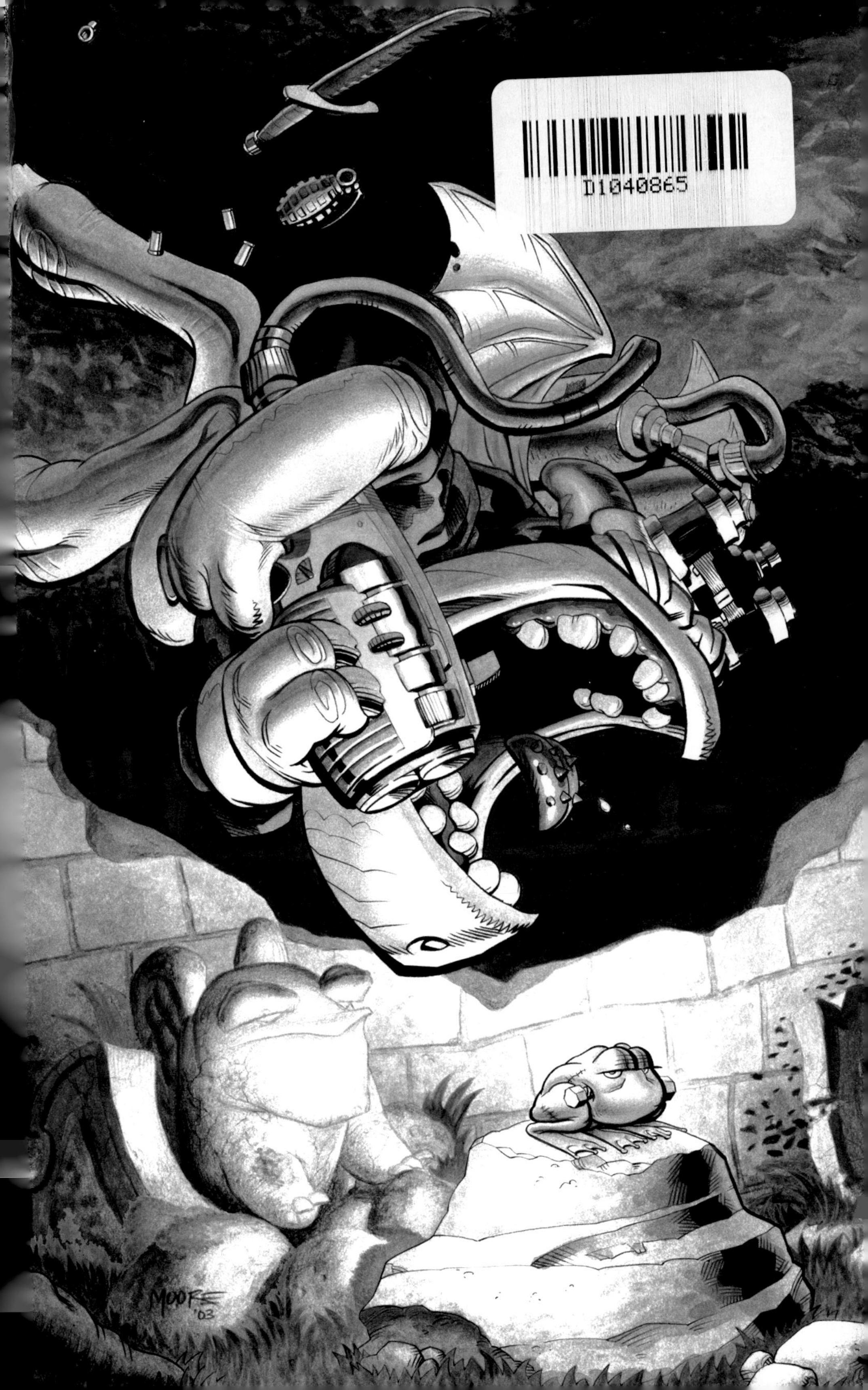
MOORE
'03

ISBN 10: 1-56163-528-6
ISBN 13: 978-1-56163-528-3
© 2003, 2004 Richard Moore
Printed in China

5    4    3    2

# BONEYARD

## VOLUME FOUR
## RICHARD MOORE

Colors by Digikore

NANTIER · BEALL · MINOUSTCHINE
Publishing inc.
new york

# SUMMARY

Michael Paris has inherited a nightmare: a cemetery filled with monsters, one of them the fetching vampiress Abbey, a whom he befriends. And as we learned in the first story arc, the real danger was not the monsters, but the fear and prejudice of the regular townsfolk. Mayor Wormwood--ultimately revealed to be the Devil himself--failed to oust Paris and the Boneyard folk from the cemetery, however, and Paris now finds himself facing an even greater evil: the I.R.S.

Sweet Roxanne, who supposedly tried to help Paris out of his debts, turns out to be the mother of all vampires and beats the holy (?) crap out of Abbey. Only a last minute intervention by Ralph with Michael's ill-fated car saves her from sure annihilation. Can Abbey recover?

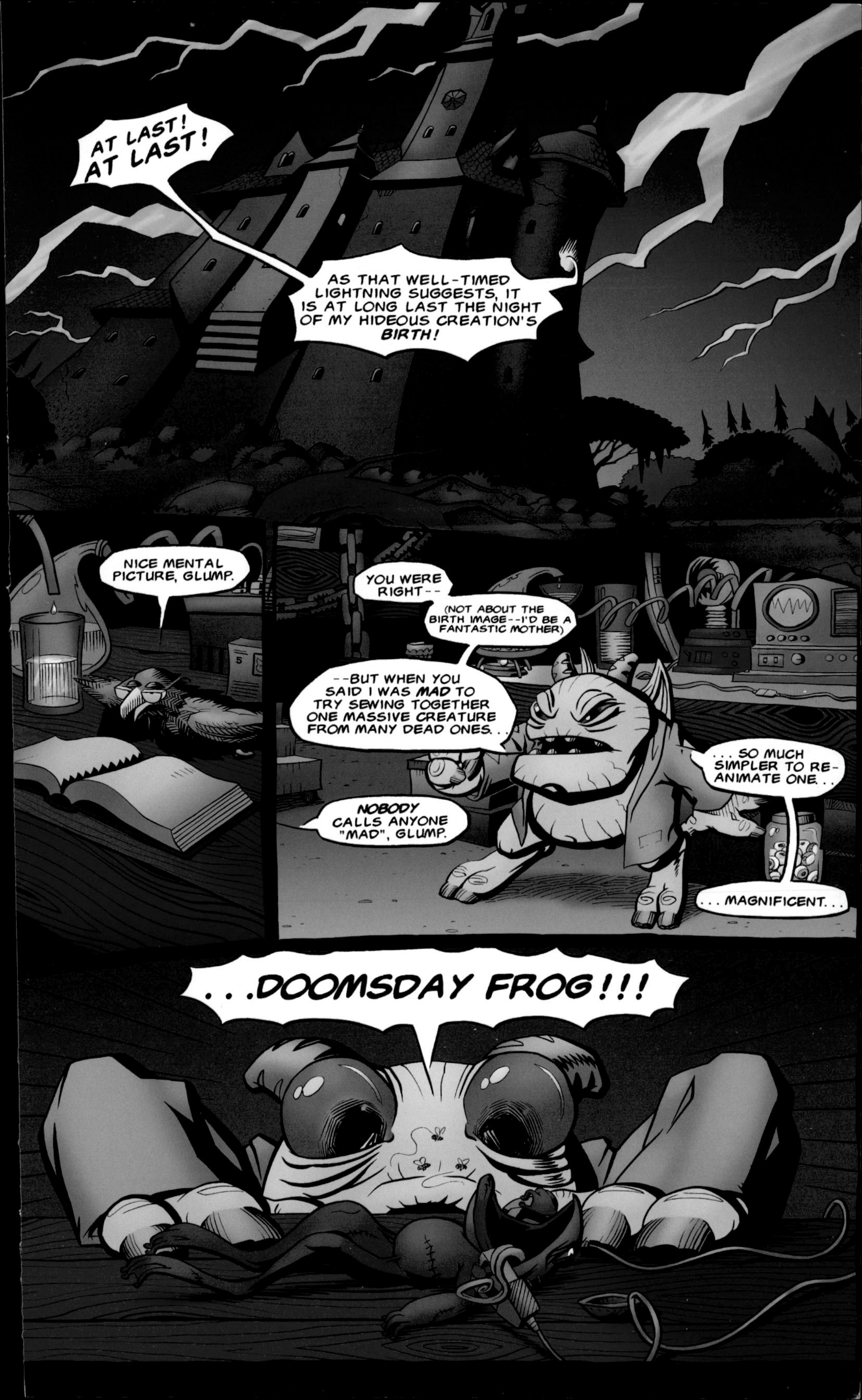
AT LAST! AT LAST!
AS THAT WELL-TIMED LIGHTNING SUGGESTS, IT IS AT LONG LAST THE NIGHT OF MY HIDEOUS CREATION'S *BIRTH!*
NICE MENTAL PICTURE, GLUMP.
YOU WERE RIGHT--
(NOT ABOUT THE BIRTH IMAGE--I'D BE A FANTASTIC MOTHER)
--BUT WHEN YOU SAID I WAS *MAD* TO TRY SEWING TOGETHER ONE MASSIVE CREATURE FROM MANY DEAD ONES...
*NOBODY* CALLS ANYONE "MAD", GLUMP.
...SO MUCH SIMPLER TO RE-ANIMATE ONE...
...MAGNIFICENT...
...DOOMSDAY FROG!!!

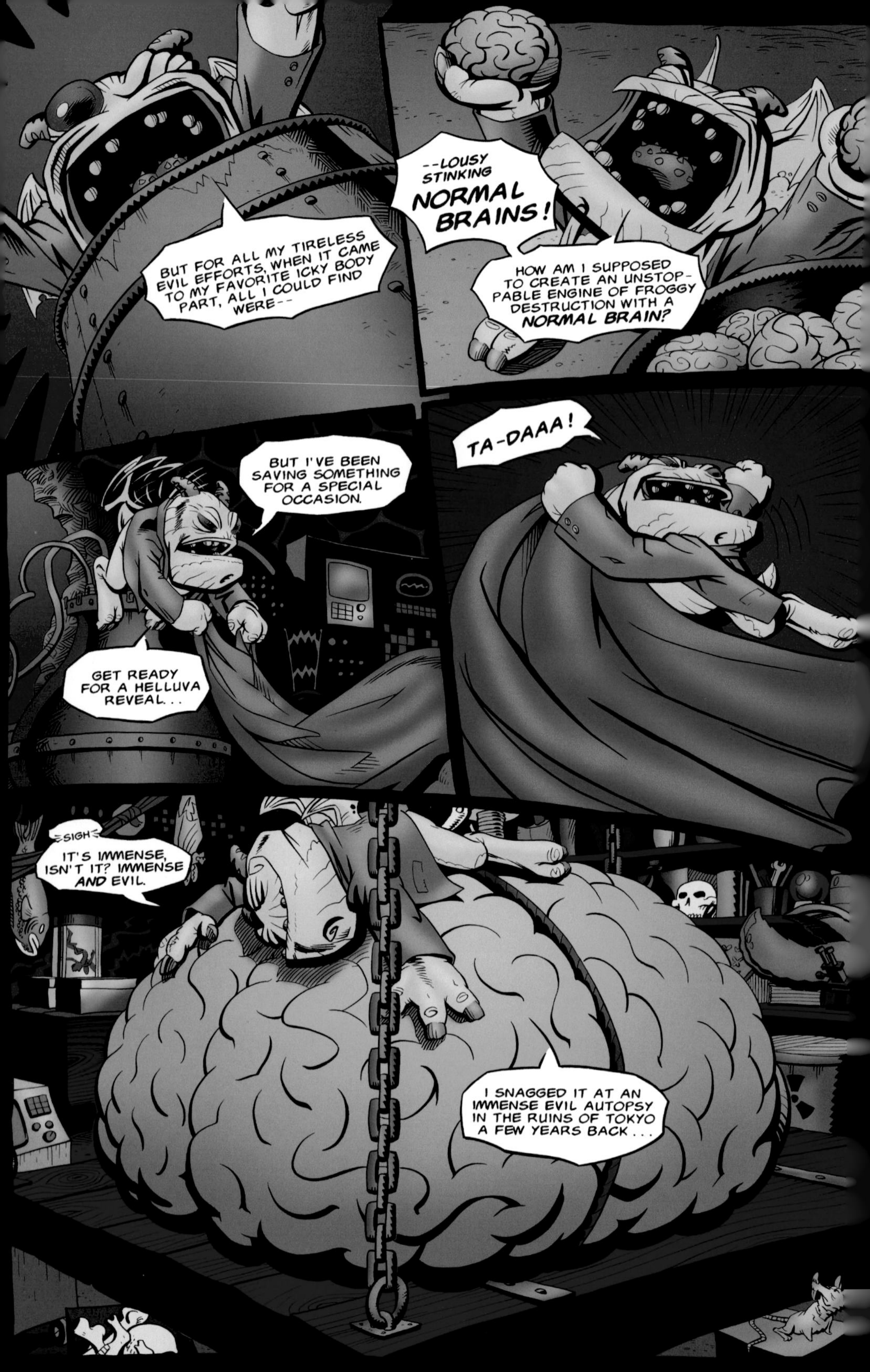
BUT FOR ALL MY TIRELESS EVIL EFFORTS, WHEN IT CAME TO MY FAVORITE ICKY BODY PART, ALL I COULD FIND WERE--
--LOUSY STINKING NORMAL BRAINS!
HOW AM I SUPPOSED TO CREATE AN UNSTOP-PABLE ENGINE OF FROGGY DESTRUCTION WITH A NORMAL BRAIN?
BUT I'VE BEEN SAVING SOMETHING FOR A SPECIAL OCCASION.
GET READY FOR A HELLUVA REVEAL...
TA-DAAA!
SIGH
IT'S IMMENSE, ISN'T IT? IMMENSE AND EVIL.
I SNAGGED IT AT AN IMMENSE EVIL AUTOPSY IN THE RUINS OF TOKYO A FEW YEARS BACK...

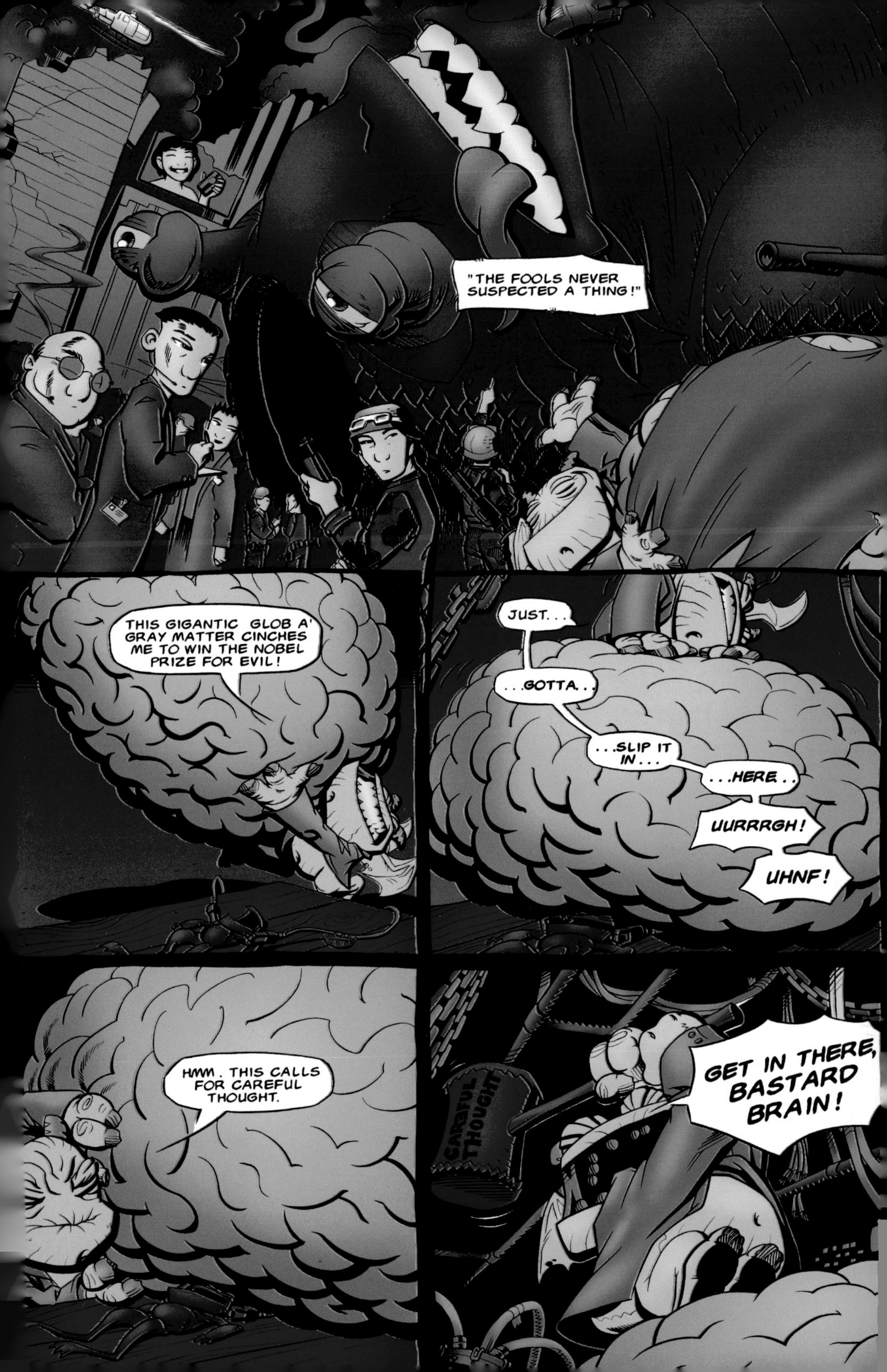
"THE FOOLS NEVER SUSPECTED A THING!"
THIS GIGANTIC GLOB A' GRAY MATTER CINCHES ME TO WIN THE NOBEL PRIZE FOR EVIL!
JUST...
...GOTTA...
...SLIP IT IN...
...HERE..
UURRRGH!
UHNF!
HMM. THIS CALLS FOR CAREFUL THOUGHT.
CAREFUL THOUGHT
GET IN THERE, BASTARD BRAIN!

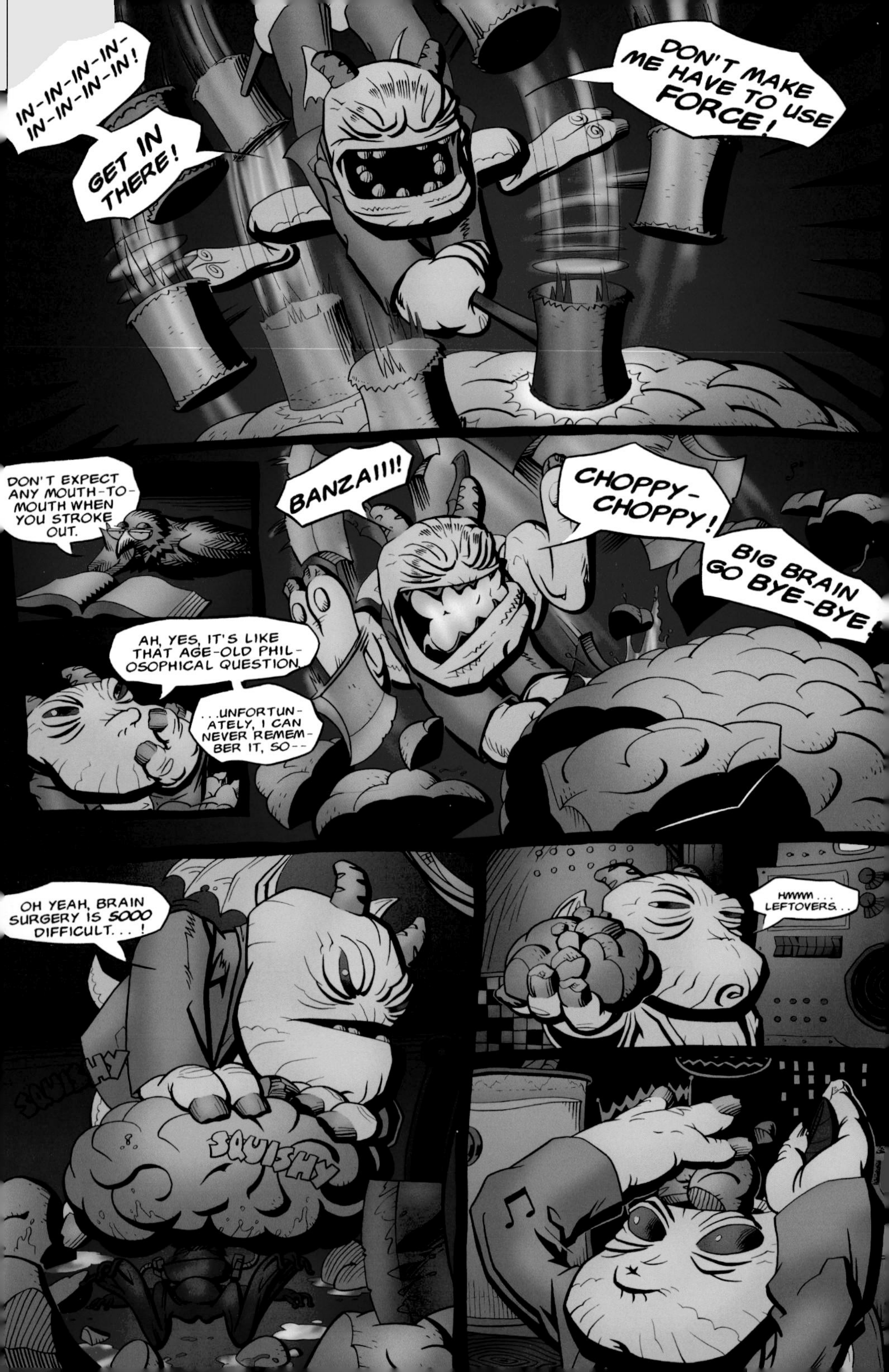
IN-IN-IN-IN-IN-IN-IN-IN!
GET IN THERE!
DON'T MAKE ME HAVE TO USE FORCE!
DON'T EXPECT ANY MOUTH-TO-MOUTH WHEN YOU STROKE OUT.
BANZAIIII!
CHOPPY-CHOPPY!
BIG BRAIN GO BYE-BYE!
AH, YES, IT'S LIKE THAT AGE-OLD PHILOSOPHICAL QUESTION.
...UNFORTUNATELY, I CAN NEVER REMEMBER IT, SO--
OH YEAH, BRAIN SURGERY IS SOOO DIFFICULT...!
SQUISHY
SQUISHY
HMMM... LEFTOVERS...

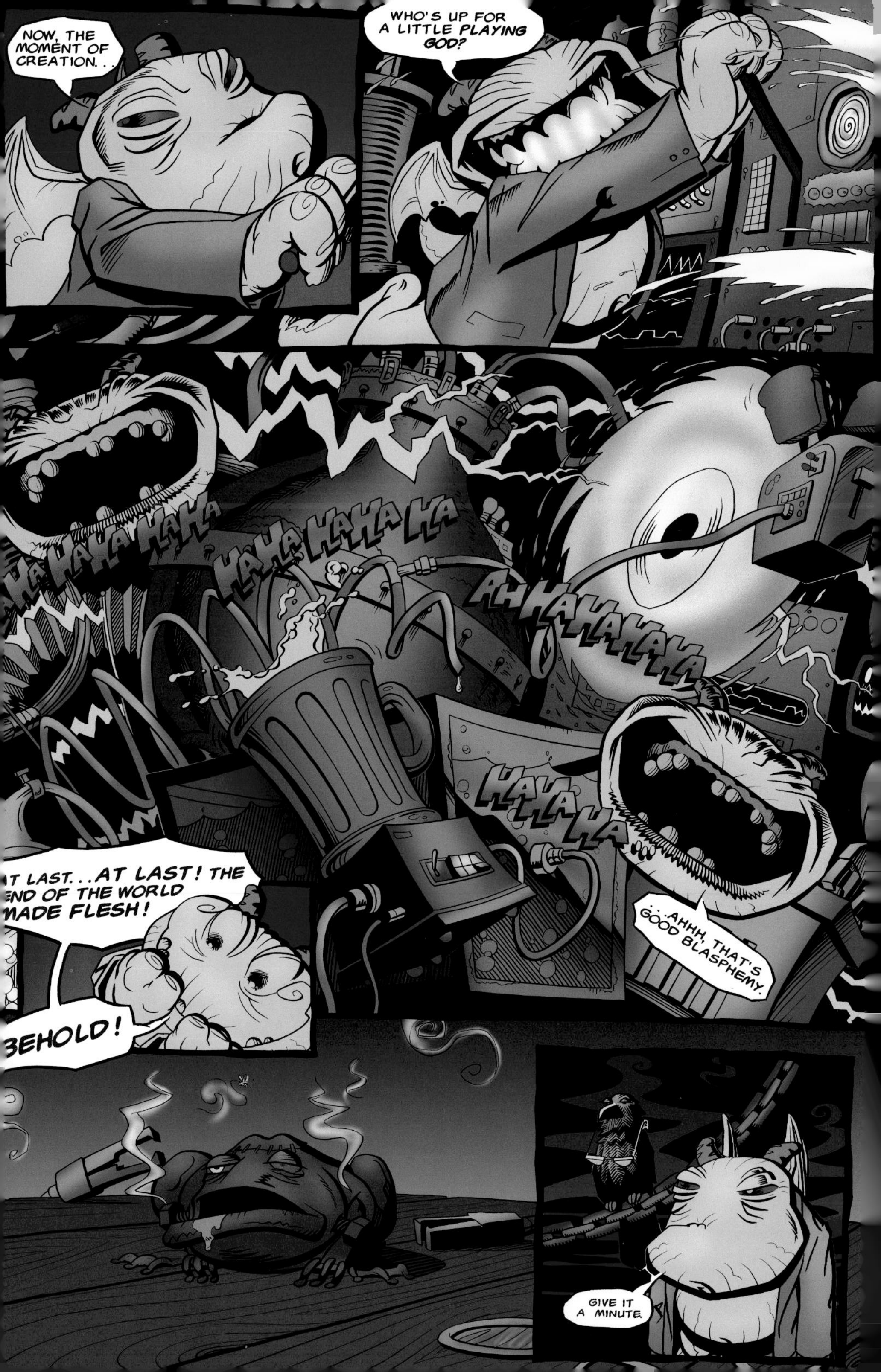

NOW, THE MOMENT OF CREATION. . .
WHO'S UP FOR A LITTLE PLAYING GOD?
HAHAHAHAHA
HAHAHAHAHAKA
AHHAHAHAHAHAHAHA
HAHAHAHA
...AT LAST...AT LAST! THE END OF THE WORLD MADE FLESH!
BEHOLD!
...AHHH, THAT'S GOOD BLASPHEMY.
GIVE IT A MINUTE.

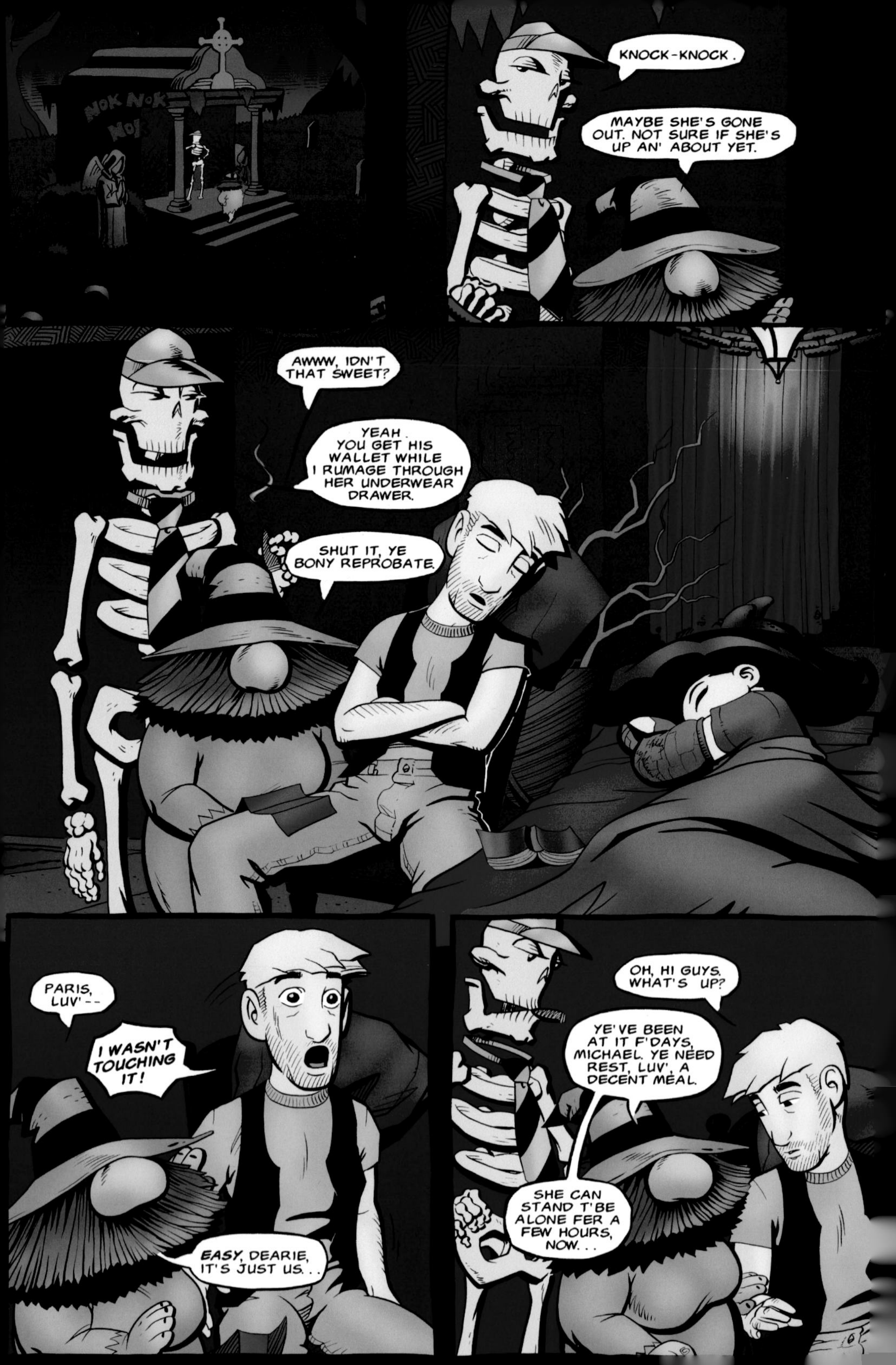
NOK NOK NOK
KNOCK-KNOCK.
MAYBE SHE'S GONE OUT. NOT SURE IF SHE'S UP AN' ABOUT YET.
AWWW, IDN'T THAT SWEET?
YEAH. YOU GET HIS WALLET WHILE I RUMAGE THROUGH HER UNDERWEAR DRAWER.
SHUT IT, YE BONY REPROBATE.
PARIS, LUV'--
I WASN'T TOUCHING IT!
EASY, DEARIE, IT'S JUST US...
OH, HI GUYS. WHAT'S UP?
YE'VE BEEN AT IT F'DAYS, MICHAEL. YE NEED REST, LUV', A DECENT MEAL.
SHE CAN STAND T'BE ALONE FER A FEW HOURS, NOW...

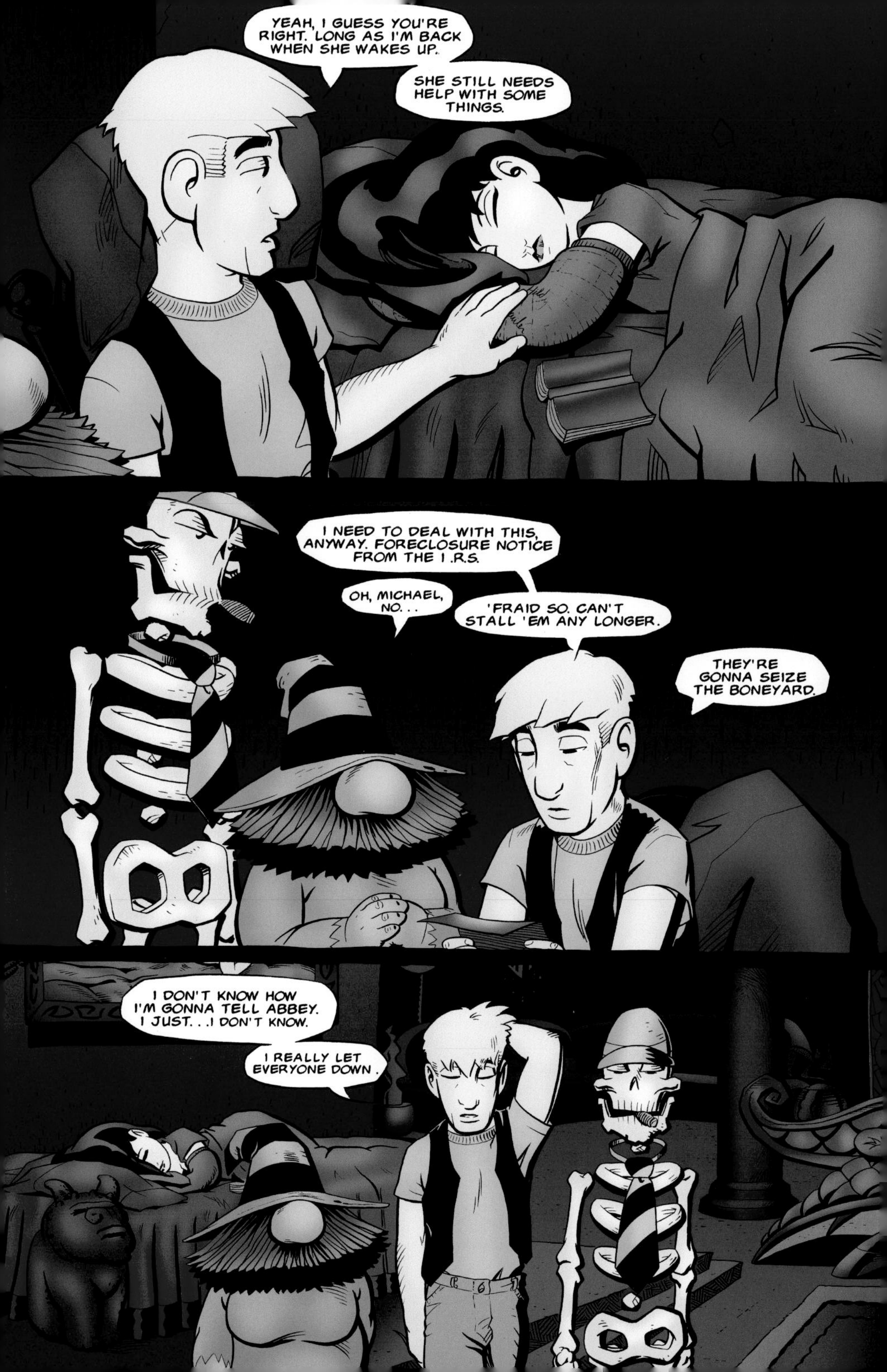
YEAH, I GUESS YOU'RE RIGHT. LONG AS I'M BACK WHEN SHE WAKES UP.
SHE STILL NEEDS HELP WITH SOME THINGS.
I NEED TO DEAL WITH THIS, ANYWAY. FORECLOSURE NOTICE FROM THE I.R.S.
OH, MICHAEL, NO...
'FRAID SO. CAN'T STALL 'EM ANY LONGER.
THEY'RE GONNA SEIZE THE BONEYARD.
I DON'T KNOW HOW I'M GONNA TELL ABBEY. I JUST...I DON'T KNOW.
I REALLY LET EVERYONE DOWN.

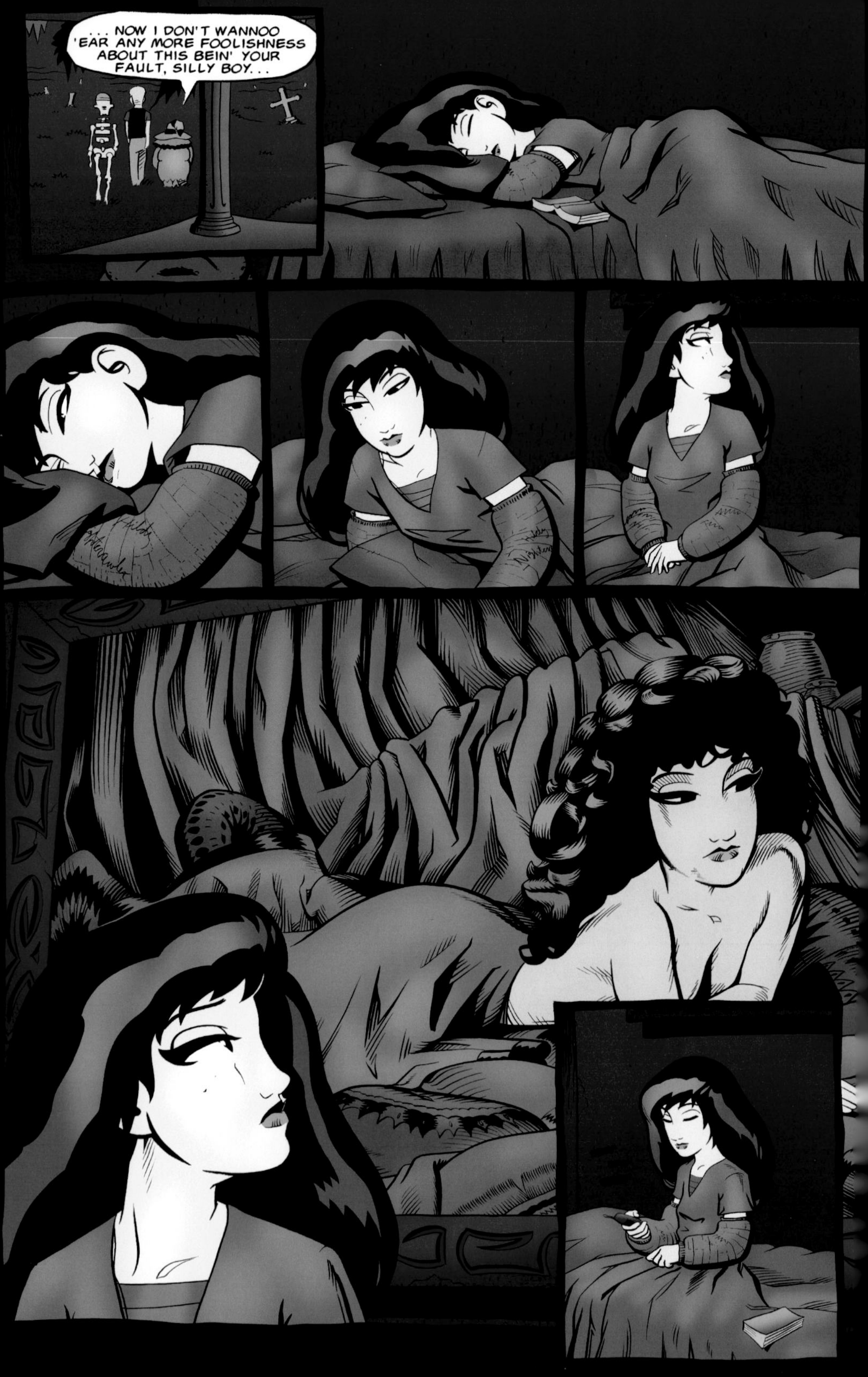

. . . NOW I DON'T WANNOO 'EAR ANY MORE FOOLISHNESS ABOUT THIS BEIN' YOUR FAULT, SILLY BOY. . .

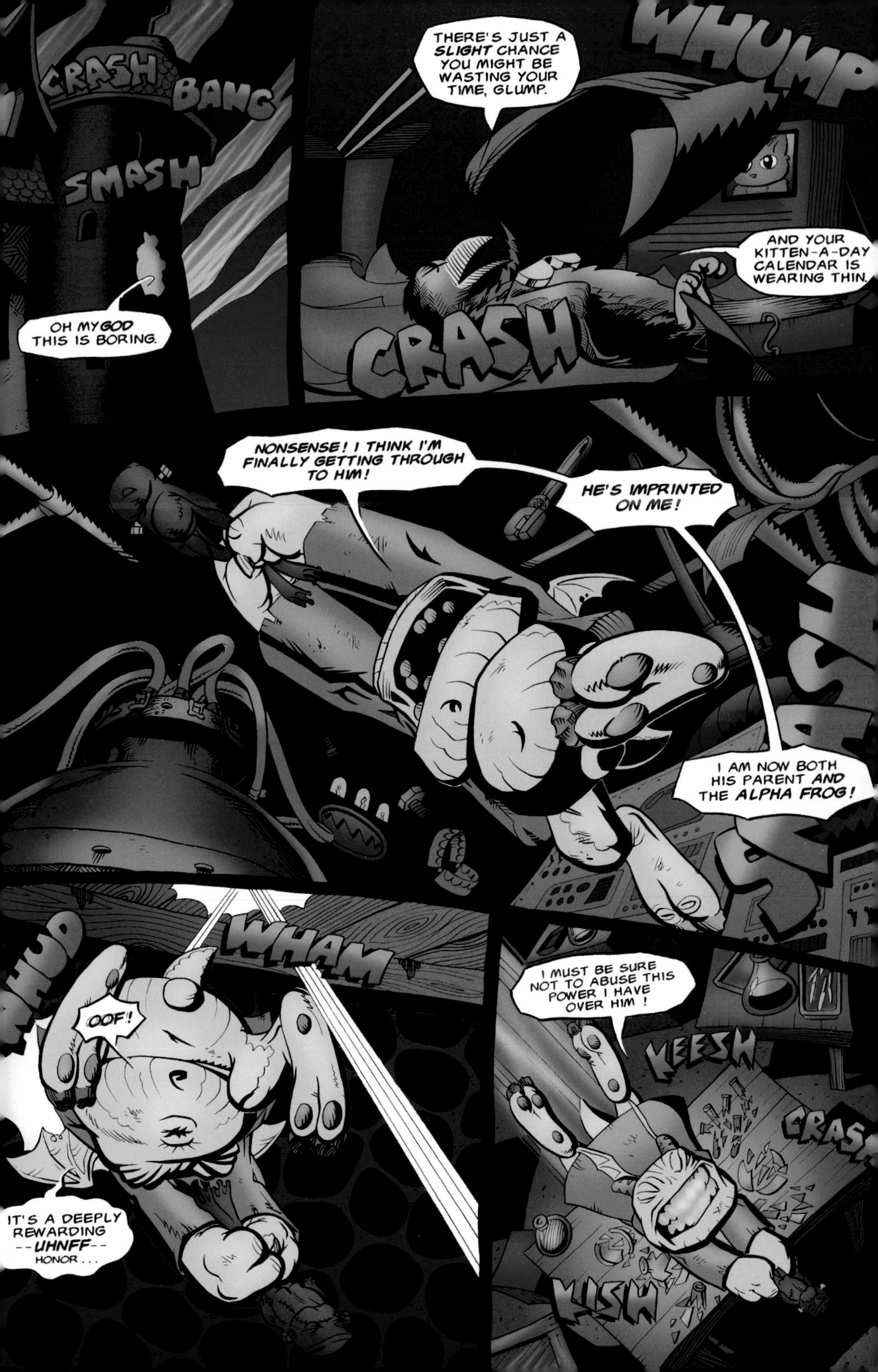

CRASH
BANG
SMASH
OH MY GOD THIS IS BORING.
THERE'S JUST A SLIGHT CHANCE YOU MIGHT BE WASTING YOUR TIME, GLUMP.
WHUMP
AND YOUR KITTEN-A-DAY CALENDAR IS WEARING THIN.
CRASH
NONSENSE! I THINK I'M FINALLY GETTING THROUGH TO HIM!
HE'S IMPRINTED ON ME!
I AM NOW BOTH HIS PARENT AND THE ALPHA FROG!
WHAM
OOF!
IT'S A DEEPLY REWARDING --UHNFF-- HONOR...
I MUST BE SURE NOT TO ABUSE THIS POWER I HAVE OVER HIM !
KEESH

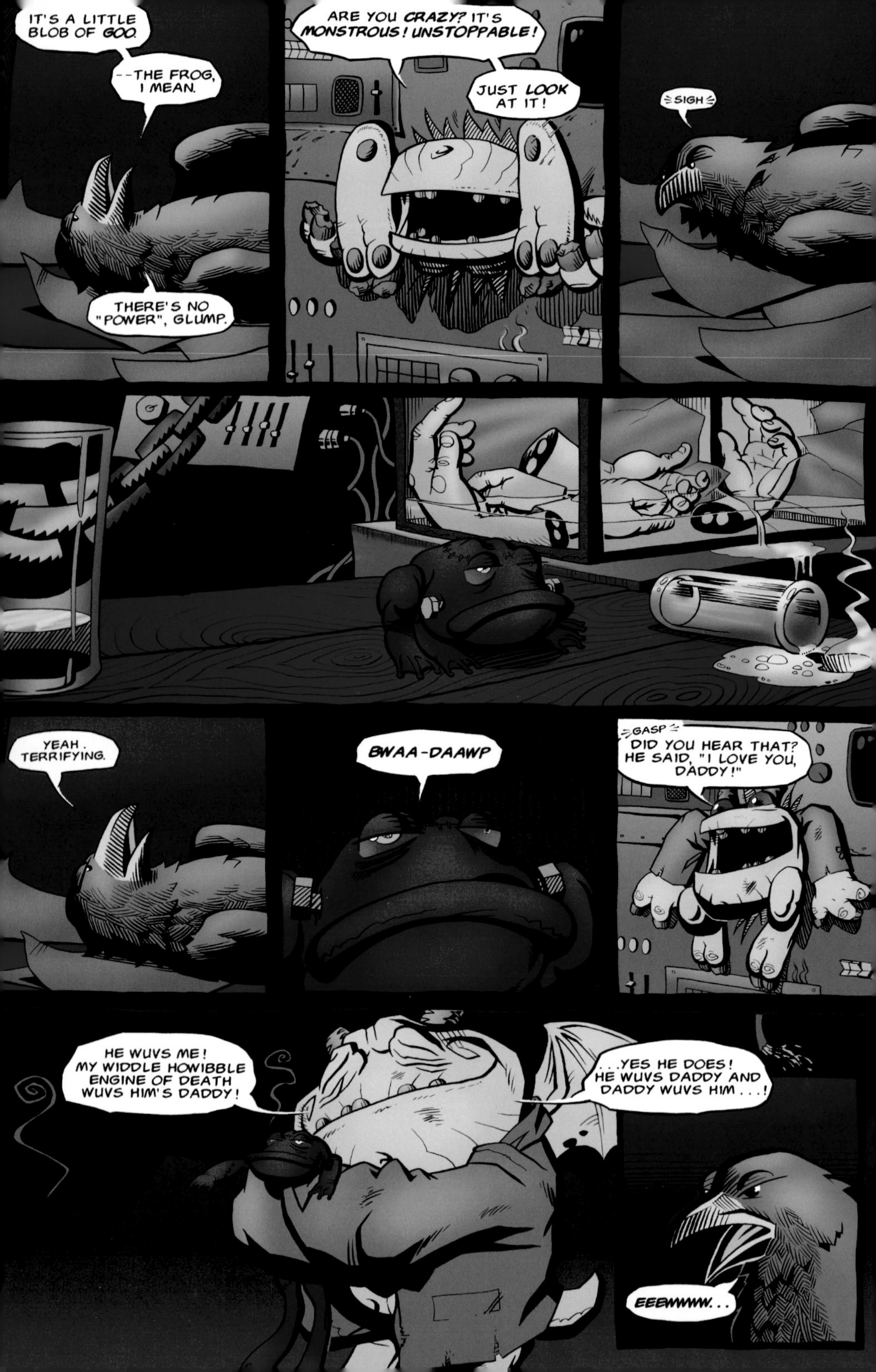
IT'S A LITTLE BLOB OF GOO.
--THE FROG, I MEAN.
THERE'S NO "POWER", GLUMP.
ARE YOU CRAZY? IT'S MONSTROUS! UNSTOPPABLE!
JUST LOOK AT IT!
SIGH
YEAH. TERRIFYING.
BWAA-DAAWP
GASP
DID YOU HEAR THAT? HE SAID, "I LOVE YOU, DADDY!"
HE WUVS ME! MY WIDDLE HOWIBBLE ENGINE OF DEATH WUVS HIM'S DADDY!
...YES HE DOES! HE WUVS DADDY AND DADDY WUVS HIM...!
EEEWWWW...

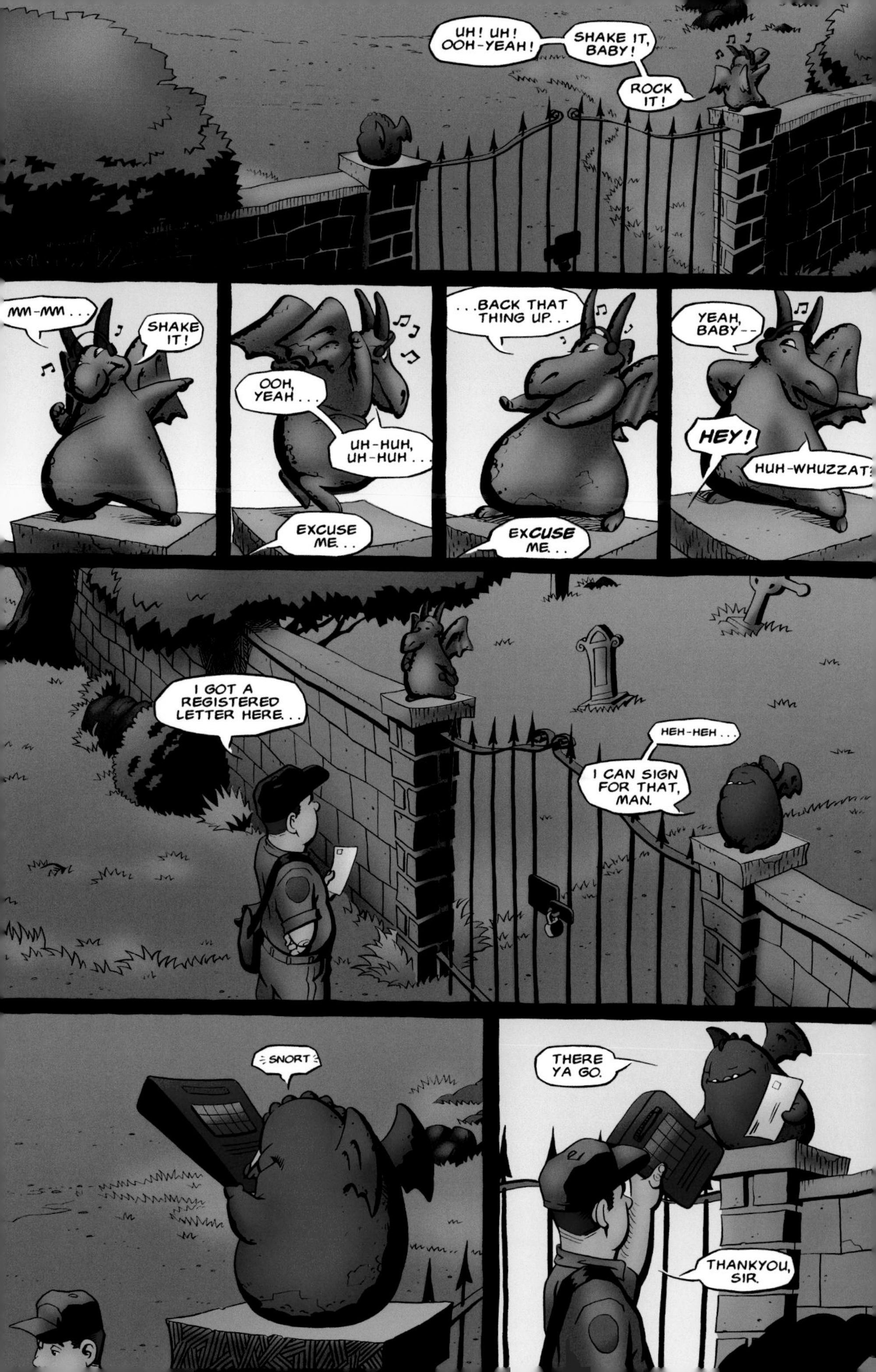
UH! UH! OOH-YEAH!
SHAKE IT, BABY!
ROCK IT!
MM-MM . . .
SHAKE IT!
OOH, YEAH . . .
UH-HUH, UH-HUH . . .
EXCUSE ME. . .
. . .BACK THAT THING UP. . .
EXCUSE ME. . .
YEAH, BABY--
HEY!
HUH-WHUZZAT?
I GOT A REGISTERED LETTER HERE. . .
HEH-HEH . . .
I CAN SIGN FOR THAT, MAN.
SNORT
THERE YA GO.
THANKYOU, SIR.

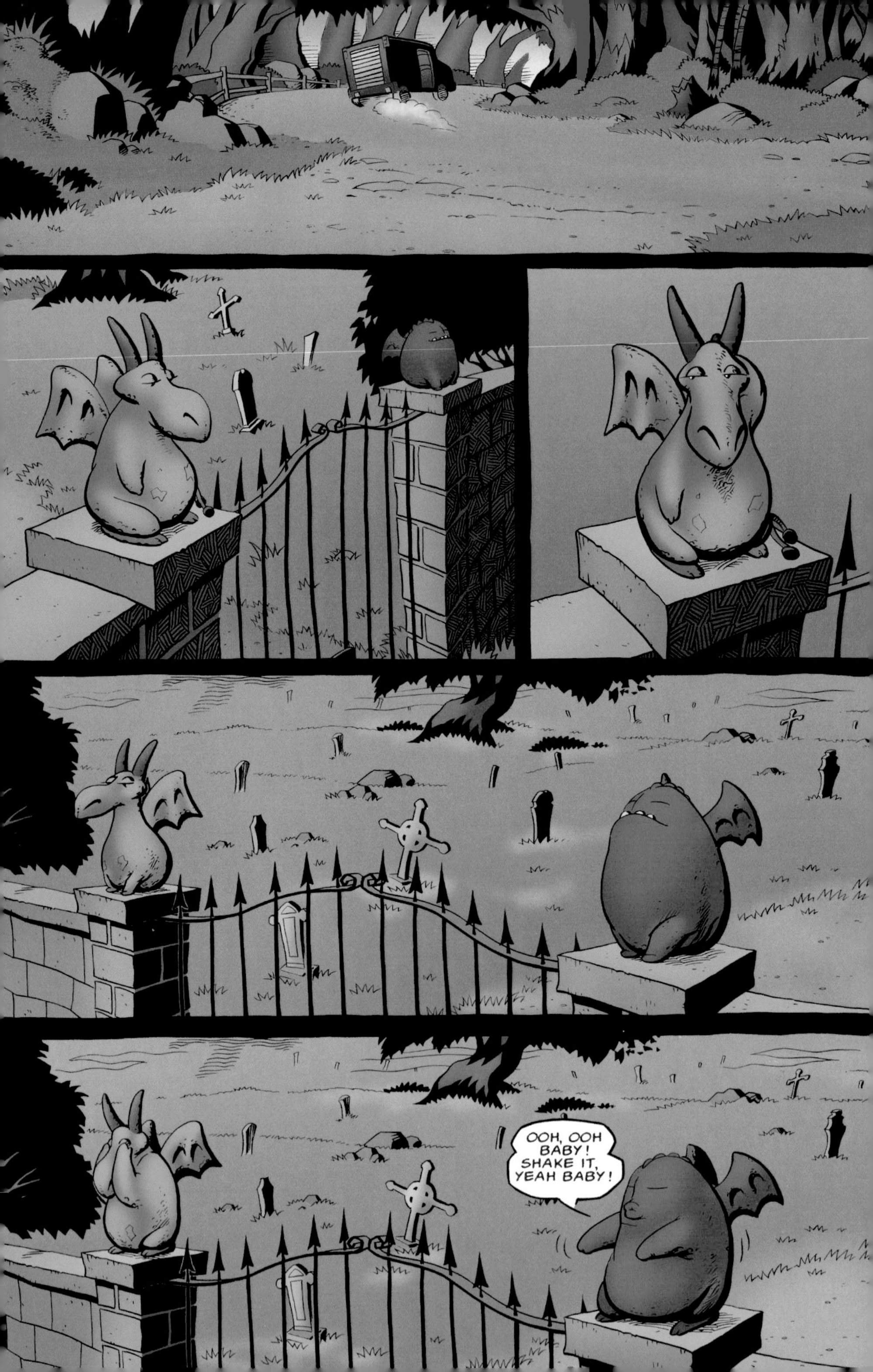
OOH, OOH BABY! SHAKE IT, YEAH BABY!

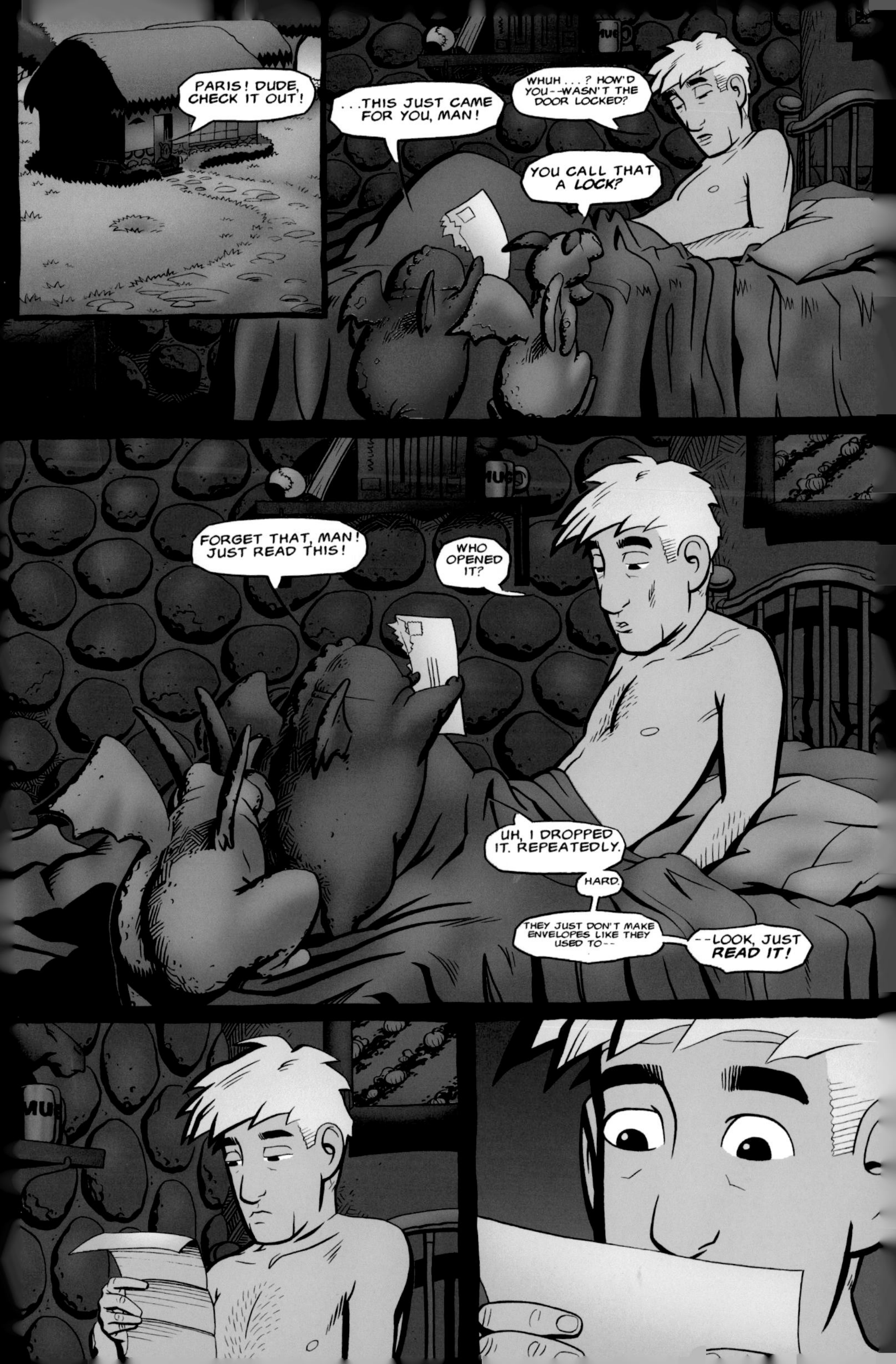
PARIS! DUDE, CHECK IT OUT!
...THIS JUST CAME FOR YOU, MAN!
WHUH...? HOW'D YOU--WASN'T THE DOOR LOCKED?
YOU CALL THAT A LOCK?
MUG
FORGET THAT, MAN! JUST READ THIS!
WHO OPENED IT?
MUG
UH, I DROPPED IT. REPEATEDLY.
HARD.
THEY JUST DON'T MAKE ENVELOPES LIKE THEY USED TO--
--LOOK, JUST READ IT!
MUG

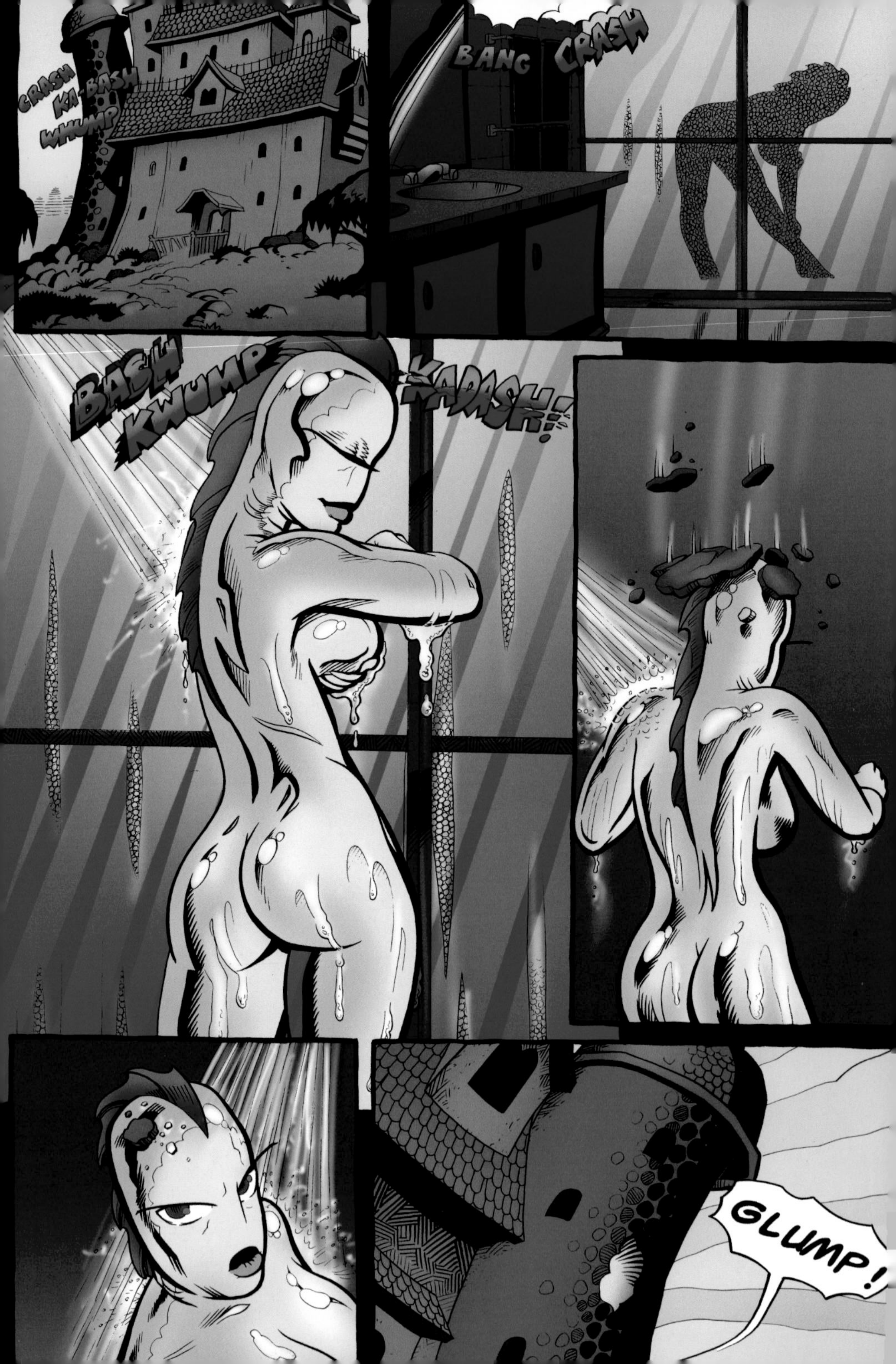
CRASH
KA-BASH
WHUMP
BANG
CRASH
BASH
KWUMP
KADASH!!
GLUMP!

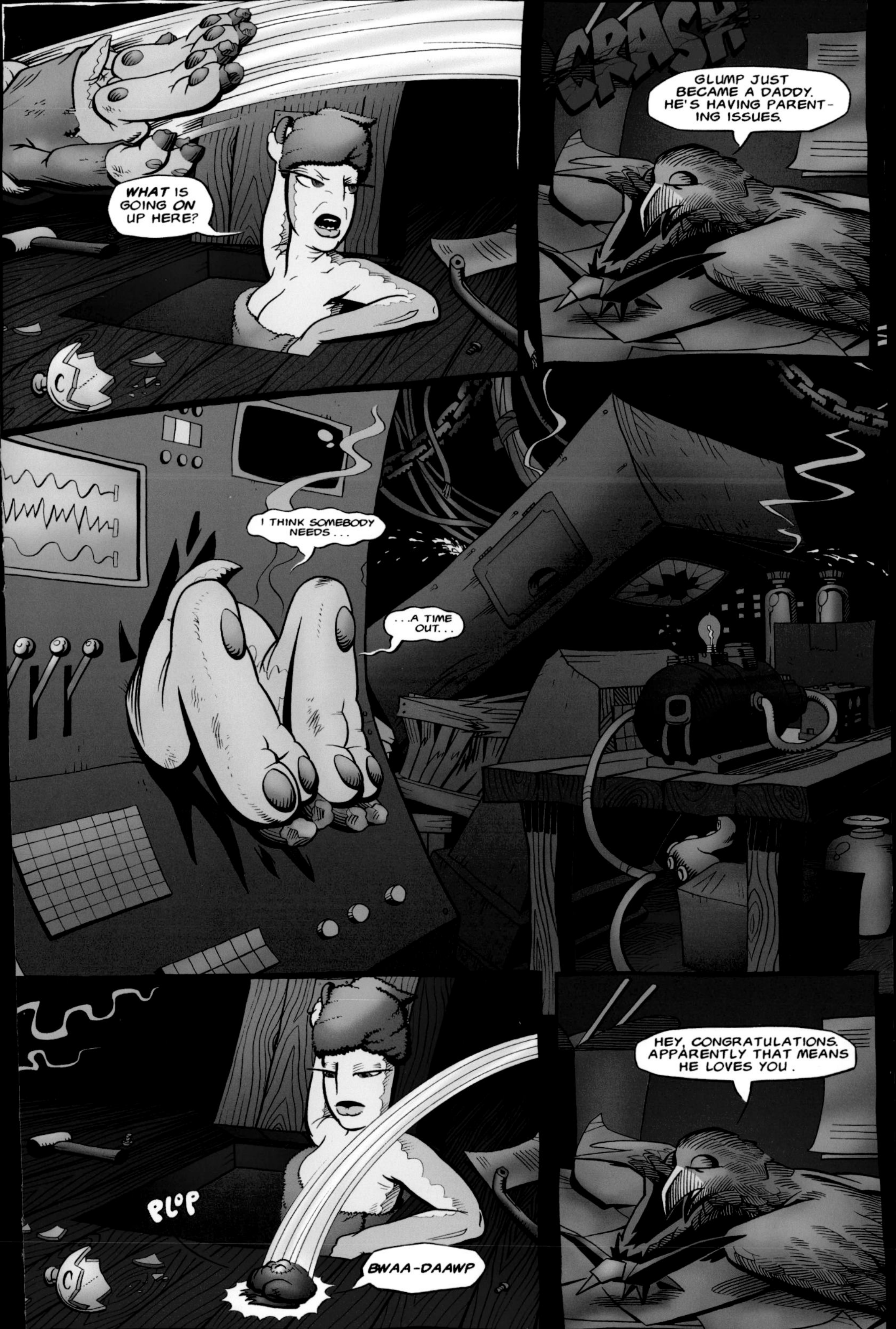
WHAT IS GOING ON UP HERE?
CRASH!
GLUMP JUST BECAME A DADDY. HE'S HAVING PARENT-ING ISSUES.
I THINK SOMEBODY NEEDS . . .
. . . A TIME OUT. . .
PLOP
BWAA-DAAWP
HEY, CONGRATULATIONS. APPARENTLY THAT MEANS HE LOVES YOU .

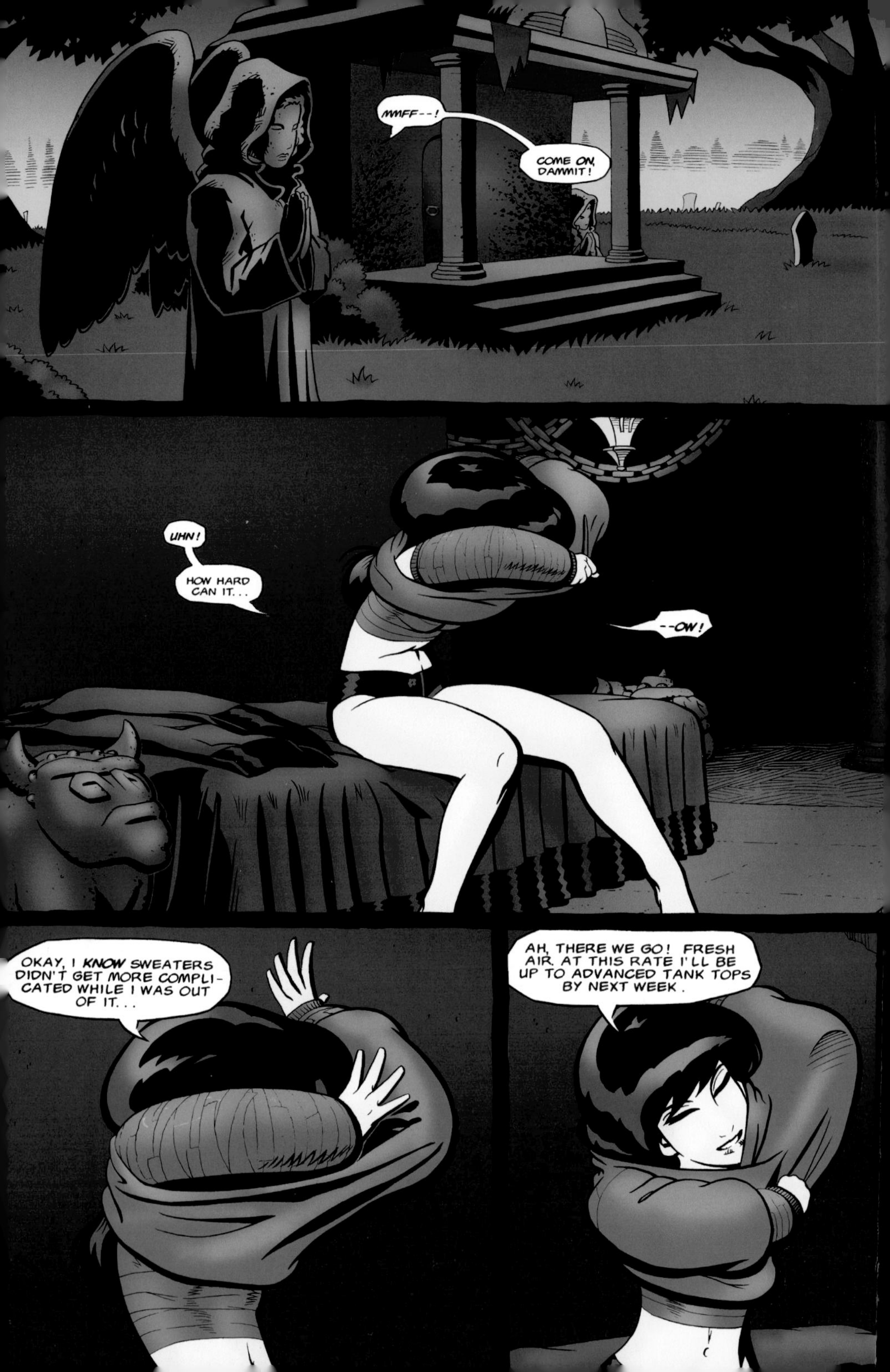
MMFF--!
COME ON, DAMMIT!
UHN!
HOW HARD CAN IT...
--OW!
OKAY, I KNOW SWEATERS DIDN'T GET MORE COMPLICATED WHILE I WAS OUT OF IT...
AH, THERE WE GO! FRESH AIR. AT THIS RATE I'LL BE UP TO ADVANCED TANK TOPS BY NEXT WEEK.

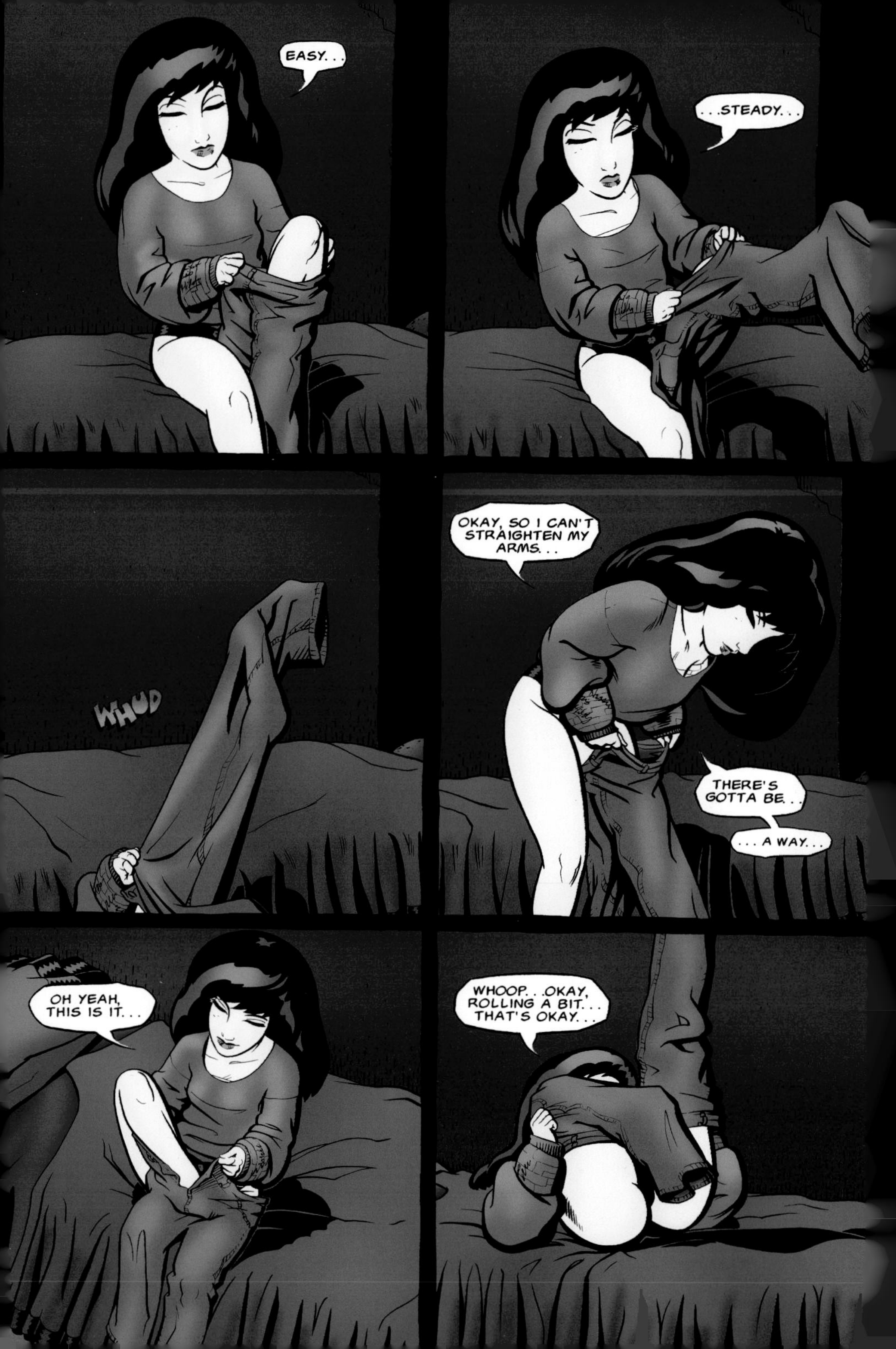
EASY. . .
. . .STEADY. . .
WHUD
OKAY, SO I CAN'T STRAIGHTEN MY ARMS. . .
THERE'S GOTTA BE. . .
. . . A WAY. . .
OH YEAH, THIS IS IT. . .
WHOOP. . .OKAY, ROLLING A BIT. . . THAT'S OKAY. . .

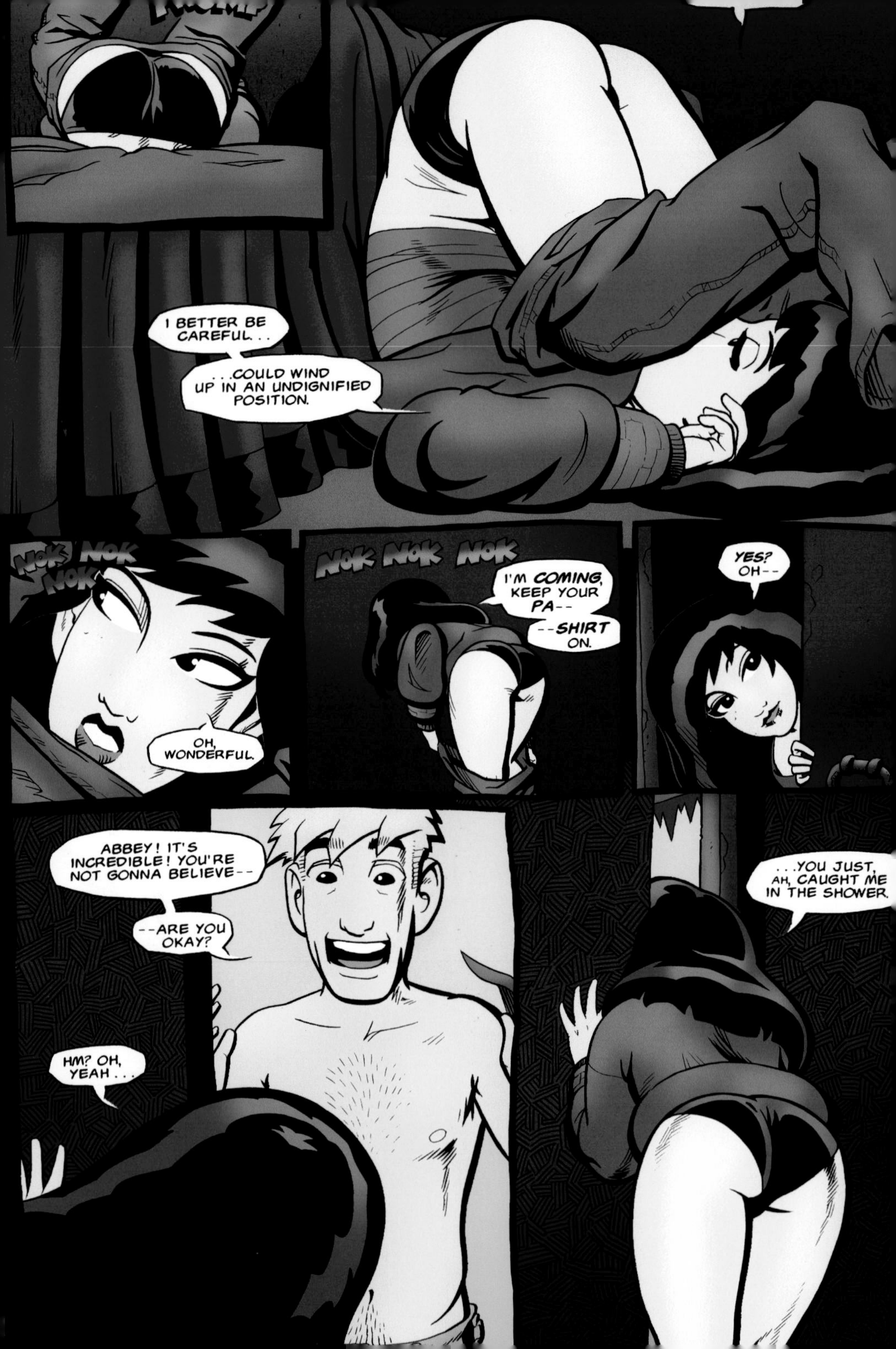
I BETTER BE CAREFUL. . .
. . .COULD WIND UP IN AN UNDIGNIFIED POSITION.
NOK NOK NOK
OH, WONDERFUL.
NOK NOK NOK
I'M COMING, KEEP YOUR PA--
--SHIRT ON.
YES? OH--
ABBEY! IT'S INCREDIBLE! YOU'RE NOT GONNA BELIEVE--
--ARE YOU OKAY?
HM? OH, YEAH . . .
. . .YOU JUST, AH, CAUGHT ME IN THE SHOWER.

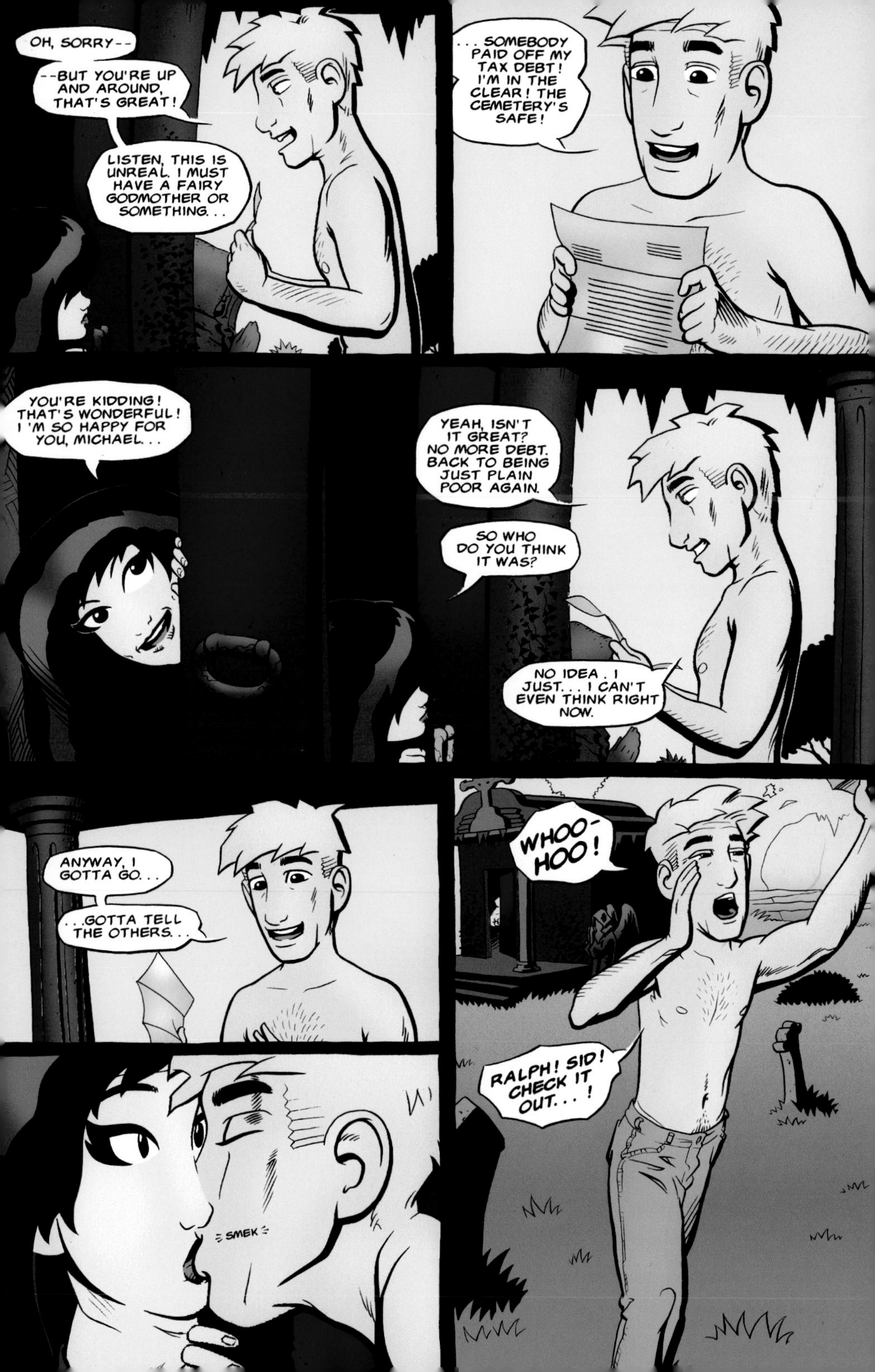
OH, SORRY--
--BUT YOU'RE UP AND AROUND, THAT'S GREAT!
LISTEN, THIS IS UNREAL. I MUST HAVE A FAIRY GODMOTHER OR SOMETHING...
...SOMEBODY PAID OFF MY TAX DEBT! I'M IN THE CLEAR! THE CEMETERY'S SAFE!
YOU'RE KIDDING! THAT'S WONDERFUL! I'M SO HAPPY FOR YOU, MICHAEL...
YEAH, ISN'T IT GREAT? NO MORE DEBT. BACK TO BEING JUST PLAIN POOR AGAIN.
SO WHO DO YOU THINK IT WAS?
NO IDEA. I JUST... I CAN'T EVEN THINK RIGHT NOW.
ANYWAY, I GOTTA GO...
...GOTTA TELL THE OTHERS...
SMEK
WHOO-HOO!
RALPH! SID! CHECK IT OUT...!

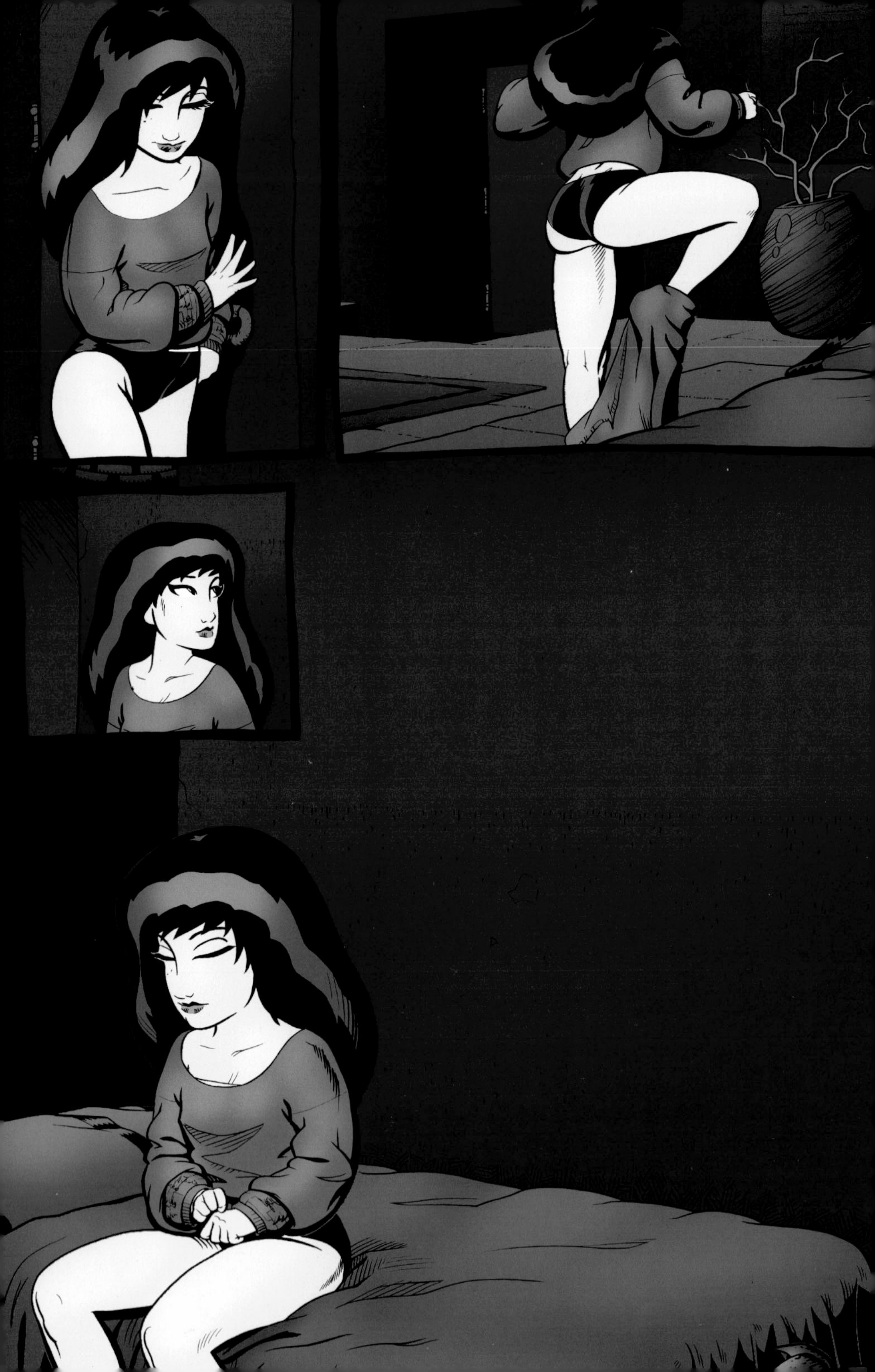

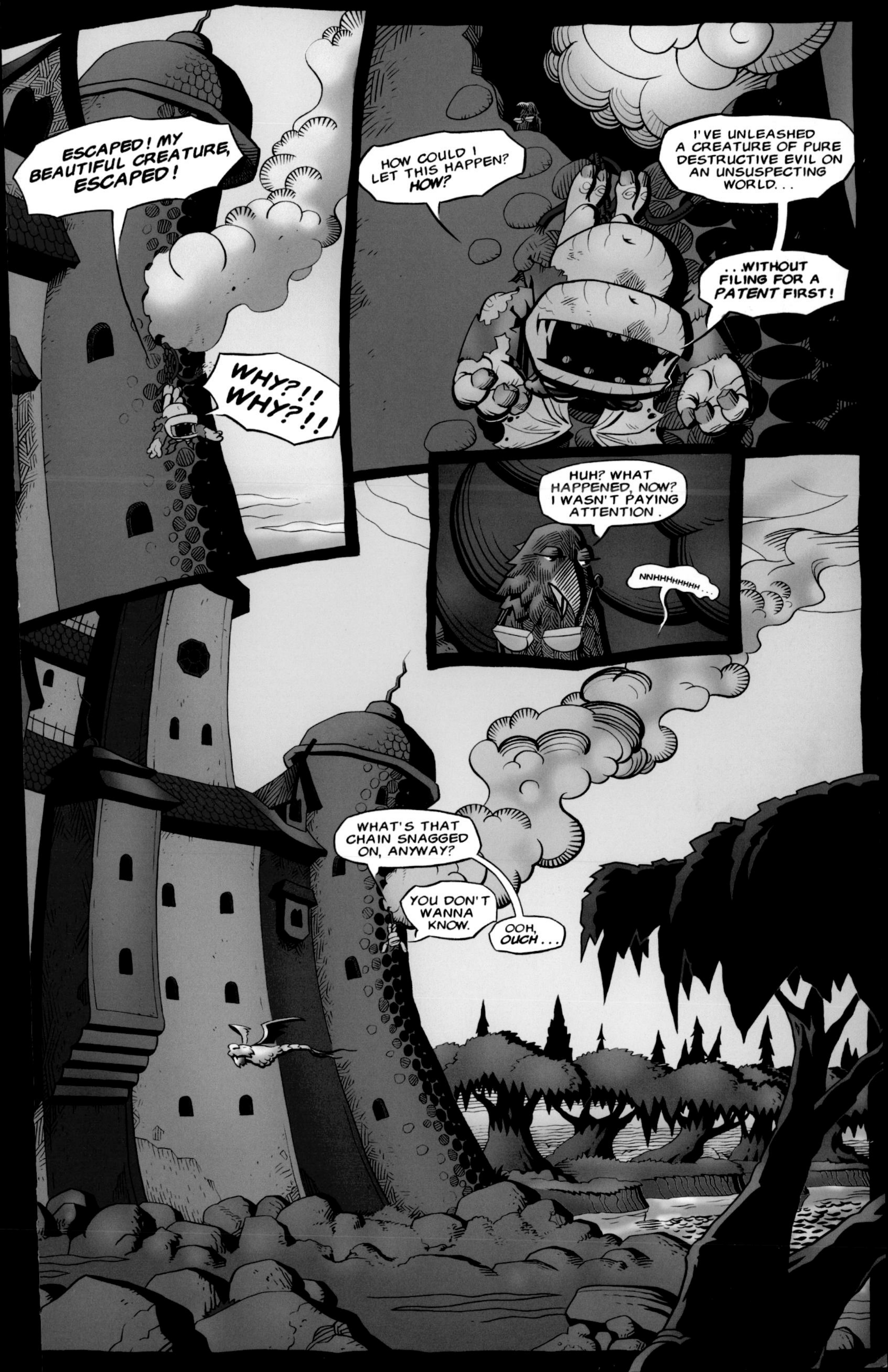
ESCAPED! MY BEAUTIFUL CREATURE, ESCAPED!
WHY?!! WHY?!!
HOW COULD I LET THIS HAPPEN? HOW?
I'VE UNLEASHED A CREATURE OF PURE DESTRUCTIVE EVIL ON AN UNSUSPECTING WORLD...
...WITHOUT FILING FOR A PATENT FIRST!
HUH? WHAT HAPPENED, NOW? I WASN'T PAYING ATTENTION.
NNHHHHHHHH...
WHAT'S THAT CHAIN SNAGGED ON, ANYWAY?
YOU DON'T WANNA KNOW.
OOH, OUCH...

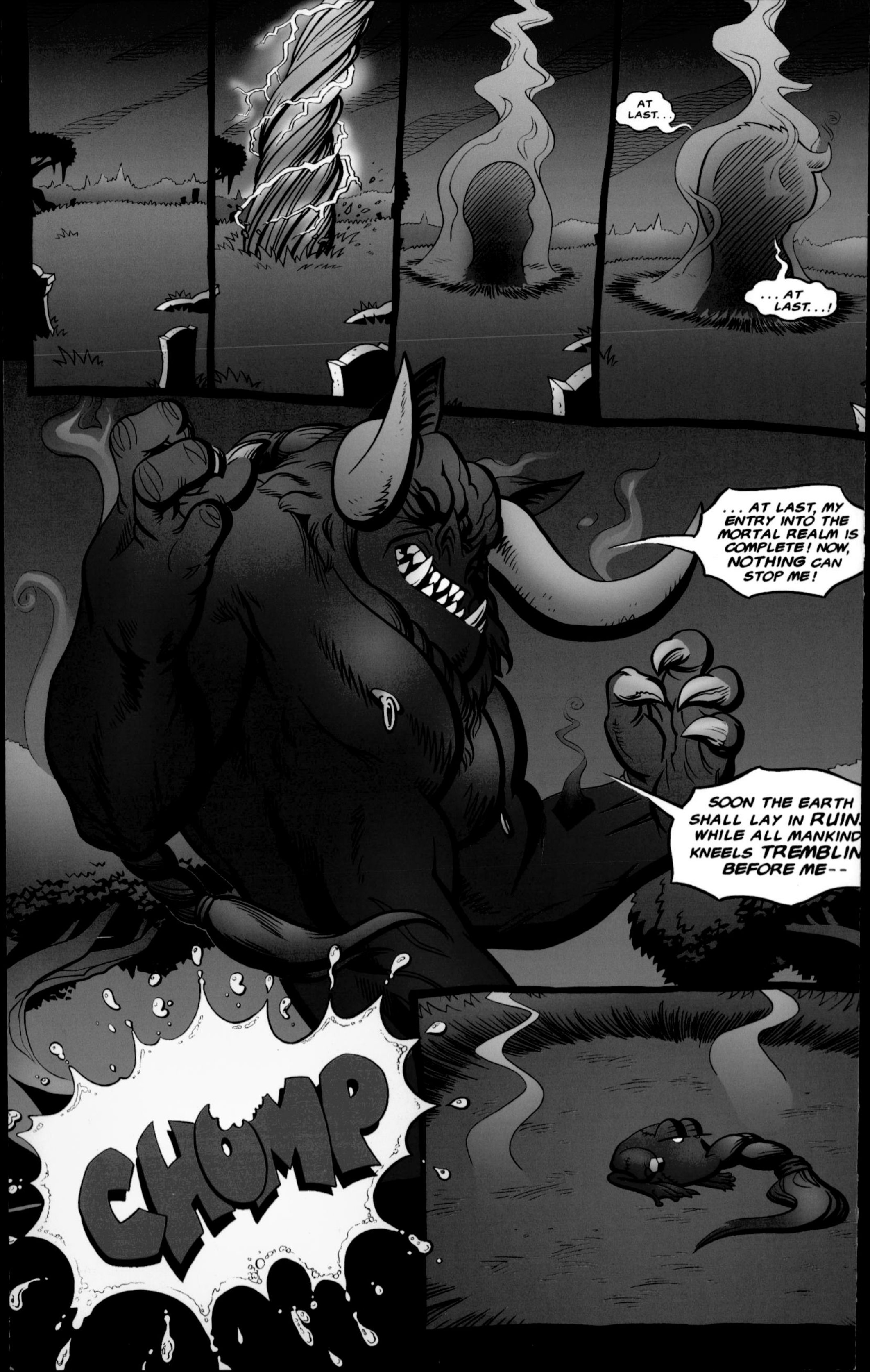
AT LAST...
...AT LAST...!
...AT LAST, MY ENTRY INTO THE MORTAL REALM IS COMPLETE! NOW, NOTHING CAN STOP ME!
SOON THE EARTH SHALL LAY IN RUIN
WHILE ALL MANKIND KNEELS TREMBLIN
BEFORE ME--
CHOMP

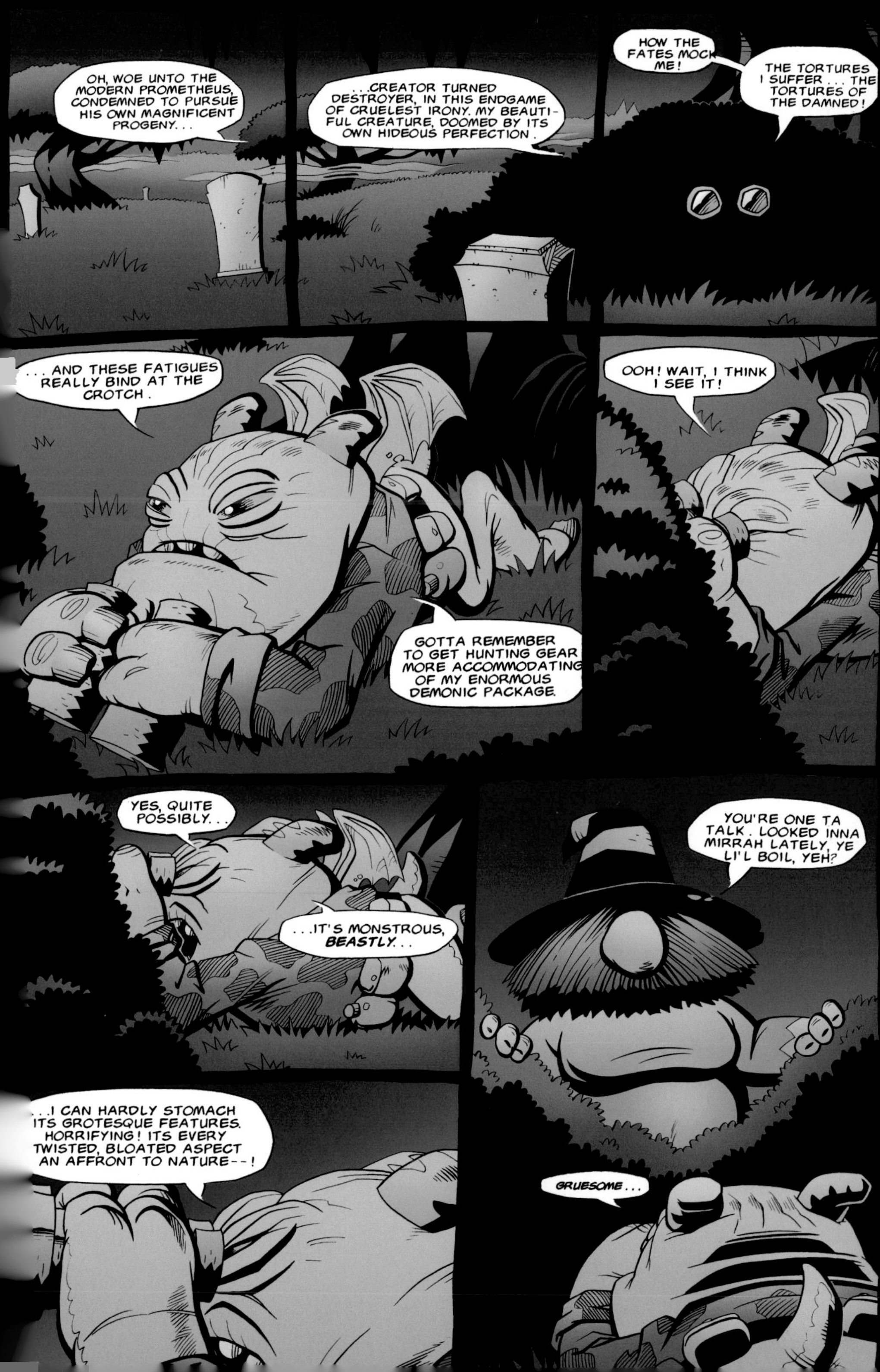
OH, WOE UNTO THE MODERN PROMETHEUS, CONDEMNED TO PURSUE HIS OWN MAGNIFICENT PROGENY...
...CREATOR TURNED DESTROYER, IN THIS ENDGAME OF CRUELEST IRONY. MY BEAUTIFUL CREATURE, DOOMED BY ITS OWN HIDEOUS PERFECTION.
HOW THE FATES MOCK ME!
THE TORTURES I SUFFER... THE TORTURES OF THE DAMNED!
...AND THESE FATIGUES REALLY BIND AT THE CROTCH.
GOTTA REMEMBER TO GET HUNTING GEAR MORE ACCOMMODATING OF MY ENORMOUS DEMONIC PACKAGE.
OOH! WAIT, I THINK I SEE IT!
YES, QUITE POSSIBLY...
...IT'S MONSTROUS, *BEASTLY*...
...I CAN HARDLY STOMACH ITS GROTESQUE FEATURES. HORRIFYING! ITS EVERY TWISTED, BLOATED ASPECT AN AFFRONT TO NATURE--!
YOU'RE ONE TA TALK. LOOKED INNA MIRRAH LATELY, YE LI'L BOIL, YEH?
GRUESOME...

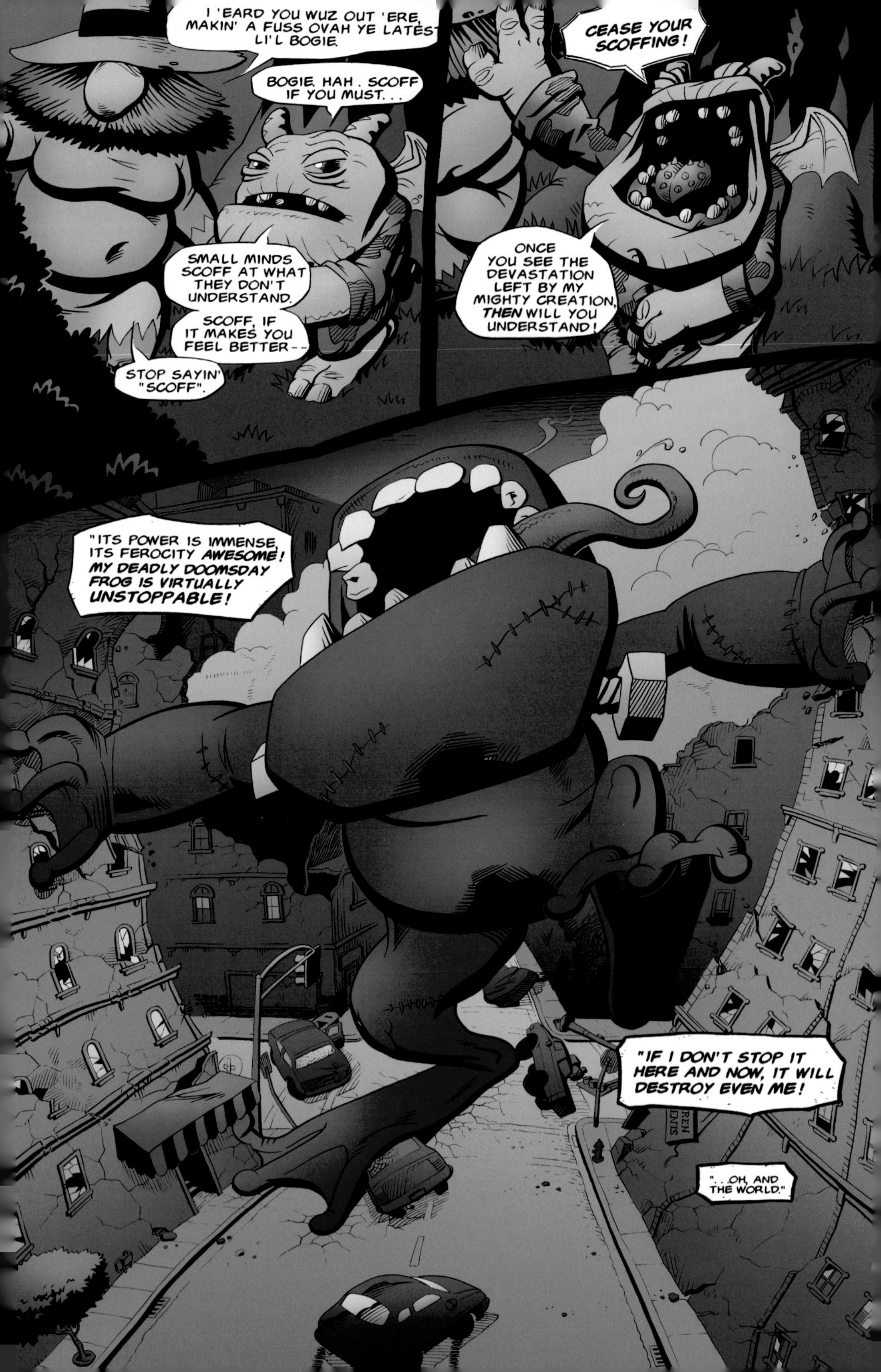
I 'EARD YOU WUZ OUT 'ERE, MAKIN' A FUSS OVAH YE LATEST LI'L BOGIE.
BOGIE. HAH. SCOFF IF YOU MUST...
SMALL MINDS SCOFF AT WHAT THEY DON'T UNDERSTAND.
SCOFF, IF IT MAKES YOU FEEL BETTER--
STOP SAYIN' "SCOFF".
CEASE YOUR SCOFFING!
ONCE YOU SEE THE DEVASTATION LEFT BY MY MIGHTY CREATION, THEN WILL YOU UNDERSTAND!
"ITS POWER IS IMMENSE, ITS FEROCITY AWESOME! MY DEADLY DOOMSDAY FROG IS VIRTUALLY UNSTOPPABLE!
"IF I DON'T STOP IT HERE AND NOW, IT WILL DESTROY EVEN ME!
"...OH, AND THE WORLD."

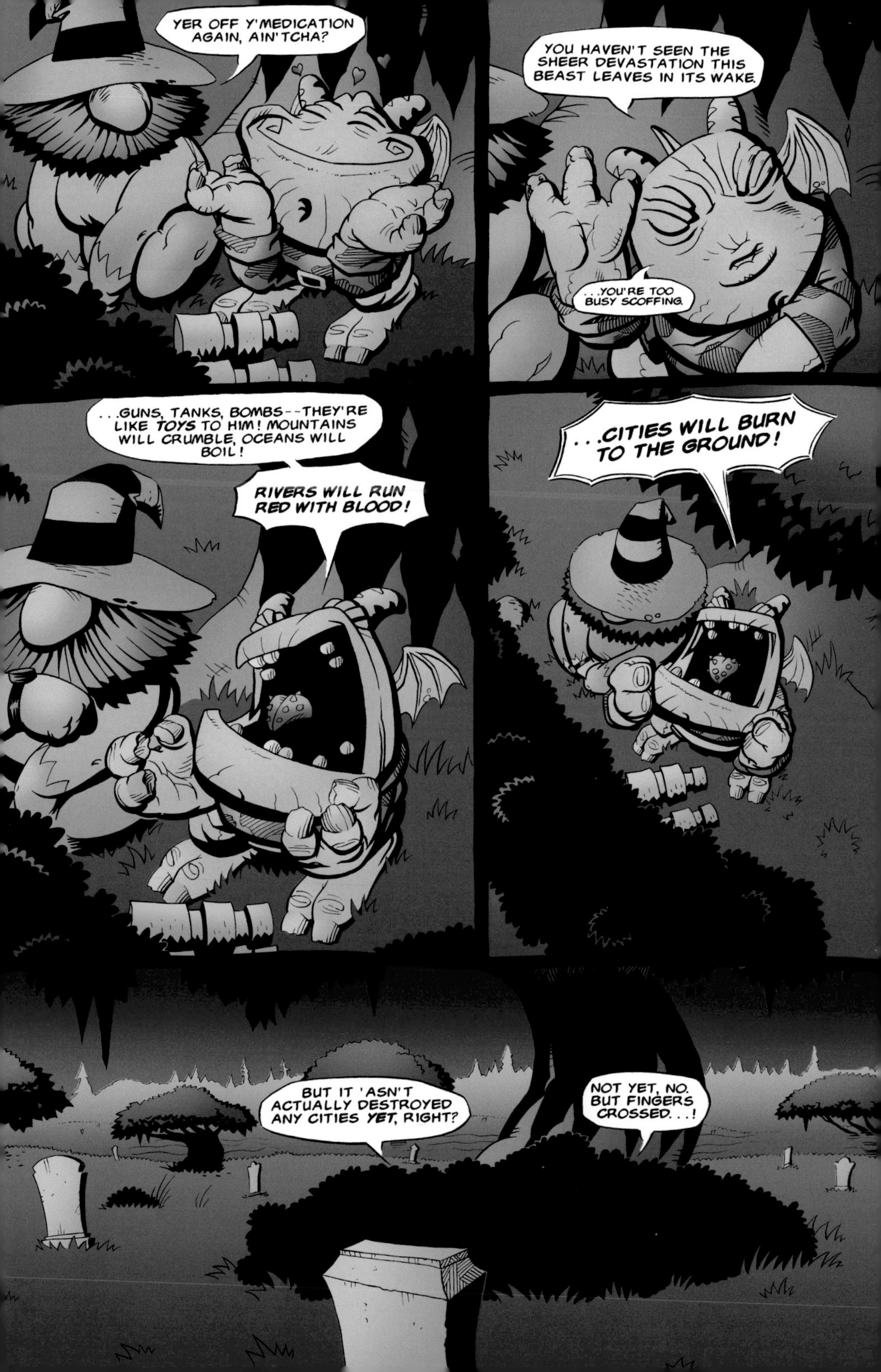

YER OFF Y'MEDICATION AGAIN, AIN'TCHA?
YOU HAVEN'T SEEN THE SHEER DEVASTATION THIS BEAST LEAVES IN ITS WAKE.
. . .YOU'RE TOO BUSY SCOFFING.
. . .GUNS, TANKS, BOMBS--THEY'RE LIKE *TOYS* TO HIM! MOUNTAINS WILL CRUMBLE, OCEANS WILL BOIL!
RIVERS WILL RUN RED WITH BLOOD!
. . .CITIES WILL BURN TO THE GROUND!
BUT IT 'ASN'T ACTUALLY DESTROYED ANY CITIES *YET*, RIGHT?
NOT YET, NO. BUT FINGERS CROSSED. . .!

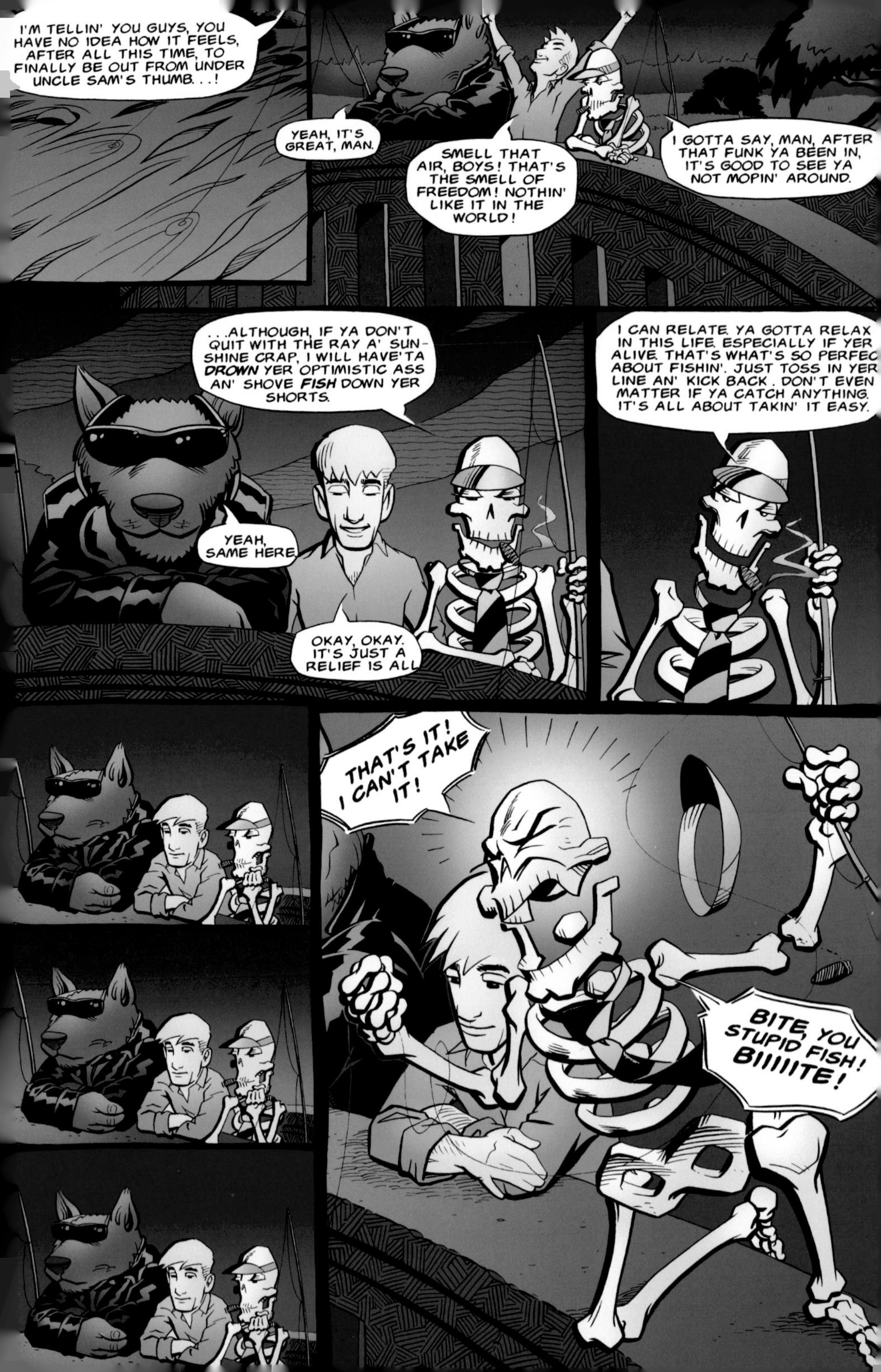
I'M TELLIN' YOU GUYS, YOU HAVE NO IDEA HOW IT FEELS, AFTER ALL THIS TIME, TO FINALLY BE OUT FROM UNDER UNCLE SAM'S THUMB...!
YEAH, IT'S GREAT, MAN.
SMELL THAT AIR, BOYS! THAT'S THE SMELL OF FREEDOM! NOTHIN' LIKE IT IN THE WORLD!
I GOTTA SAY, MAN, AFTER THAT FUNK YA BEEN IN, IT'S GOOD TO SEE YA NOT MOPIN' AROUND.
...ALTHOUGH, IF YA DON'T QUIT WITH THE RAY A' SUNSHINE CRAP, I WILL HAVE'TA DROWN YER OPTIMISTIC ASS AN' SHOVE FISH DOWN YER SHORTS.
YEAH, SAME HERE
OKAY, OKAY. IT'S JUST A RELIEF IS ALL
I CAN RELATE. YA GOTTA RELAX IN THIS LIFE. ESPECIALLY IF YER ALIVE. THAT'S WHAT'S SO PERFEC ABOUT FISHIN'. JUST TOSS IN YER LINE AN' KICK BACK. DON'T EVEN MATTER IF YA CATCH ANYTHING. IT'S ALL ABOUT TAKIN' IT EASY.
THAT'S IT! I CAN'T TAKE IT!
BITE, YOU STUPID FISH! BIIIIITE!

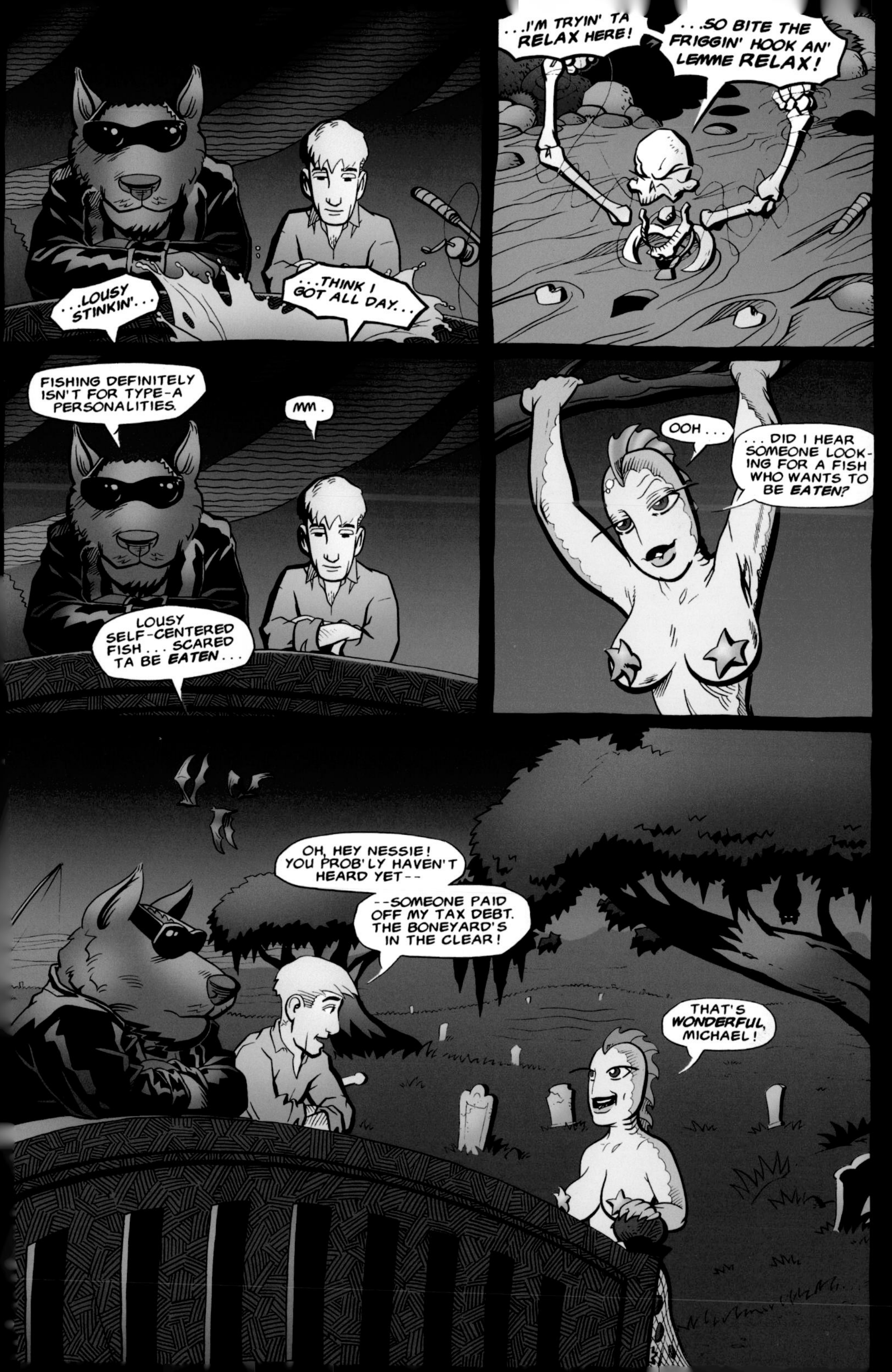
...LOUSY STINKIN'...
...THINK I GOT ALL DAY...
...I'M TRYIN' TA RELAX HERE!
...SO BITE THE FRIGGIN' HOOK AN' LEMME RELAX!
FISHING DEFINITELY ISN'T FOR TYPE-A PERSONALITIES.
MM.
LOUSY SELF-CENTERED FISH... SCARED TA BE EATEN...
OOH...
...DID I HEAR SOMEONE LOOKING FOR A FISH WHO WANTS TO BE EATEN?
OH, HEY NESSIE! YOU PROB'LY HAVEN'T HEARD YET--
--SOMEONE PAID OFF MY TAX DEBT. THE BONEYARD'S IN THE CLEAR!
THAT'S WONDERFUL, MICHAEL!

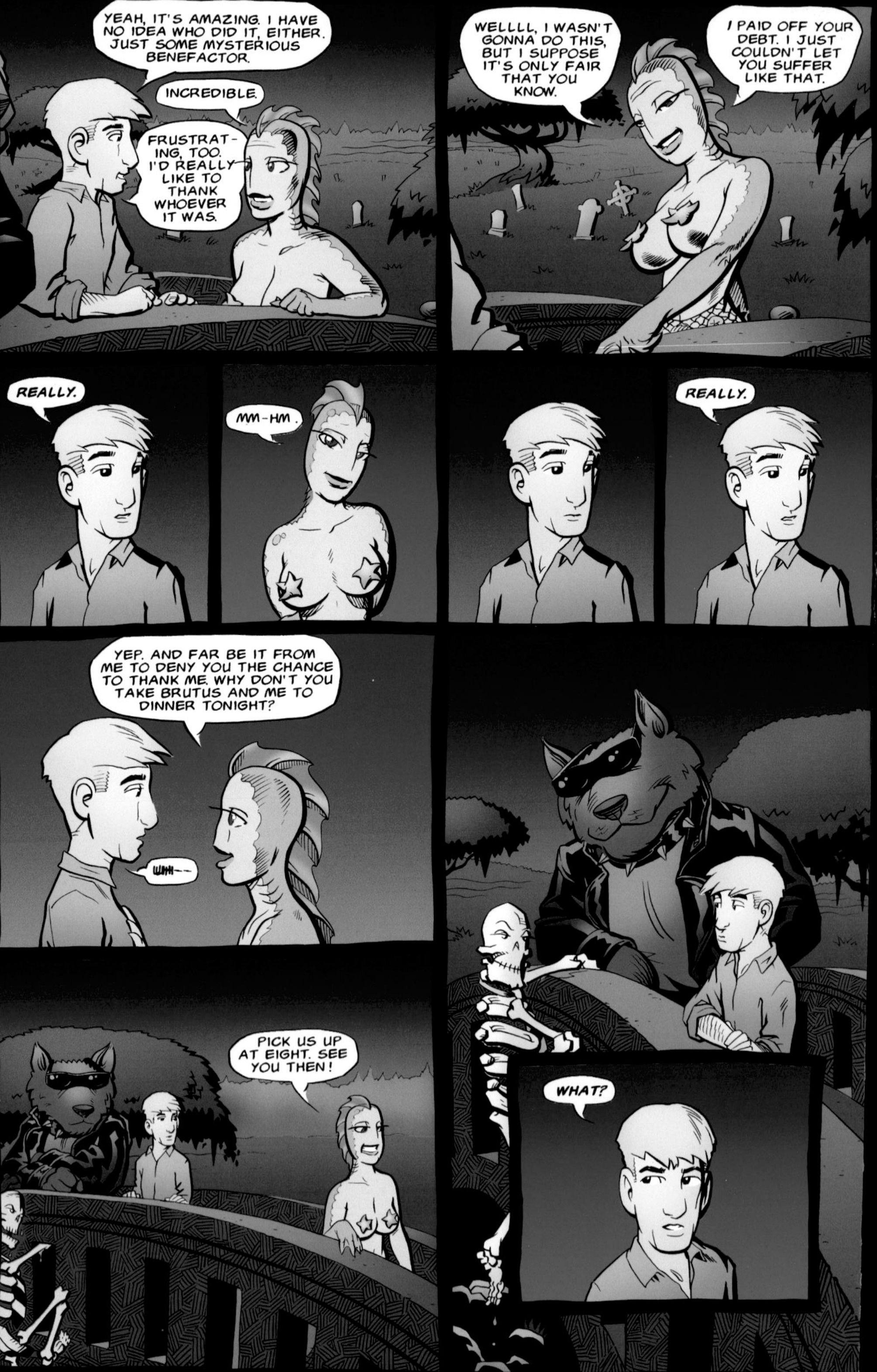
YEAH, IT'S AMAZING. I HAVE NO IDEA WHO DID IT, EITHER. JUST SOME MYSTERIOUS BENEFACTOR.
INCREDIBLE.
FRUSTRATING, TOO. I'D REALLY LIKE TO THANK WHOEVER IT WAS.
WELLLL, I WASN'T GONNA DO THIS, BUT I SUPPOSE IT'S ONLY FAIR THAT YOU KNOW.
I PAID OFF YOUR DEBT. I JUST COULDN'T LET YOU SUFFER LIKE THAT.
REALLY.
MM-HM.
REALLY.
YEP. AND FAR BE IT FROM ME TO DENY YOU THE CHANCE TO THANK ME. WHY DON'T YOU TAKE BRUTUS AND ME TO DINNER TONIGHT?
PICK US UP AT EIGHT. SEE YOU THEN!
WHAT?

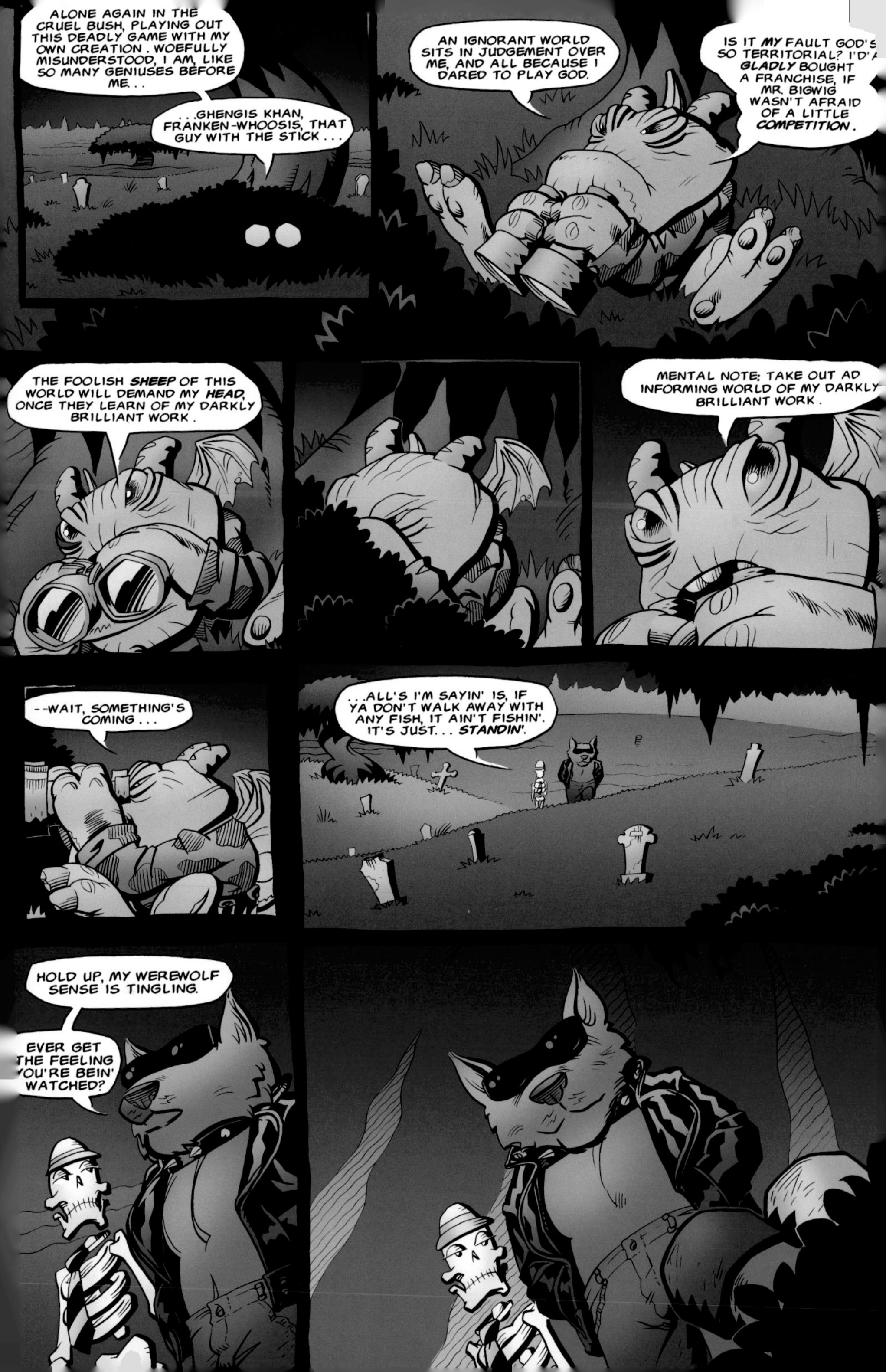

ALONE AGAIN IN THE CRUEL BUSH, PLAYING OUT THIS DEADLY GAME WITH MY OWN CREATION. WOEFULLY MISUNDERSTOOD, I AM, LIKE SO MANY GENIUSES BEFORE ME...
...GHENGIS KHAN, FRANKEN-WHOOSIS, THAT GUY WITH THE STICK...
AN IGNORANT WORLD SITS IN JUDGEMENT OVER ME, AND ALL BECAUSE I DARED TO PLAY GOD.
IS IT MY FAULT GOD'S SO TERRITORIAL? I'D'A GLADLY BOUGHT A FRANCHISE, IF MR. BIGWIG WASN'T AFRAID OF A LITTLE COMPETITION.
THE FOOLISH SHEEP OF THIS WORLD WILL DEMAND MY HEAD, ONCE THEY LEARN OF MY DARKLY BRILLIANT WORK.
MENTAL NOTE: TAKE OUT AD INFORMING WORLD OF MY DARKLY BRILLIANT WORK.
--WAIT, SOMETHING'S COMING...
...ALL'S I'M SAYIN' IS, IF YA DON'T WALK AWAY WITH ANY FISH, IT AIN'T FISHIN'. IT'S JUST... STANDIN'.
HOLD UP, MY WEREWOLF SENSE IS TINGLING.
EVER GET THE FEELING YOU'RE BEIN' WATCHED?

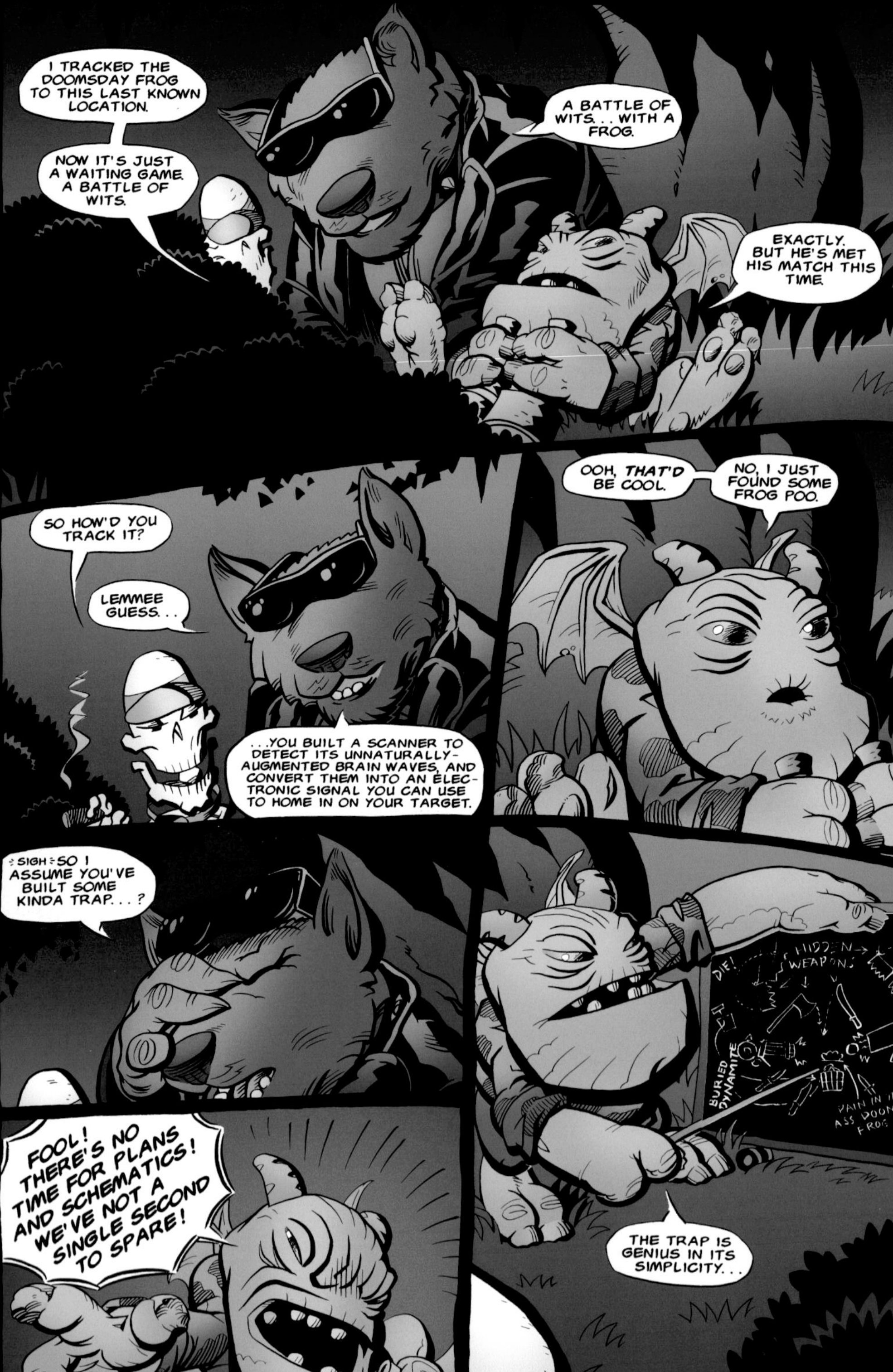
I TRACKED THE DOOMSDAY FROG TO THIS LAST KNOWN LOCATION.
NOW IT'S JUST A WAITING GAME. A BATTLE OF WITS.
A BATTLE OF WITS... WITH A FROG.
EXACTLY. BUT HE'S MET HIS MATCH THIS TIME.
SO HOW'D YOU TRACK IT?
LEMMEE GUESS...
...YOU BUILT A SCANNER TO DETECT ITS UNNATURALLY-AUGMENTED BRAIN WAVES, AND CONVERT THEM INTO AN ELECTRONIC SIGNAL YOU CAN USE TO HOME IN ON YOUR TARGET.
OOH, THAT'D BE COOL.
NO, I JUST FOUND SOME FROG POO.
÷SIGH÷ SO I ASSUME YOU'VE BUILT SOME KINDA TRAP...?
DIE!
HIDDEN WEAPONS
BURIED DYNAMITE
THE TRAP IS GENIUS IN ITS SIMPLICITY...
FOOL! THERE'S NO TIME FOR PLANS AND SCHEMATICS! WE'VE NOT A SINGLE SECOND TO SPARE!

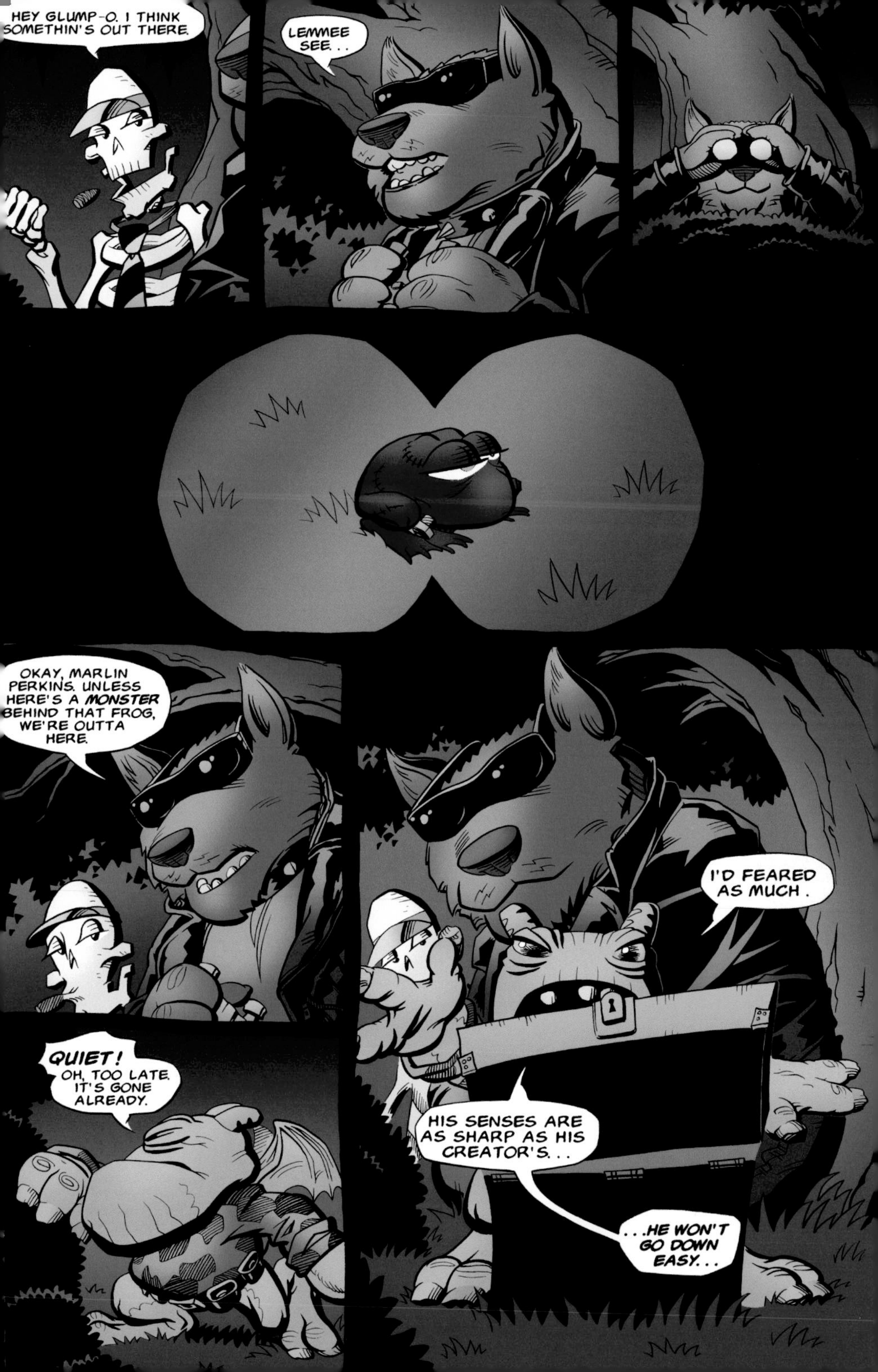
HEY GLUMP-O. I THINK SOMETHIN'S OUT THERE.
LEMMEE SEE. . .
OKAY, MARLIN PERKINS. UNLESS HERE'S A MONSTER BEHIND THAT FROG, WE'RE OUTTA HERE.
I'D FEARED AS MUCH.
QUIET! OH, TOO LATE. IT'S GONE ALREADY.
HIS SENSES ARE AS SHARP AS HIS CREATOR'S. . .
. . .HE WON'T GO DOWN EASY. . .

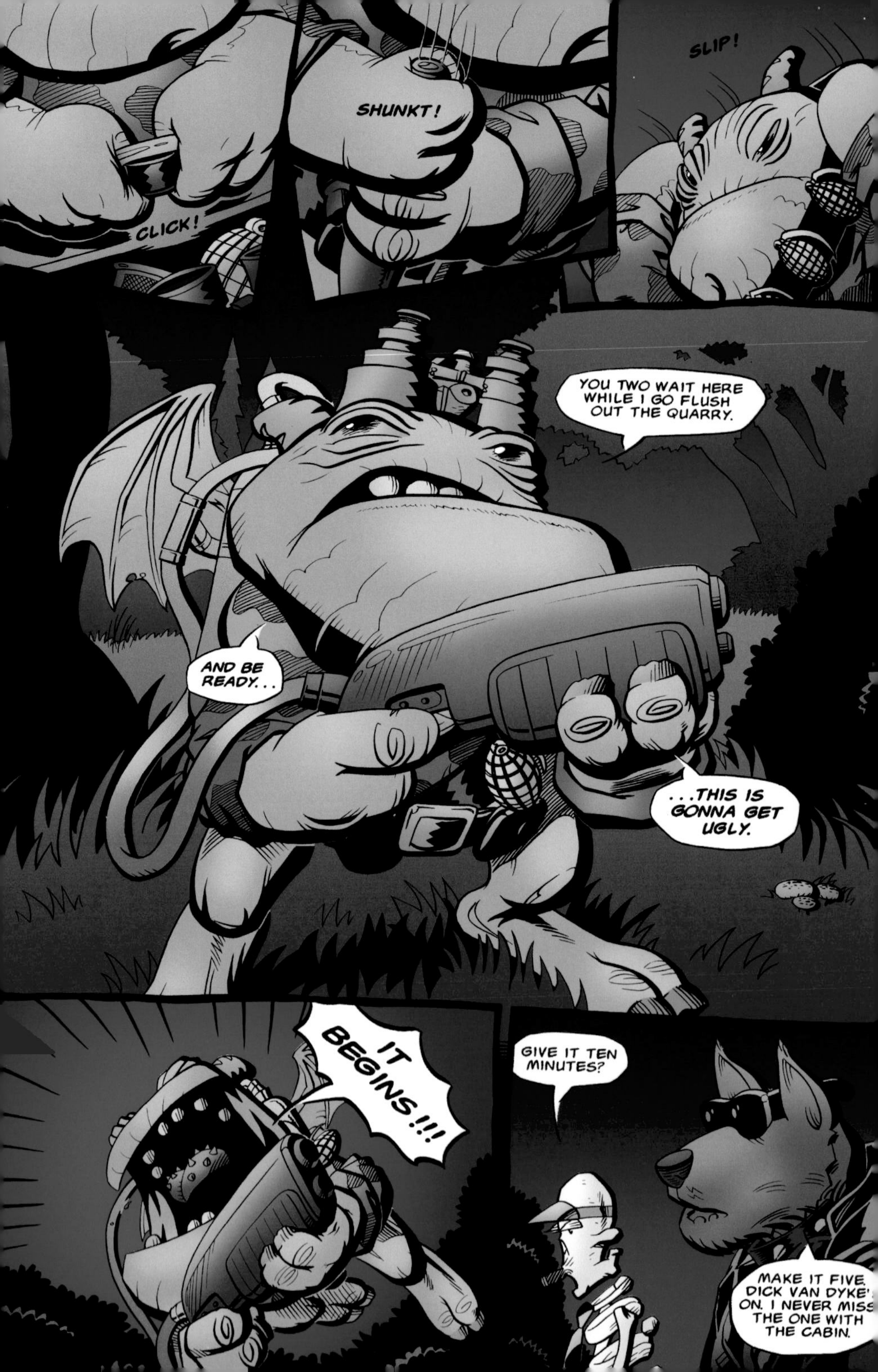
CLICK!
SHUNKT!
SLIP!
YOU TWO WAIT HERE WHILE I GO FLUSH OUT THE QUARRY.
AND BE READY...
...THIS IS GONNA GET UGLY.
IT BEGINS!!!
GIVE IT TEN MINUTES?
MAKE IT FIVE. DICK VAN DYKE'S ON. I NEVER MISS THE ONE WITH THE CABIN.

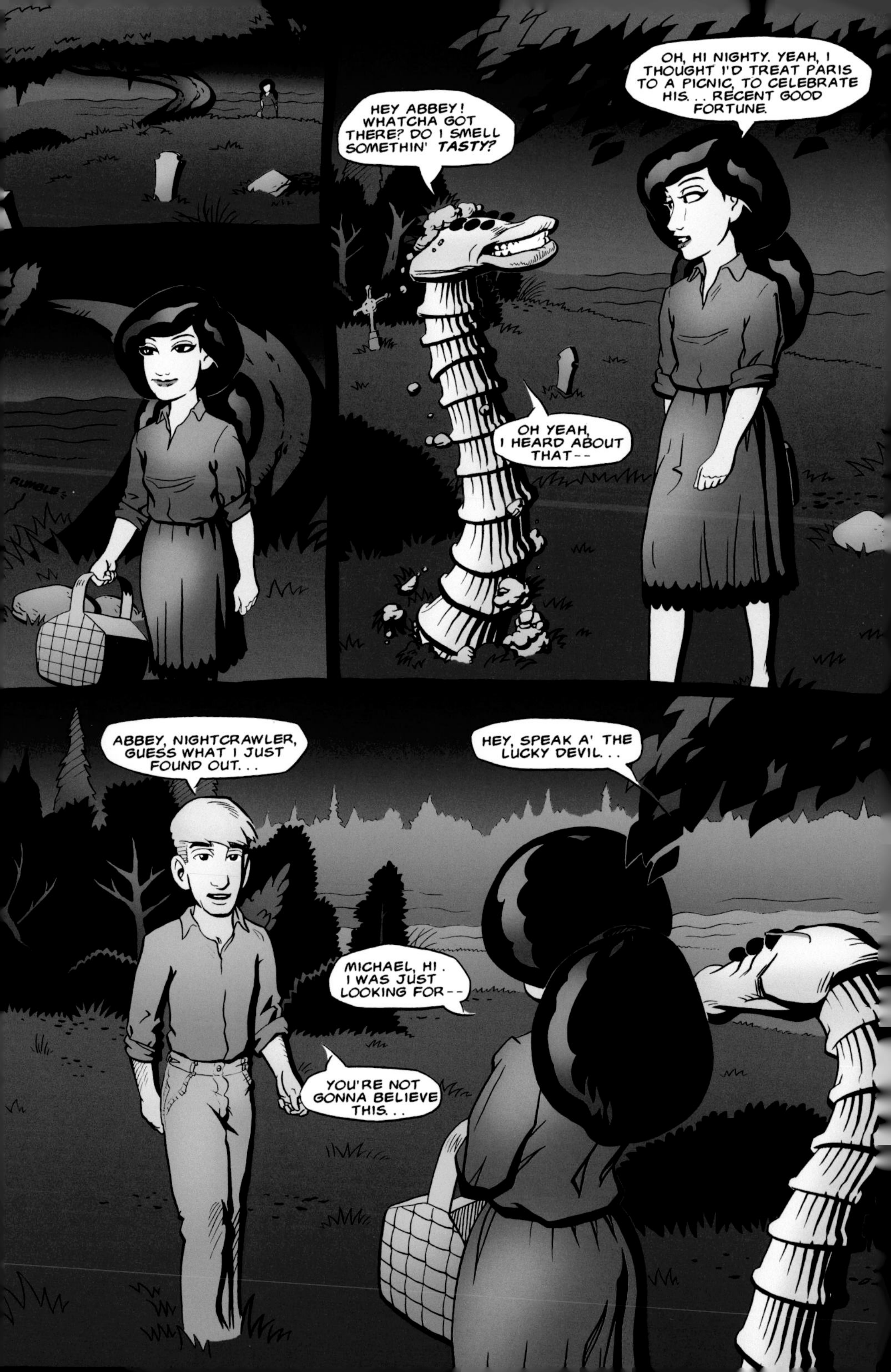
RUMBLE
HEY ABBEY! WHATCHA GOT THERE? DO I SMELL SOMETHIN' *TASTY?*
OH, HI NIGHTY. YEAH, I THOUGHT I'D TREAT PARIS TO A PICNIC, TO CELEBRATE HIS. . . RECENT GOOD FORTUNE.
OH YEAH, I HEARD ABOUT THAT--
ABBEY, NIGHTCRAWLER, GUESS WHAT I JUST FOUND OUT. . .
HEY, SPEAK A' THE LUCKY DEVIL. . .
MICHAEL, HI. I WAS JUST LOOKING FOR--
YOU'RE NOT GONNA BELIEVE THIS. . .

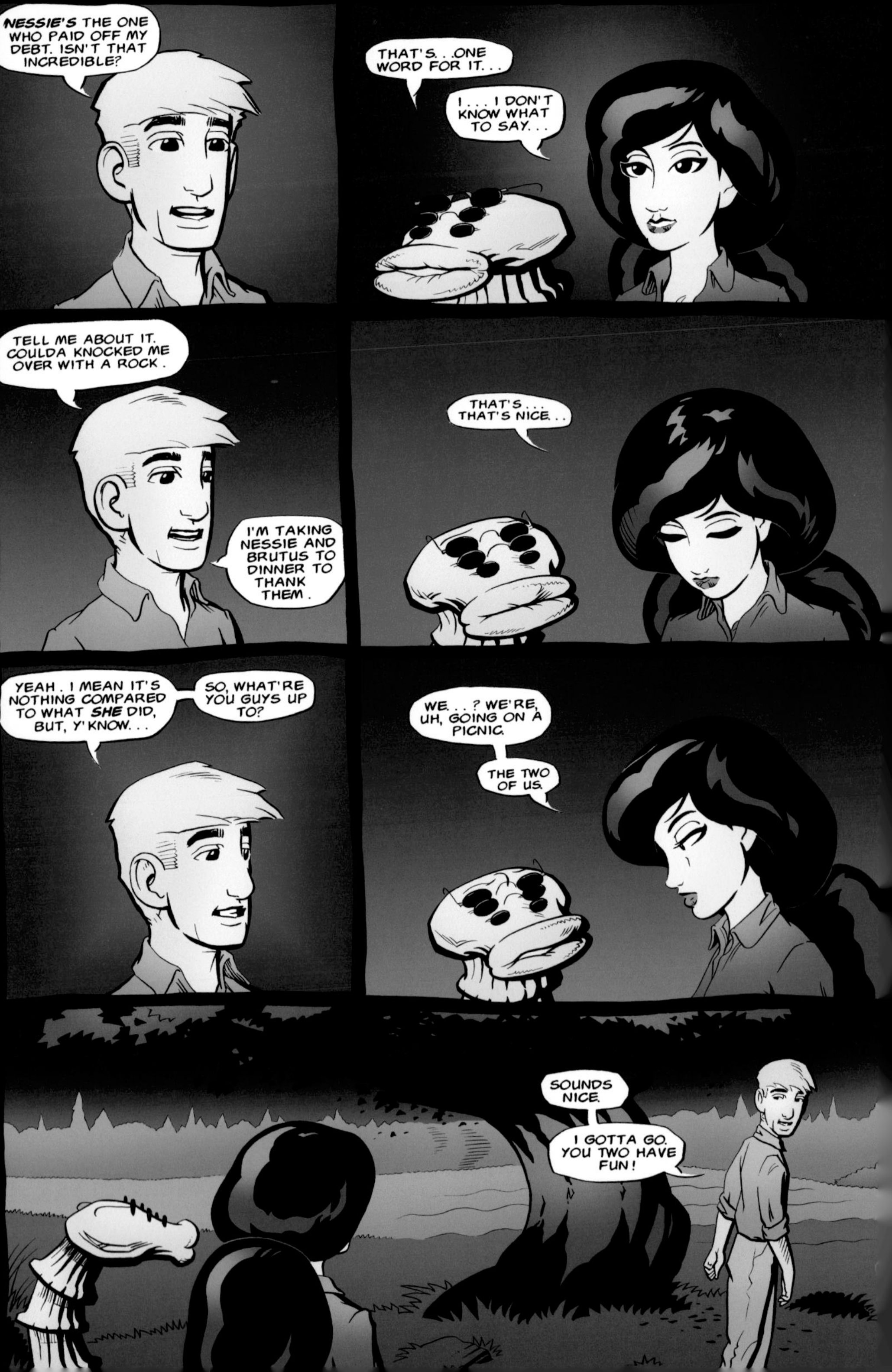

NESSIE'S THE ONE WHO PAID OFF MY DEBT. ISN'T THAT INCREDIBLE?
THAT'S. . .ONE WORD FOR IT. . .
I. . . I DON'T KNOW WHAT TO SAY. . .
TELL ME ABOUT IT. COULDA KNOCKED ME OVER WITH A ROCK.
I'M TAKING NESSIE AND BRUTUS TO DINNER TO THANK THEM.
THAT'S. . . THAT'S NICE. . .
YEAH. I MEAN IT'S NOTHING COMPARED TO WHAT SHE DID, BUT, Y'KNOW. . .
SO, WHAT'RE YOU GUYS UP TO?
WE. . .? WE'RE, UH, GOING ON A PICNIC.
THE TWO OF US.
SOUNDS NICE.
I GOTTA GO. YOU TWO HAVE FUN!

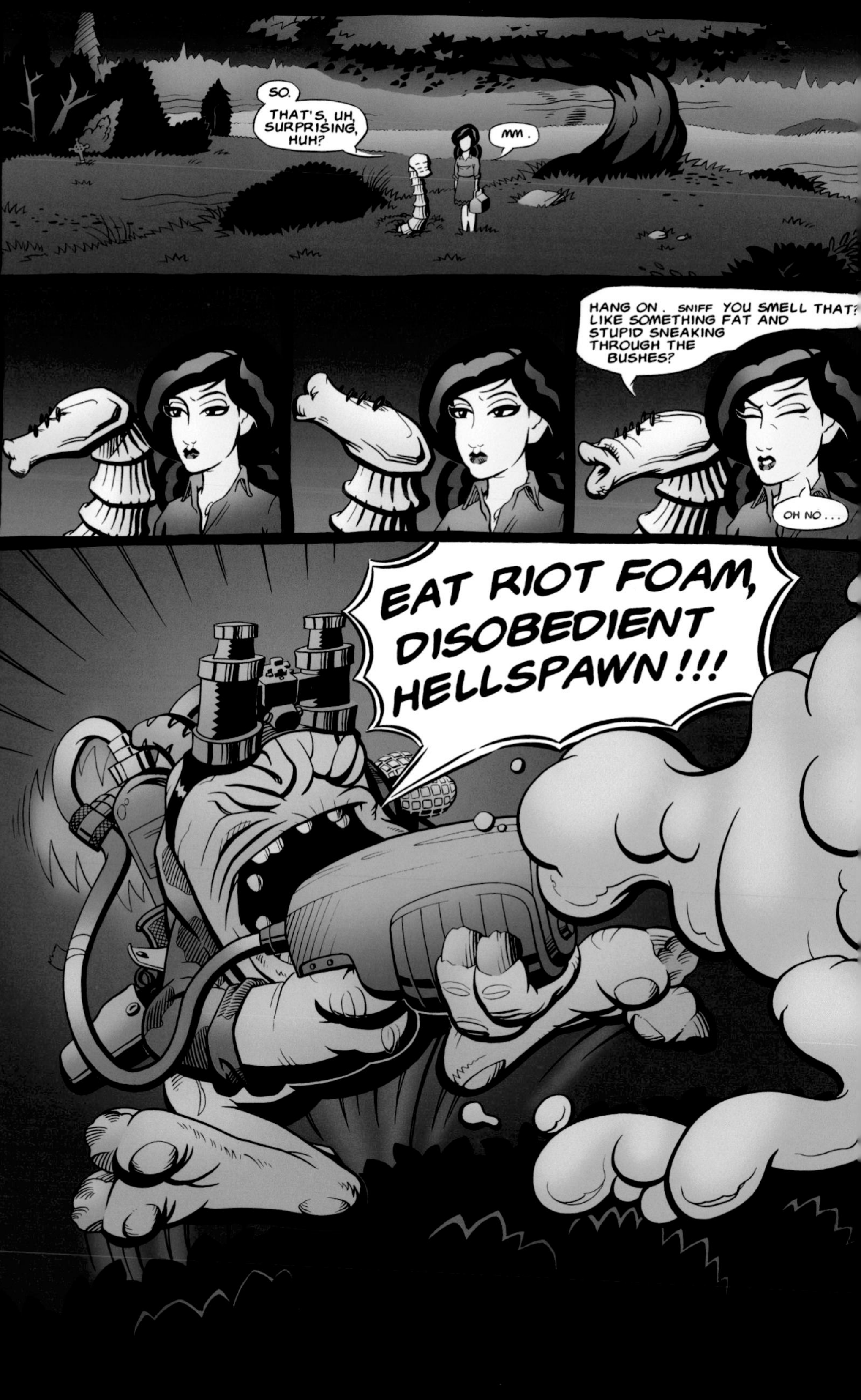
SO.
THAT'S, UH, SURPRISING, HUH?
MM.
HANG ON. SNIFF YOU SMELL THAT? LIKE SOMETHING FAT AND STUPID SNEAKING THROUGH THE BUSHES?
OH NO...
EAT RIOT FOAM, DISOBEDIENT HELLSPAWN!!!

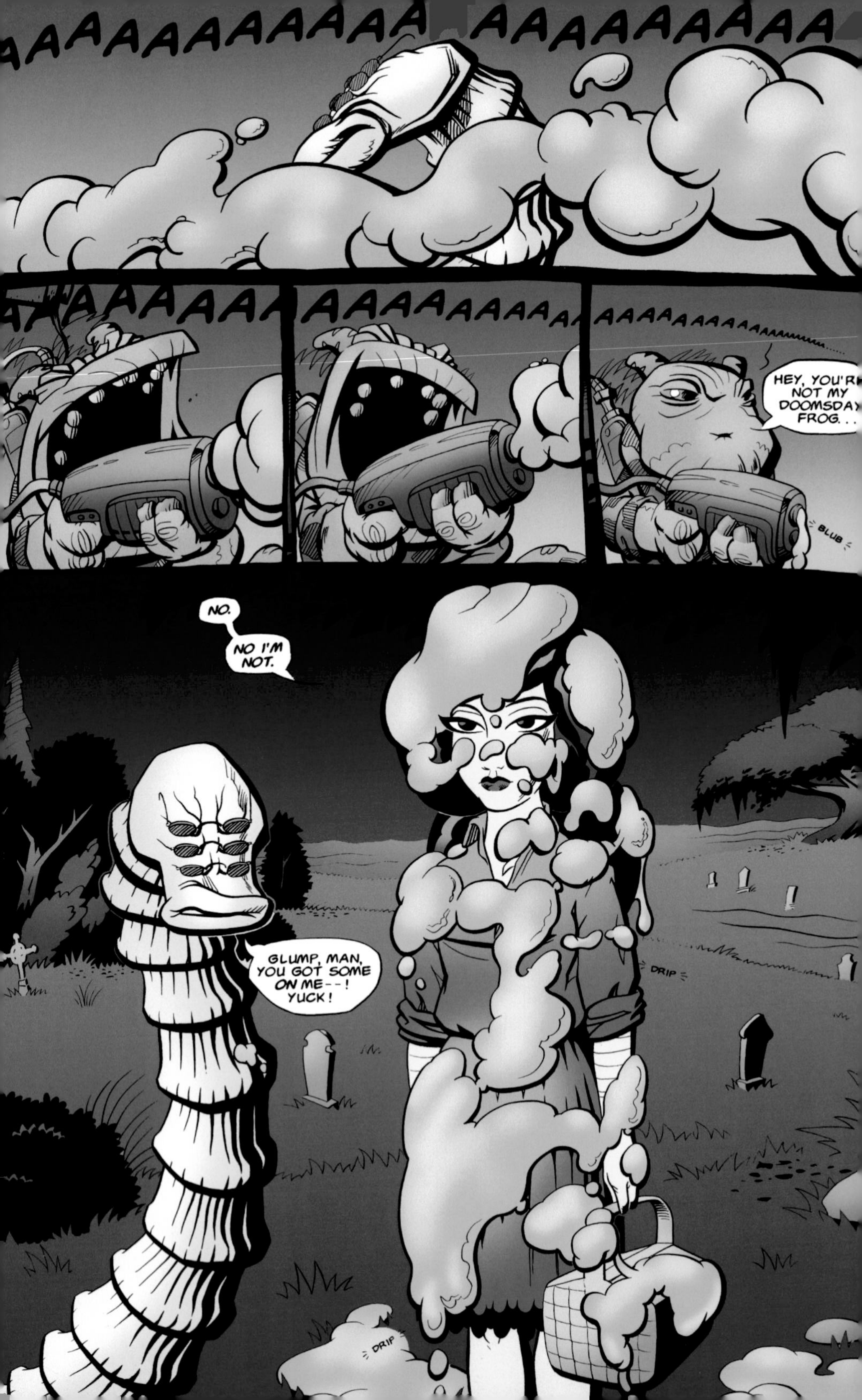
AAAAAAAAAAAA AAAAAAAAAA
AAAAAAAA
AAAAAAAAAA
AAAAAAAAAAAAAA
HEY, YOU'RE NOT MY DOOMSDAY FROG...
BLUB
NO.
NO I'M NOT.
GLUMP, MAN, YOU GOT SOME ON ME--! YUCK!
DRIP
DRIP

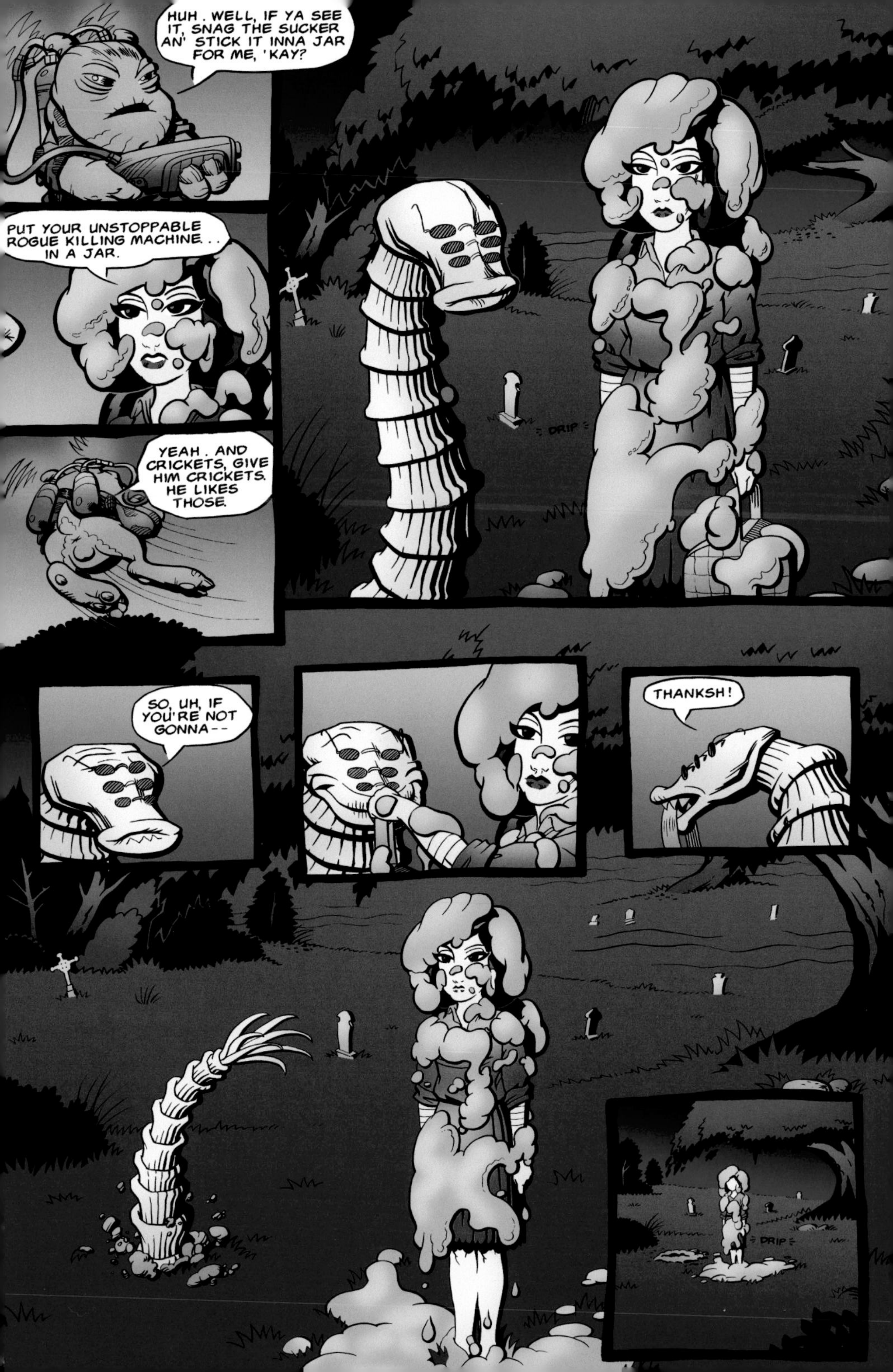
HUH. WELL, IF YA SEE IT, SNAG THE SUCKER AN' STICK IT INNA JAR FOR ME, 'KAY?
PUT YOUR UNSTOPPABLE ROGUE KILLING MACHINE... IN A JAR.
YEAH. AND CRICKETS, GIVE HIM CRICKETS. HE LIKES THOSE.
DRIP
SO, UH, IF YOU'RE NOT GONNA--
THANKSH!
DRIP

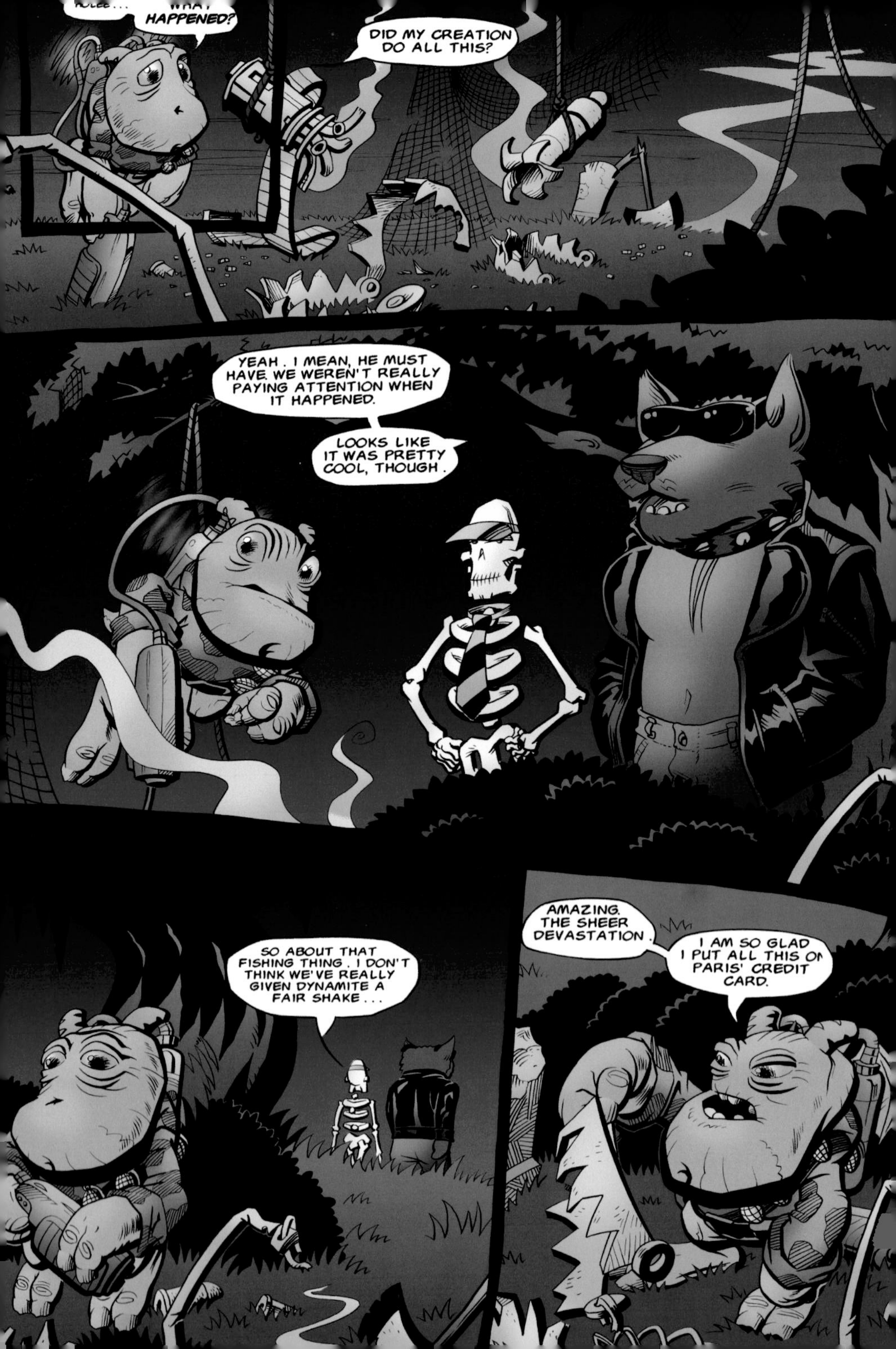
HAPPENED?
DID MY CREATION DO ALL THIS?
YEAH . I MEAN, HE MUST HAVE. WE WEREN'T REALLY PAYING ATTENTION WHEN IT HAPPENED.
LOOKS LIKE IT WAS PRETTY COOL, THOUGH .
SO ABOUT THAT FISHING THING . I DON'T THINK WE'VE REALLY GIVEN DYNAMITE A FAIR SHAKE . . .
AMAZING. THE SHEER DEVASTATION .
I AM SO GLAD I PUT ALL THIS ON PARIS' CREDIT CARD.

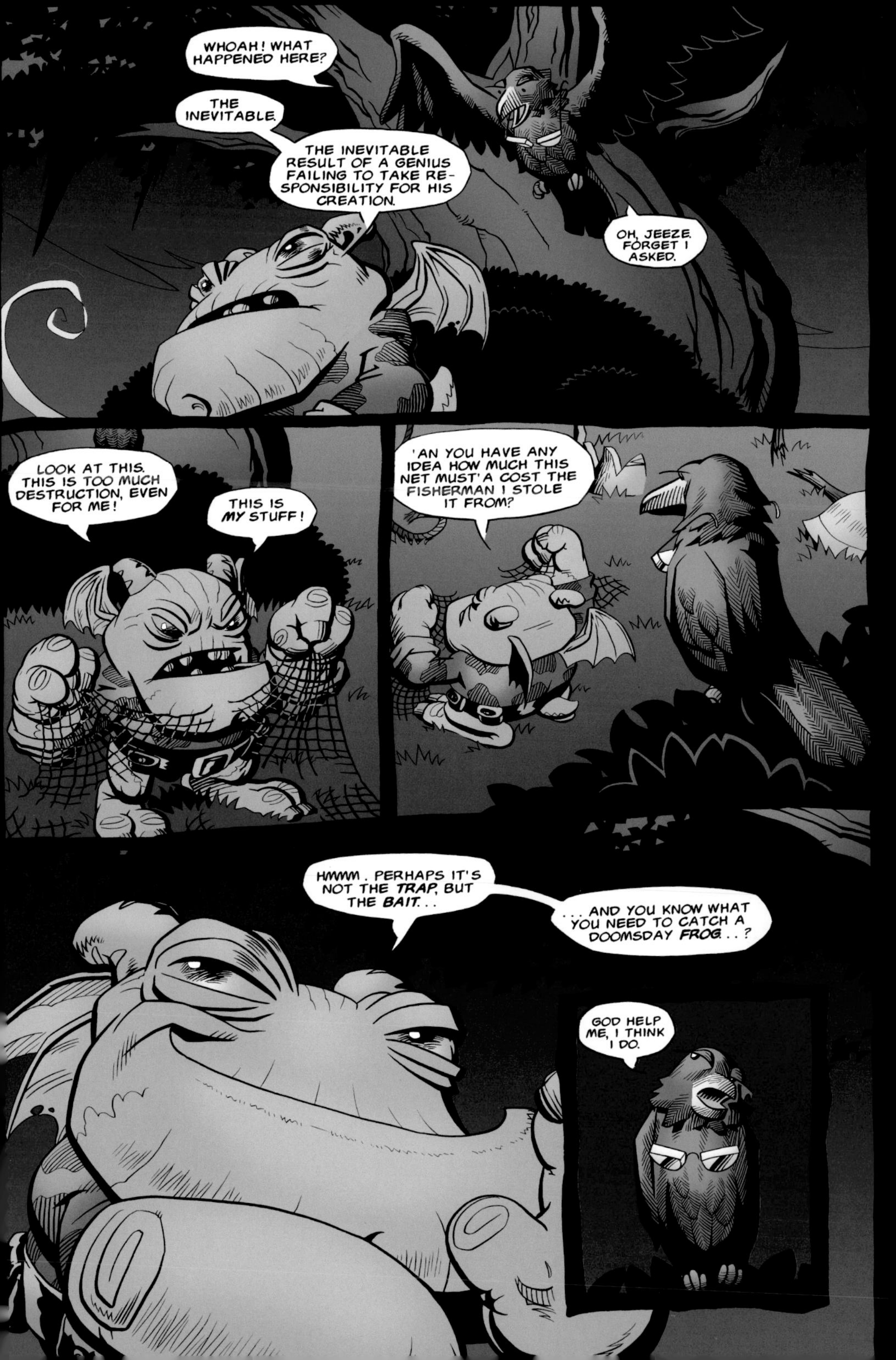
WHOAH! WHAT HAPPENED HERE?
THE INEVITABLE.
THE INEVITABLE RESULT OF A GENIUS FAILING TO TAKE RE-SPONSIBILITY FOR HIS CREATION.
OH, JEEZE. FORGET I ASKED.
LOOK AT THIS. THIS IS TOO MUCH DESTRUCTION, EVEN FOR ME!
THIS IS MY STUFF!
'AN YOU HAVE ANY IDEA HOW MUCH THIS NET MUST'A COST THE FISHERMAN I STOLE IT FROM?
HMMM. PERHAPS IT'S NOT THE TRAP, BUT THE BAIT...
...AND YOU KNOW WHAT YOU NEED TO CATCH A DOOMSDAY FROG...?
GOD HELP ME, I THINK I DO.

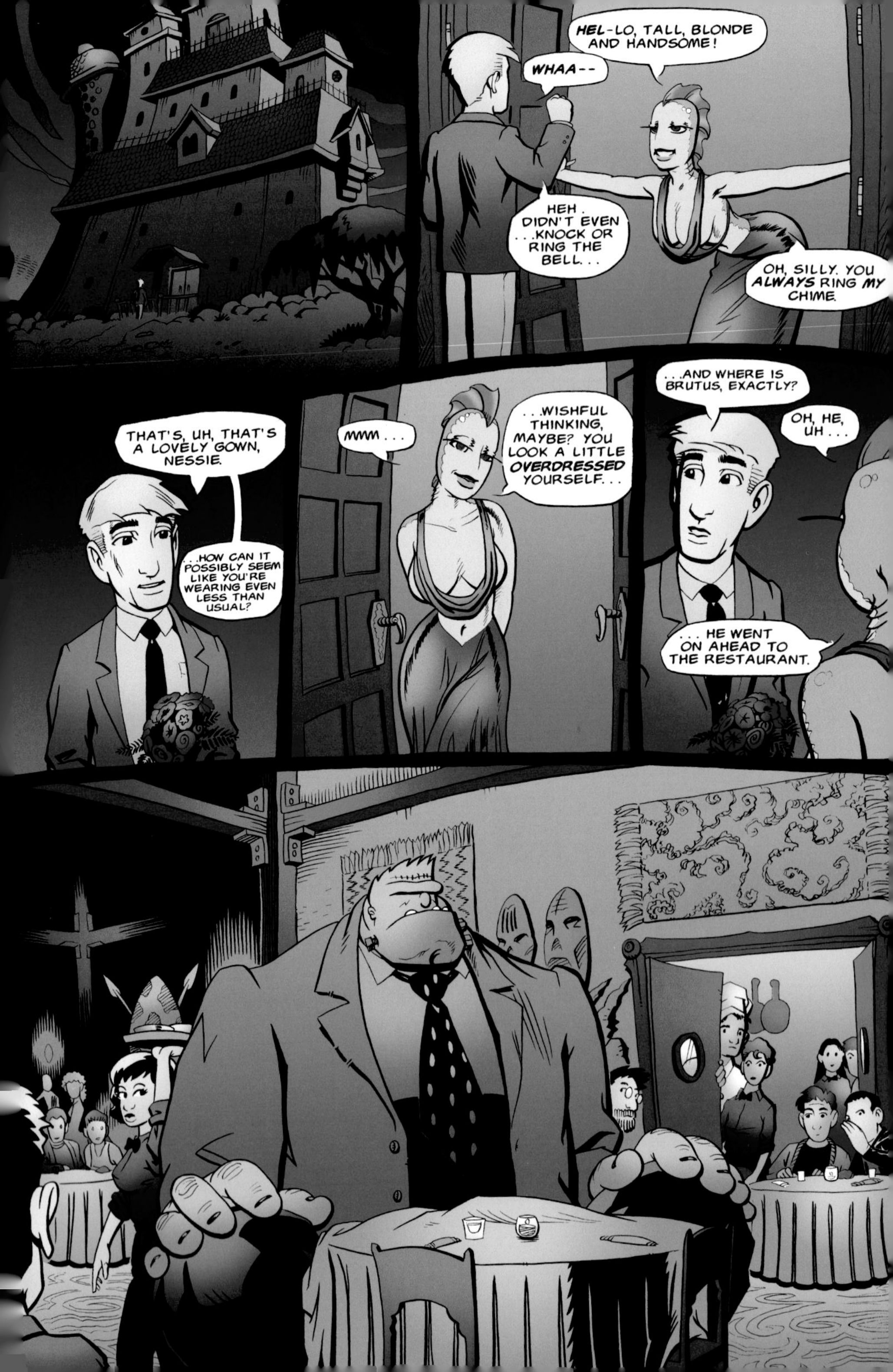
HEL-LO, TALL, BLONDE AND HANDSOME!
WHAA--
HEH. DIDN'T EVEN ...KNOCK OR RING THE BELL...
OH, SILLY. YOU ALWAYS RING MY CHIME.
THAT'S, UH, THAT'S A LOVELY GOWN, NESSIE.
...HOW CAN IT POSSIBLY SEEM LIKE YOU'RE WEARING EVEN LESS THAN USUAL?
MMM...
...WISHFUL THINKING, MAYBE? YOU LOOK A LITTLE OVERDRESSED YOURSELF...
...AND WHERE IS BRUTUS, EXACTLY?
OH, HE, UH...
...HE WENT ON AHEAD TO THE RESTAURANT.

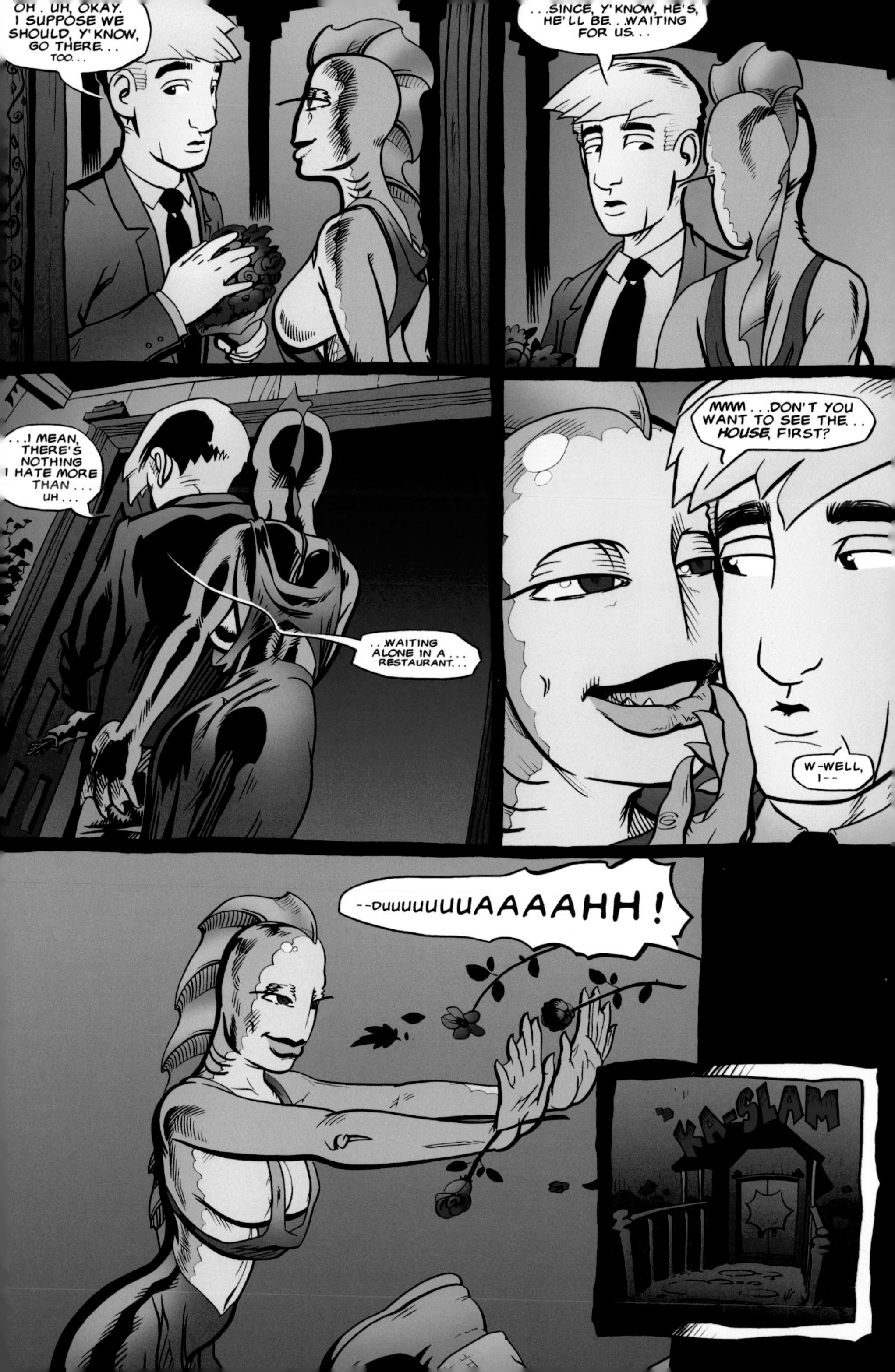
OH . UH, OKAY. I SUPPOSE WE SHOULD, Y' KNOW, GO THERE. . . TOO. . .
. . .SINCE, Y' KNOW, HE'S, HE'LL BE. . .WAITING FOR US. . .
. . .I MEAN, THERE'S NOTHING I HATE MORE THAN . . . UH . . .
. . .WAITING ALONE IN A. . . RESTAURANT. . .
MMM . . .DON'T YOU WANT TO SEE THE. . . HOUSE, FIRST?
W-WELL, I--
--DUUUUUUUAAAAAHH!
KA-SLAM

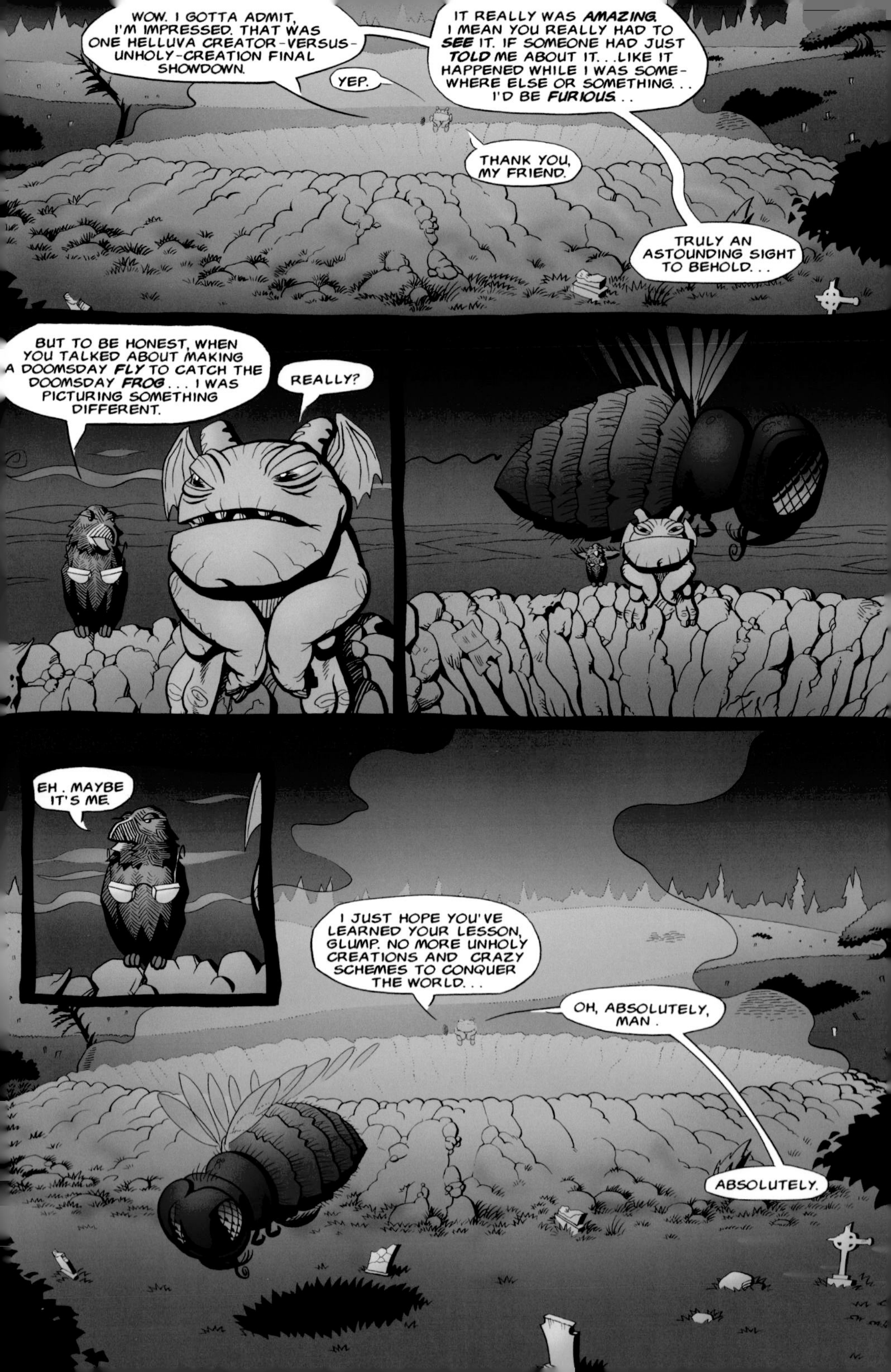
WOW. I GOTTA ADMIT, I'M IMPRESSED. THAT WAS ONE HELLUVA CREATOR-VERSUS-UNHOLY-CREATION FINAL SHOWDOWN.
YEP.
IT REALLY WAS AMAZING. I MEAN YOU REALLY HAD TO SEE IT. IF SOMEONE HAD JUST TOLD ME ABOUT IT... LIKE IT HAPPENED WHILE I WAS SOME-WHERE ELSE OR SOMETHING... I'D BE FURIOUS...
THANK YOU, MY FRIEND.
TRULY AN ASTOUNDING SIGHT TO BEHOLD...
BUT TO BE HONEST, WHEN YOU TALKED ABOUT MAKING A DOOMSDAY FLY TO CATCH THE DOOMSDAY FROG... I WAS PICTURING SOMETHING DIFFERENT.
REALLY?
EH. MAYBE IT'S ME.
I JUST HOPE YOU'VE LEARNED YOUR LESSON, GLUMP. NO MORE UNHOLY CREATIONS AND CRAZY SCHEMES TO CONQUER THE WORLD...
OH, ABSOLUTELY, MAN.
ABSOLUTELY.

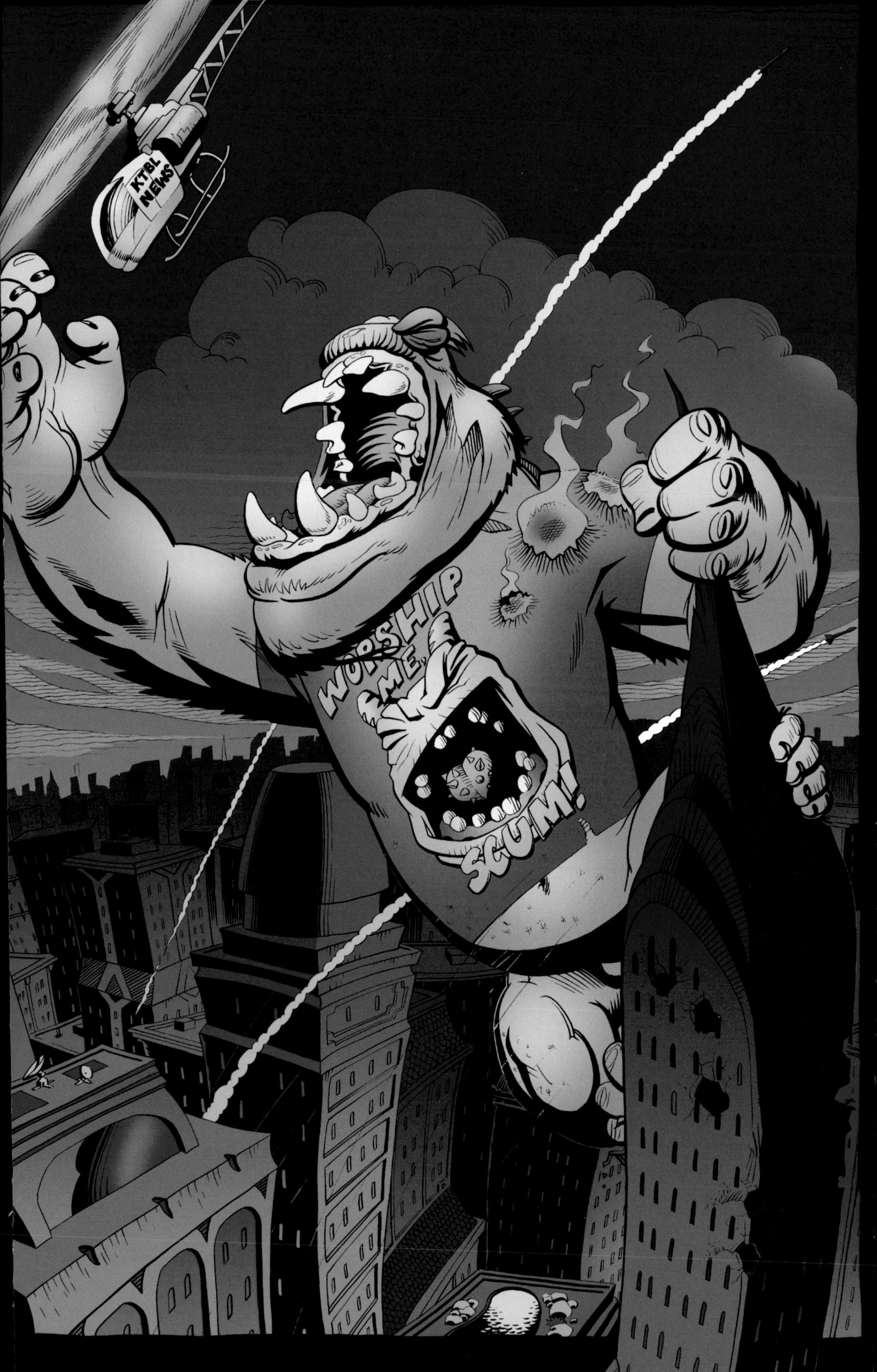
KTBL NEWS
WORSHIP ME, SCUM!

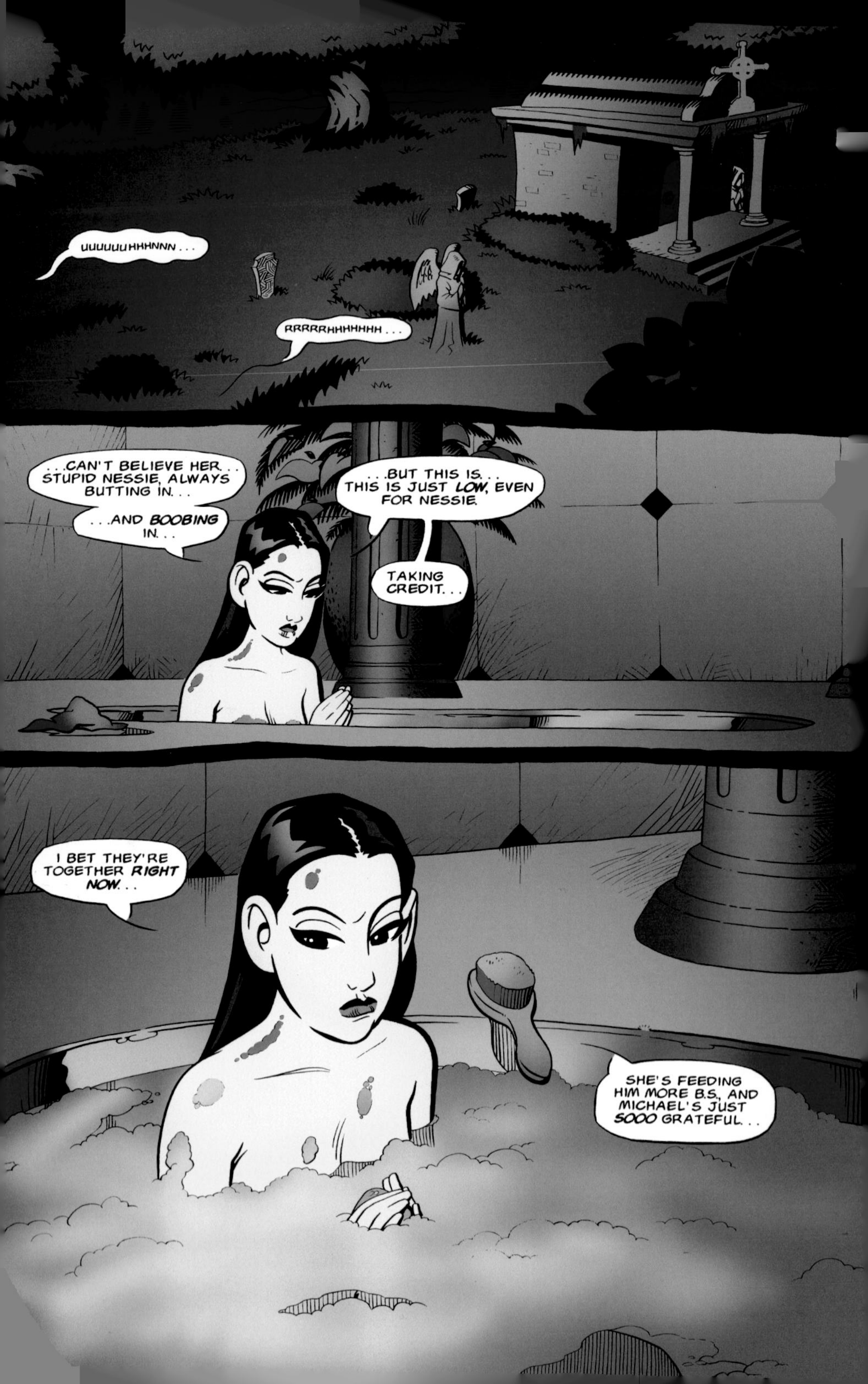
UUUUUUHHHNNN...
RRRRRHHHHHHH...
...CAN'T BELIEVE HER... STUPID NESSIE, ALWAYS BUTTING IN...
...AND BOOBING IN...
...BUT THIS IS... THIS IS JUST LOW, EVEN FOR NESSIE.
TAKING CREDIT...
I BET THEY'RE TOGETHER RIGHT NOW...
SHE'S FEEDING HIM MORE B.S., AND MICHAEL'S JUST SOOO GRATEFUL...

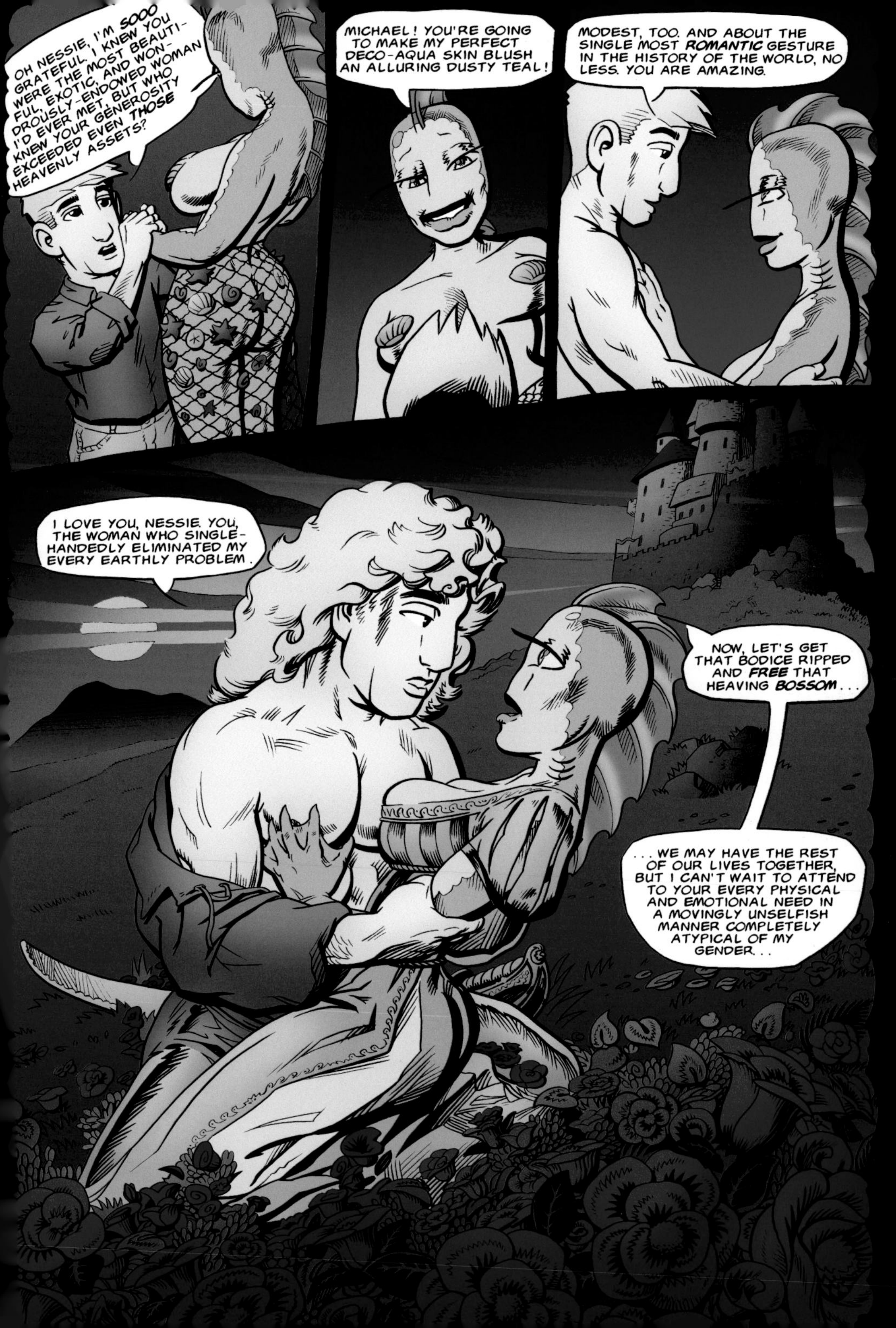
OH NESSIE, I'M SOOO GRATEFUL. I KNEW YOU WERE THE MOST BEAUTIFUL, EXOTIC, AND WONDROUSLY-ENDOWED WOMAN I'D EVER MET, BUT WHO KNEW YOUR GENEROSITY EXCEEDED EVEN THOSE HEAVENLY ASSETS?
MICHAEL! YOU'RE GOING TO MAKE MY PERFECT DECO-AQUA SKIN BLUSH AN ALLURING DUSTY TEAL!
MODEST, TOO. AND ABOUT THE SINGLE MOST ROMANTIC GESTURE IN THE HISTORY OF THE WORLD, NO LESS. YOU ARE AMAZING.
I LOVE YOU, NESSIE. YOU, THE WOMAN WHO SINGLE-HANDEDLY ELIMINATED MY EVERY EARTHLY PROBLEM.
NOW, LET'S GET THAT BODICE RIPPED AND FREE THAT HEAVING BOSSOM...
...WE MAY HAVE THE REST OF OUR LIVES TOGETHER, BUT I CAN'T WAIT TO ATTEND TO YOUR EVERY PHYSICAL AND EMOTIONAL NEED IN A MOVINGLY UNSELFISH MANNER COMPLETELY ATYPICAL OF MY GENDER...

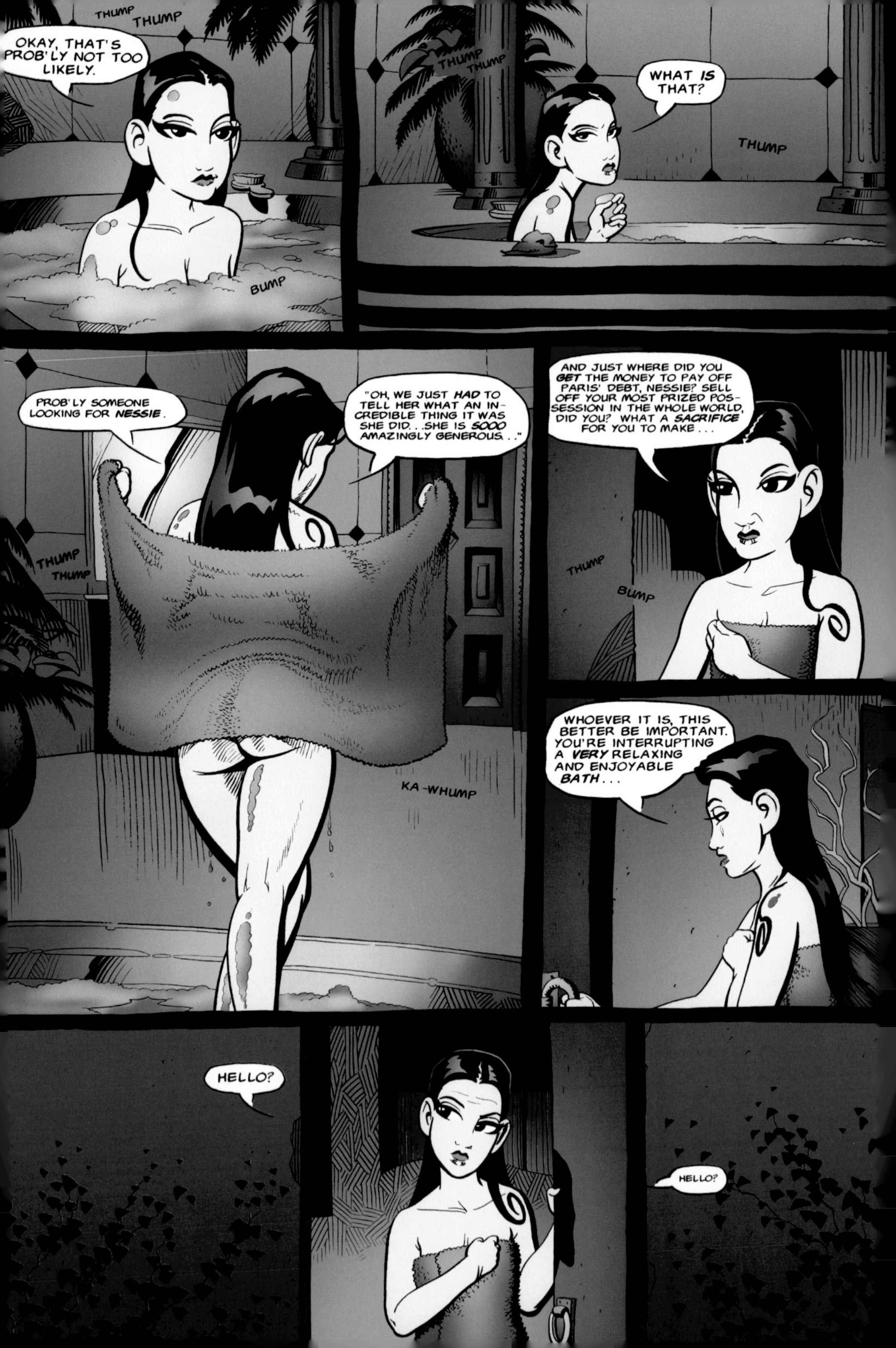
THUMP
THUMP
OKAY, THAT'S PROB'LY NOT TOO LIKELY.
BUMP
THUMP
THUMP
WHAT IS THAT?
THUMP
PROB'LY SOMEONE LOOKING FOR NESSIE.
"OH, WE JUST HAD TO TELL HER WHAT AN INCREDIBLE THING IT WAS SHE DID. . .SHE IS SOOO AMAZINGLY GENEROUS. . ."
THUMP
THUMP
KA-WHUMP
AND JUST WHERE DID YOU GET THE MONEY TO PAY OFF PARIS' DEBT, NESSIE? SELL OFF YOUR MOST PRIZED POSSESSION IN THE WHOLE WORLD, DID YOU? WHAT A SACRIFICE FOR YOU TO MAKE . . .
THUMP
BUMP
WHOEVER IT IS, THIS BETTER BE IMPORTANT. YOU'RE INTERRUPTING A VERY RELAXING AND ENJOYABLE BATH . . .
HELLO?
HELLO?

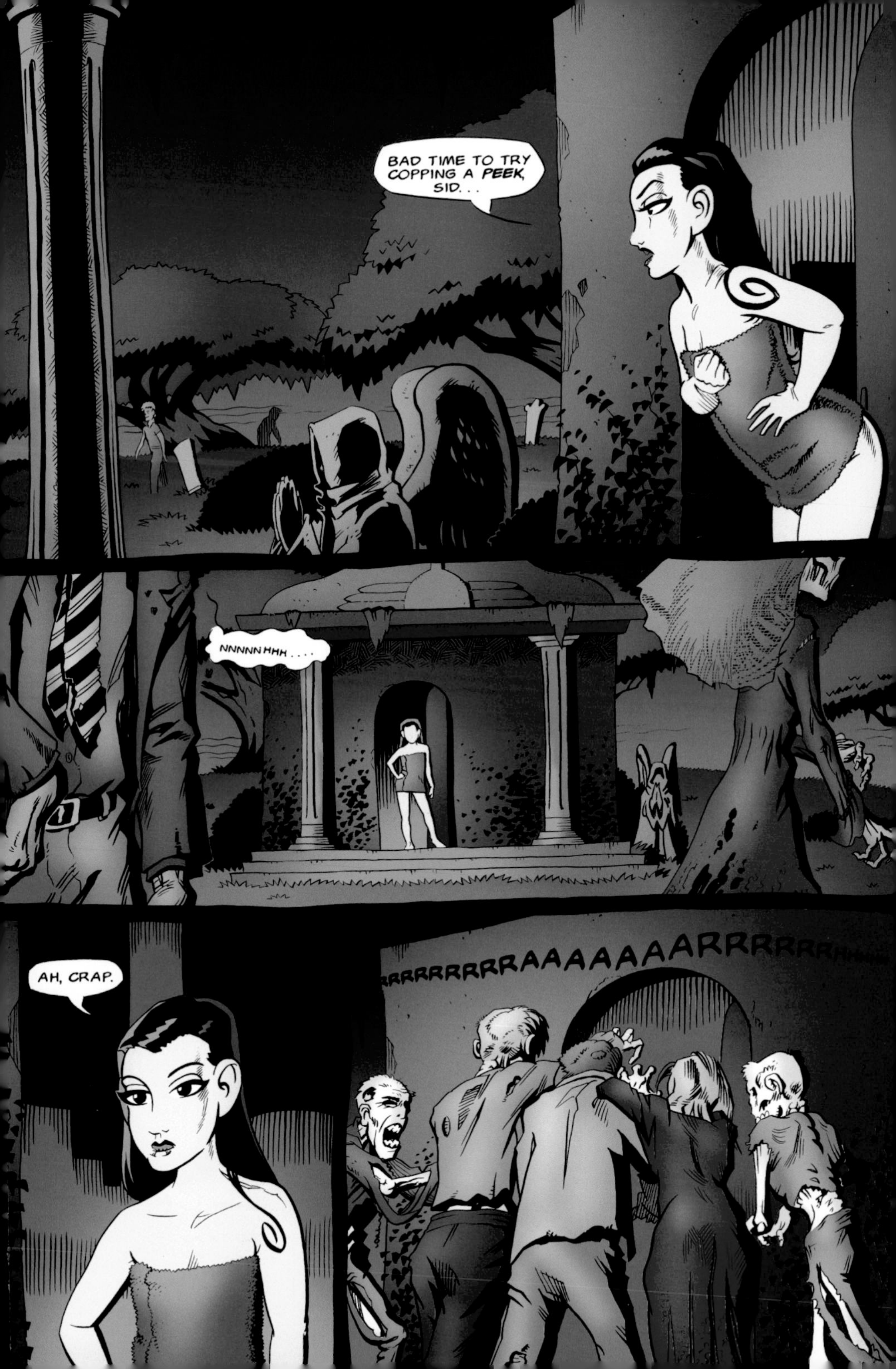
BAD TIME TO TRY COPPING A PEEK, SID...
NNNNNHHH....
AH, CRAP.
RRRRRRRRRRAAAAAAAARRRRRR

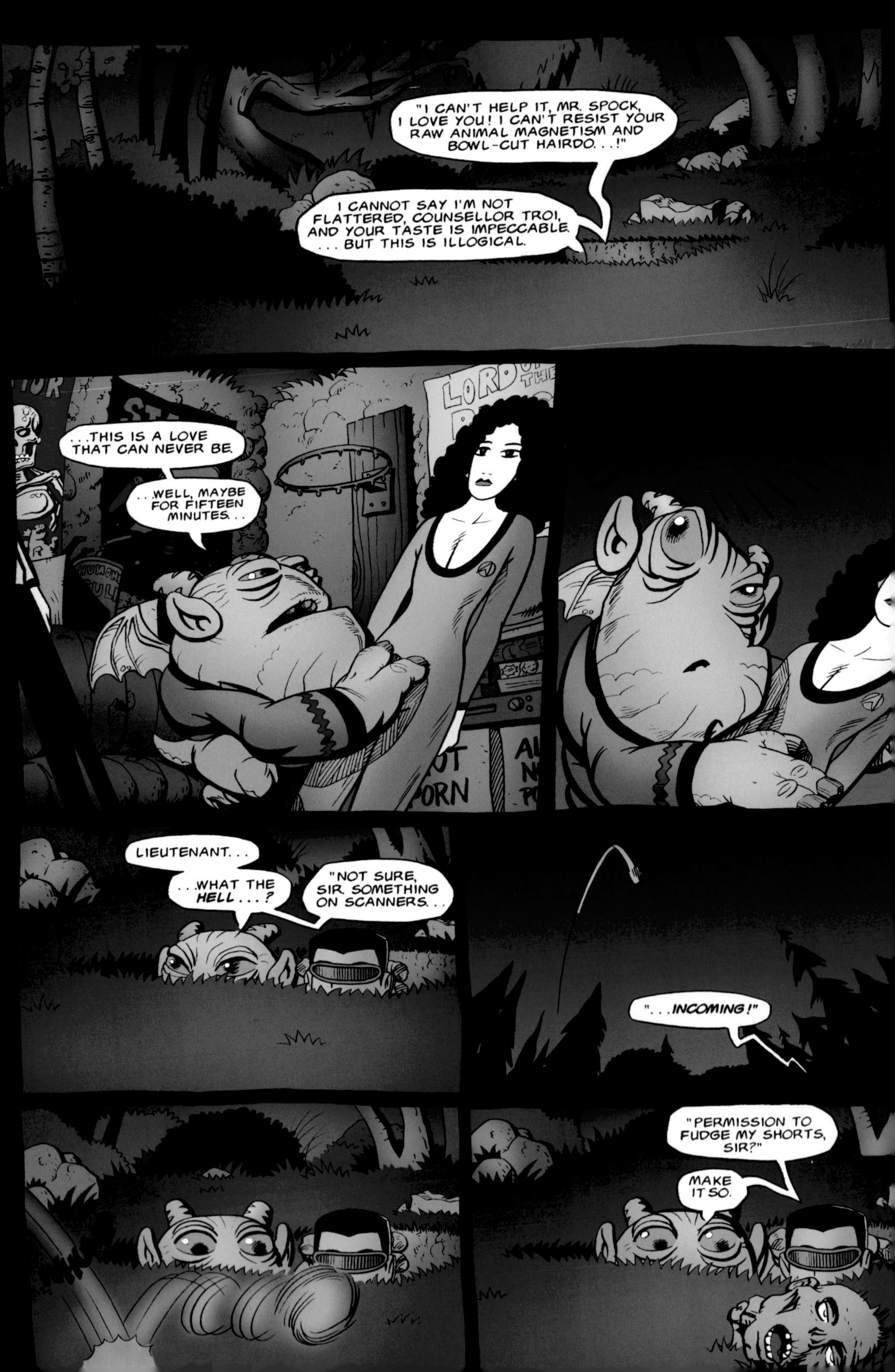
"I CAN'T HELP IT, MR. SPOCK, I LOVE YOU! I CAN'T RESIST YOUR RAW ANIMAL MAGNETISM AND BOWL-CUT HAIRDO. . .!"
I CANNOT SAY I'M NOT FLATTERED, COUNSELLOR TROI, AND YOUR TASTE IS IMPECCABLE. . . . BUT THIS IS ILLOGICAL.
. . .THIS IS A LOVE THAT CAN NEVER BE.
. . .WELL, MAYBE FOR FIFTEEN MINUTES. . .
LIEUTENANT. . .
. . .WHAT THE HELL . . .?
"NOT SURE, SIR. SOMETHING ON SCANNERS. . .
". . .INCOMING!"
"PERMISSION TO FUDGE MY SHORTS, SIR?"
MAKE IT SO.

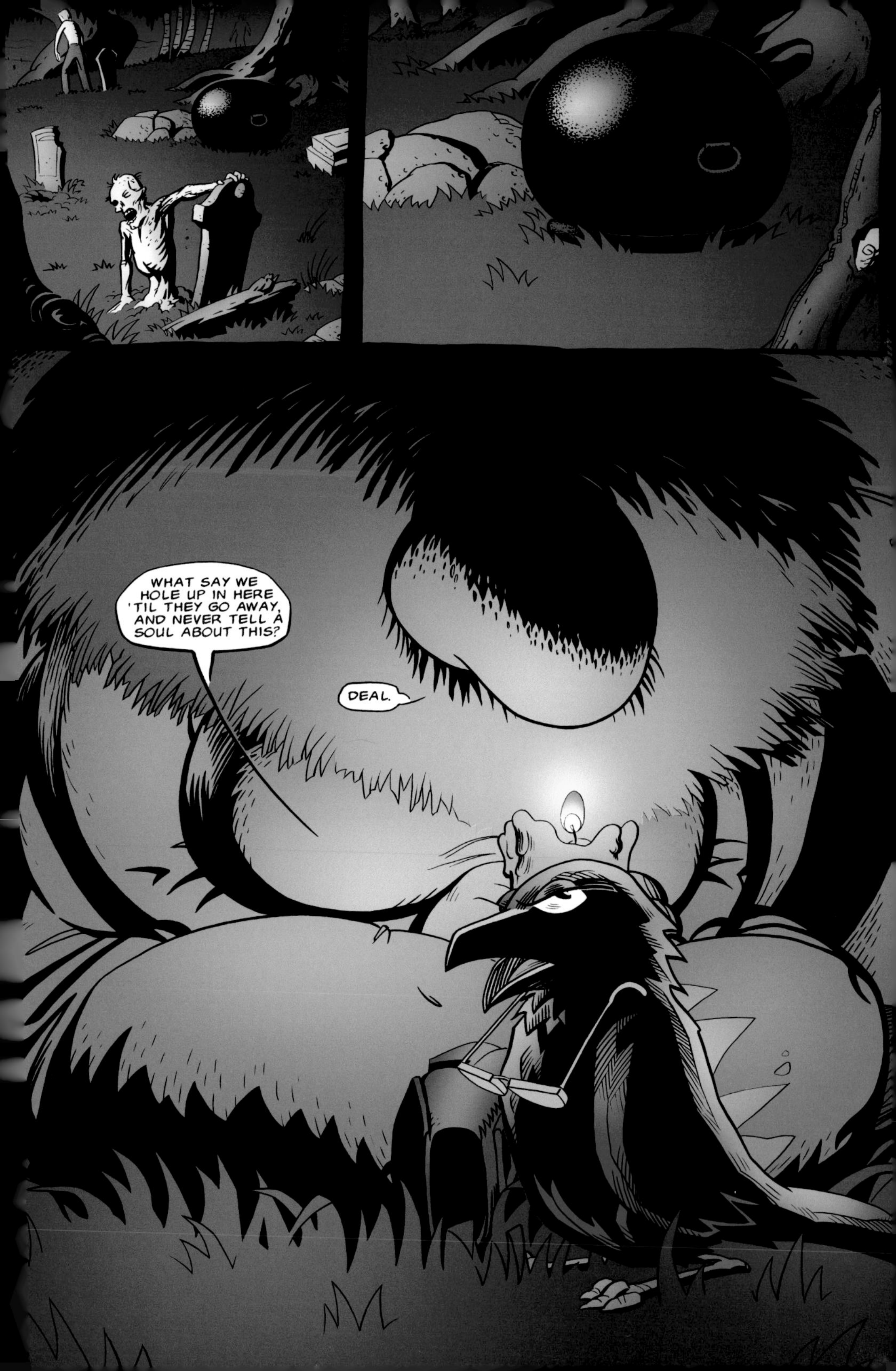
WHAT SAY WE HOLE UP IN HERE 'TIL THEY GO AWAY, AND NEVER TELL A SOUL ABOUT THIS?
DEAL.

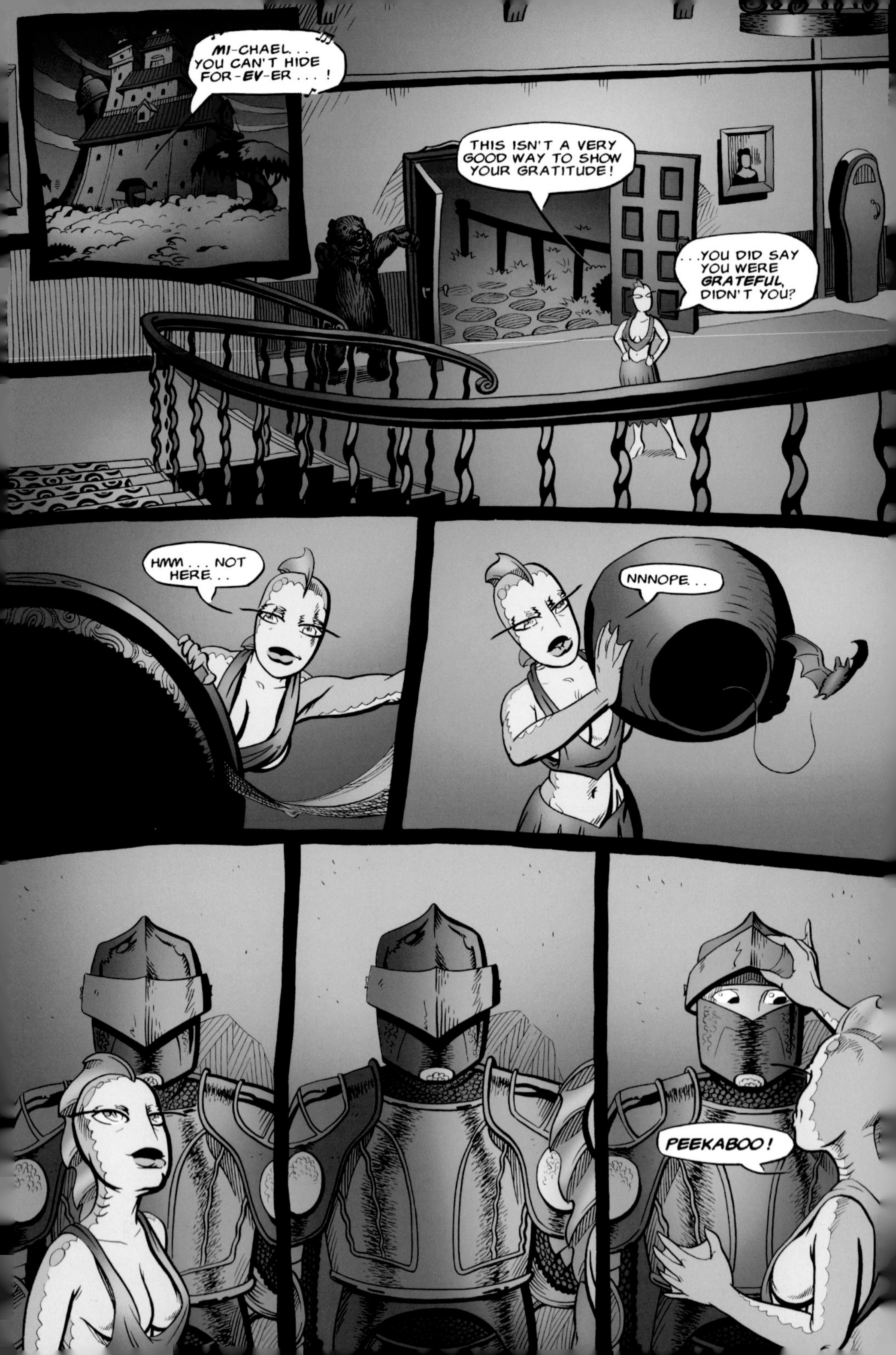
MI-CHAEL. . . YOU CAN'T HIDE FOR-EV-ER . . . !
THIS ISN'T A VERY GOOD WAY TO SHOW YOUR GRATITUDE!
. . .YOU DID SAY YOU WERE GRATEFUL, DIDN'T YOU?
HMM . . . NOT HERE. . .
NNNOPE. . .
PEEKABOO!

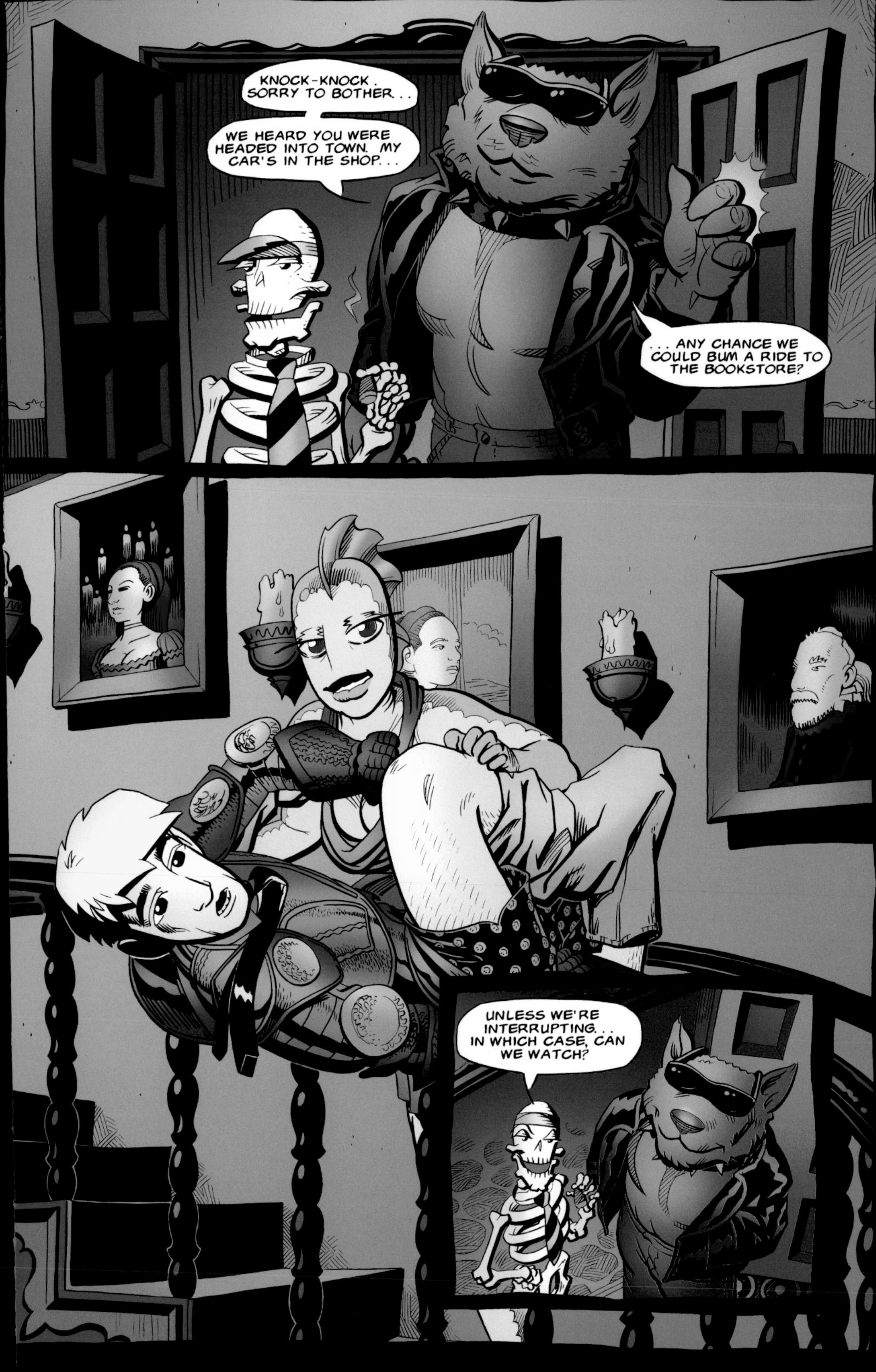
KNOCK-KNOCK. SORRY TO BOTHER...
WE HEARD YOU WERE HEADED INTO TOWN. MY CAR'S IN THE SHOP...
...ANY CHANCE WE COULD BUM A RIDE TO THE BOOKSTORE?
UNLESS WE'RE INTERRUPTING... IN WHICH CASE, CAN WE WATCH?

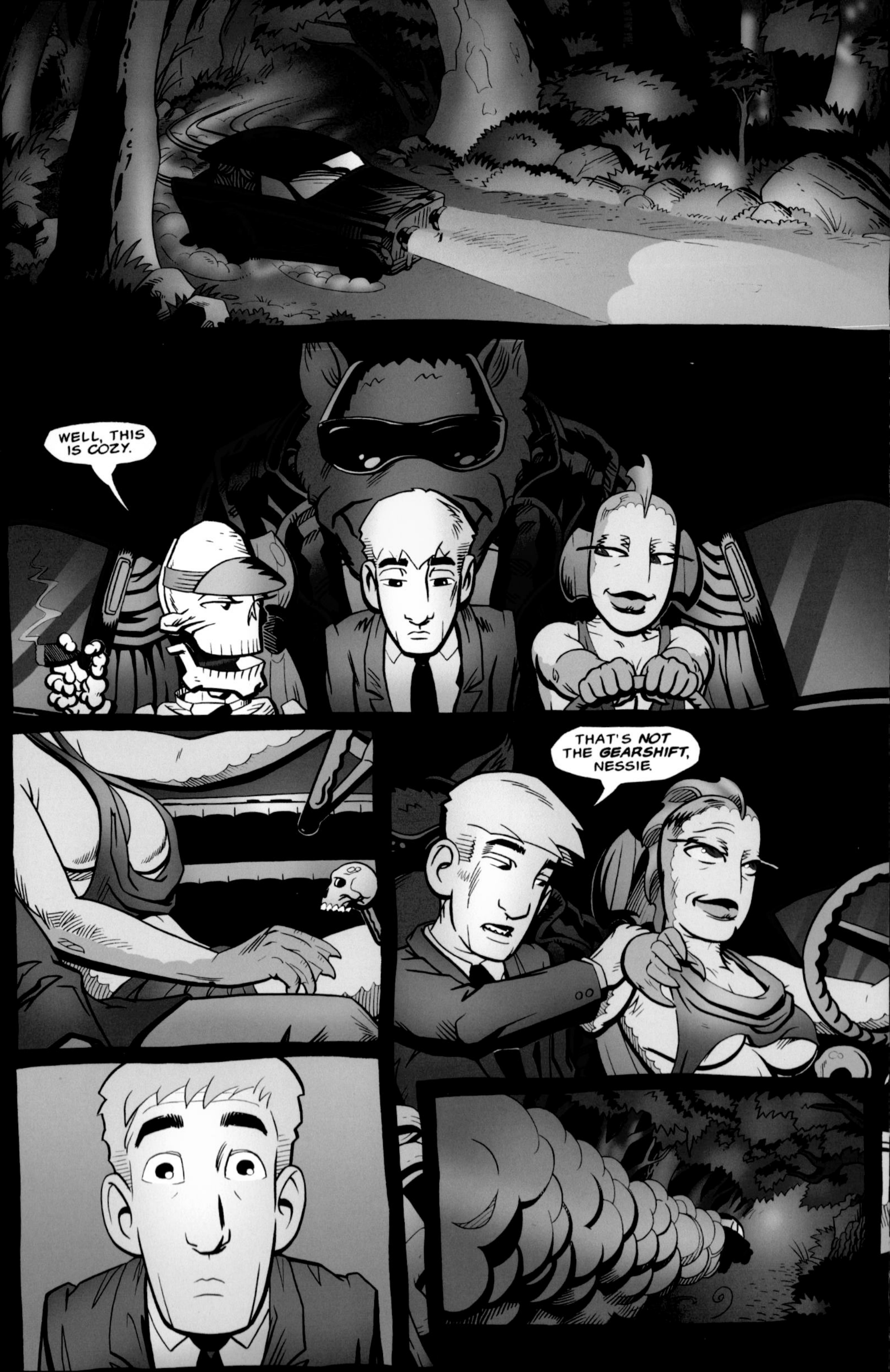
WELL, THIS IS COZY.
THAT'S NOT THE GEARSHIFT, NESSIE.

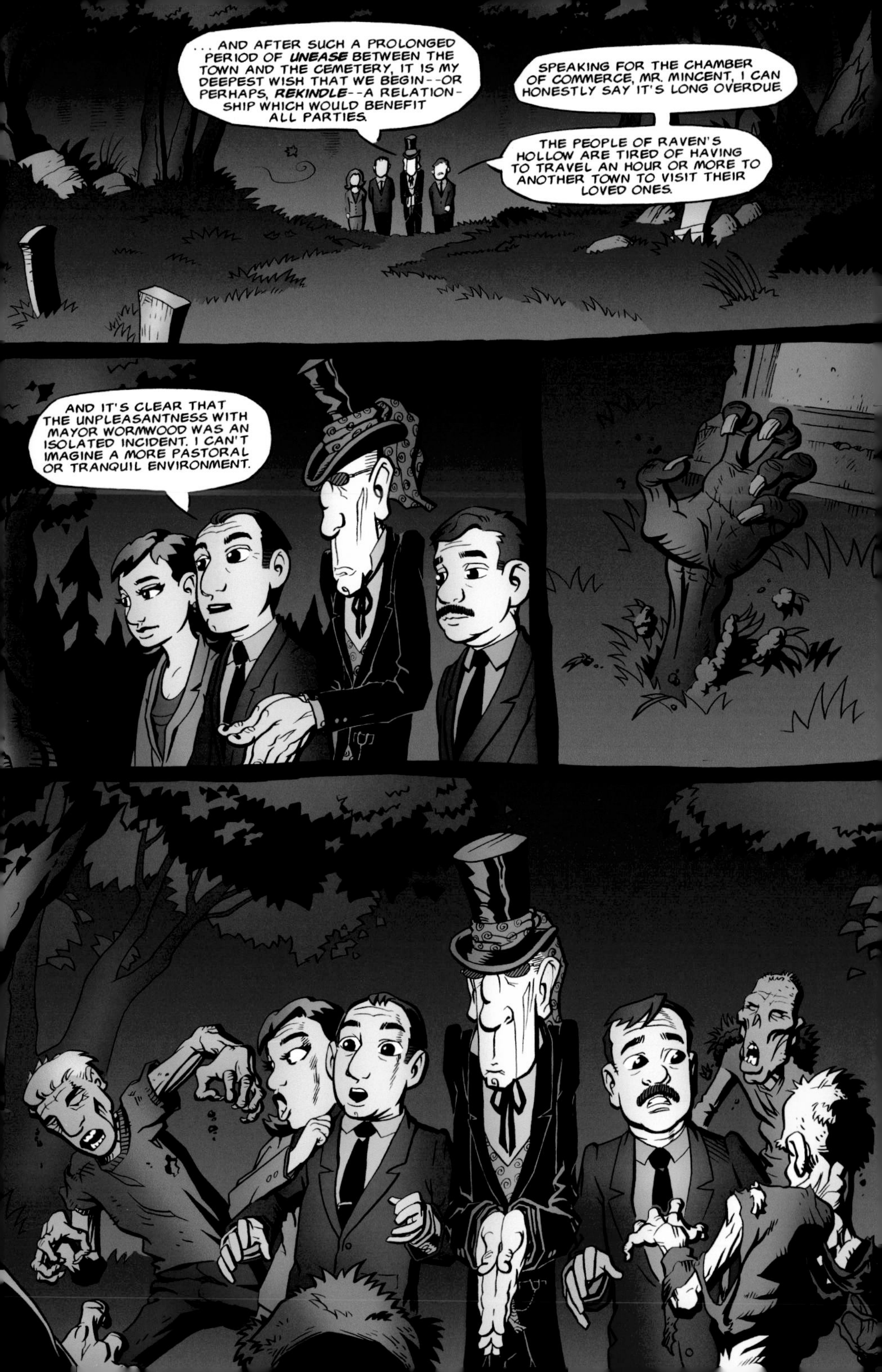
. . . AND AFTER SUCH A PROLONGED PERIOD OF UNEASE BETWEEN THE TOWN AND THE CEMETERY, IT IS MY DEEPEST WISH THAT WE BEGIN--OR PERHAPS, REKINDLE--A RELATIONSHIP WHICH WOULD BENEFIT ALL PARTIES.
SPEAKING FOR THE CHAMBER OF COMMERCE, MR. MINCENT, I CAN HONESTLY SAY IT'S LONG OVERDUE.
THE PEOPLE OF RAVEN'S HOLLOW ARE TIRED OF HAVING TO TRAVEL AN HOUR OR MORE TO ANOTHER TOWN TO VISIT THEIR LOVED ONES.
AND IT'S CLEAR THAT THE UNPLEASANTNESS WITH MAYOR WORMWOOD WAS AN ISOLATED INCIDENT. I CAN'T IMAGINE A MORE PASTORAL OR TRANQUIL ENVIRONMENT.

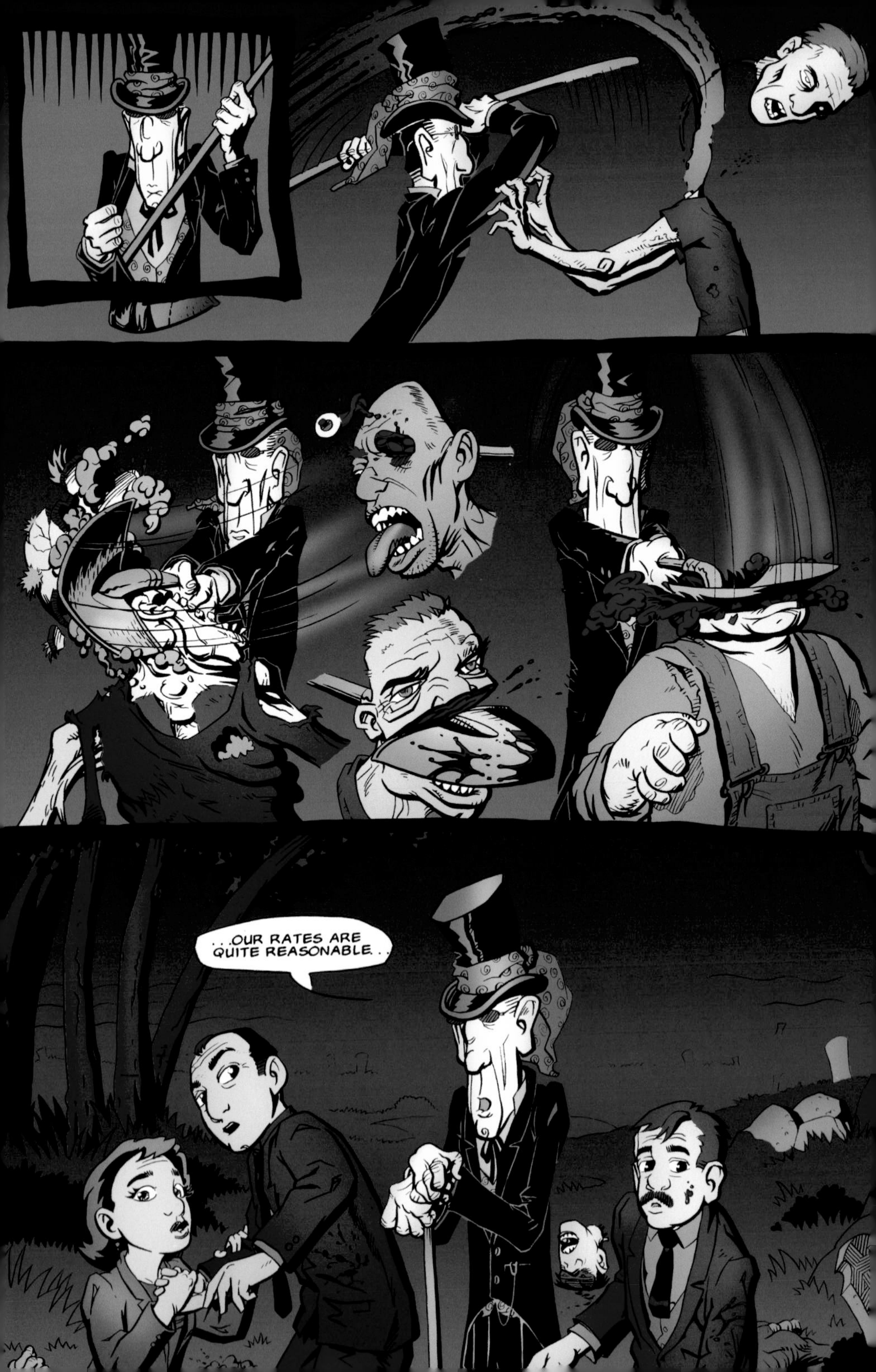
. . .OUR RATES ARE QUITE REASONABLE. . .

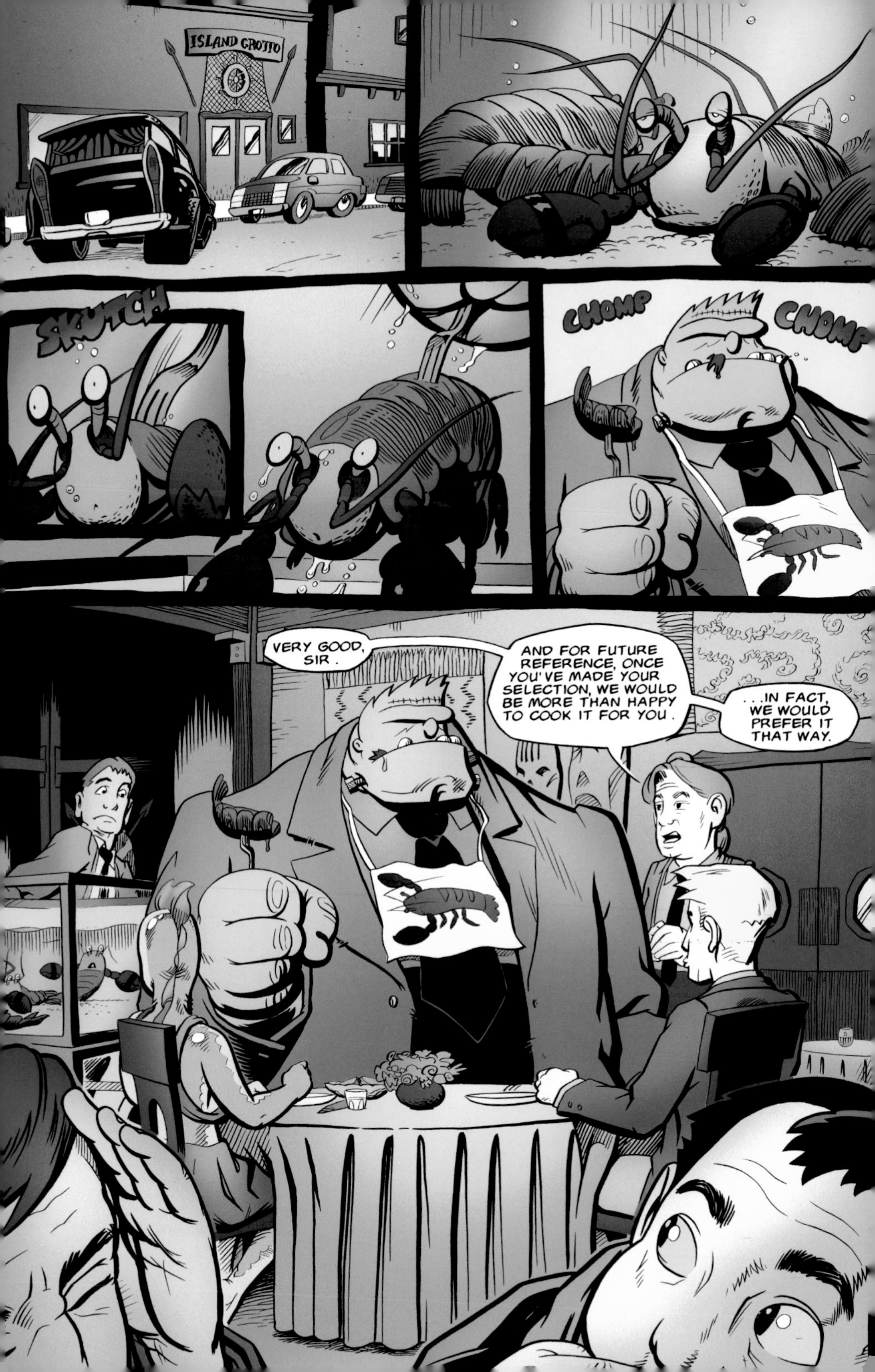
ISLAND GROTTO
SKUTCH
CHOMP
CHOMP
VERY GOOD, SIR.
AND FOR FUTURE REFERENCE, ONCE YOU'VE MADE YOUR SELECTION, WE WOULD BE MORE THAN HAPPY TO COOK IT FOR YOU.
...IN FACT, WE WOULD PREFER IT THAT WAY.

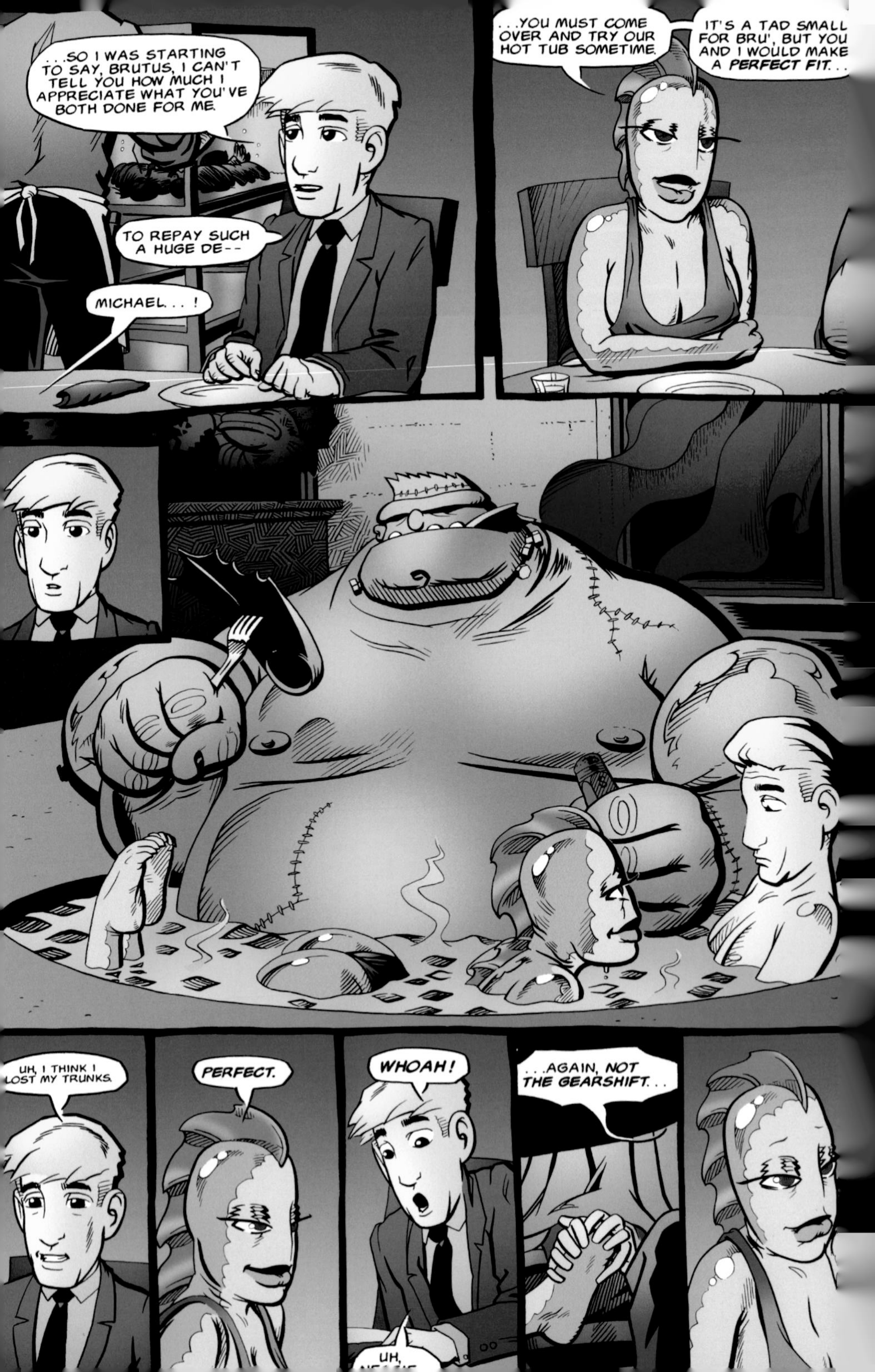

...SO I WAS STARTING TO SAY, BRUTUS, I CAN'T TELL YOU HOW MUCH I APPRECIATE WHAT YOU'VE BOTH DONE FOR ME.
TO REPAY SUCH A HUGE DE--
MICHAEL...!
...YOU MUST COME OVER AND TRY OUR HOT TUB SOMETIME.
IT'S A TAD SMALL FOR BRU', BUT YOU AND I WOULD MAKE A PERFECT FIT...
UH, I THINK I LOST MY TRUNKS.
PERFECT.
WHOAH!
UH,
...AGAIN, NOT THE GEARSHIFT...

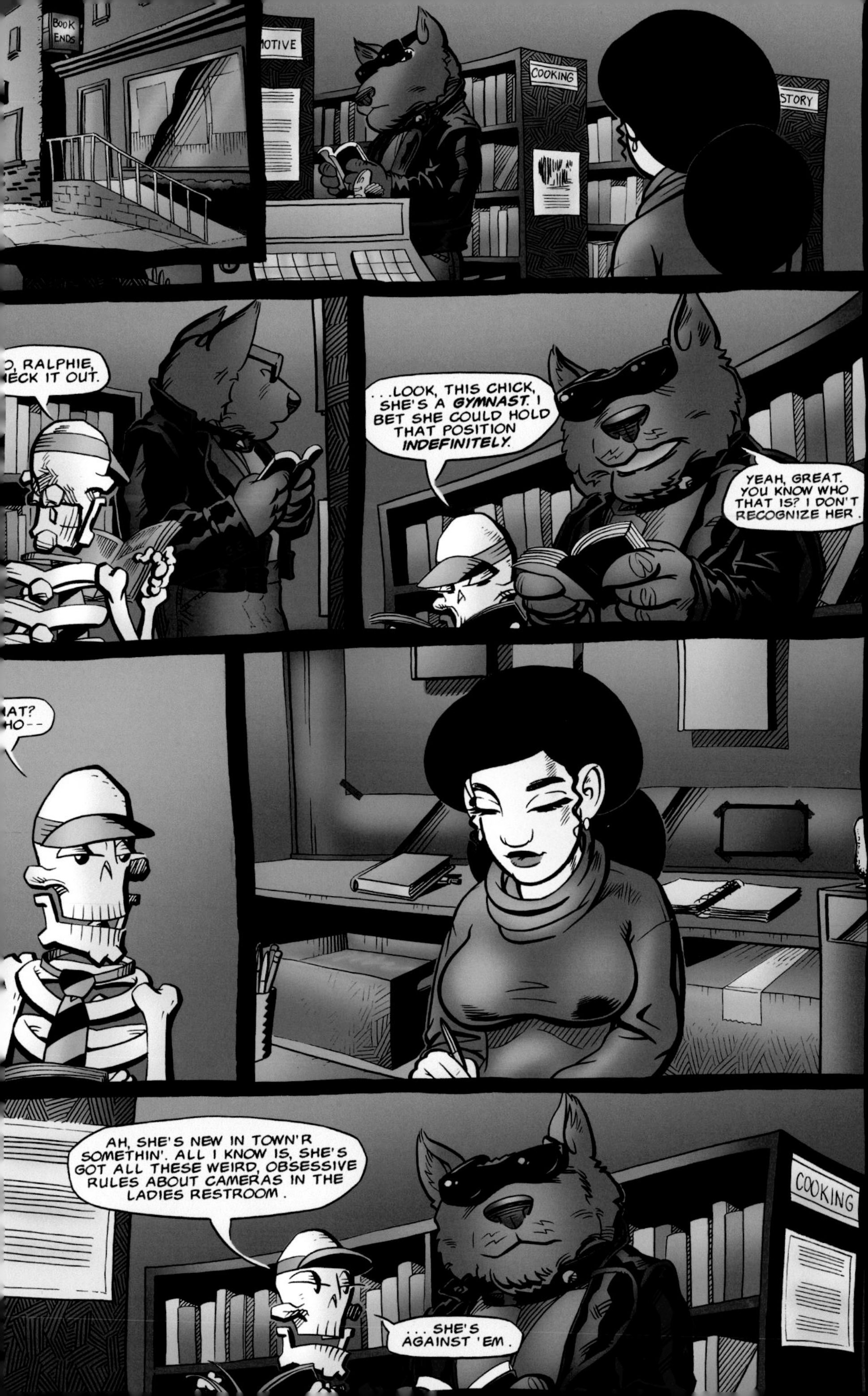
BOOK ENDS
MOTIVE
COOKING
STORY
O, RALPHIE,
ECK IT OUT.
...LOOK, THIS CHICK, SHE'S A GYMNAST. I BET SHE COULD HOLD THAT POSITION INDEFINITELY.
YEAH, GREAT. YOU KNOW WHO THAT IS? I DON'T RECOGNIZE HER.
AT?
HO--
AH, SHE'S NEW IN TOWN'R SOMETHIN'. ALL I KNOW IS, SHE'S GOT ALL THESE WEIRD, OBSESSIVE RULES ABOUT CAMERAS IN THE LADIES RESTROOM.
COOKING
...SHE'S AGAINST 'EM.

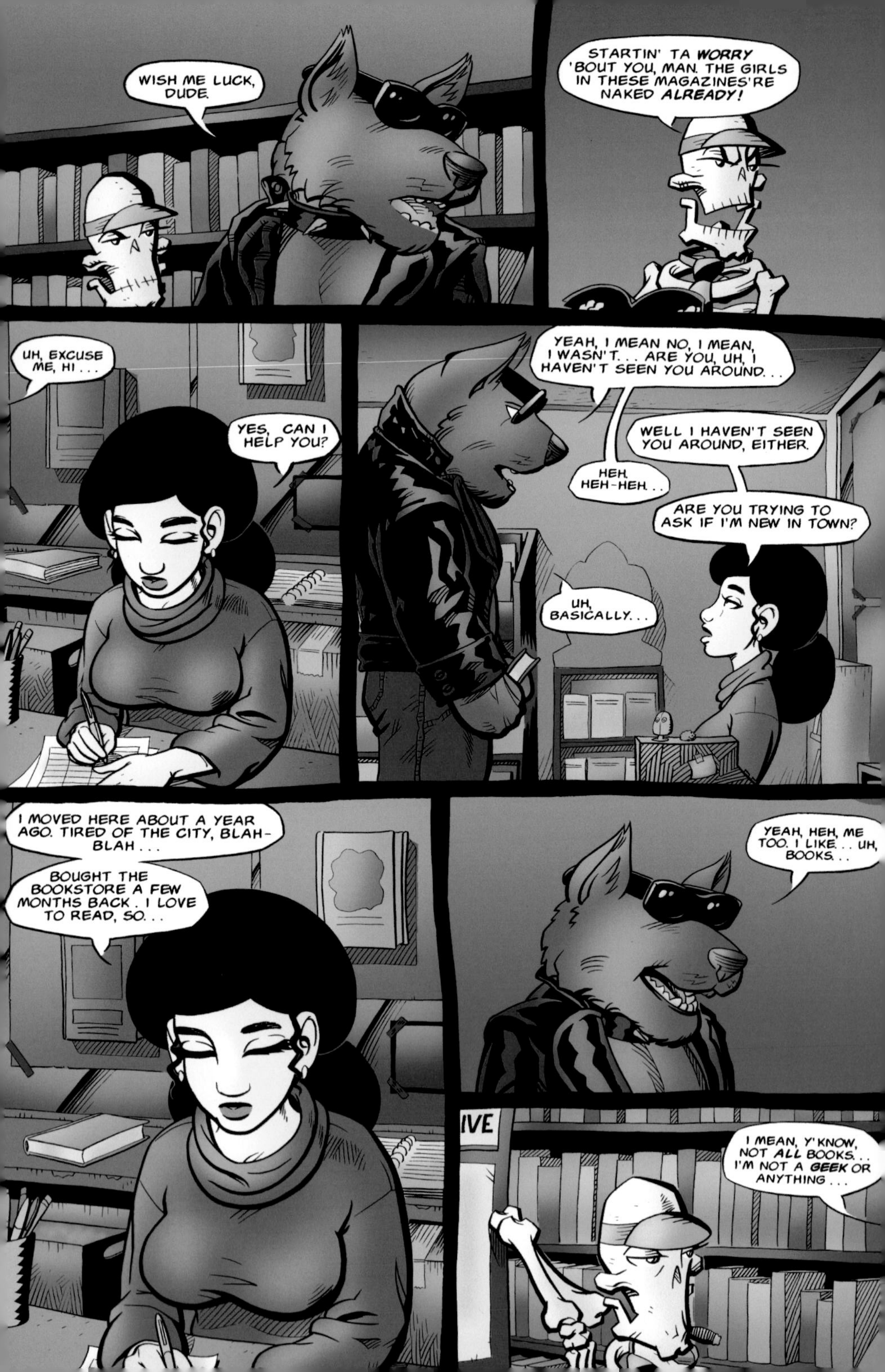
WISH ME LUCK, DUDE.
STARTIN' TA WORRY 'BOUT YOU, MAN. THE GIRLS IN THESE MAGAZINES'RE NAKED ALREADY!
UH, EXCUSE ME, HI . . .
YES, CAN I HELP YOU?
YEAH, I MEAN NO, I MEAN, I WASN'T. . . ARE YOU, UH, I HAVEN'T SEEN YOU AROUND. . .
HEH. HEH-HEH. . .
WELL I HAVEN'T SEEN YOU AROUND, EITHER.
ARE YOU TRYING TO ASK IF I'M NEW IN TOWN?
UH, BASICALLY. . .
I MOVED HERE ABOUT A YEAR AGO. TIRED OF THE CITY, BLAH-BLAH . . .
BOUGHT THE BOOKSTORE A FEW MONTHS BACK. I LOVE TO READ, SO. . .
YEAH, HEH, ME TOO. I LIKE. . . UH, BOOKS. . .
IVE
I MEAN, Y'KNOW, NOT ALL BOOKS. . . I'M NOT A GEEK OR ANYTHING . . .

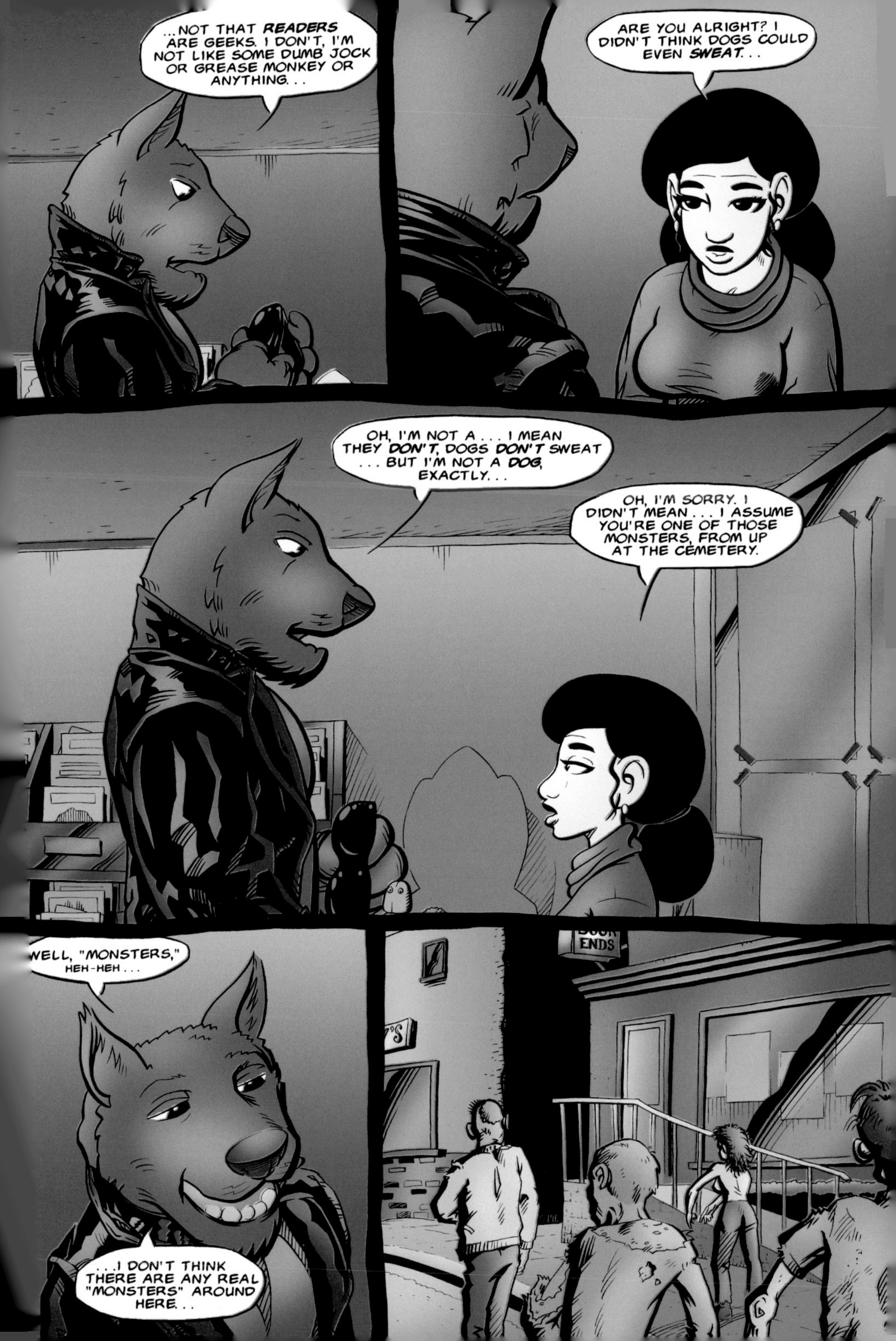
...NOT THAT READERS ARE GEEKS. I DON'T, I'M NOT LIKE SOME DUMB JOCK OR GREASE MONKEY OR ANYTHING...
ARE YOU ALRIGHT? I DIDN'T THINK DOGS COULD EVEN SWEAT...
OH, I'M NOT A... I MEAN THEY DON'T, DOGS DON'T SWEAT ... BUT I'M NOT A DOG, EXACTLY...
OH, I'M SORRY. I DIDN'T MEAN... I ASSUME YOU'RE ONE OF THOSE MONSTERS, FROM UP AT THE CEMETERY.
WELL, "MONSTERS," HEH-HEH...
...I DON'T THINK THERE ARE ANY REAL "MONSTERS" AROUND HERE...
ENDS

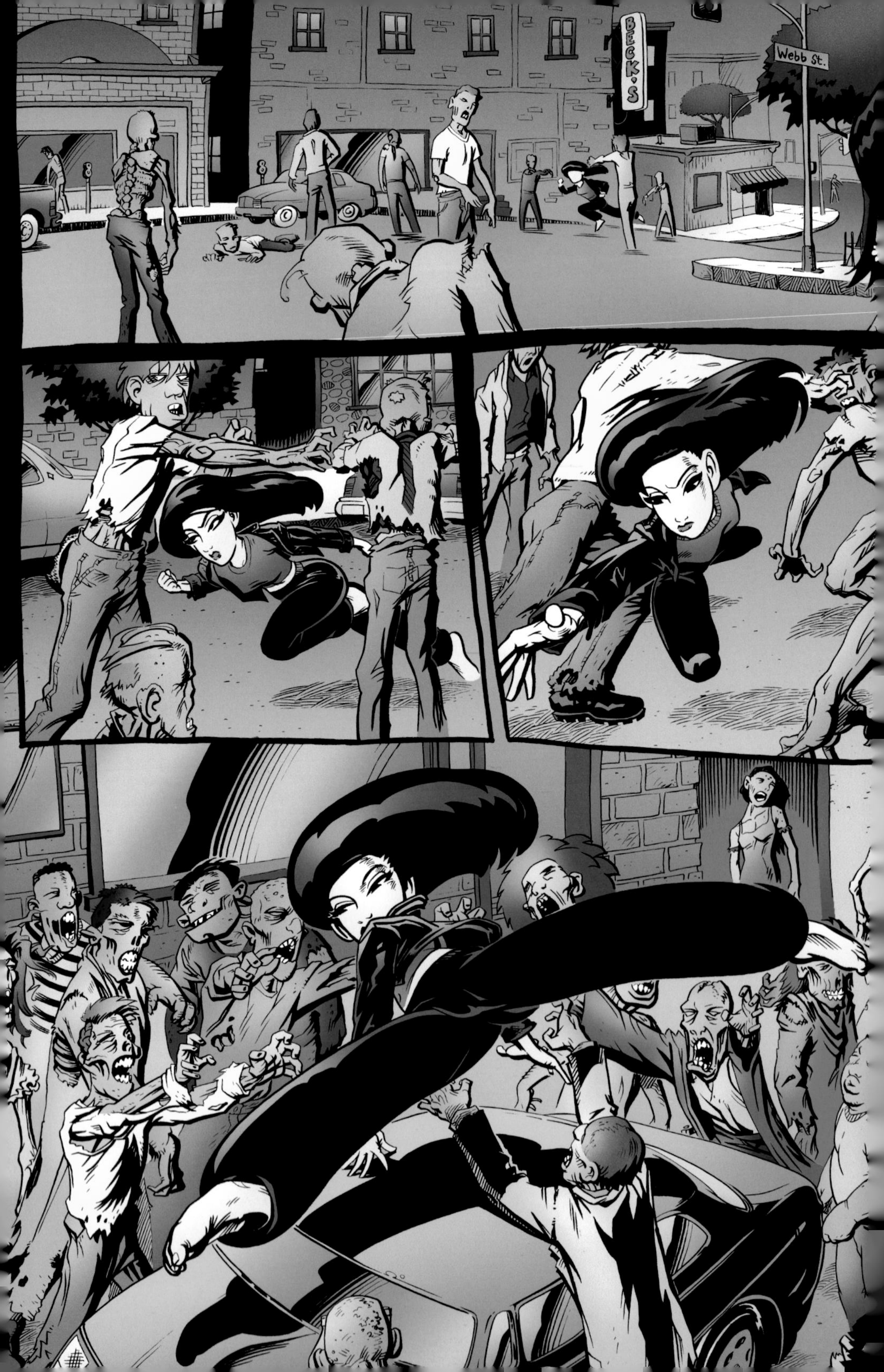
BECK'S
Webb St.

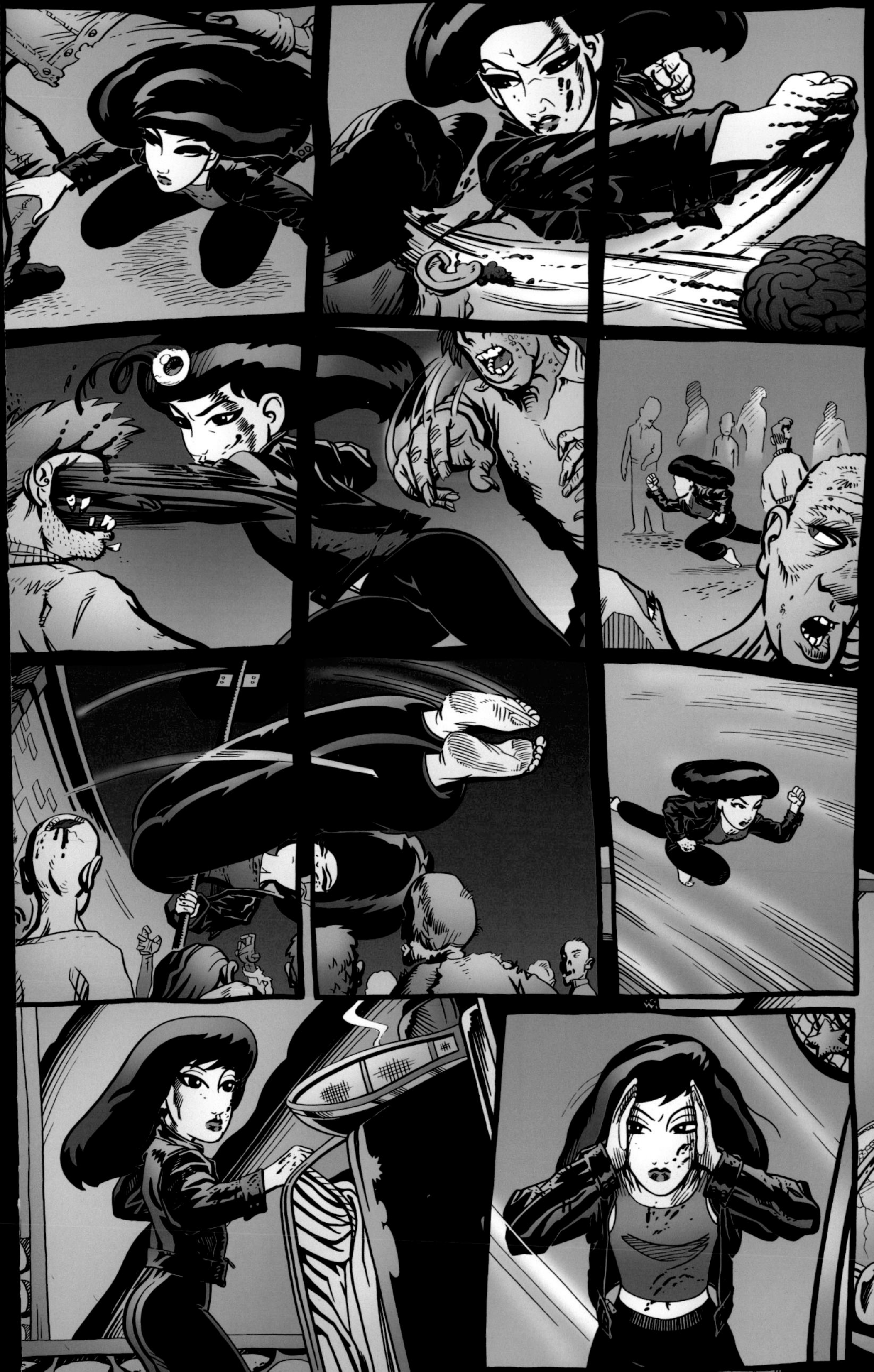

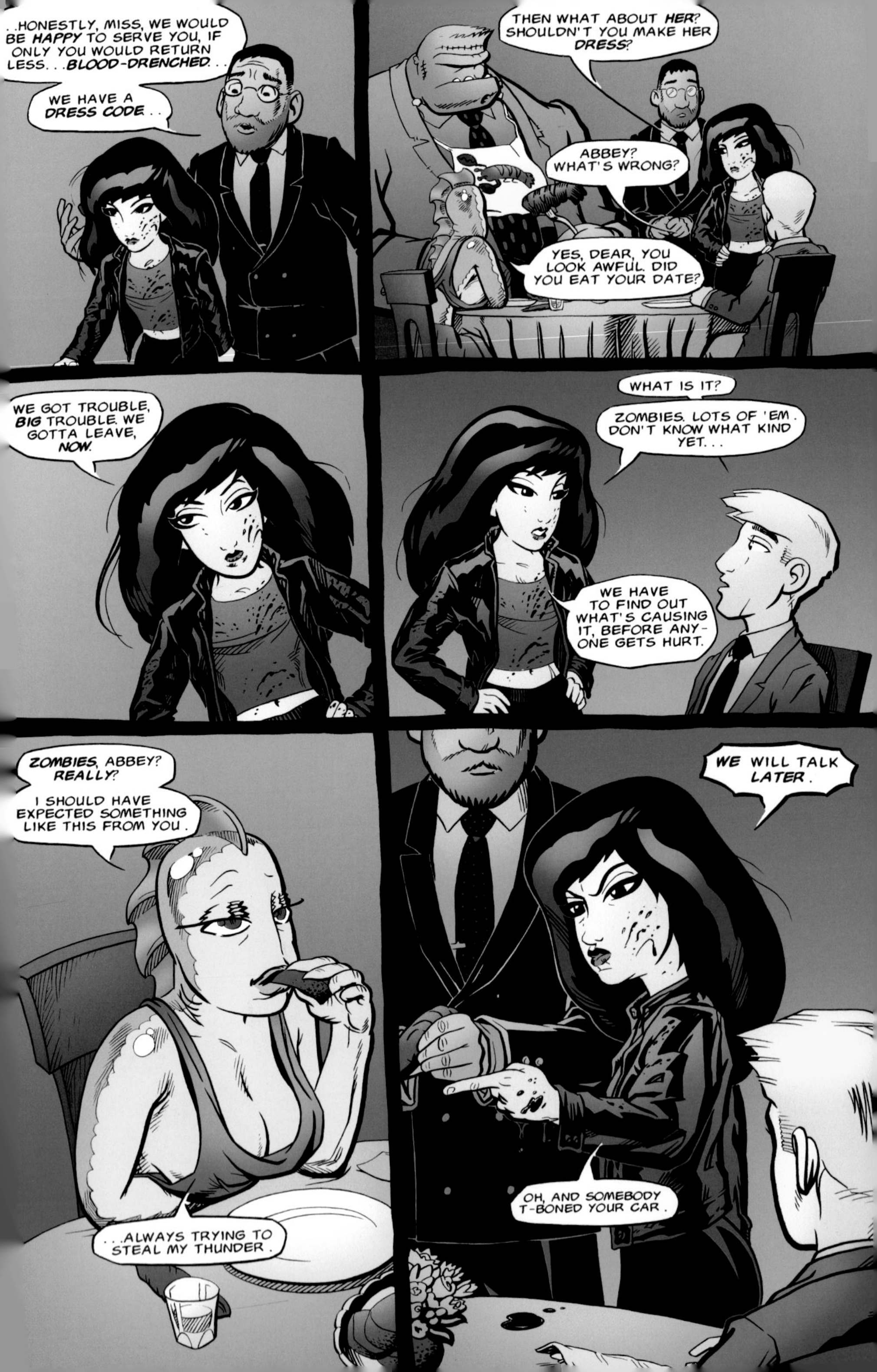
..HONESTLY, MISS, WE WOULD BE HAPPY TO SERVE YOU, IF ONLY YOU WOULD RETURN LESS...BLOOD-DRENCHED...
WE HAVE A DRESS CODE..
THEN WHAT ABOUT HER? SHOULDN'T YOU MAKE HER DRESS?
ABBEY? WHAT'S WRONG?
YES, DEAR, YOU LOOK AWFUL. DID YOU EAT YOUR DATE?
WE GOT TROUBLE, BIG TROUBLE. WE GOTTA LEAVE, NOW.
WHAT IS IT?
ZOMBIES. LOTS OF 'EM. DON'T KNOW WHAT KIND YET...
WE HAVE TO FIND OUT WHAT'S CAUSING IT, BEFORE ANY-ONE GETS HURT.
ZOMBIES, ABBEY? REALLY?
I SHOULD HAVE EXPECTED SOMETHING LIKE THIS FROM YOU.
...ALWAYS TRYING TO STEAL MY THUNDER.
WE WILL TALK LATER.
OH, AND SOMEBODY T-BONED YOUR CAR.

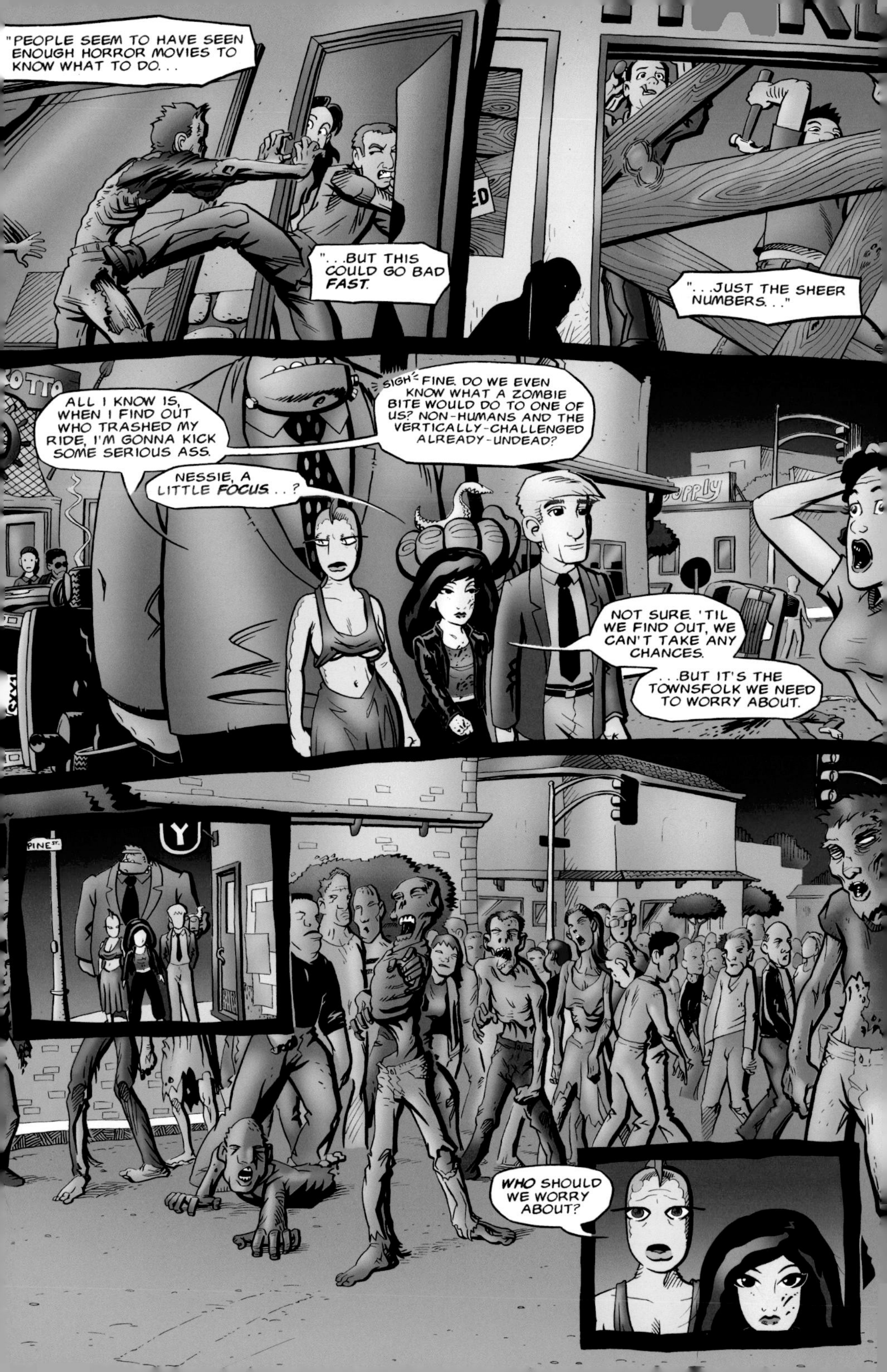
"PEOPLE SEEM TO HAVE SEEN ENOUGH HORROR MOVIES TO KNOW WHAT TO DO. . .
". . .BUT THIS COULD GO BAD FAST.
". . .JUST THE SHEER NUMBERS. . ."
ALL I KNOW IS, WHEN I FIND OUT WHO TRASHED MY RIDE, I'M GONNA KICK SOME SERIOUS ASS.
SIGH
FINE. DO WE EVEN KNOW WHAT A ZOMBIE BITE WOULD DO TO ONE OF US? NON-HUMANS AND THE VERTICALLY-CHALLENGED ALREADY-UNDEAD?
NESSIE, A LITTLE FOCUS. . .?
NOT SURE. 'TIL WE FIND OUT, WE CAN'T TAKE ANY CHANCES.
. . .BUT IT'S THE TOWNSFOLK WE NEED TO WORRY ABOUT.
PINE ST.
WHO SHOULD WE WORRY ABOUT?

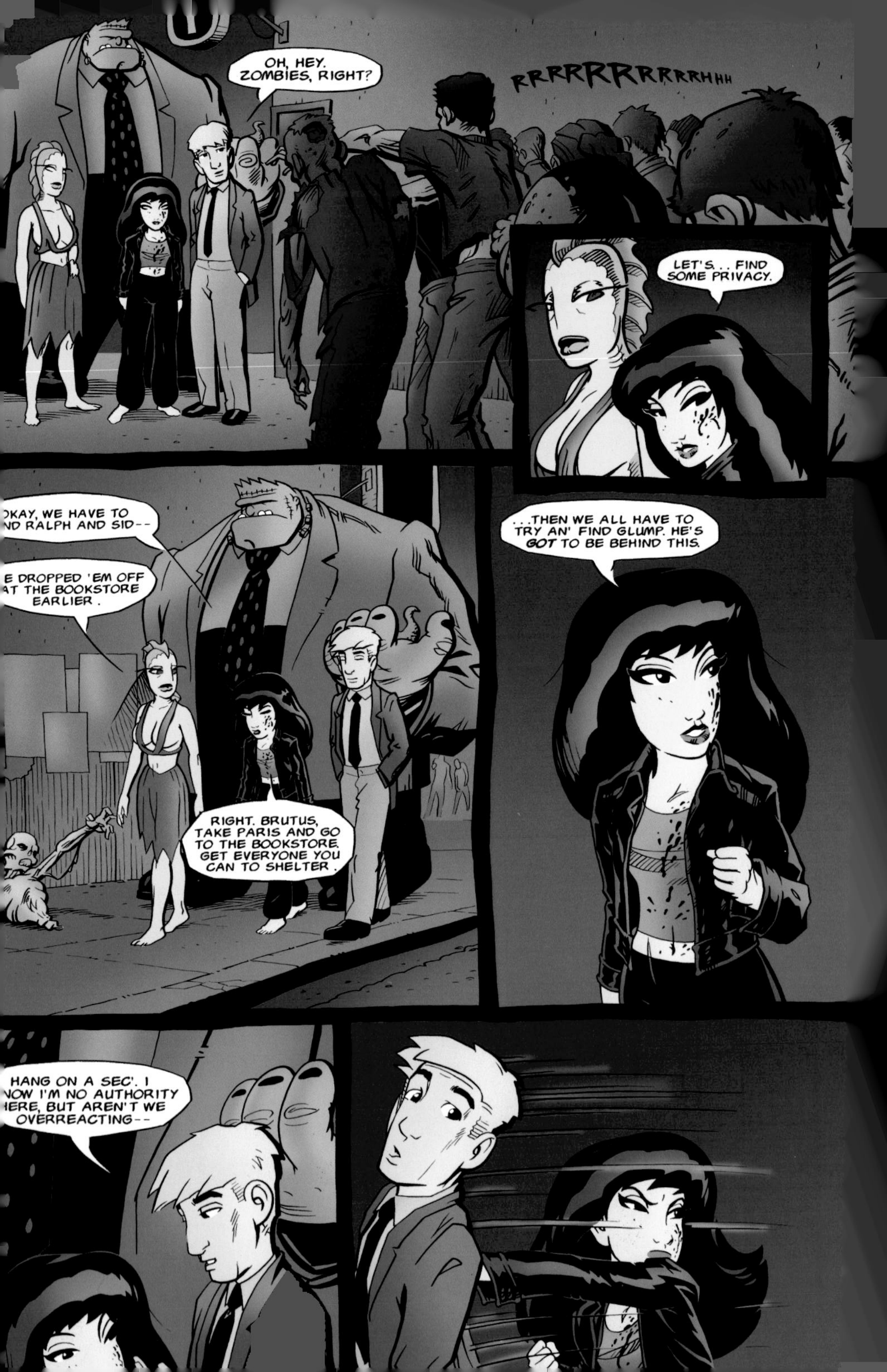

OH, HEY. ZOMBIES, RIGHT?
RRRRRRRRRRRHHH
LET'S... FIND SOME PRIVACY.
OKAY, WE HAVE TO ND RALPH AND SID--
E DROPPED 'EM OFF AT THE BOOKSTORE EARLIER.
RIGHT. BRUTUS, TAKE PARIS AND GO TO THE BOOKSTORE. GET EVERYONE YOU CAN TO SHELTER.
...THEN WE ALL HAVE TO TRY AN' FIND GLUMP. HE'S GOT TO BE BEHIND THIS.
HANG ON A SEC'. I NOW I'M NO AUTHORITY HERE, BUT AREN'T WE OVERREACTING--

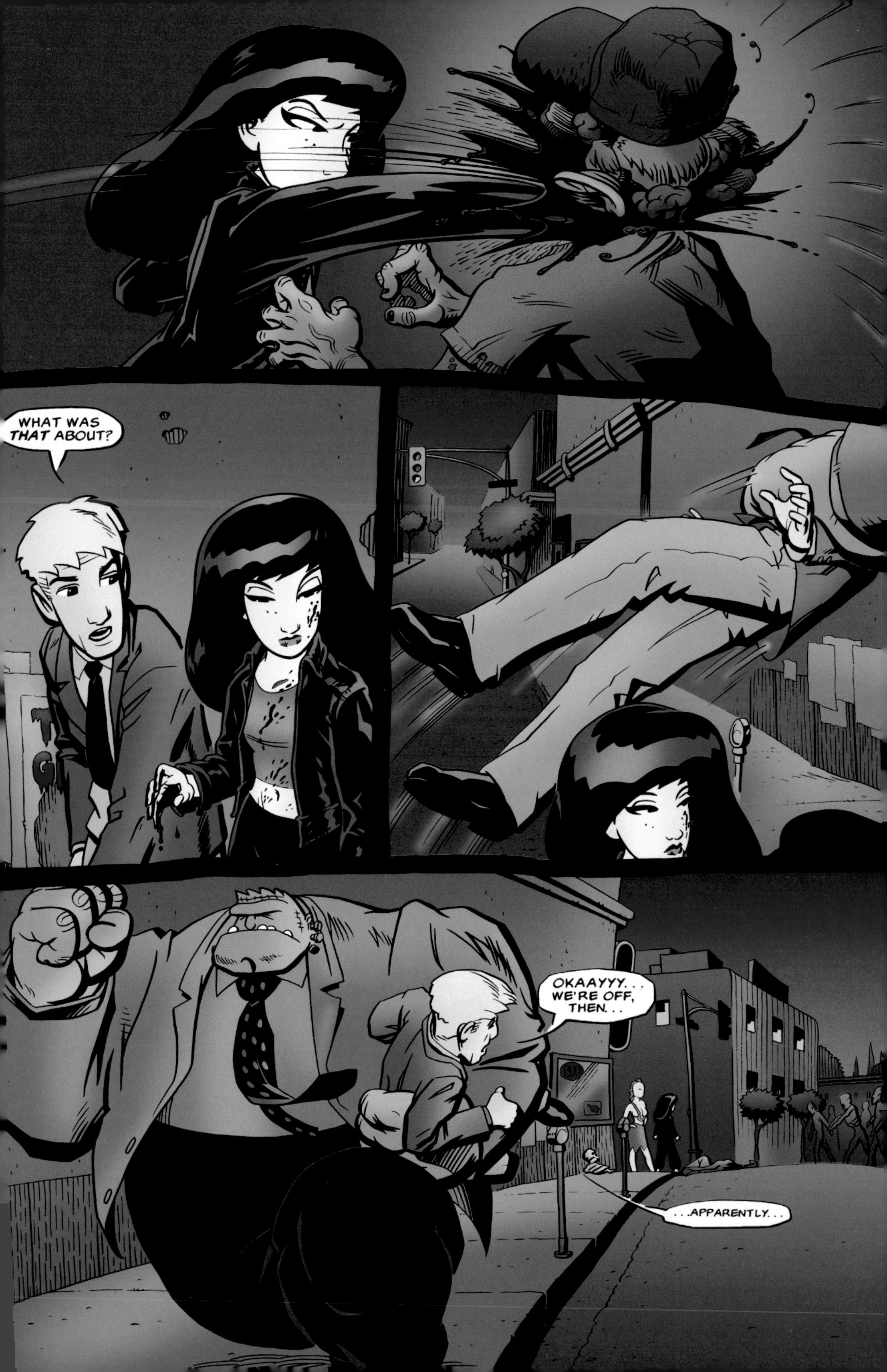
WHAT WAS *THAT* ABOUT?
OKAAYYY. . . WE'RE OFF, THEN. . .
. . .APPARENTLY. . .

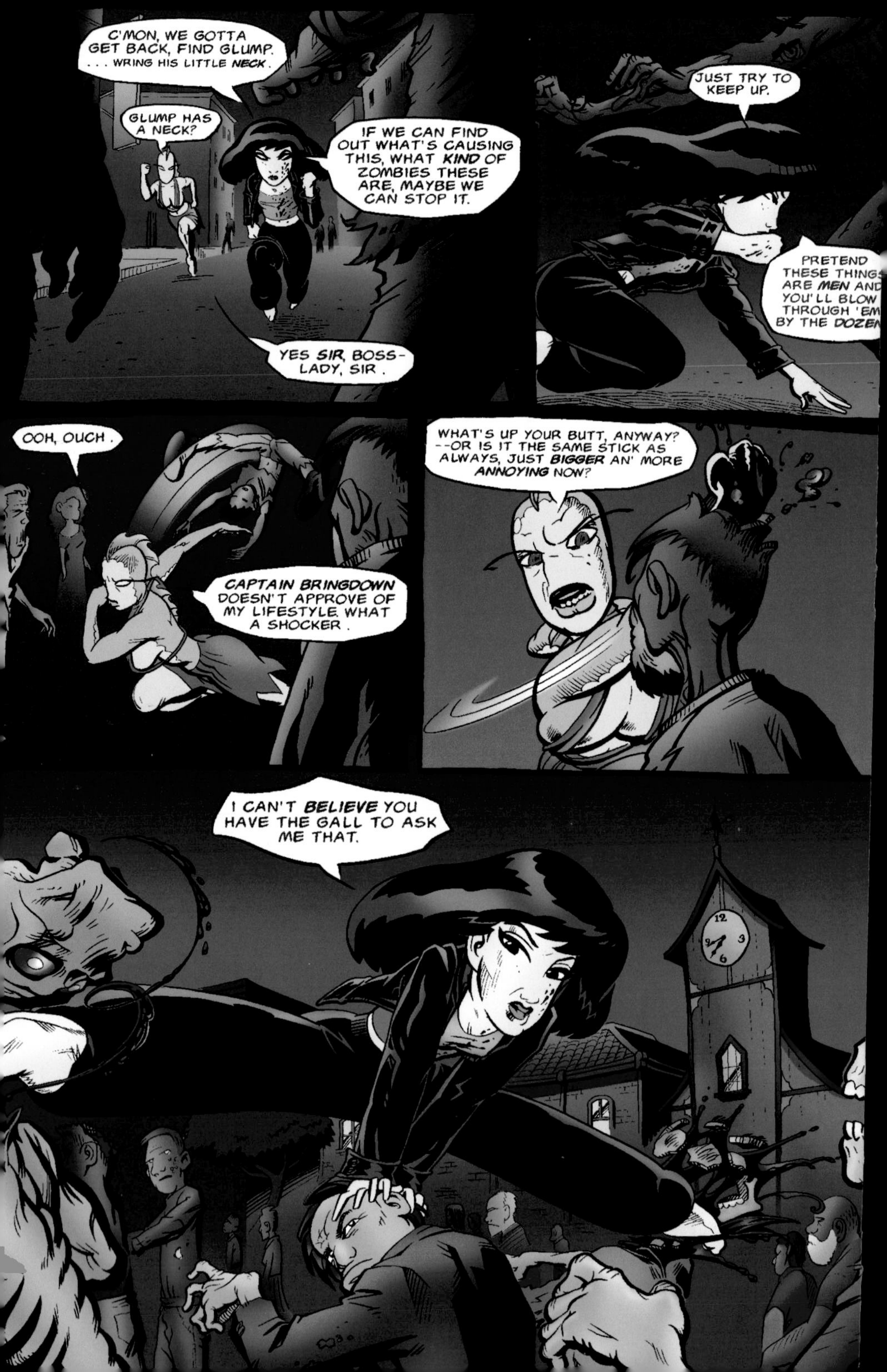
C'MON, WE GOTTA GET BACK, FIND GLUMP. . . . WRING HIS LITTLE NECK.
GLUMP HAS A NECK?
IF WE CAN FIND OUT WHAT'S CAUSING THIS, WHAT KIND OF ZOMBIES THESE ARE, MAYBE WE CAN STOP IT.
YES SIR, BOSS-LADY, SIR.
JUST TRY TO KEEP UP.
PRETEND THESE THINGS ARE MEN AND YOU'LL BLOW THROUGH 'EM BY THE DOZEN
OOH, OUCH.
CAPTAIN BRINGDOWN DOESN'T APPROVE OF MY LIFESTYLE. WHAT A SHOCKER.
WHAT'S UP YOUR BUTT, ANYWAY? --OR IS IT THE SAME STICK AS ALWAYS, JUST BIGGER AN' MORE ANNOYING NOW?
I CAN'T BELIEVE YOU HAVE THE GALL TO ASK ME THAT.

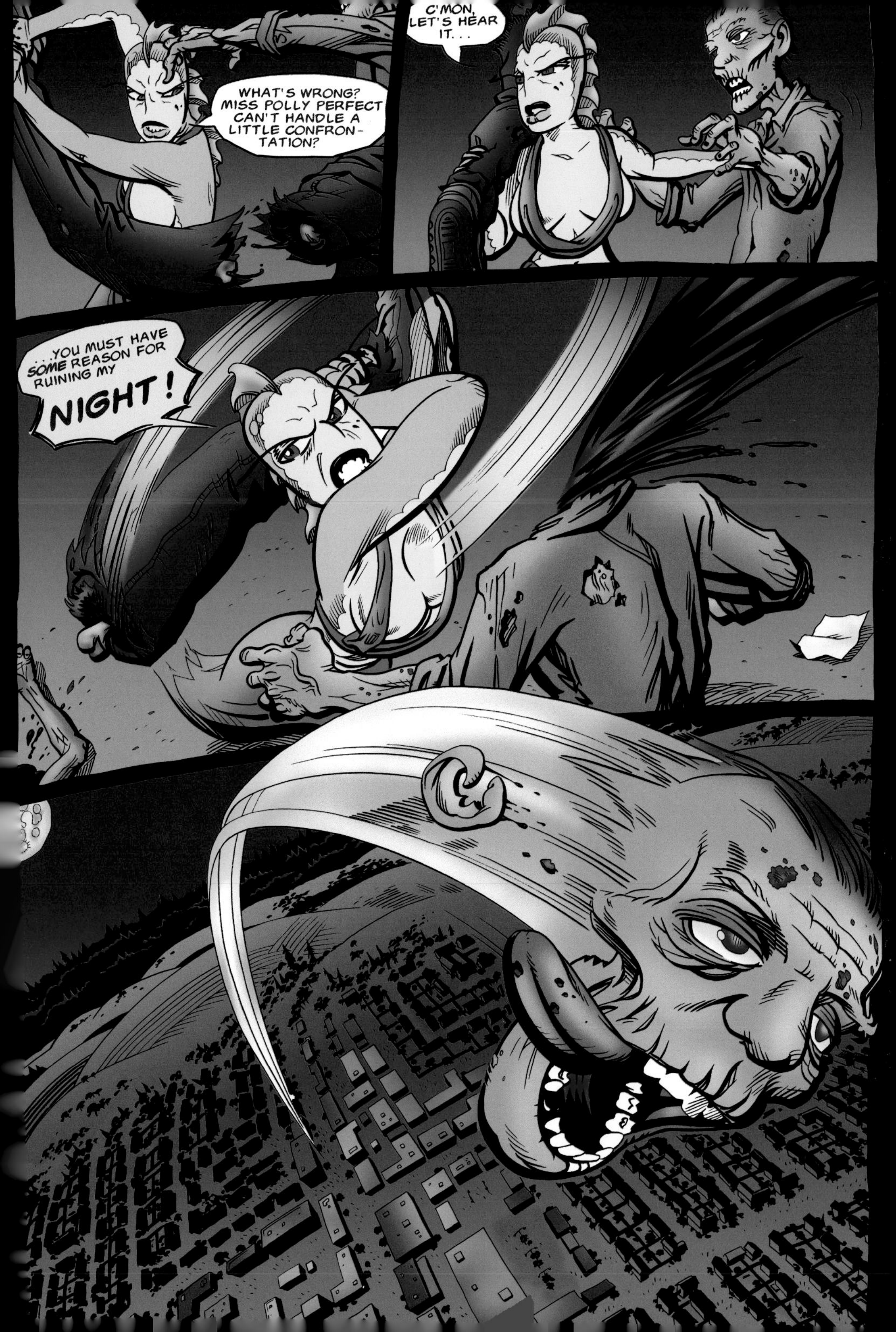
WHAT'S WRONG? MISS POLLY PERFECT CAN'T HANDLE A LITTLE CONFRON-TATION?
C'MON, LET'S HEAR IT. . .
. . .YOU MUST HAVE SOME REASON FOR RUINING MY NIGHT!

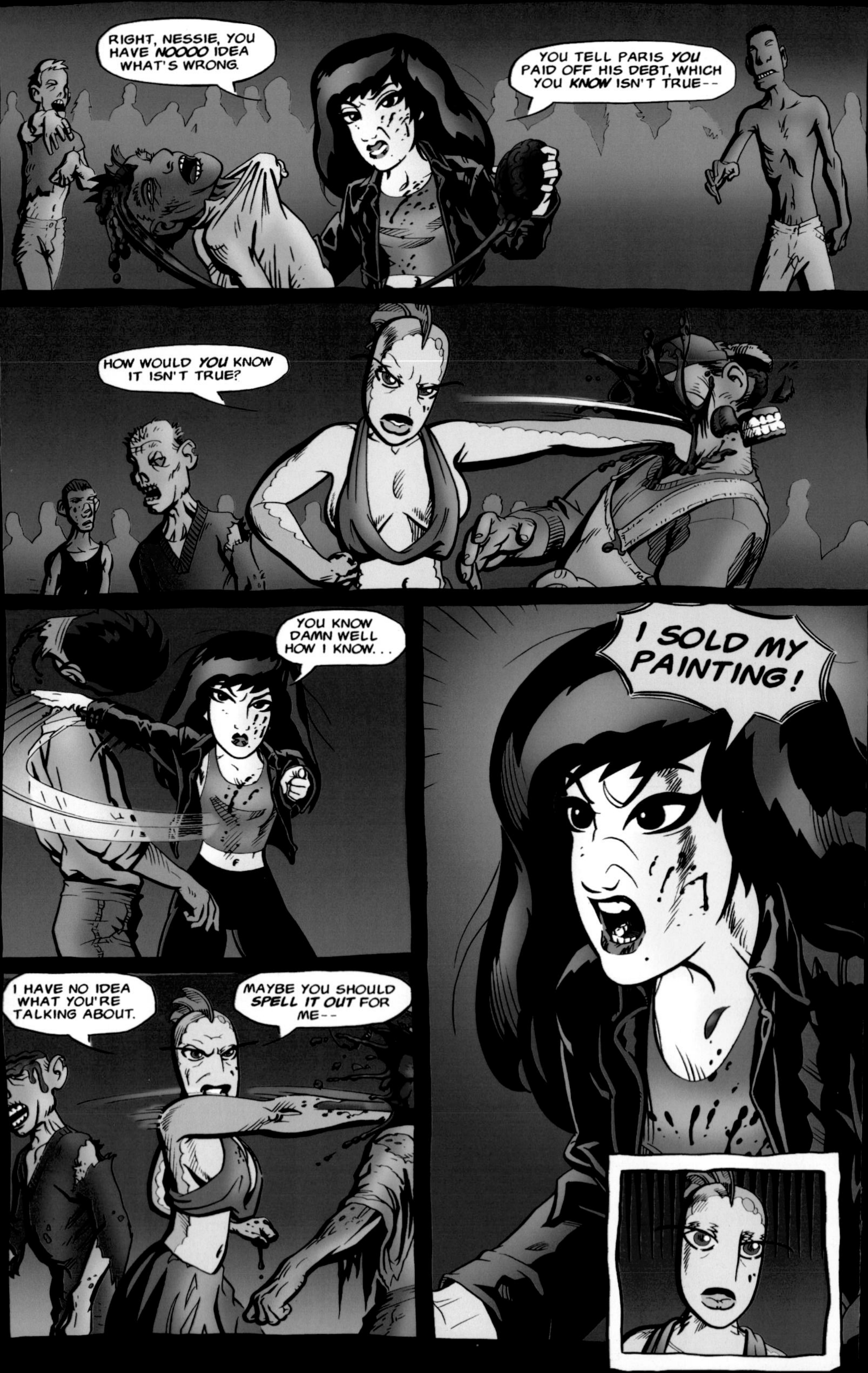
RIGHT, NESSIE, YOU HAVE NOOOO IDEA WHAT'S WRONG.
YOU TELL PARIS YOU PAID OFF HIS DEBT, WHICH YOU KNOW ISN'T TRUE--
HOW WOULD YOU KNOW IT ISN'T TRUE?
YOU KNOW DAMN WELL HOW I KNOW...
I HAVE NO IDEA WHAT YOU'RE TALKING ABOUT.
MAYBE YOU SHOULD SPELL IT OUT FOR ME--
I SOLD MY PAINTING!

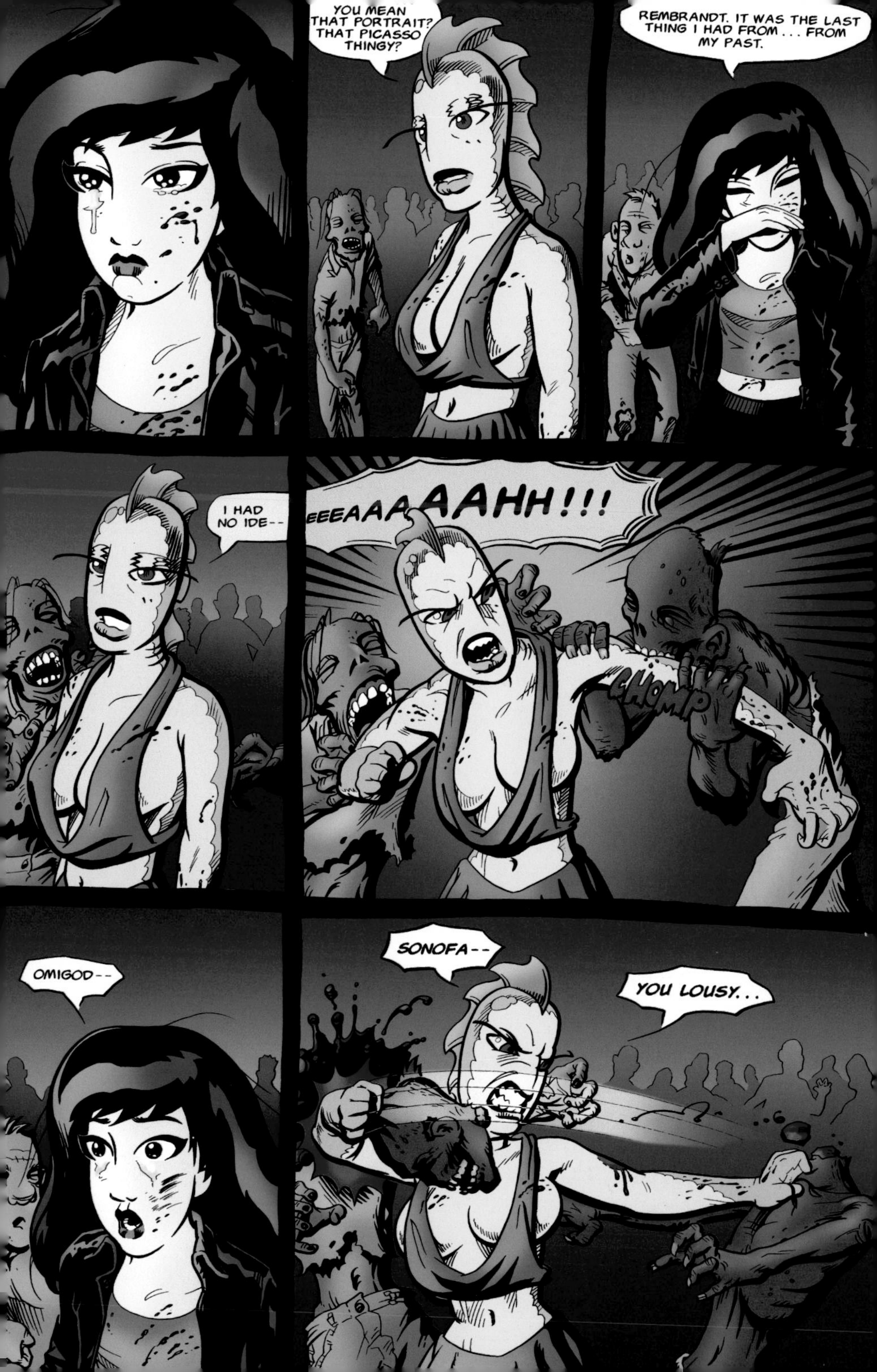
YOU MEAN THAT PORTRAIT? THAT PICASSO THINGY?
REMBRANDT. IT WAS THE LAST THING I HAD FROM . . . FROM MY PAST.
I HAD NO IDE--
EEEAAAAAHH!!!
CHOMP
OMIGOD--
SONOFA--
YOU LOUSY...

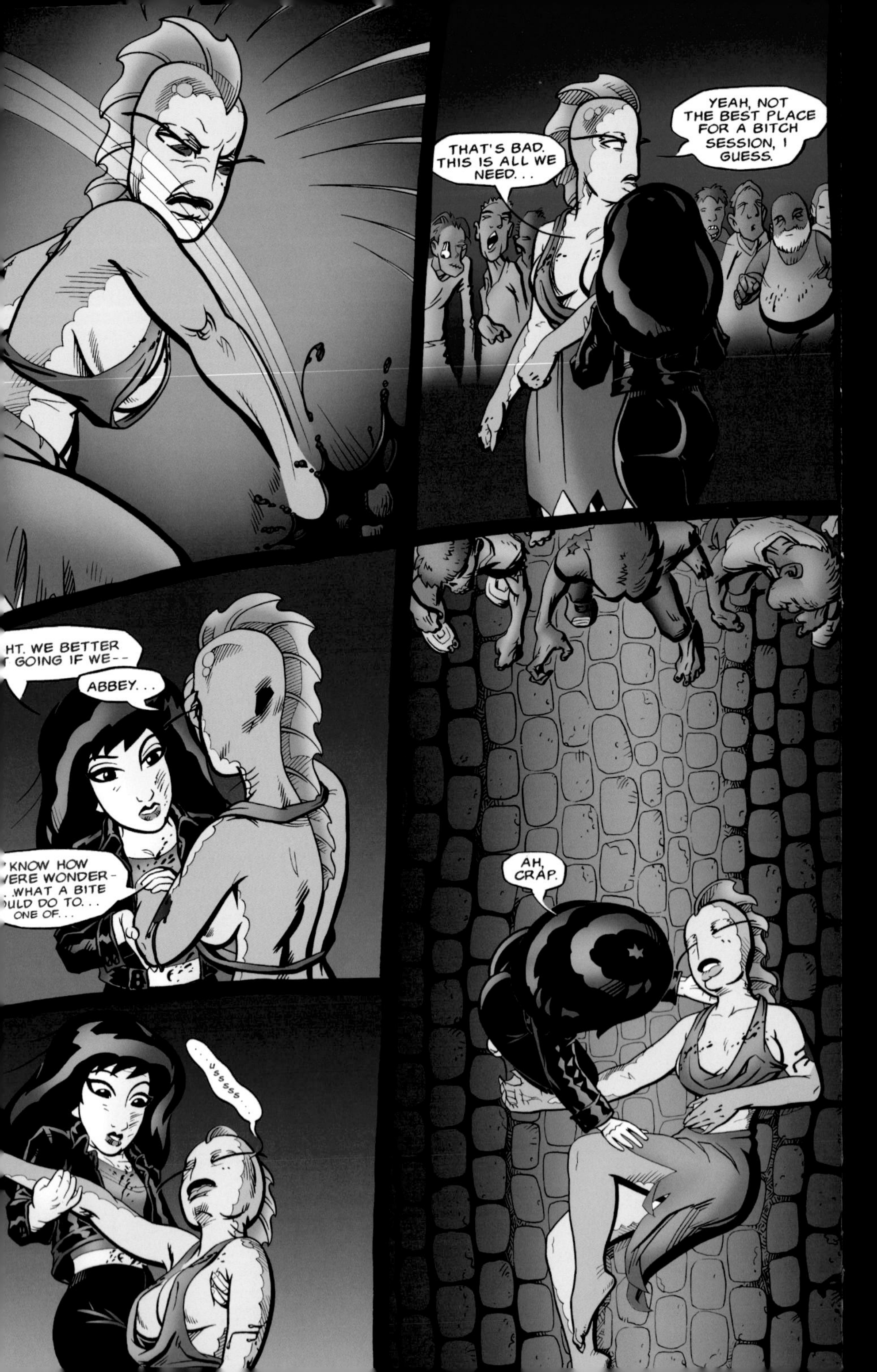
THAT'S BAD. THIS IS ALL WE NEED. . .
YEAH, NOT THE BEST PLACE FOR A BITCH SESSION, I GUESS.
HT. WE BETTER
GOING IF WE--
ABBEY. . .
KNOW HOW
ERE WONDER-
. .WHAT A BITE
ULD DO TO. . .
ONE OF. . .
. . .USSSSS. . .
AH, CRAP.

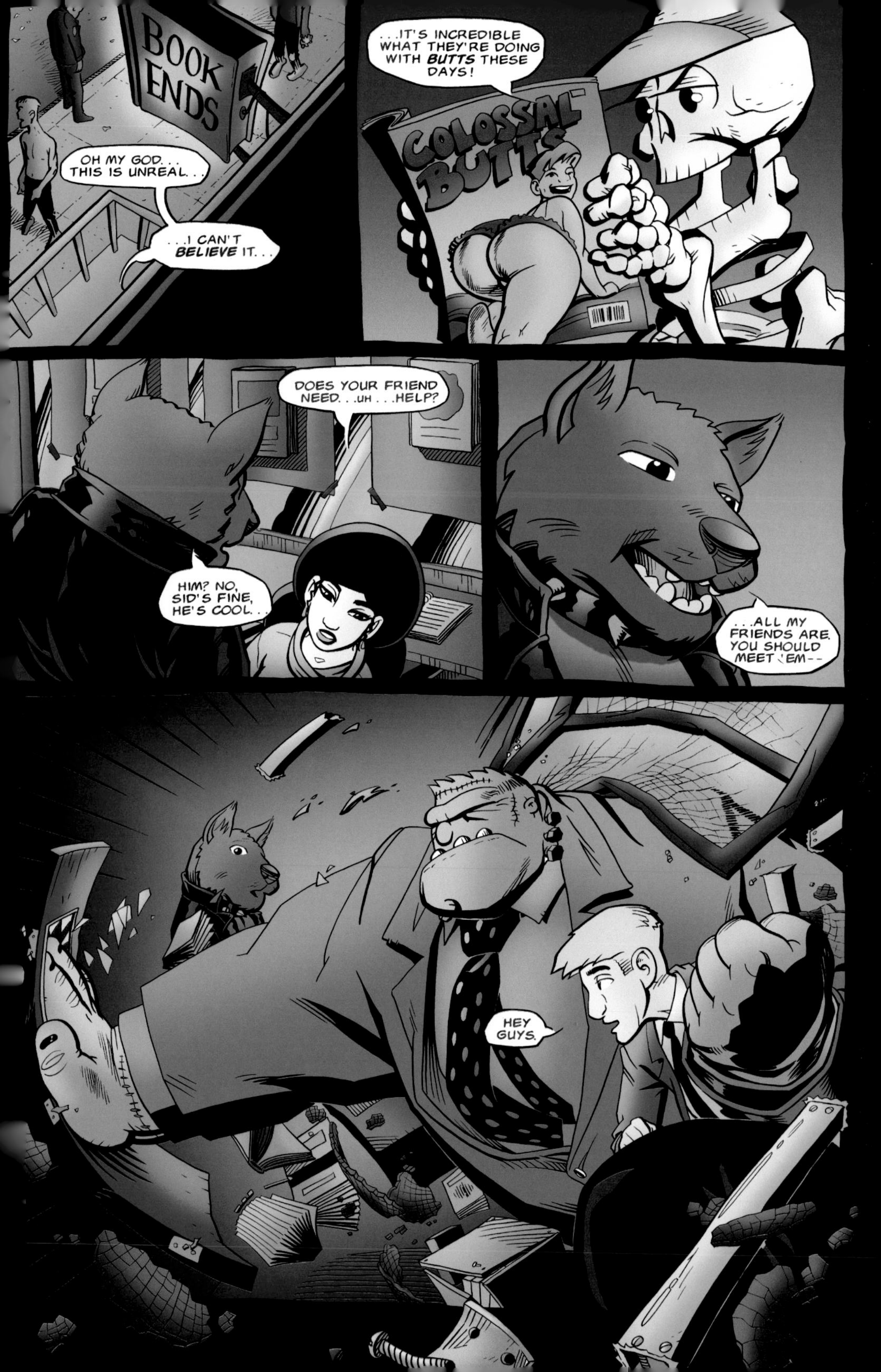
BOOK ENDS
OH MY GOD... THIS IS UNREAL...
...I CAN'T BELIEVE IT...
...IT'S INCREDIBLE WHAT THEY'RE DOING WITH BUTTS THESE DAYS!
COLOSSAL BUTTS
DOES YOUR FRIEND NEED...UH...HELP?
HIM? NO, SID'S FINE, HE'S COOL...
...ALL MY FRIENDS ARE. YOU SHOULD MEET 'EM--
HEY GUYS.

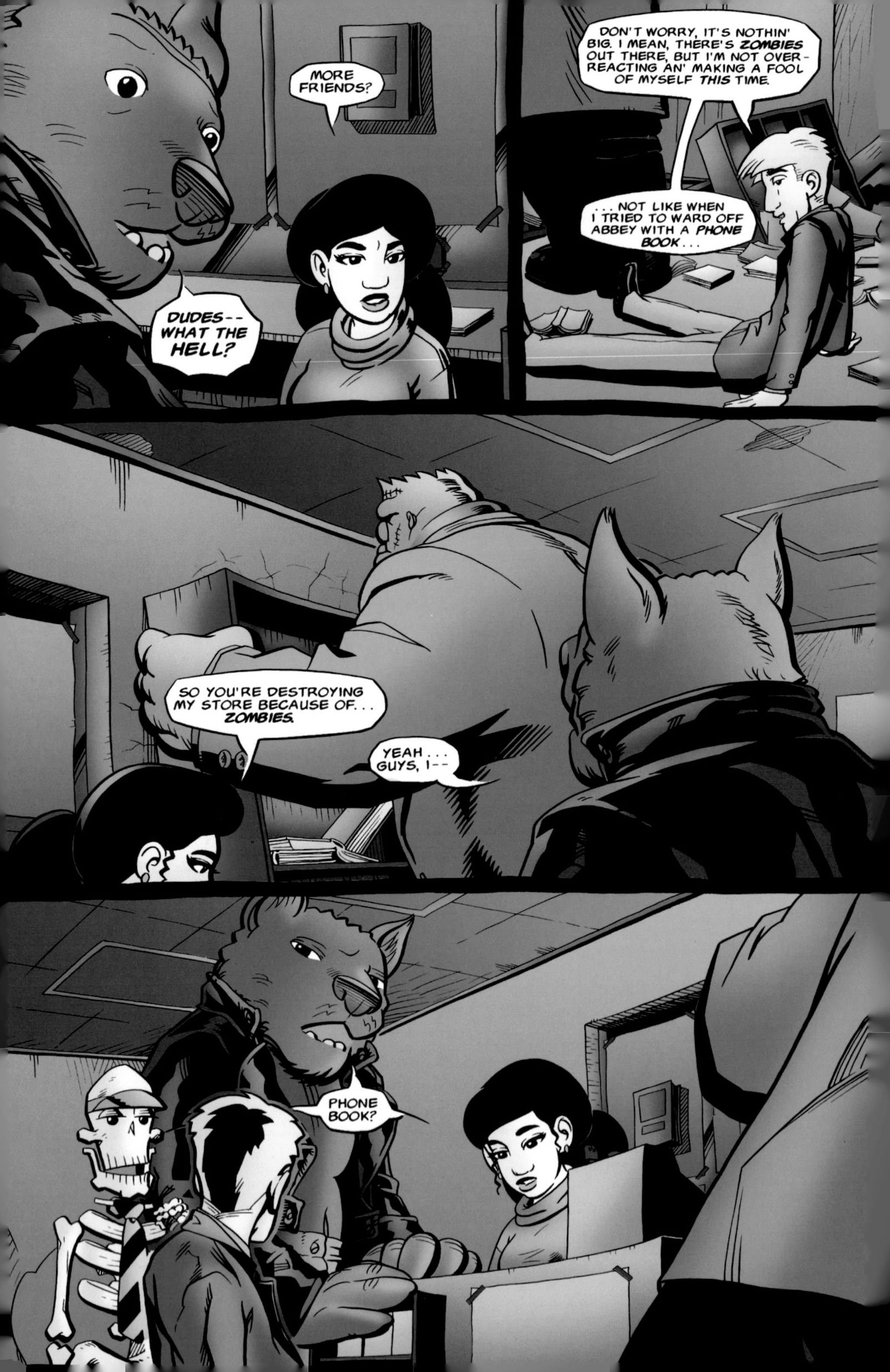
MORE FRIENDS?
DUDES-- WHAT THE HELL?
DON'T WORRY, IT'S NOTHIN' BIG. I MEAN, THERE'S ZOMBIES OUT THERE, BUT I'M NOT OVER-REACTING AN' MAKING A FOOL OF MYSELF THIS TIME.
...NOT LIKE WHEN I TRIED TO WARD OFF ABBEY WITH A PHONE BOOK...
SO YOU'RE DESTROYING MY STORE BECAUSE OF... ZOMBIES.
YEAH... GUYS, I--
PHONE BOOK?

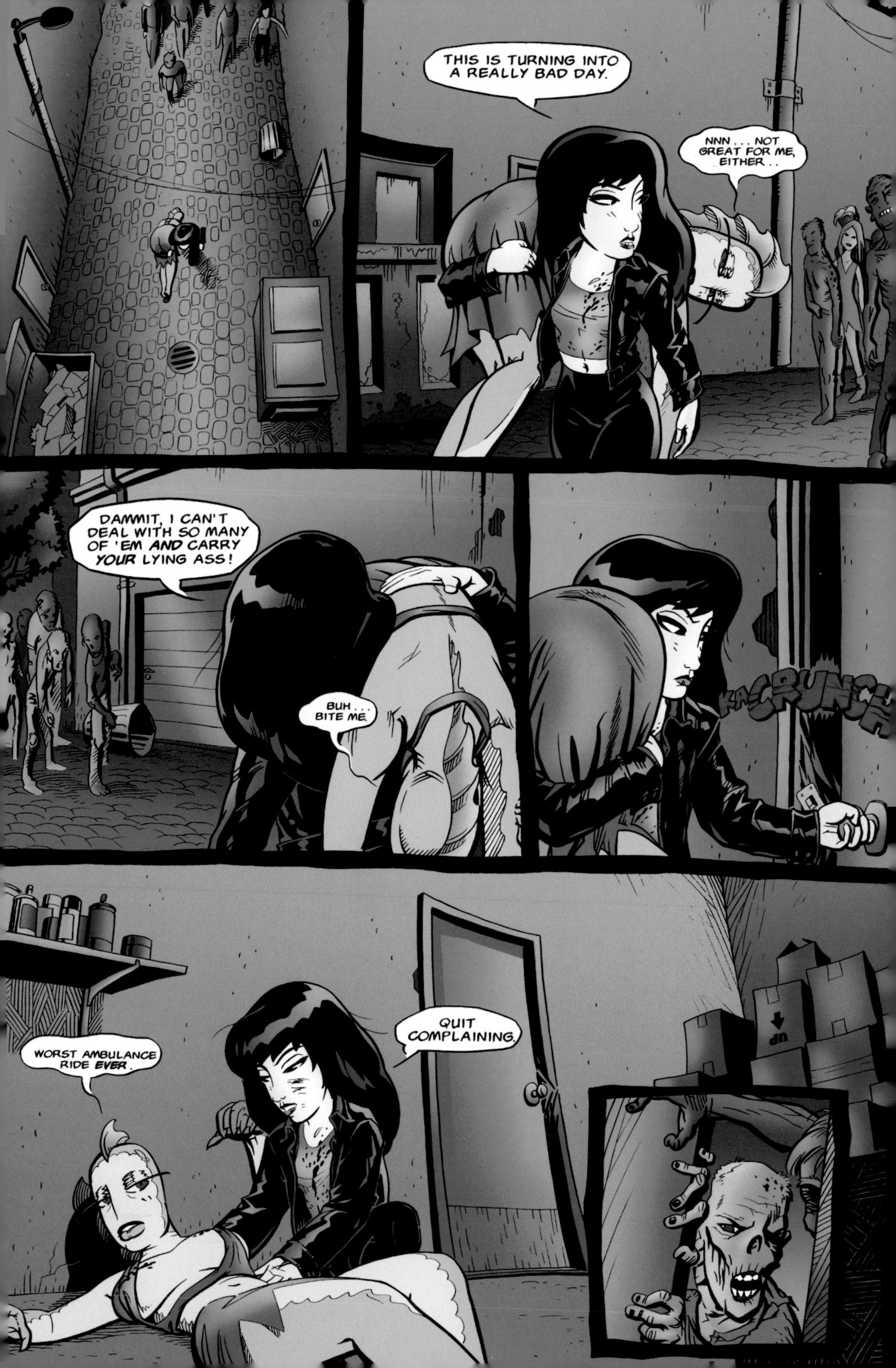
THIS IS TURNING INTO A REALLY BAD DAY.
NNN . . . NOT GREAT FOR ME, EITHER . .
DAMMIT, I CAN'T DEAL WITH SO MANY OF 'EM AND CARRY YOUR LYING ASS!
BUH . . BITE ME.
KACRUNCH
WORST AMBULANCE RIDE EVER.
QUIT COMPLAINING.
dn

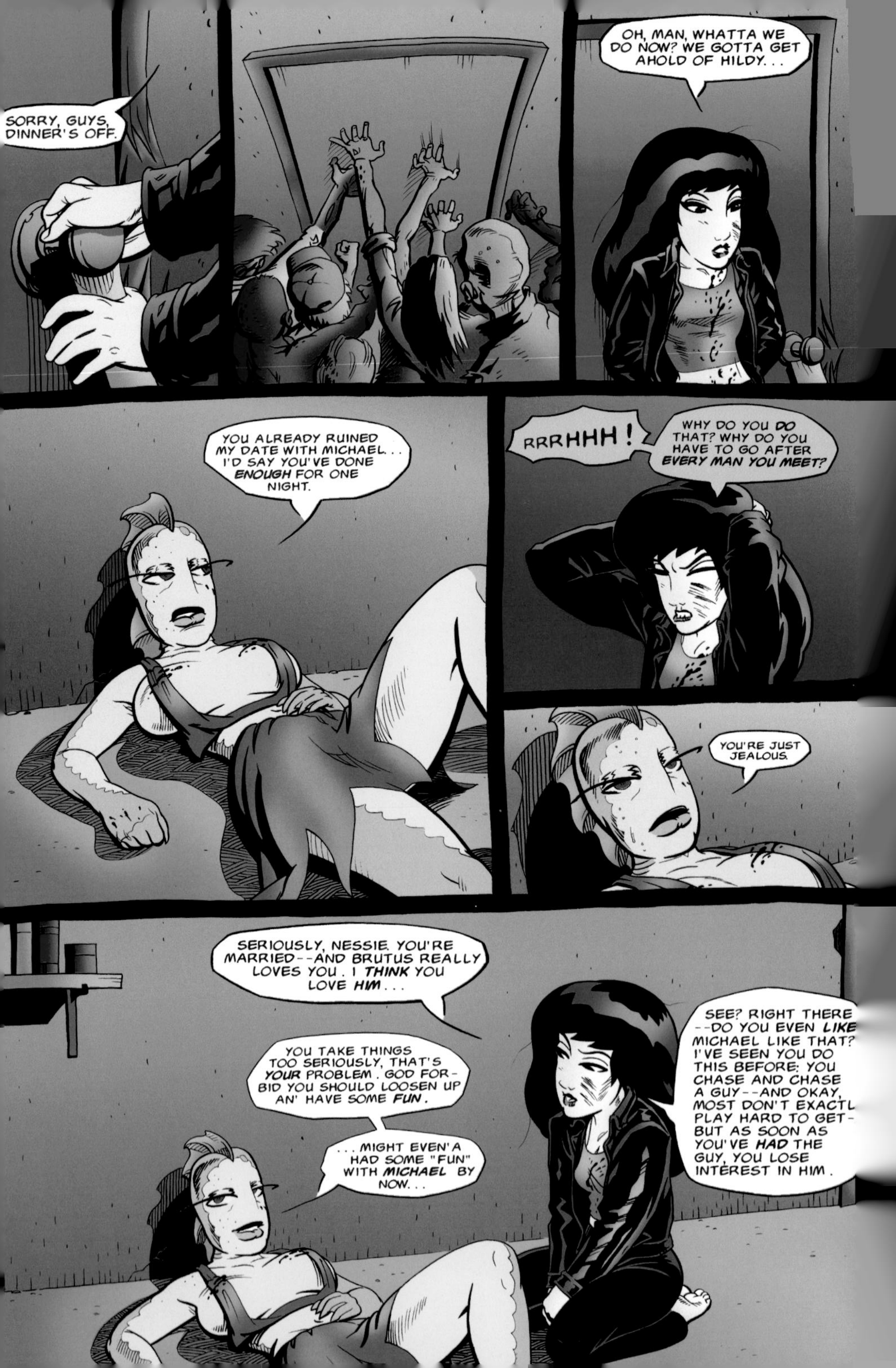
SORRY, GUYS, DINNER'S OFF.
OH, MAN, WHATTA WE DO NOW? WE GOTTA GET AHOLD OF HILDY...
YOU ALREADY RUINED MY DATE WITH MICHAEL... I'D SAY YOU'VE DONE ENOUGH FOR ONE NIGHT.
RRRHHH!
WHY DO YOU DO THAT? WHY DO YOU HAVE TO GO AFTER EVERY MAN YOU MEET?
YOU'RE JUST JEALOUS.
SERIOUSLY, NESSIE. YOU'RE MARRIED--AND BRUTUS REALLY LOVES YOU. I THINK YOU LOVE HIM...
YOU TAKE THINGS TOO SERIOUSLY, THAT'S YOUR PROBLEM. GOD FOR-BID YOU SHOULD LOOSEN UP AN' HAVE SOME FUN.
...MIGHT EVEN'A HAD SOME "FUN" WITH MICHAEL BY NOW...
SEE? RIGHT THERE --DO YOU EVEN LIKE MICHAEL LIKE THAT? I'VE SEEN YOU DO THIS BEFORE: YOU CHASE AND CHASE A GUY--AND OKAY, MOST DON'T EXACTL PLAY HARD TO GET-BUT AS SOON AS YOU'VE HAD THE GUY, YOU LOSE INTEREST IN HIM.

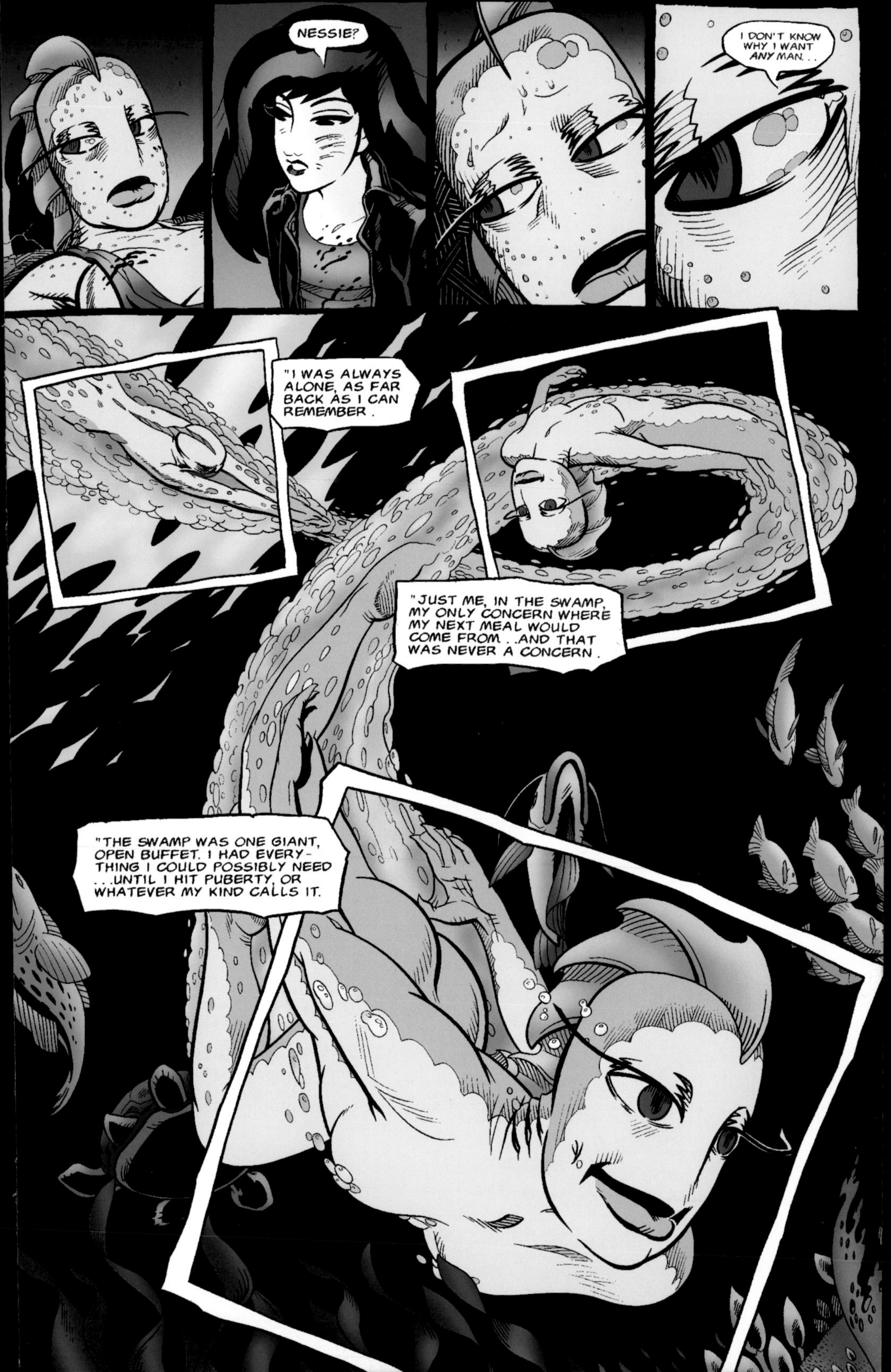
NESSIE?
I DON'T KNOW WHY I WANT ANY MAN. . .
"I WAS ALWAYS ALONE, AS FAR BACK AS I CAN REMEMBER.
"JUST ME, IN THE SWAMP, MY ONLY CONCERN WHERE MY NEXT MEAL WOULD COME FROM. . AND THAT WAS NEVER A CONCERN.
"THE SWAMP WAS ONE GIANT, OPEN BUFFET. I HAD EVERY-THING I COULD POSSIBLY NEED . . .UNTIL I HIT PUBERTY, OR WHATEVER MY KIND CALLS IT.

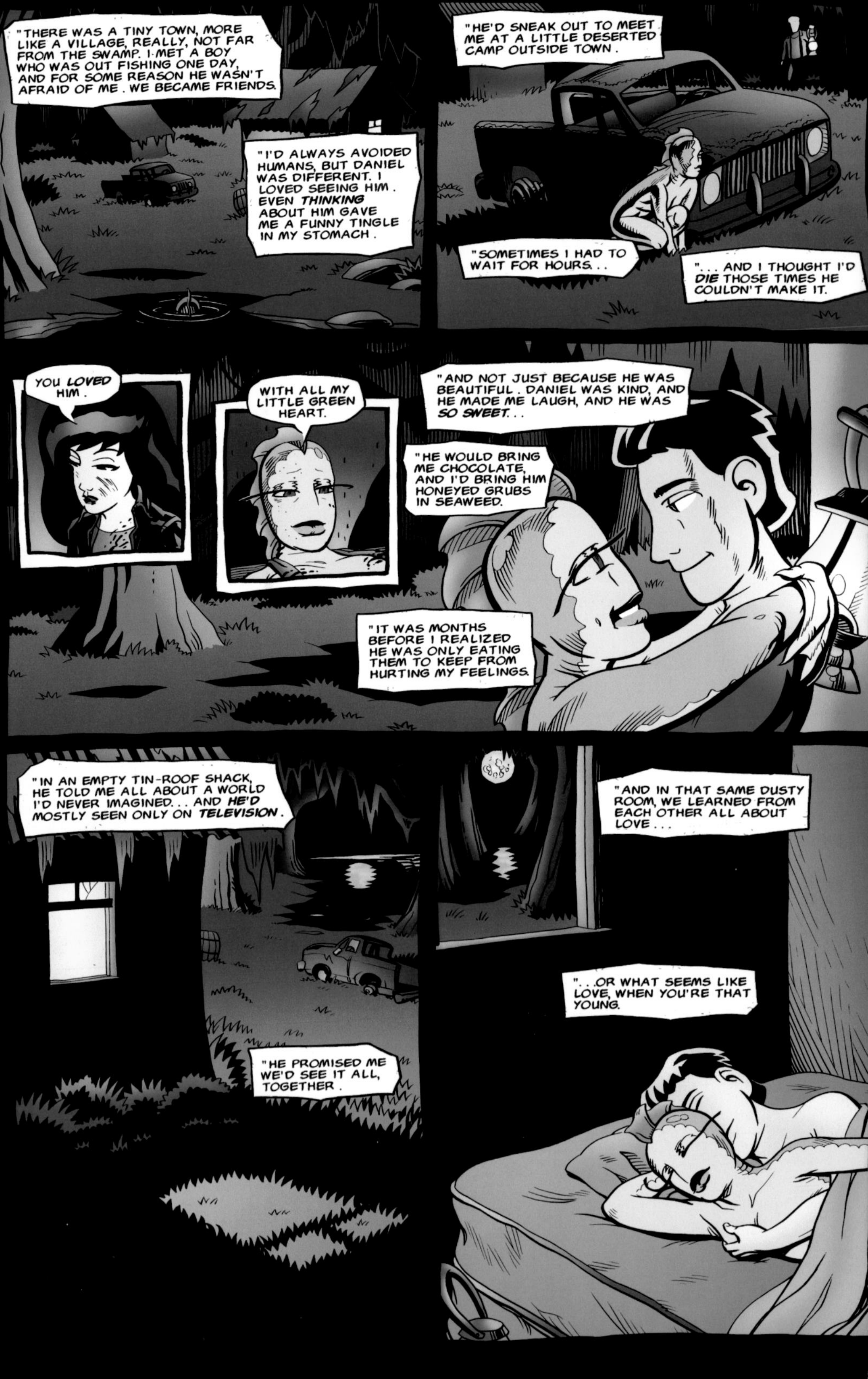

"THERE WAS A TINY TOWN, MORE LIKE A VILLAGE, REALLY, NOT FAR FROM THE SWAMP. I MET A BOY WHO WAS OUT FISHING ONE DAY, AND FOR SOME REASON HE WASN'T AFRAID OF ME. WE BECAME FRIENDS.
"I'D ALWAYS AVOIDED HUMANS, BUT DANIEL WAS DIFFERENT. I LOVED SEEING HIM. EVEN THINKING ABOUT HIM GAVE ME A FUNNY TINGLE IN MY STOMACH.
"HE'D SNEAK OUT TO MEET ME AT A LITTLE DESERTED CAMP OUTSIDE TOWN.
"SOMETIMES I HAD TO WAIT FOR HOURS...
"... AND I THOUGHT I'D DIE THOSE TIMES HE COULDN'T MAKE IT.
YOU LOVED HIM.
WITH ALL MY LITTLE GREEN HEART.
"AND NOT JUST BECAUSE HE WAS BEAUTIFUL. DANIEL WAS KIND, AND HE MADE ME LAUGH, AND HE WAS SO SWEET...
"HE WOULD BRING ME CHOCOLATE, AND I'D BRING HIM HONEYED GRUBS IN SEAWEED.
"IT WAS MONTHS BEFORE I REALIZED HE WAS ONLY EATING THEM TO KEEP FROM HURTING MY FEELINGS.
"IN AN EMPTY TIN-ROOF SHACK, HE TOLD ME ALL ABOUT A WORLD I'D NEVER IMAGINED... AND HE'D MOSTLY SEEN ONLY ON TELEVISION.
"HE PROMISED ME WE'D SEE IT ALL, TOGETHER.
"AND IN THAT SAME DUSTY ROOM, WE LEARNED FROM EACH OTHER ALL ABOUT LOVE...
"...OR WHAT SEEMS LIKE LOVE, WHEN YOU'RE THAT YOUNG.

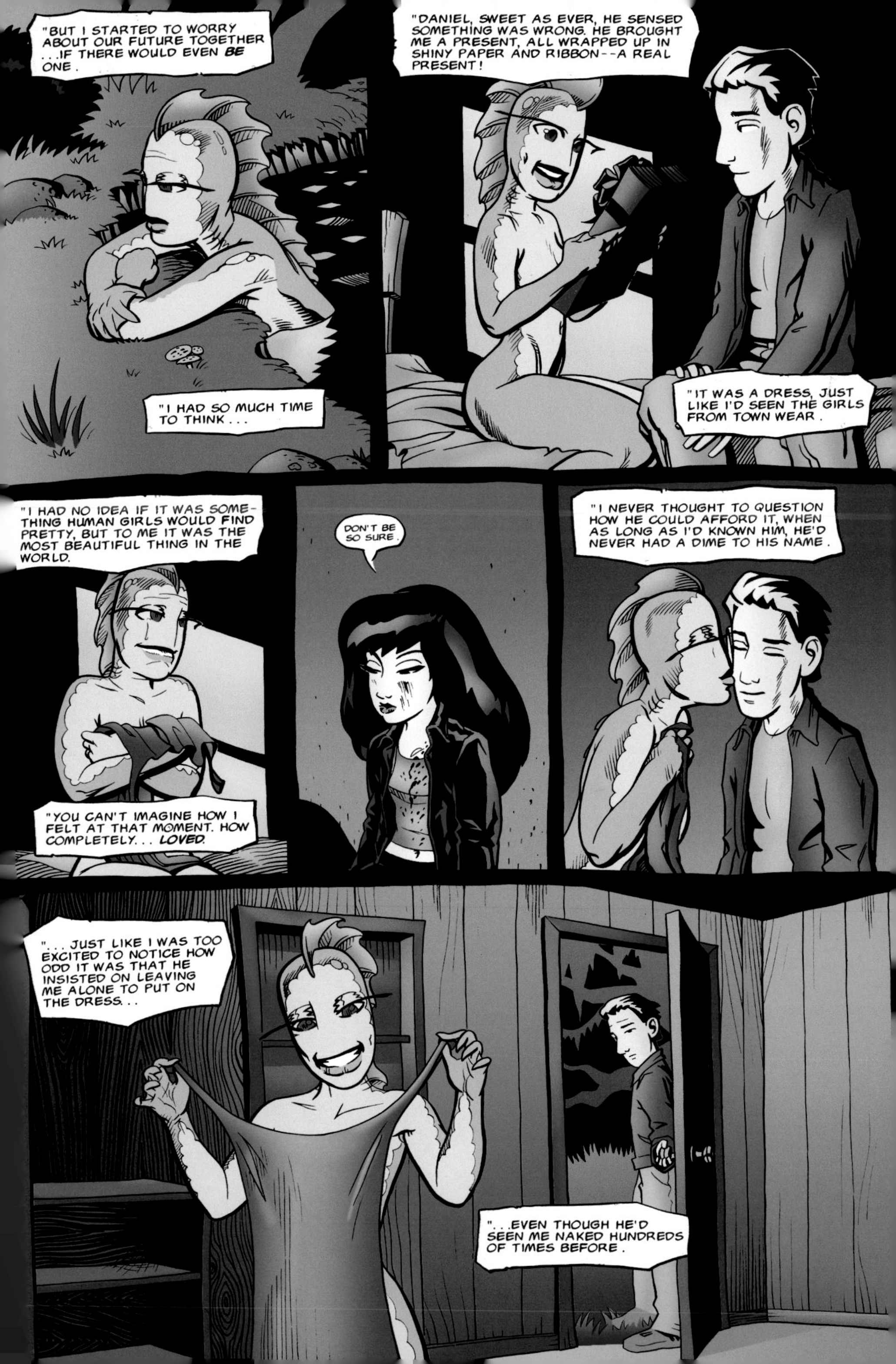
"BUT I STARTED TO WORRY ABOUT OUR FUTURE TOGETHER . . .IF THERE WOULD EVEN *BE* ONE .
"I HAD SO MUCH TIME TO THINK . . .
"DANIEL, SWEET AS EVER, HE SENSED SOMETHING WAS WRONG. HE BROUGHT ME A PRESENT, ALL WRAPPED UP IN SHINY PAPER AND RIBBON--A REAL PRESENT!
"IT WAS A DRESS, JUST LIKE I'D SEEN THE GIRLS FROM TOWN WEAR .
"I HAD NO IDEA IF IT WAS SOME-THING HUMAN GIRLS WOULD **FIND** PRETTY, BUT TO ME IT WAS THE MOST BEAUTIFUL THING IN THE WORLD.
"YOU CAN'T IMAGINE HOW I FELT AT THAT MOMENT. HOW COMPLETELY. . . ***LOVED***.
DON'T BE SO SURE.
"I NEVER THOUGHT TO QUESTION HOW HE COULD AFFORD IT, WHEN AS LONG AS I'D KNOWN HIM, HE'D NEVER HAD A DIME TO HIS NAME .
". . . JUST LIKE I WAS TOO EXCITED TO NOTICE HOW ODD IT WAS THAT HE INSISTED ON LEAVING ME ALONE TO PUT ON THE DRESS. . .
". . .EVEN THOUGH HE'D SEEN ME NAKED HUNDREDS OF TIMES BEFORE .

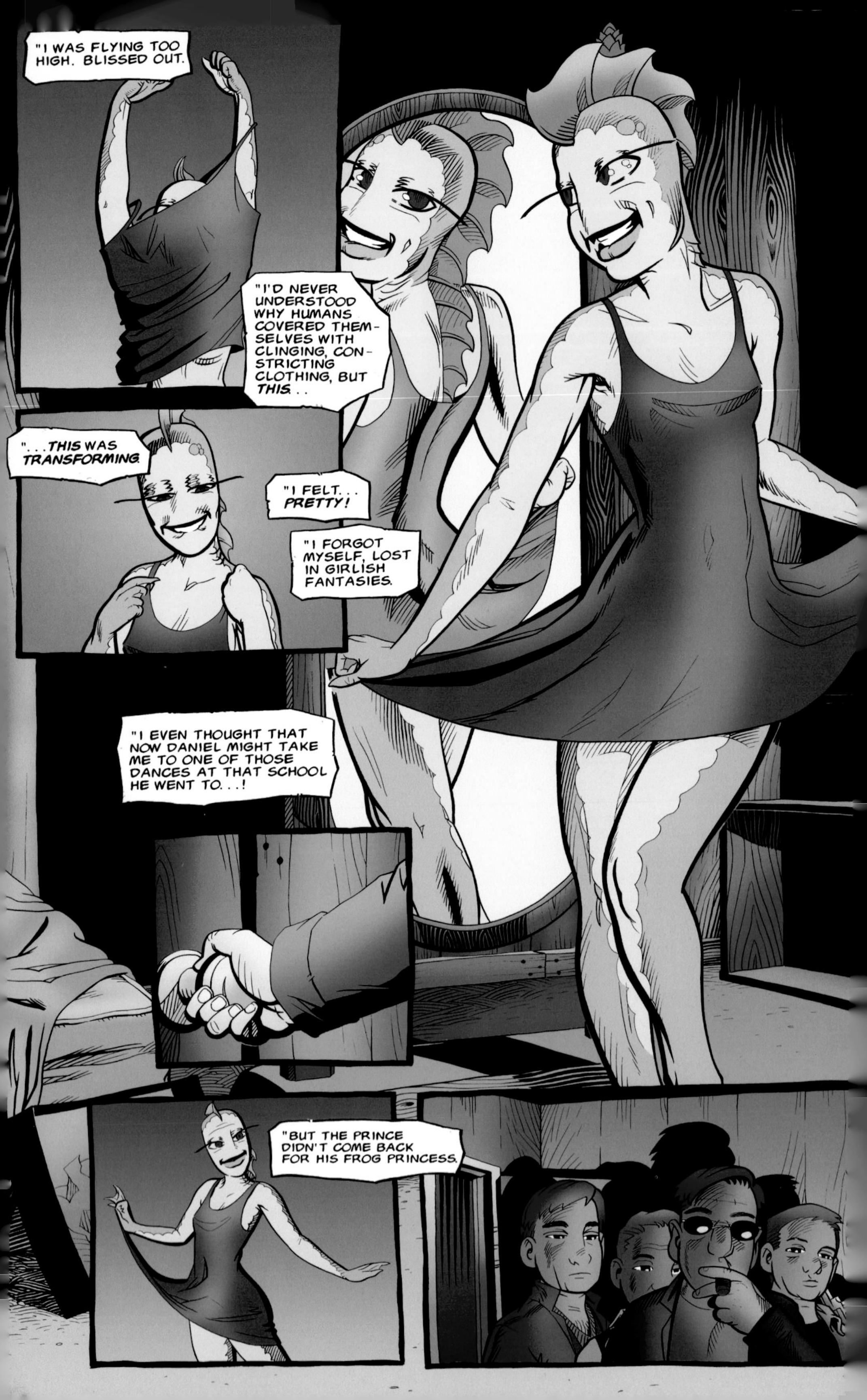
"I WAS FLYING TOO HIGH. BLISSED OUT.
"I'D NEVER UNDERSTOOD WHY HUMANS COVERED THEMSELVES WITH CLINGING, CONSTRICTING CLOTHING, BUT *THIS*. . .
". . .*THIS* WAS *TRANSFORMING*.
"I FELT. . . *PRETTY!*
"I FORGOT MYSELF, LOST IN GIRLISH FANTASIES.
"I EVEN THOUGHT THAT NOW DANIEL MIGHT TAKE ME TO ONE OF THOSE DANCES AT THAT SCHOOL HE WENT TO. . .!
"BUT THE PRINCE DIDN'T COME BACK FOR HIS FROG PRINCESS.

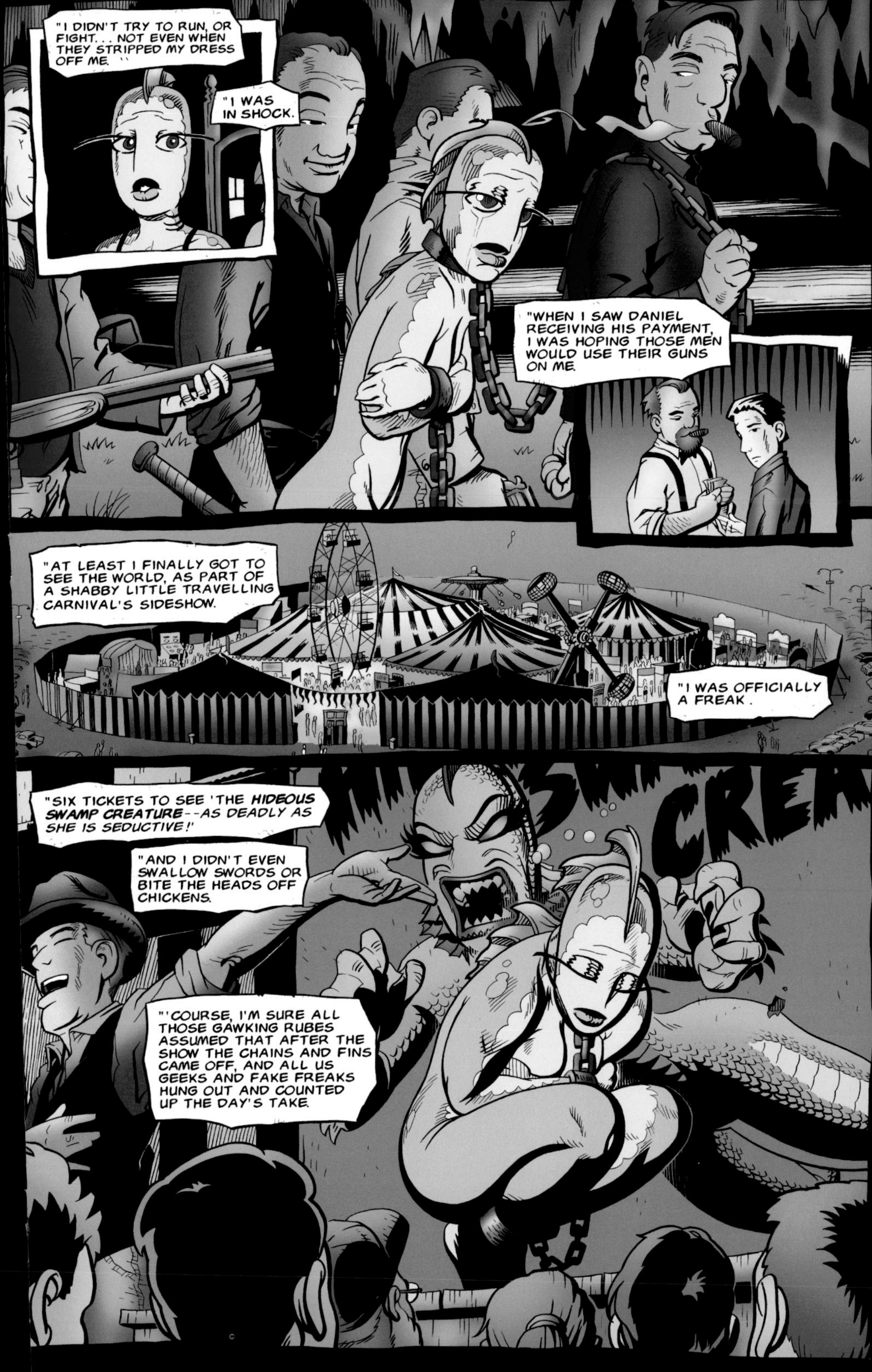

"I DIDN'T TRY TO RUN, OR FIGHT... NOT EVEN WHEN THEY STRIPPED MY DRESS OFF ME.
"I WAS IN SHOCK.
"WHEN I SAW DANIEL RECEIVING HIS PAYMENT, I WAS HOPING THOSE MEN WOULD USE THEIR GUNS ON ME.
"AT LEAST I FINALLY GOT TO SEE THE WORLD, AS PART OF A SHABBY LITTLE TRAVELLING CARNIVAL'S SIDESHOW.
"I WAS OFFICIALLY A FREAK.
"SIX TICKETS TO SEE 'THE *HIDEOUS SWAMP CREATURE*--AS DEADLY AS SHE IS SEDUCTIVE!'
"AND I DIDN'T EVEN SWALLOW SWORDS OR BITE THE HEADS OFF CHICKENS.
"'COURSE, I'M SURE ALL THOSE GAWKING RUBES ASSUMED THAT AFTER THE SHOW THE CHAINS AND FINS CAME OFF, AND ALL US GEEKS AND FAKE FREAKS HUNG OUT AND COUNTED UP THE DAY'S TAKE.

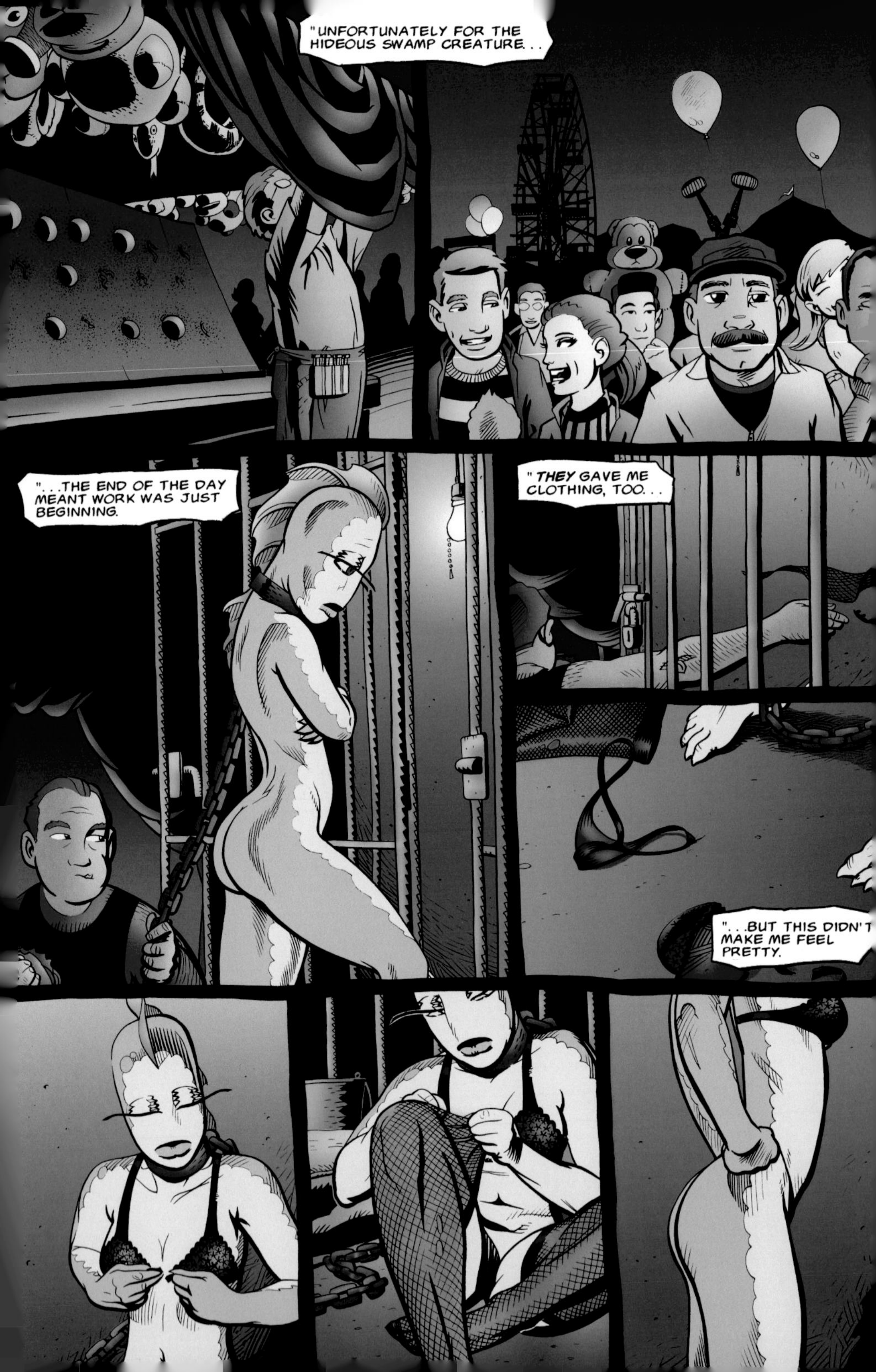
"UNFORTUNATELY FOR THE HIDEOUS SWAMP CREATURE. . .
". . .THE END OF THE DAY MEANT WORK WAS JUST BEGINNING.
"THEY GAVE ME CLOTHING, TOO. . .
". . .BUT THIS DIDN'T MAKE ME FEEL PRETTY.

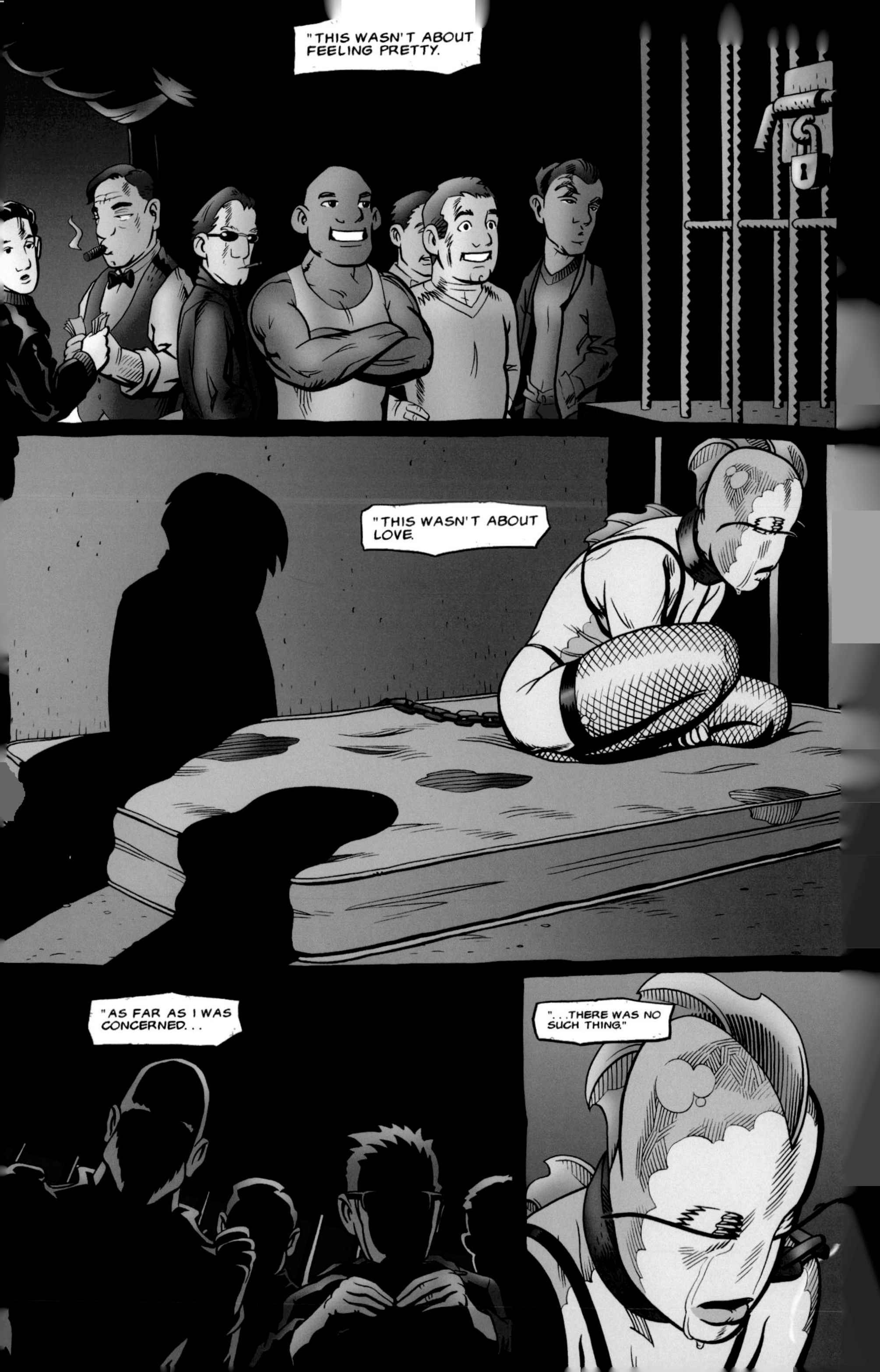
"THIS WASN'T ABOUT FEELING PRETTY.
"THIS WASN'T ABOUT LOVE.
"AS FAR AS I WAS CONCERNED. . .
". . .THERE WAS NO SUCH THING."

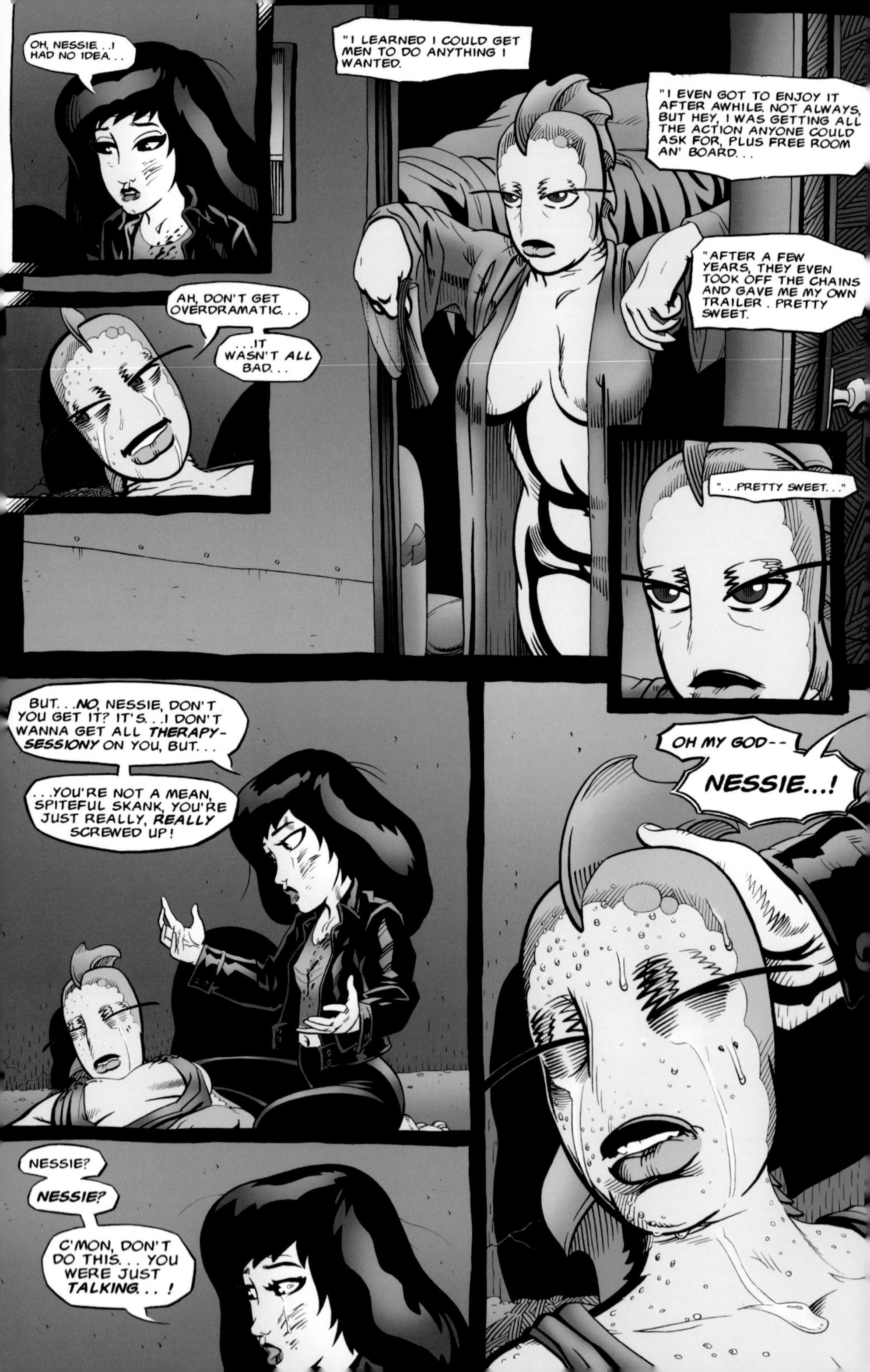
OH, NESSIE. . .I HAD NO IDEA. . .
"I LEARNED I COULD GET MEN TO DO ANYTHING I WANTED.
"I EVEN GOT TO ENJOY IT AFTER AWHILE. NOT ALWAYS, BUT HEY, I WAS GETTING ALL THE ACTION ANYONE COULD ASK FOR, PLUS FREE ROOM AN' BOARD. . .
AH, DON'T GET OVERDRAMATIC. . .
. . .IT WASN'T ALL BAD. . .
"AFTER A FEW YEARS, THEY EVEN TOOK OFF THE CHAINS AND GAVE ME MY OWN TRAILER . PRETTY SWEET.
". . .PRETTY SWEET. . ."
BUT. . .NO, NESSIE, DON'T YOU GET IT? IT'S. . .I DON'T WANNA GET ALL THERAPY-SESSIONY ON YOU, BUT. . .
. . .YOU'RE NOT A MEAN, SPITEFUL SKANK, YOU'RE JUST REALLY, REALLY SCREWED UP!
OH MY GOD--
NESSIE...!
NESSIE?
NESSIE?
C'MON, DON'T DO THIS. . . YOU WERE JUST TALKING. . . !

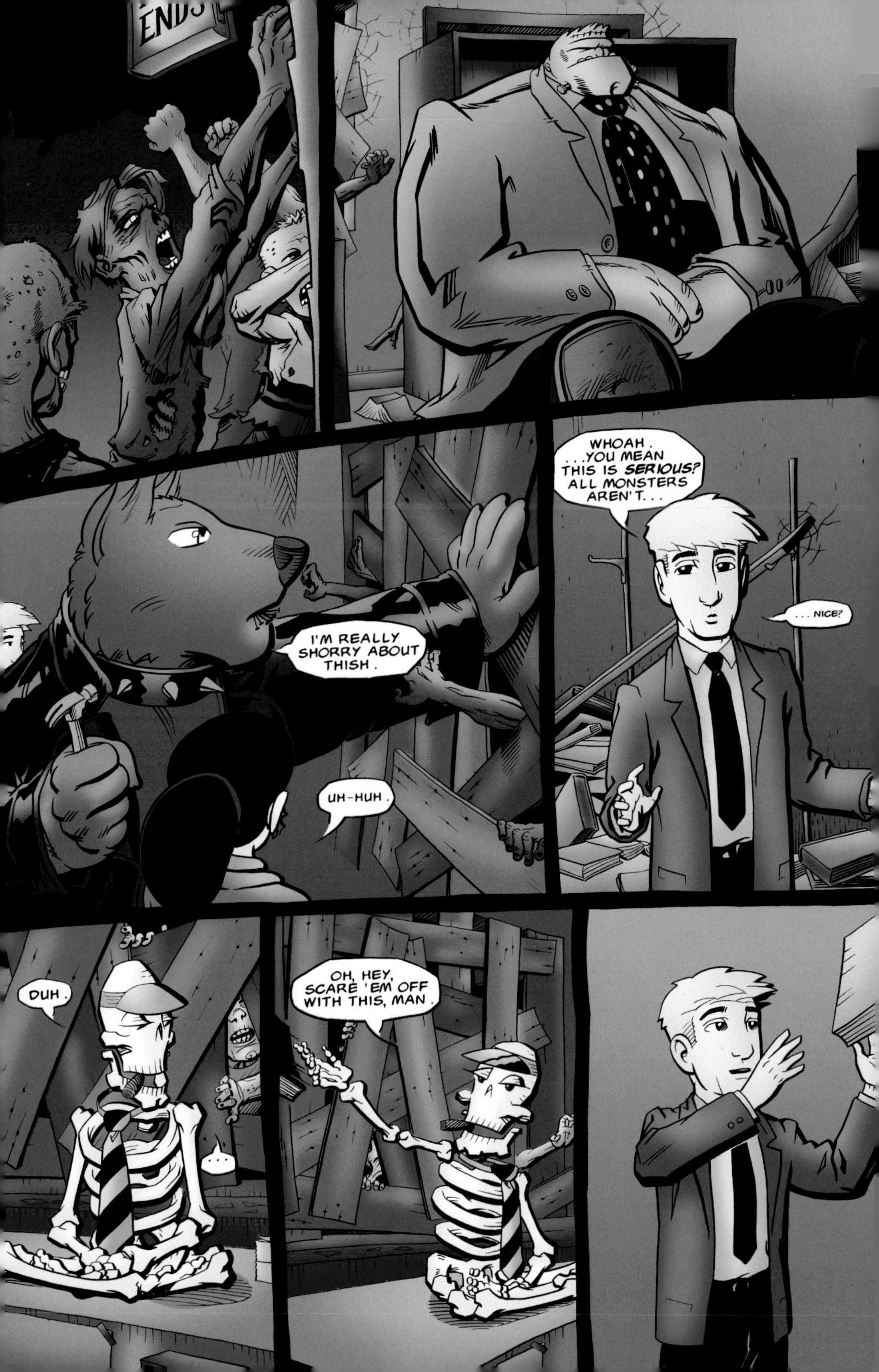
ENDS
I'M REALLY SHORRY ABOUT THISH.
UH-HUH.
WHOAH. ...YOU MEAN THIS IS SERIOUS? ALL MONSTERS AREN'T...
...NICE?
DUH.
...
OH, HEY, SCARE 'EM OFF WITH THIS, MAN.

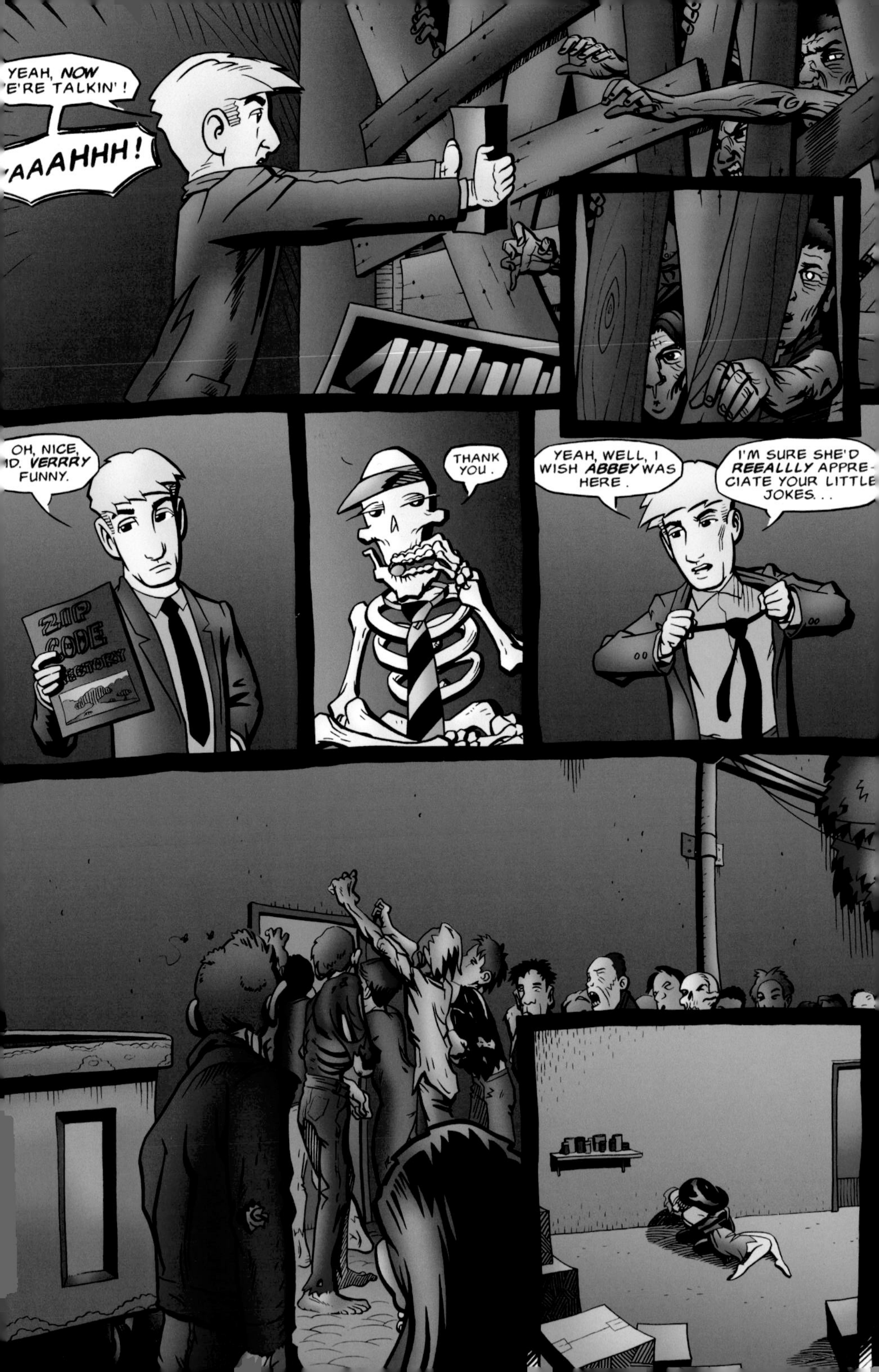

YEAH, NOW
'E'RE TALKIN' !
'AAAHHH !
OH, NICE,
ID. VERRRY
FUNNY.
THANK
YOU.
YEAH, WELL, I
WISH ABBEY WAS
HERE.
I'M SURE SHE'D
REEALLLY APPRE-
CIATE YOUR LITTLE
JOKES. . .
ZIP
CODE

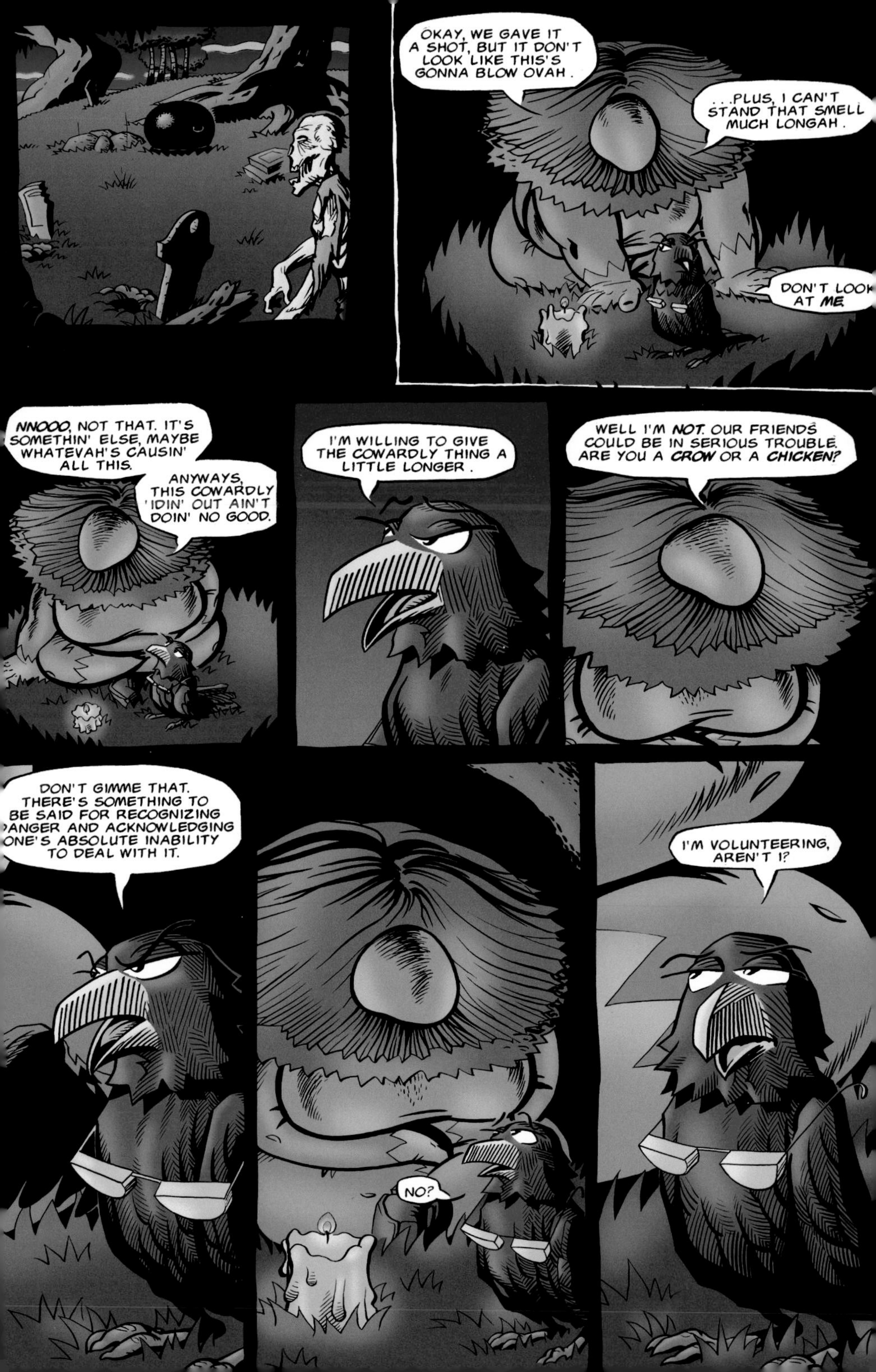
OKAY, WE GAVE IT A SHOT, BUT IT DON'T LOOK LIKE THIS'S GONNA BLOW OVAH.
...PLUS, I CAN'T STAND THAT SMELL MUCH LONGAH.
DON'T LOOK AT ME.
NNOOO, NOT THAT. IT'S SOMETHIN' ELSE, MAYBE WHATEVAH'S CAUSIN' ALL THIS.
ANYWAYS, THIS COWARDLY 'IDIN' OUT AIN'T DOIN' NO GOOD.
I'M WILLING TO GIVE THE COWARDLY THING A LITTLE LONGER.
WELL I'M NOT. OUR FRIENDS COULD BE IN SERIOUS TROUBLE. ARE YOU A CROW OR A CHICKEN?
DON'T GIMME THAT. THERE'S SOMETHING TO BE SAID FOR RECOGNIZING DANGER AND ACKNOWLEDGING ONE'S ABSOLUTE INABILITY TO DEAL WITH IT.
NO?
I'M VOLUNTEERING, AREN'T I?

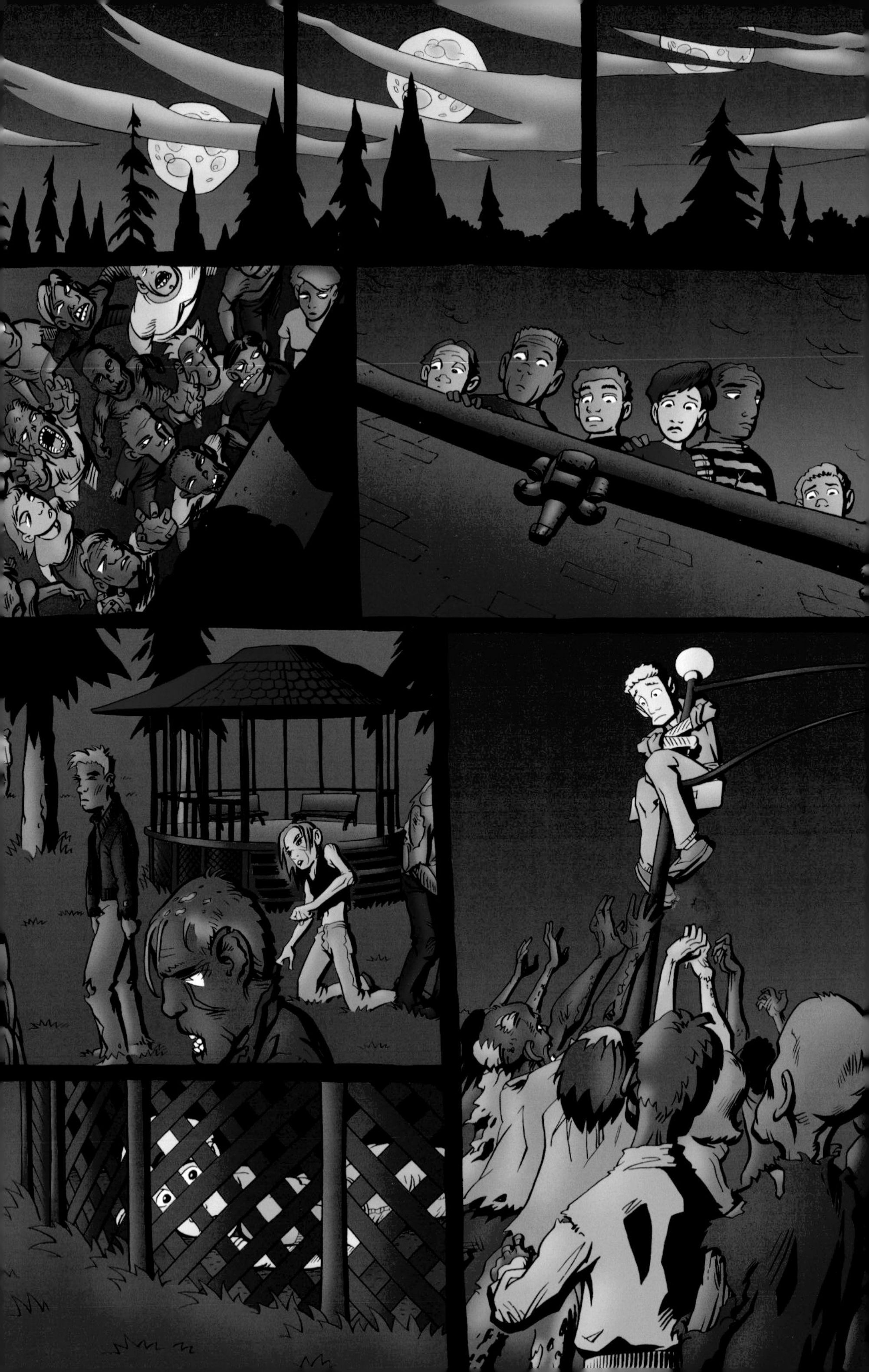

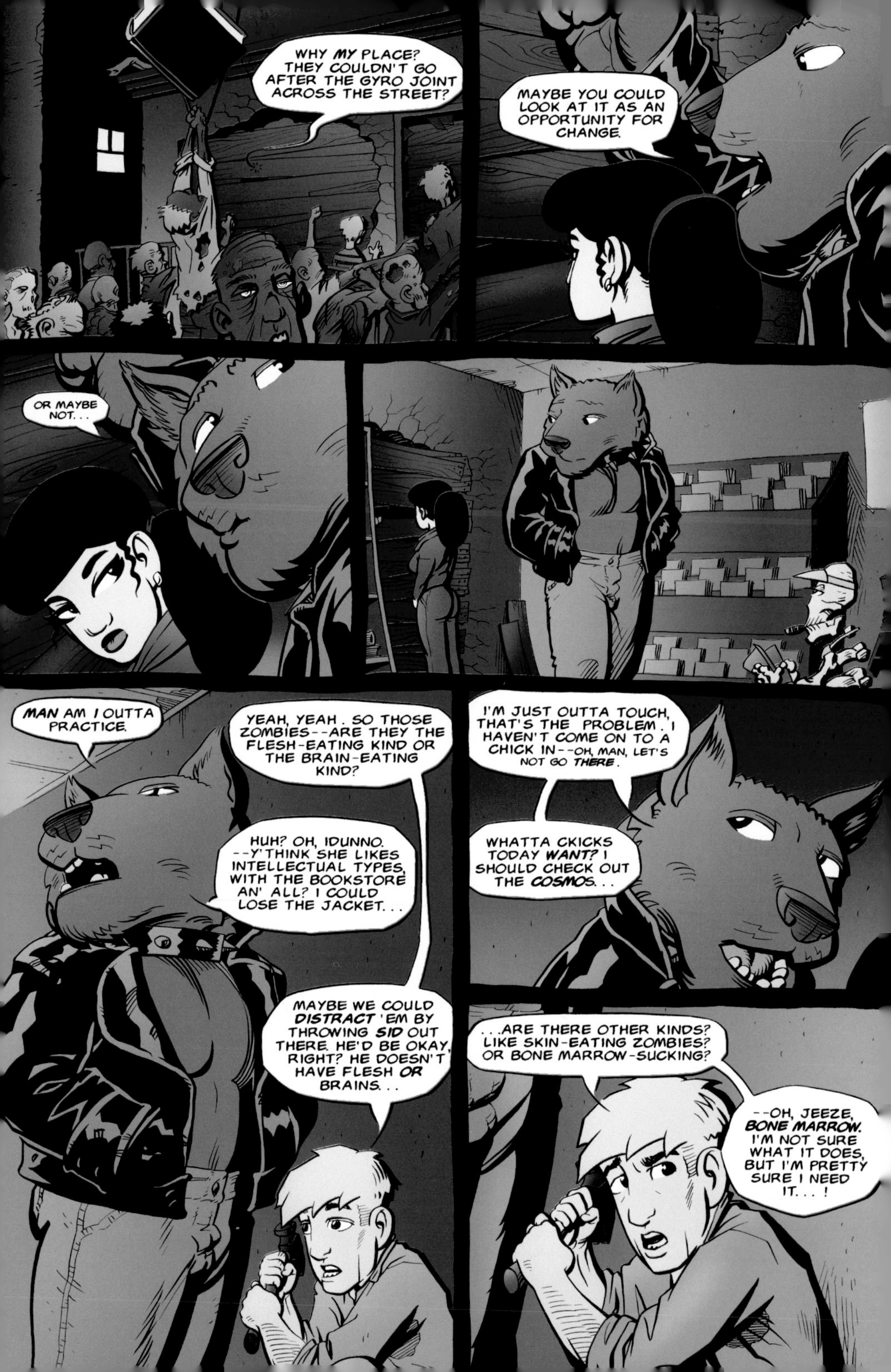
WHY MY PLACE? THEY COULDN'T GO AFTER THE GYRO JOINT ACROSS THE STREET?
MAYBE YOU COULD LOOK AT IT AS AN OPPORTUNITY FOR CHANGE.
OR MAYBE NOT. . .
MAN AM I OUTTA PRACTICE.
YEAH, YEAH . SO THOSE ZOMBIES--ARE THEY THE FLESH-EATING KIND OR THE BRAIN-EATING KIND?
HUH? OH, IDUNNO. --Y'THINK SHE LIKES INTELLECTUAL TYPES, WITH THE BOOKSTORE AN' ALL? I COULD LOSE THE JACKET. . .
MAYBE WE COULD DISTRACT 'EM BY THROWING SID OUT THERE. HE'D BE OKAY, RIGHT? HE DOESN'T HAVE FLESH OR BRAINS. . .
I'M JUST OUTTA TOUCH, THAT'S THE PROBLEM. I HAVEN'T COME ON TO A CHICK IN--OH, MAN, LET'S NOT GO THERE.
WHATTA CKICKS TODAY WANT? I SHOULD CHECK OUT THE COSMOS. . .
. . .ARE THERE OTHER KINDS? LIKE SKIN-EATING ZOMBIES? OR BONE MARROW-SUCKING?
--OH, JEEZE, BONE MARROW. I'M NOT SURE WHAT IT DOES, BUT I'M PRETTY SURE I NEED IT. . . !

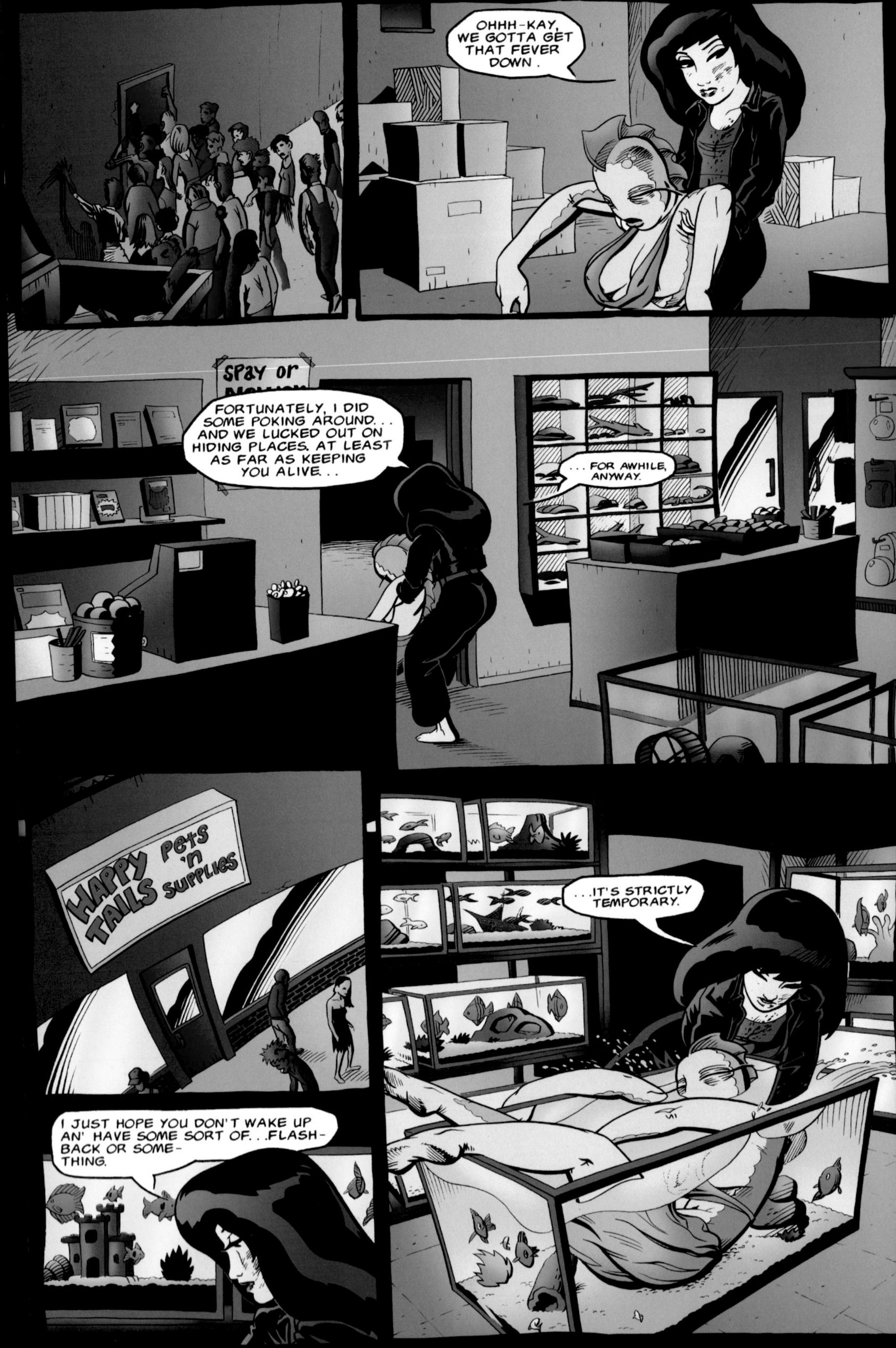
OHHH-KAY, WE GOTTA GET THAT FEVER DOWN.
Spay or
FORTUNATELY, I DID SOME POKING AROUND. . . AND WE LUCKED OUT ON HIDING PLACES. AT LEAST AS FAR AS KEEPING YOU ALIVE. . .
. . . FOR AWHILE, ANYWAY.
HAPPY TAILS Pets 'n Supplies
. . .IT'S STRICTLY TEMPORARY.
I JUST HOPE YOU DON'T WAKE UP AN' HAVE SOME SORT OF. . .FLASH-BACK OR SOME-THING.

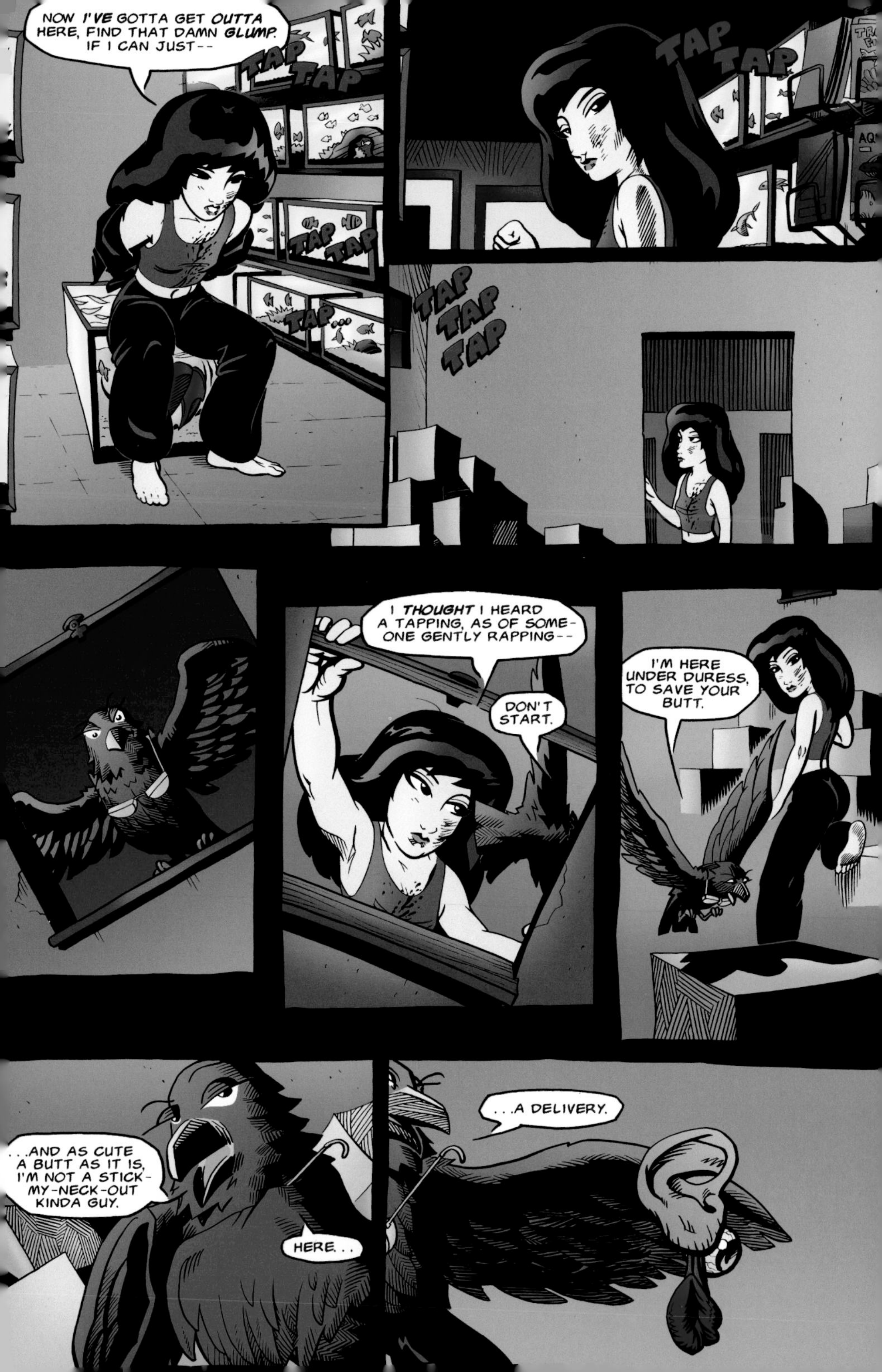
NOW I'VE GOTTA GET OUTTA HERE, FIND THAT DAMN GLUMP. IF I CAN JUST--
TAP TAP
TAP TAP
TAP...
TAP TAP
TAP TAP TAP
I THOUGHT I HEARD A TAPPING, AS OF SOME-ONE GENTLY RAPPING--
DON'T START.
I'M HERE UNDER DURESS, TO SAVE YOUR BUTT.
...AND AS CUTE A BUTT AS IT IS, I'M NOT A STICK-MY-NECK-OUT KINDA GUY.
HERE...
...A DELIVERY.

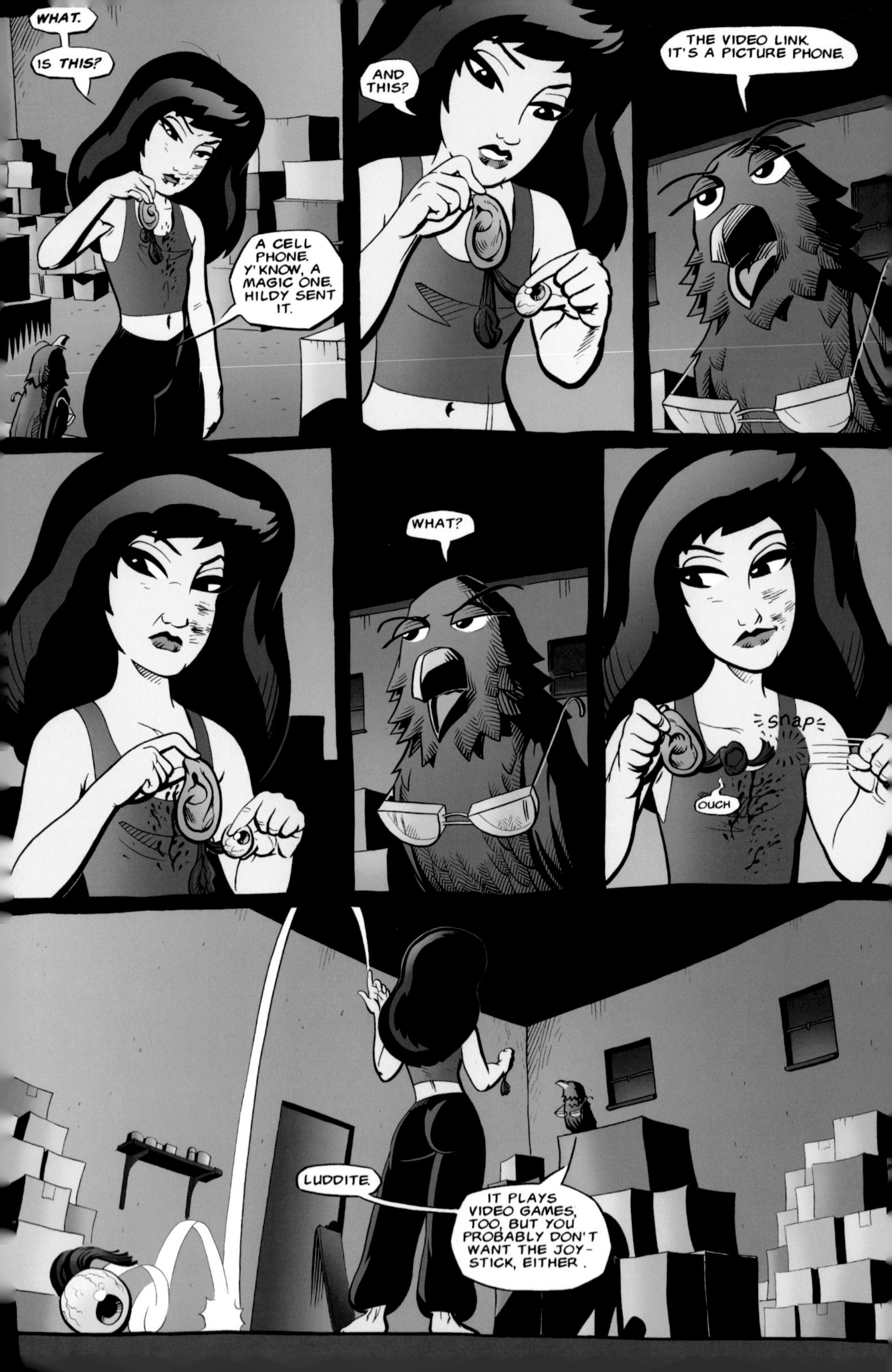
WHAT.
IS THIS?
A CELL PHONE. Y'KNOW, A MAGIC ONE. HILDY SENT IT.
AND THIS?
THE VIDEO LINK. IT'S A PICTURE PHONE.
WHAT?
SNAP
OUCH
LUDDITE.
IT PLAYS VIDEO GAMES, TOO, BUT YOU PROBABLY DON'T WANT THE JOY-STICK, EITHER.

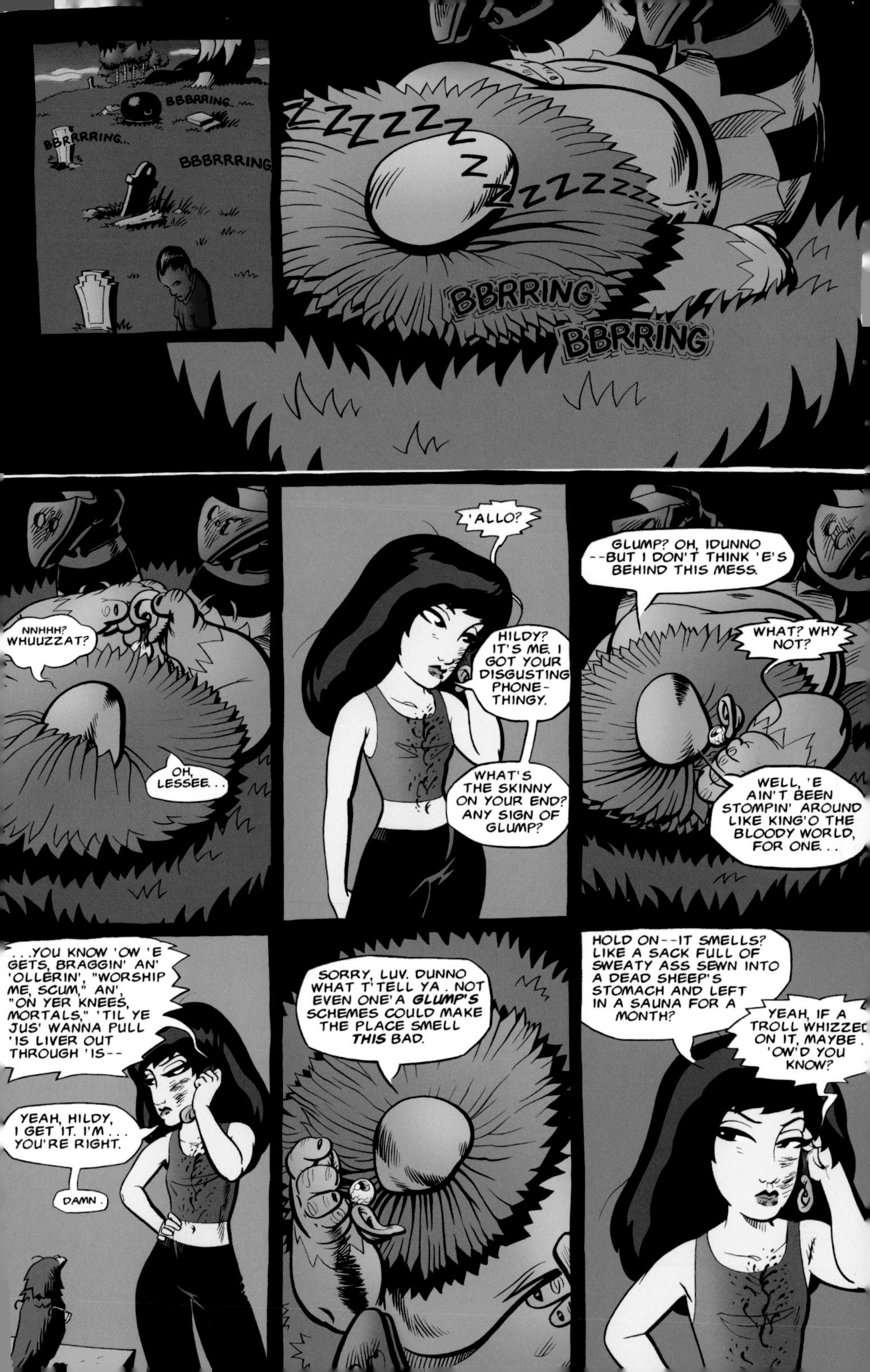
BBBRRING...
BBRRRRING...
BBBRRRRING
ZZZZZZZZ
ZZZZZZZZ
BBRRING
BBRRING
NNHHH? WHUUZZAT?
OH, LESSEE...
'ALLO?
HILDY? IT'S ME. I GOT YOUR DISGUSTING PHONE-THINGY.
WHAT'S THE SKINNY ON YOUR END? ANY SIGN OF GLUMP?
GLUMP? OH, IDUNNO --BUT I DON'T THINK 'E'S BEHIND THIS MESS.
WHAT? WHY NOT?
WELL, 'E AIN'T BEEN STOMPIN' AROUND LIKE KING'O THE BLOODY WORLD, FOR ONE...
...YOU KNOW 'OW 'E GETS, BRAGGIN' AN' 'OLLERIN', "WORSHIP ME, SCUM," AN', "ON YER KNEES, MORTALS," 'TIL YE JUS' WANNA PULL 'IS LIVER OUT THROUGH 'IS--
YEAH, HILDY, I GET IT. I'M... YOU'RE RIGHT.
DAMN.
SORRY, LUV. DUNNO WHAT T'TELL YA. NOT EVEN ONE'A GLUMP'S SCHEMES COULD MAKE THE PLACE SMELL THIS BAD.
HOLD ON--IT SMELLS? LIKE A SACK FULL OF SWEATY ASS SEWN INTO A DEAD SHEEP'S STOMACH AND LEFT IN A SAUNA FOR A MONTH?
YEAH, IF A TROLL WHIZZED ON IT, MAYBE. 'OW'D YOU KNOW?

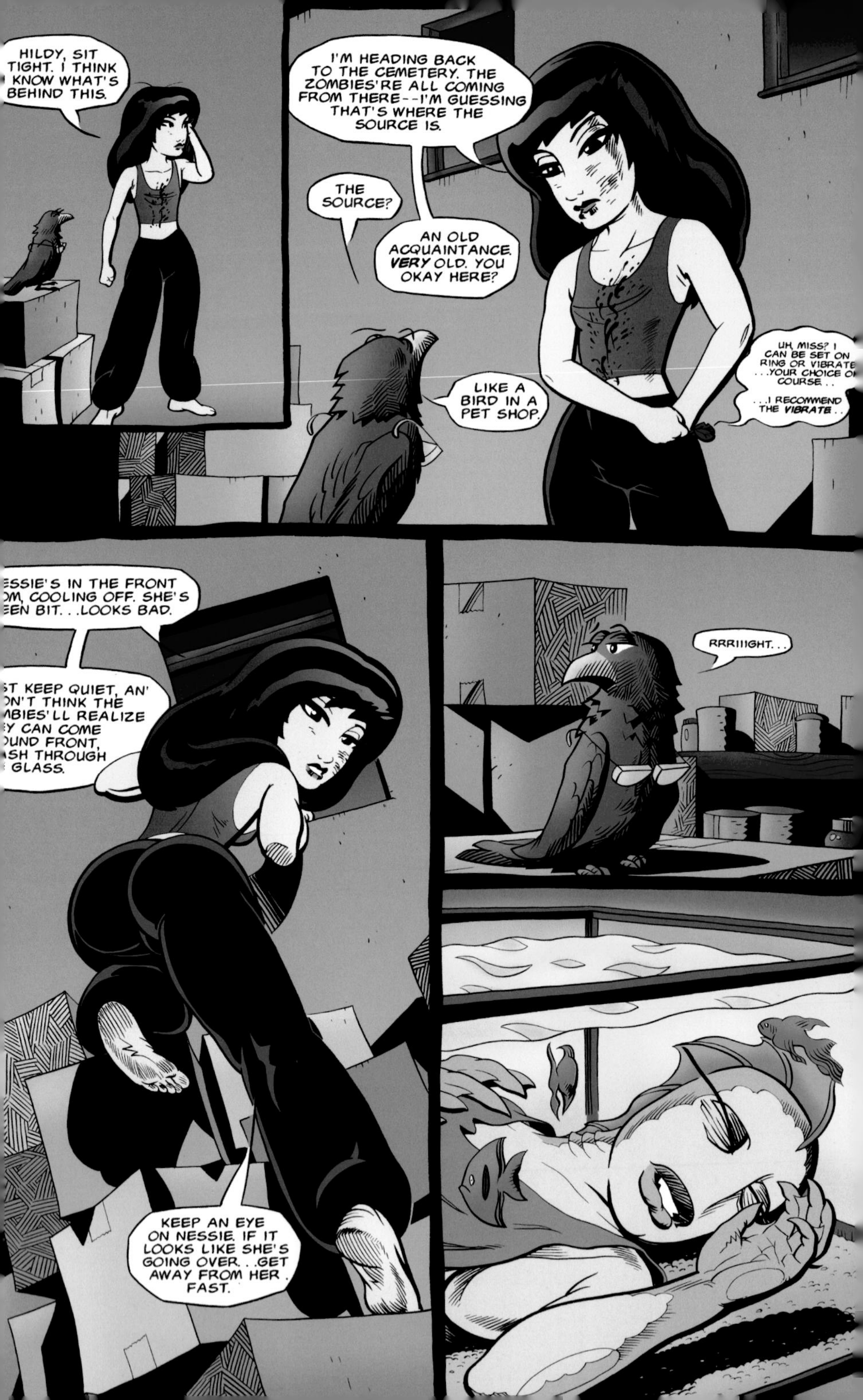
HILDY, SIT TIGHT. I THINK I KNOW WHAT'S BEHIND THIS.
I'M HEADING BACK TO THE CEMETERY. THE ZOMBIES'RE ALL COMING FROM THERE--I'M GUESSING THAT'S WHERE THE SOURCE IS.
THE SOURCE?
AN OLD ACQUAINTANCE. VERY OLD. YOU OKAY HERE?
LIKE A BIRD IN A PET SHOP.
UH, MISS? I CAN BE SET ON RING OR VIBRATE ...YOUR CHOICE OF COURSE...
...I RECOMMEND THE VIBRATE...
ESSIE'S IN THE FRONT OM, COOLING OFF. SHE'S EEN BIT...LOOKS BAD.
ST KEEP QUIET, AN' ON'T THINK THE MBIES'LL REALIZE EY CAN COME OUND FRONT, ASH THROUGH GLASS.
RRRIIIGHT...
KEEP AN EYE ON NESSIE. IF IT LOOKS LIKE SHE'S GOING OVER...GET AWAY FROM HER. FAST.

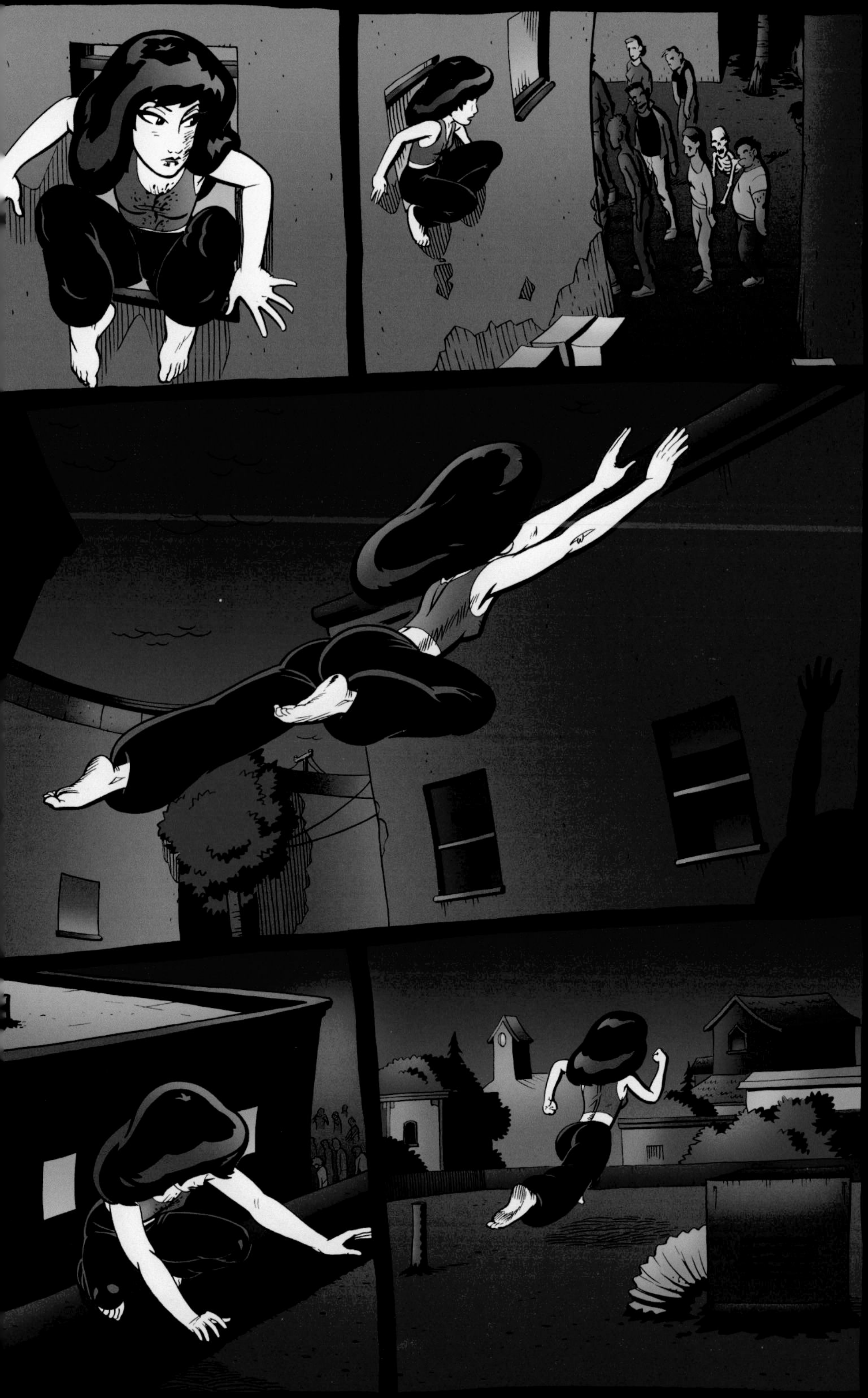

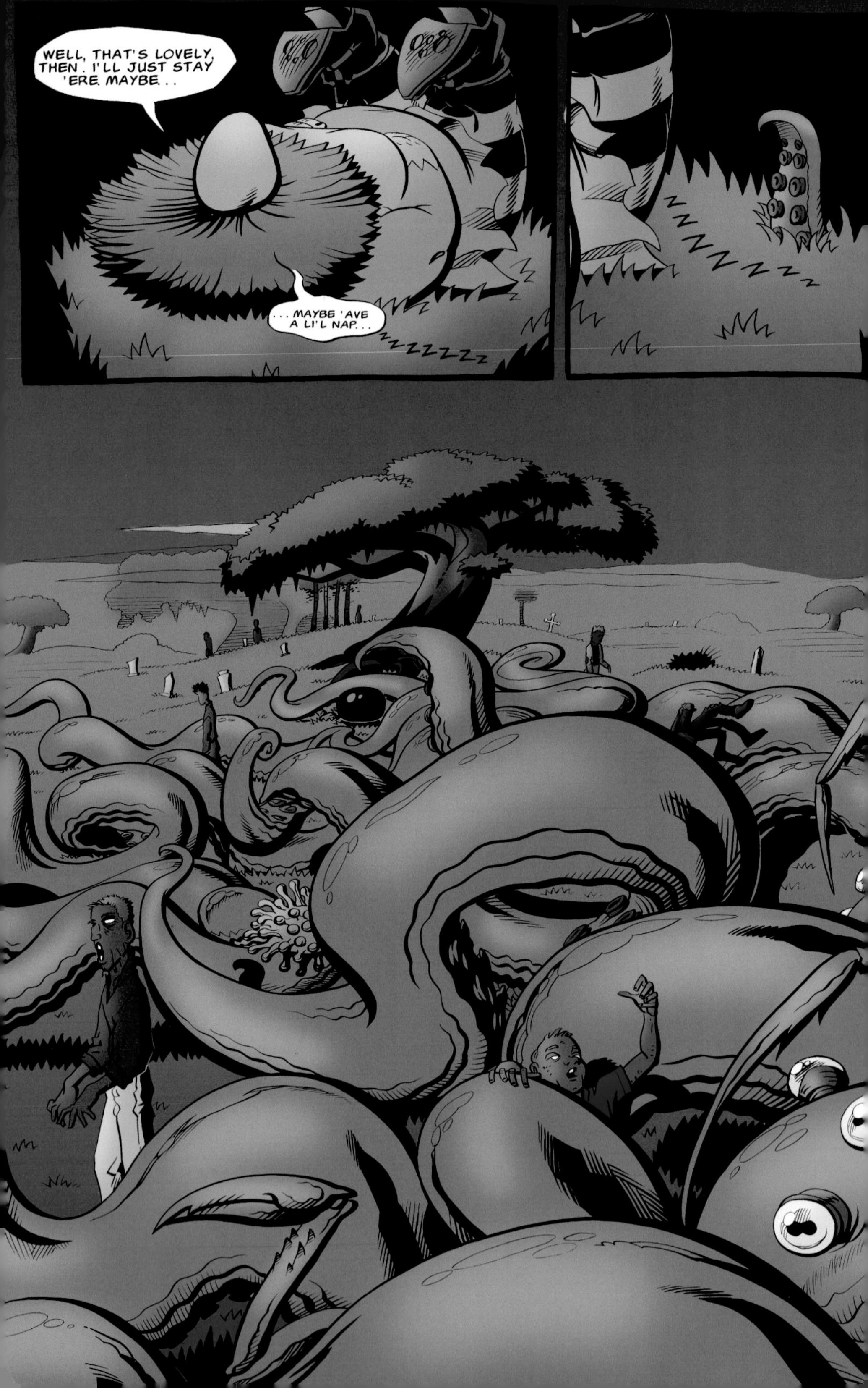
WELL, THAT'S LOVELY, THEN. I'LL JUST STAY 'ERE. MAYBE...
...MAYBE 'AVE A LI'L NAP...
ZZZZZZZ
ZZZZZZZZ

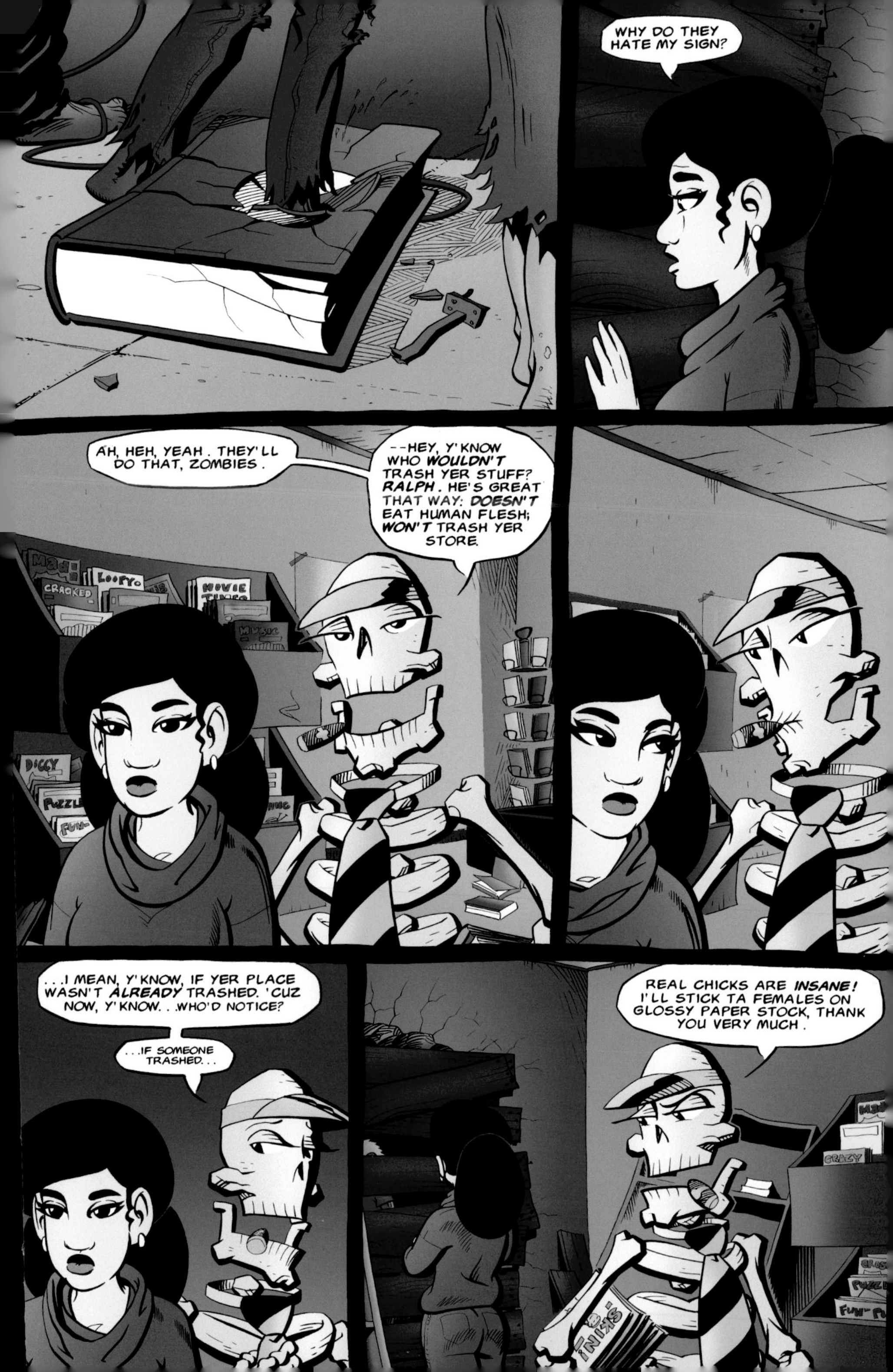
WHY DO THEY HATE MY SIGN?
AH, HEH, YEAH. THEY'LL DO THAT, ZOMBIES.
--HEY, Y'KNOW WHO WOULDN'T TRASH YER STUFF? RALPH. HE'S GREAT THAT WAY: DOESN'T EAT HUMAN FLESH; WON'T TRASH YER STORE.
MAD
LOOPY
CRACKED
MOVIE
MUSIC
DIGGY
PUZZLE
FUN-
...I MEAN, Y'KNOW, IF YER PLACE WASN'T ALREADY TRASHED. 'CUZ NOW, Y'KNOW...WHO'D NOTICE?
...IF SOMEONE TRASHED...
REAL CHICKS ARE INSANE! I'LL STICK TA FEMALES ON GLOSSY PAPER STOCK, THANK YOU VERY MUCH.
CRAZY
SKIN!
PUZZLE
FUN-

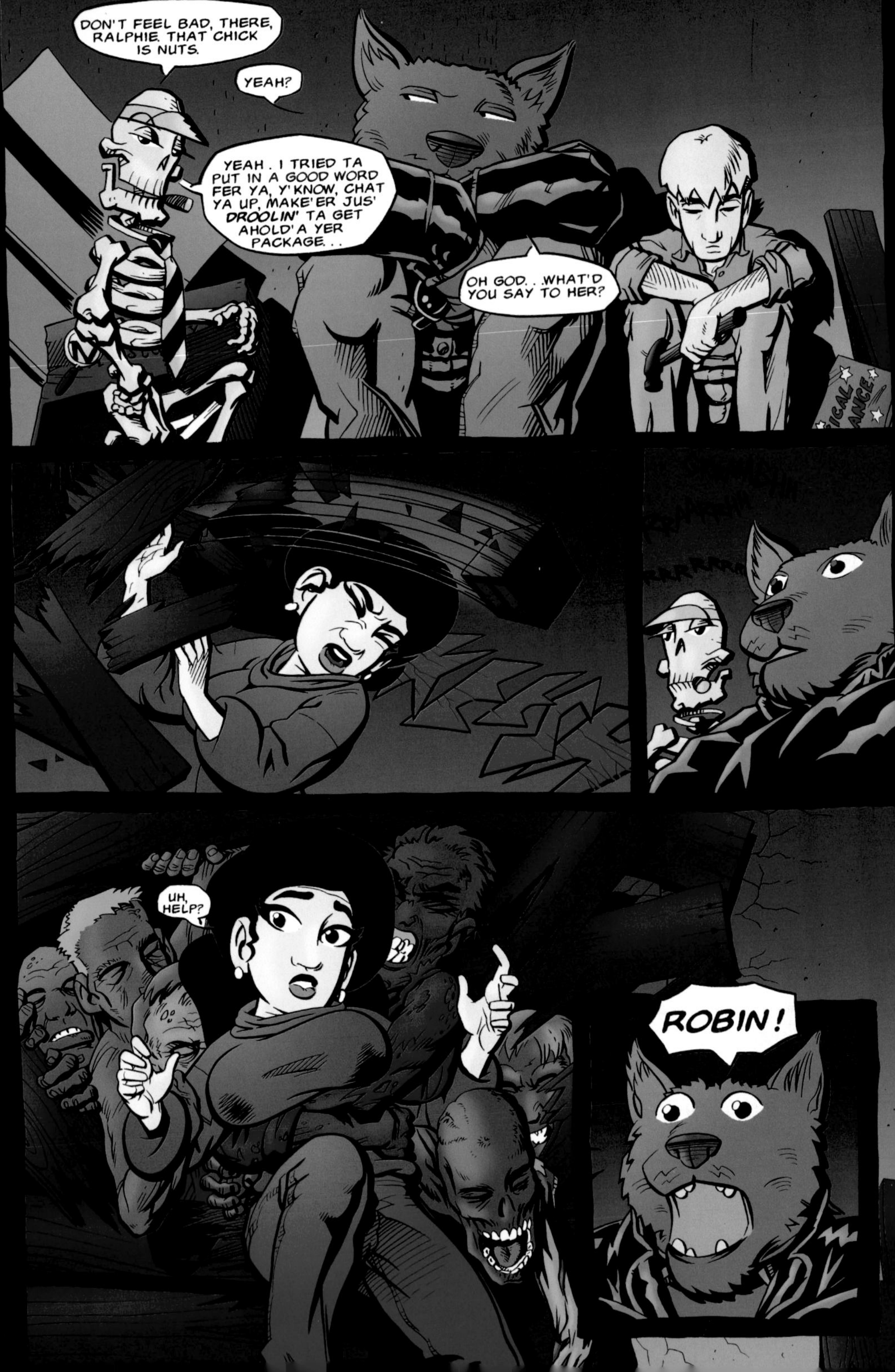
DON'T FEEL BAD, THERE, RALPHIE. THAT CHICK IS NUTS.
YEAH?
YEAH . I TRIED TA PUT IN A GOOD WORD FER YA, Y'KNOW, CHAT YA UP, MAKE'ER JUS' DROOLIN' TA GET AHOLD'A YER PACKAGE . .
OH GOD. . WHAT'D YOU SAY TO HER?
UH, HELP?
ROBIN!

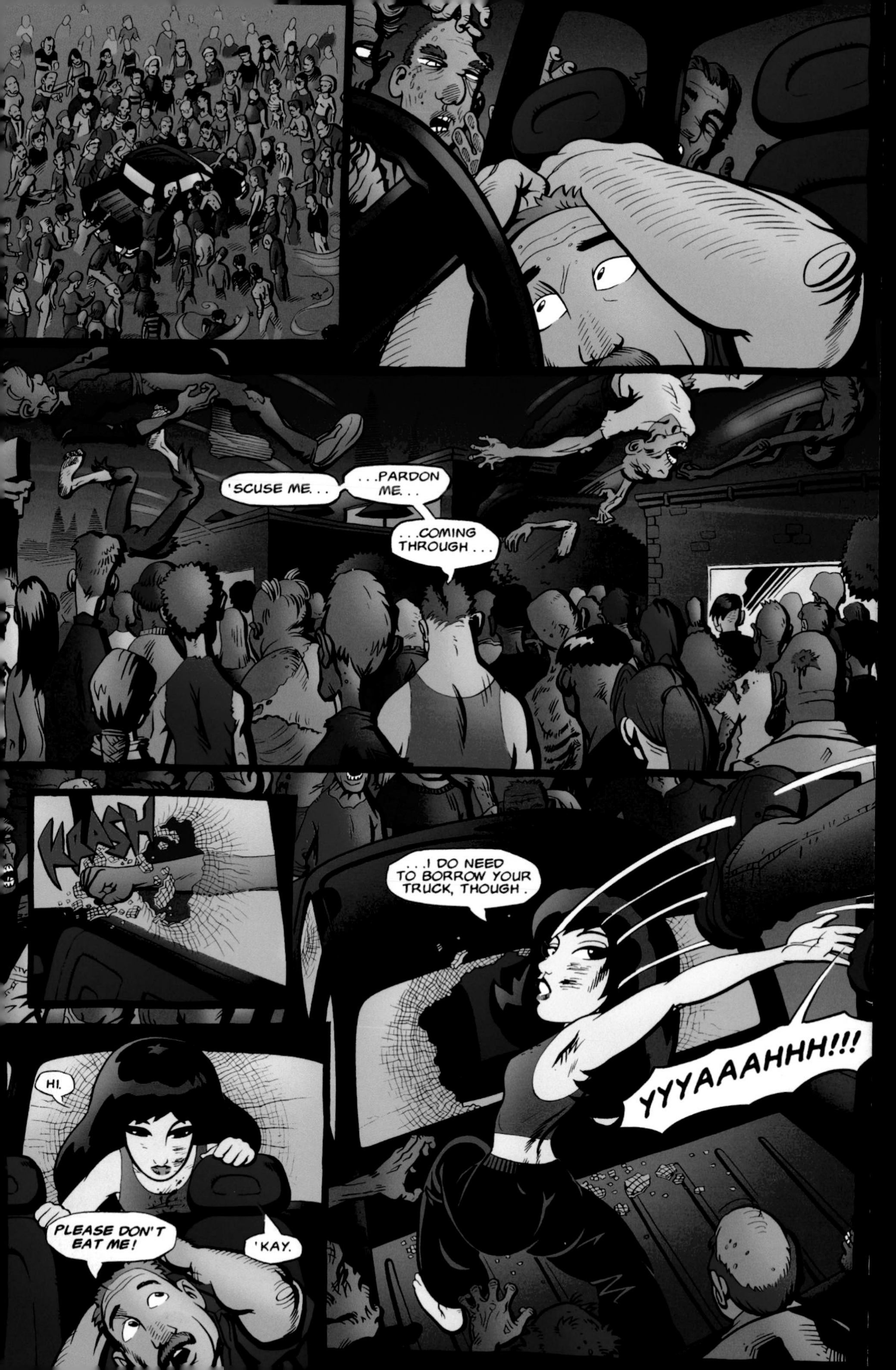
'SCUSE ME...
...PARDON ME...
...COMING THROUGH...
KRASH
...I DO NEED TO BORROW YOUR TRUCK, THOUGH.
YYYAAAHHH!!!
HI.
PLEASE DON'T EAT ME!
'KAY.

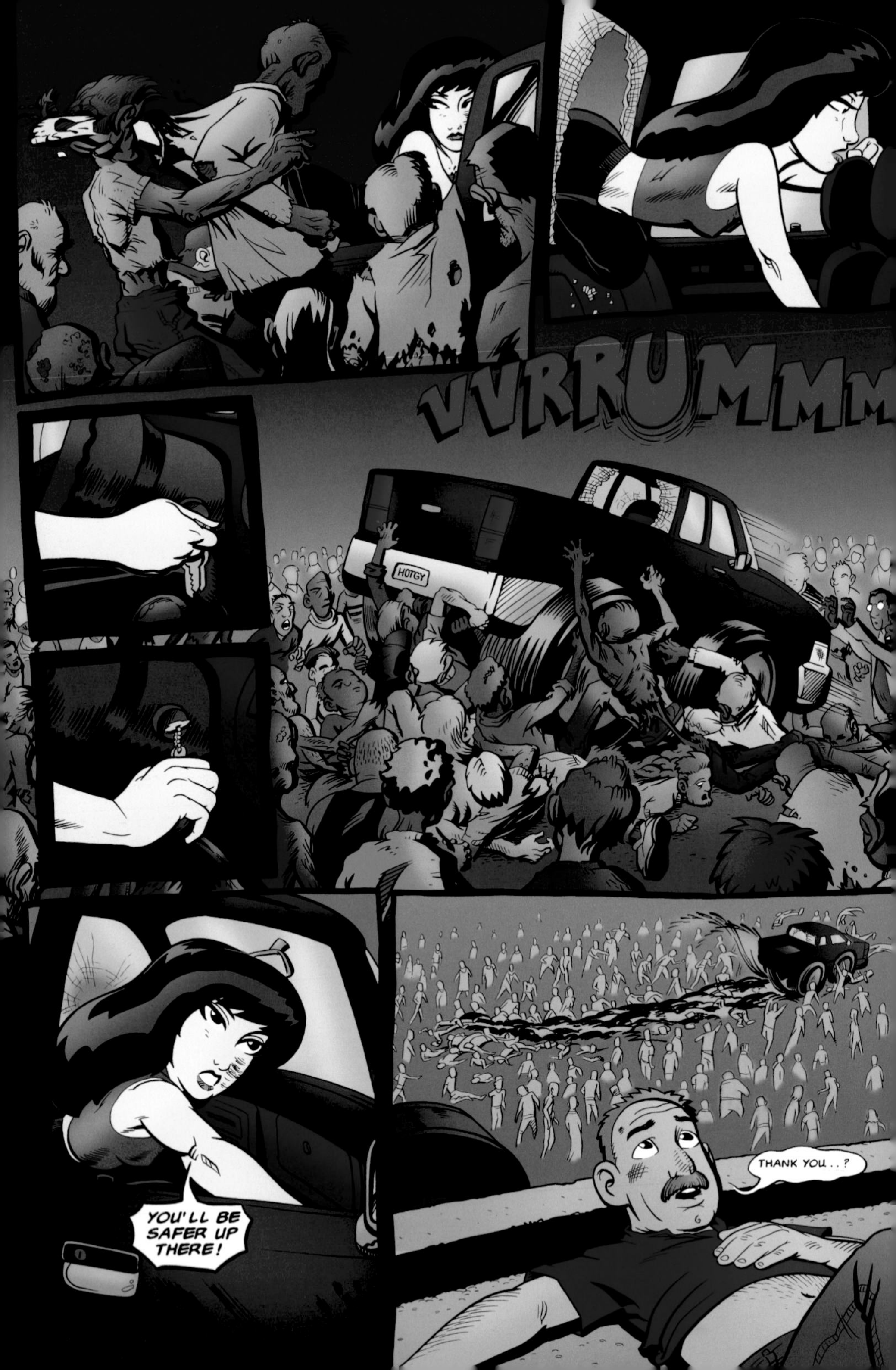
VVRRUMMM
HOTGY
YOU'LL BE SAFER UP THERE!
THANK YOU..?

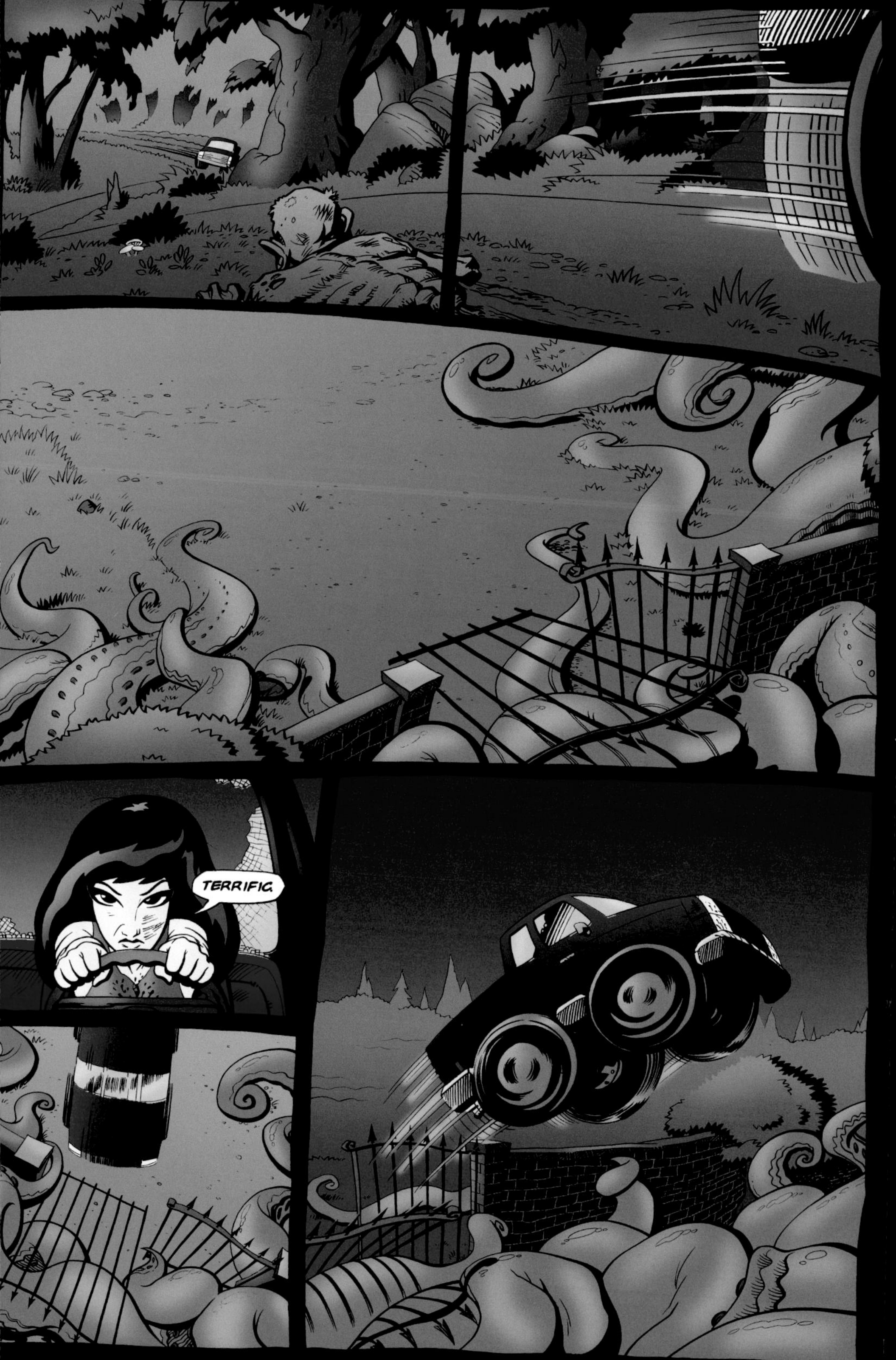
TERRIFIC.

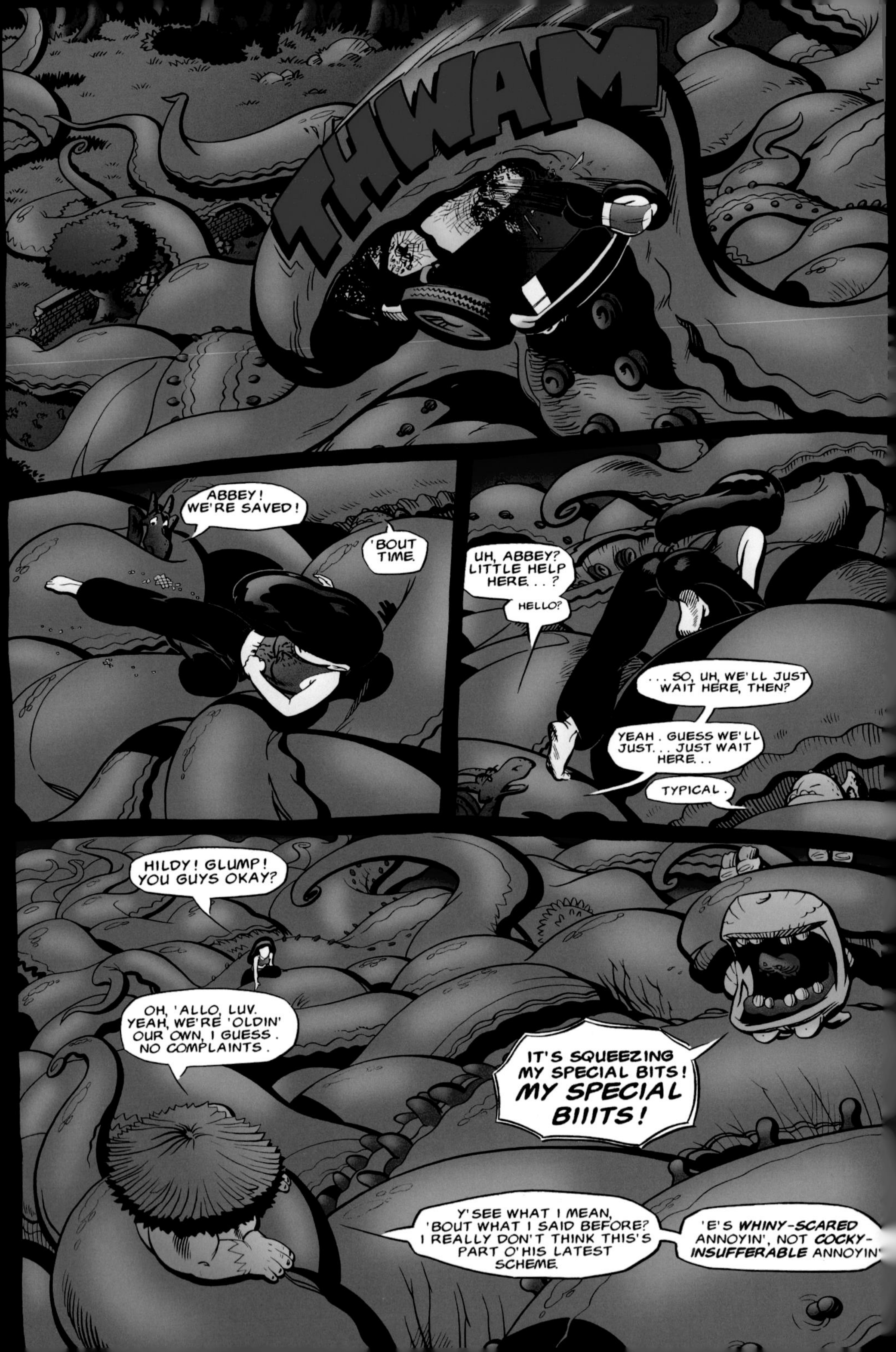
THWAM
ABBEY! WE'RE SAVED!
'BOUT TIME.
UH, ABBEY? LITTLE HELP HERE. . . ?
HELLO?
. . . SO, UH, WE'LL JUST WAIT HERE, THEN?
YEAH. GUESS WE'LL JUST. . . JUST WAIT HERE. . .
TYPICAL.
HILDY! GLUMP! YOU GUYS OKAY?
OH, 'ALLO, LUV. YEAH, WE'RE 'OLDIN' OUR OWN, I GUESS. NO COMPLAINTS.
IT'S SQUEEZING MY SPECIAL BITS! MY SPECIAL BIIITS!
Y'SEE WHAT I MEAN, 'BOUT WHAT I SAID BEFORE? I REALLY DON'T THINK THIS'S PART O'HIS LATEST SCHEME.
'E'S WHINY-SCARED ANNOYIN', NOT COCKY-INSUFFERABLE ANNOYIN'

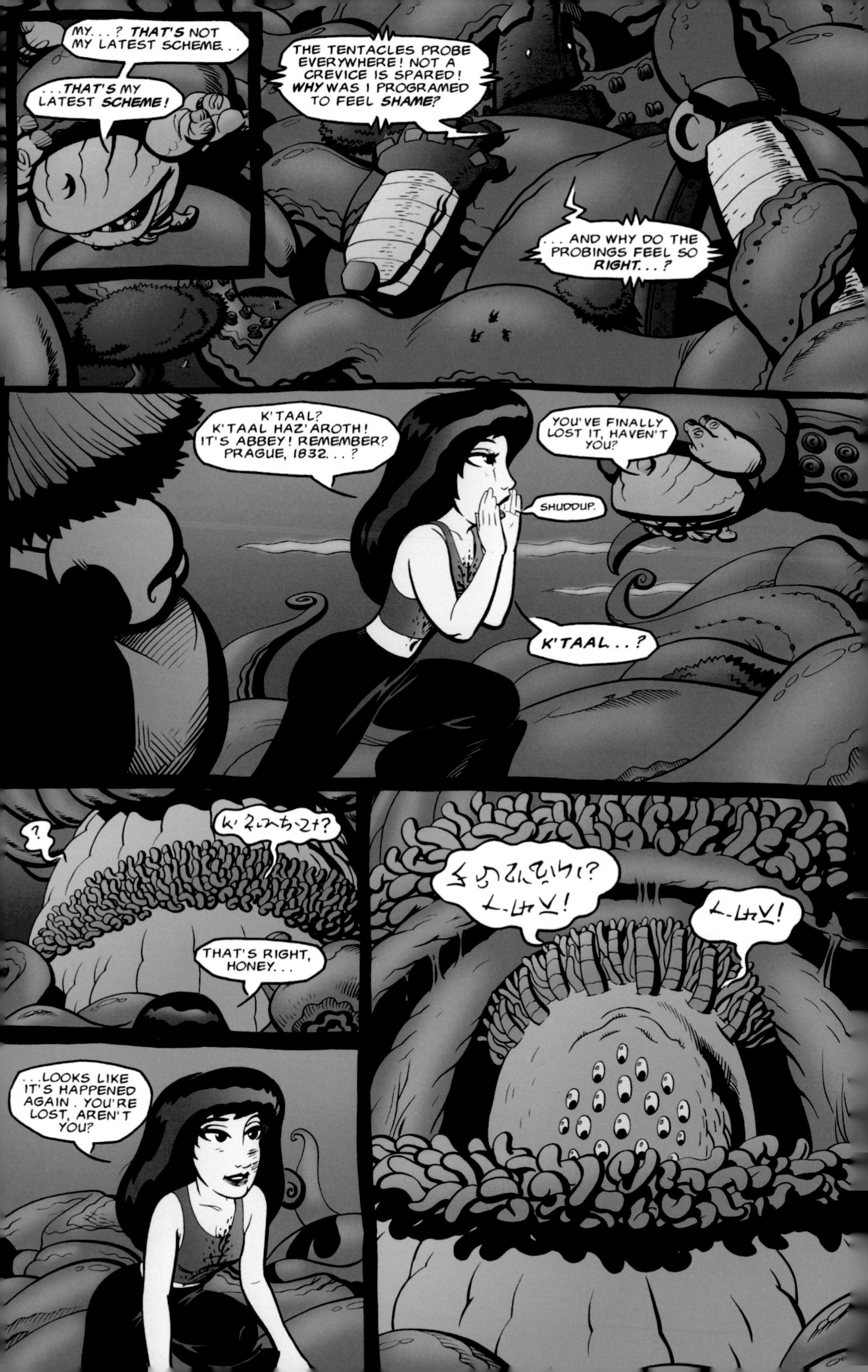
MY. . . ? THAT'S NOT MY LATEST SCHEME. . .
. . .THAT'S MY LATEST SCHEME!
THE TENTACLES PROBE EVERYWHERE! NOT A CREVICE IS SPARED! WHY WAS I PROGRAMED TO FEEL SHAME?
. . . AND WHY DO THE PROBINGS FEEL SO RIGHT. . . ?
K'TAAL? K'TAAL HAZ'AROTH! IT'S ABBEY! REMEMBER? PRAGUE, 1832. . . ?
YOU'VE FINALLY LOST IT, HAVEN'T YOU?
SHUDDUP.
K'TAAL. . . ?
?
THAT'S RIGHT, HONEY. . .
. . .LOOKS LIKE IT'S HAPPENED AGAIN. YOU'RE LOST, AREN'T YOU?

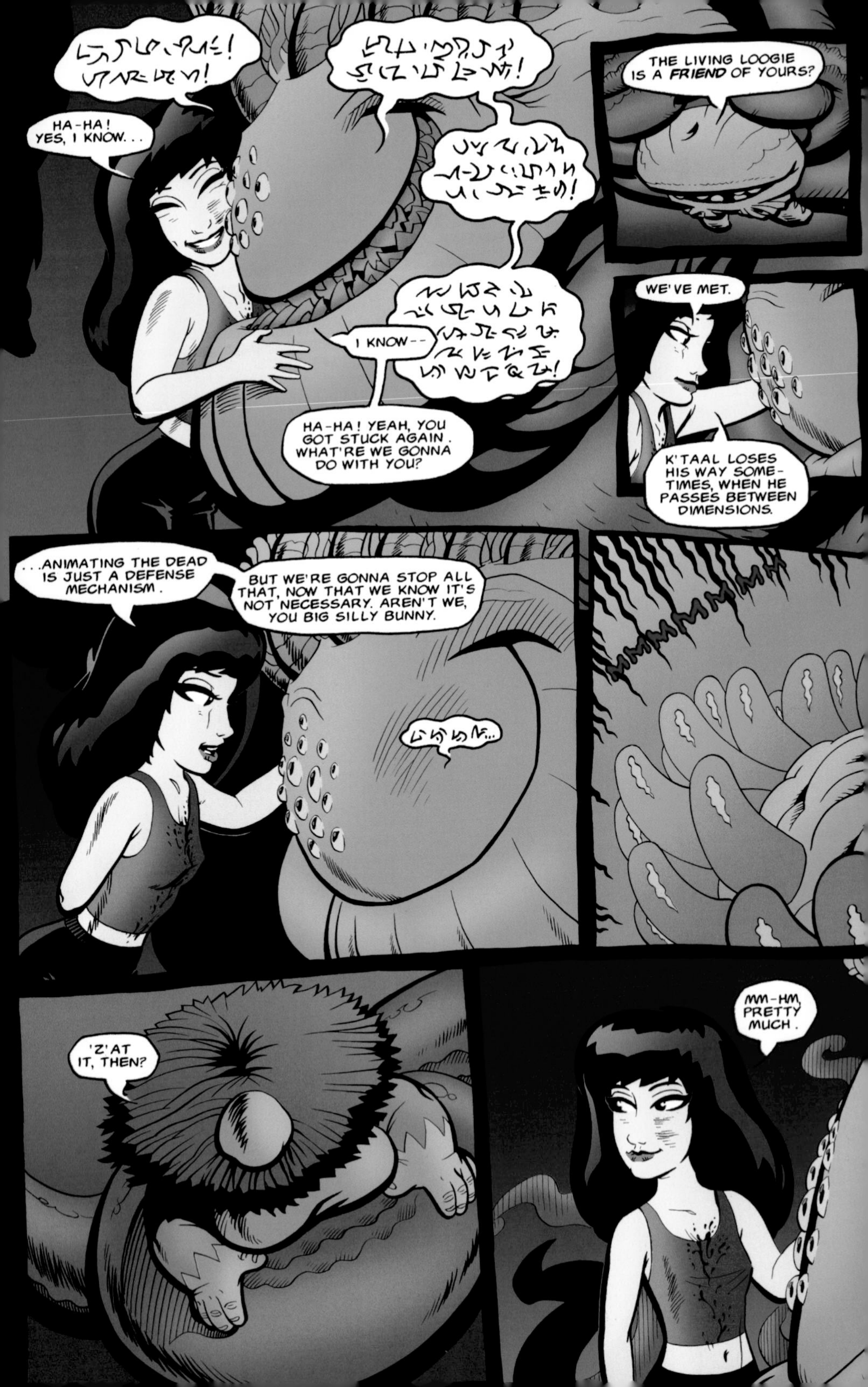
HA-HA! YES, I KNOW...
I KNOW--
HA-HA! YEAH, YOU GOT STUCK AGAIN. WHAT'RE WE GONNA DO WITH YOU?
THE LIVING LOOGIE IS A *FRIEND* OF YOURS?
WE'VE MET.
K'TAAL LOSES HIS WAY SOMETIMES, WHEN HE PASSES BETWEEN DIMENSIONS.
...ANIMATING THE DEAD IS JUST A DEFENSE MECHANISM.
BUT WE'RE GONNA STOP ALL THAT, NOW THAT WE KNOW IT'S NOT NECESSARY. AREN'T WE, YOU BIG SILLY BUNNY.
'Z'AT IT, THEN?
MM-HM, PRETTY MUCH.

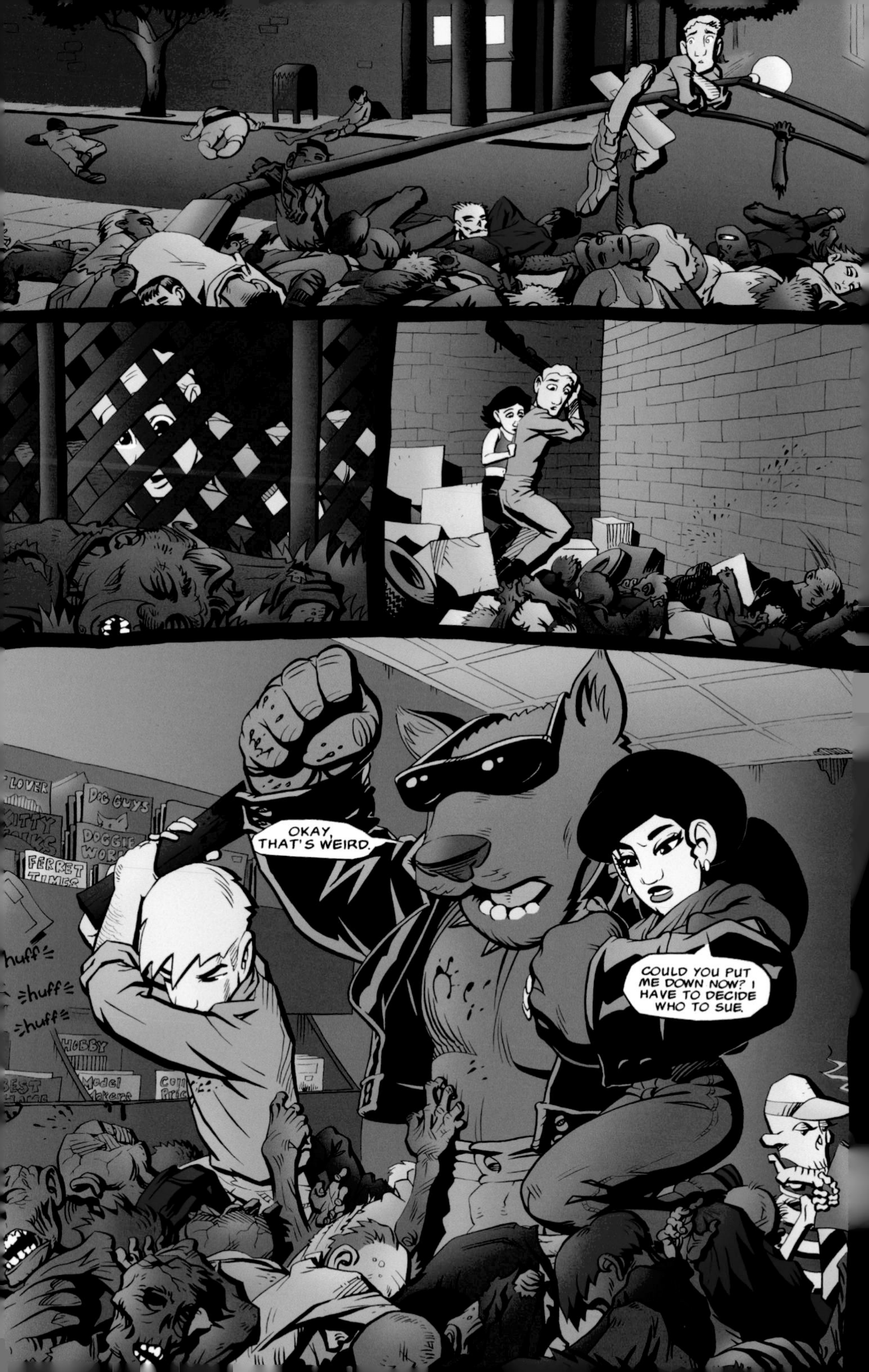
DOG GUYS
FERRET TIMES
OKAY, THAT'S WEIRD.
huff
huff
huff
HOBBY
COULD YOU PUT ME DOWN NOW? I HAVE TO DECIDE WHO TO SUE.

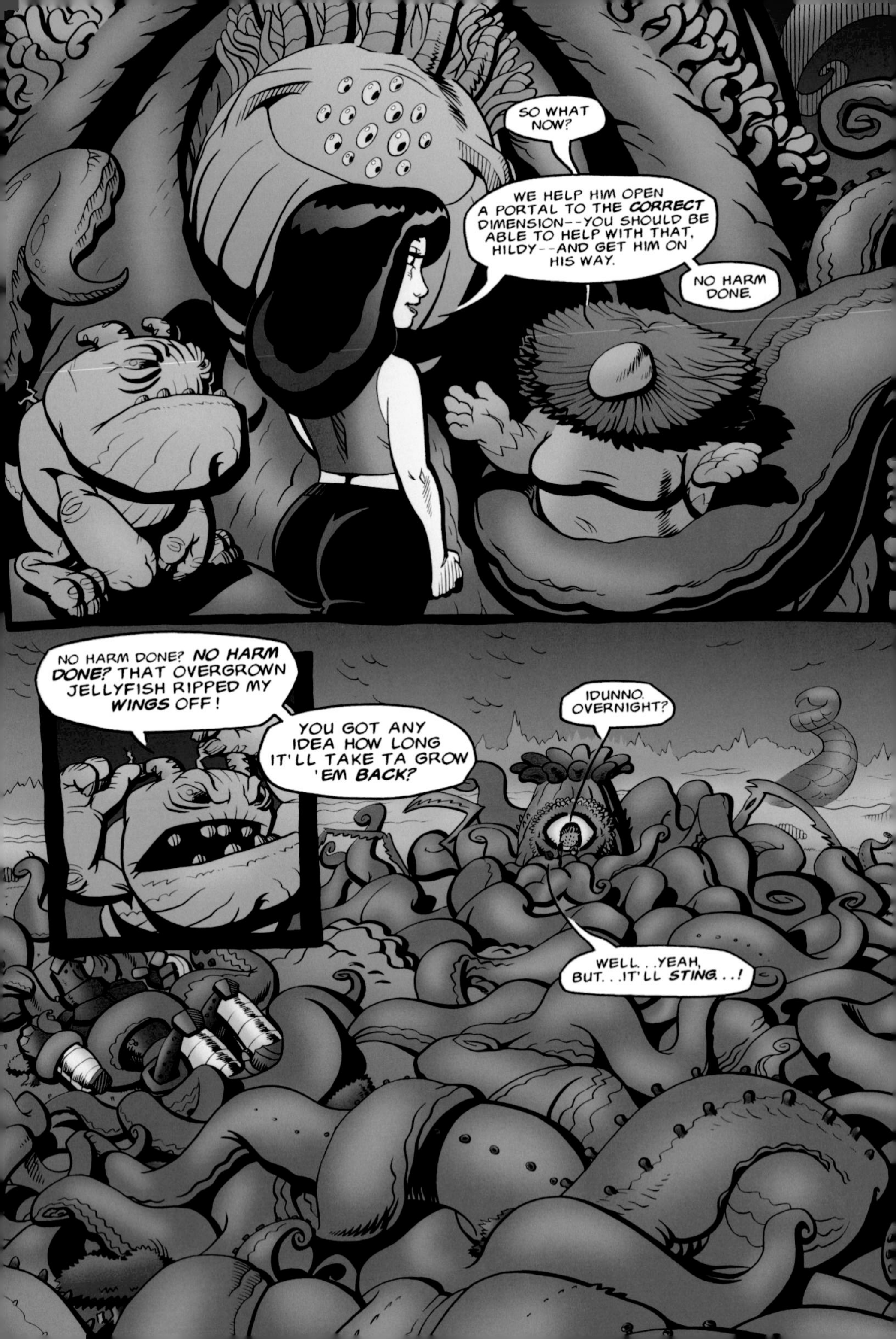
SO WHAT NOW?
WE HELP HIM OPEN A PORTAL TO THE CORRECT DIMENSION--YOU SHOULD BE ABLE TO HELP WITH THAT, HILDY--AND GET HIM ON HIS WAY.
NO HARM DONE.
NO HARM DONE? NO HARM DONE? THAT OVERGROWN JELLYFISH RIPPED MY WINGS OFF!
YOU GOT ANY IDEA HOW LONG IT'LL TAKE TA GROW 'EM BACK?
IDUNNO. OVERNIGHT?
WELL. . .YEAH, BUT. . .IT'LL STING. . .!

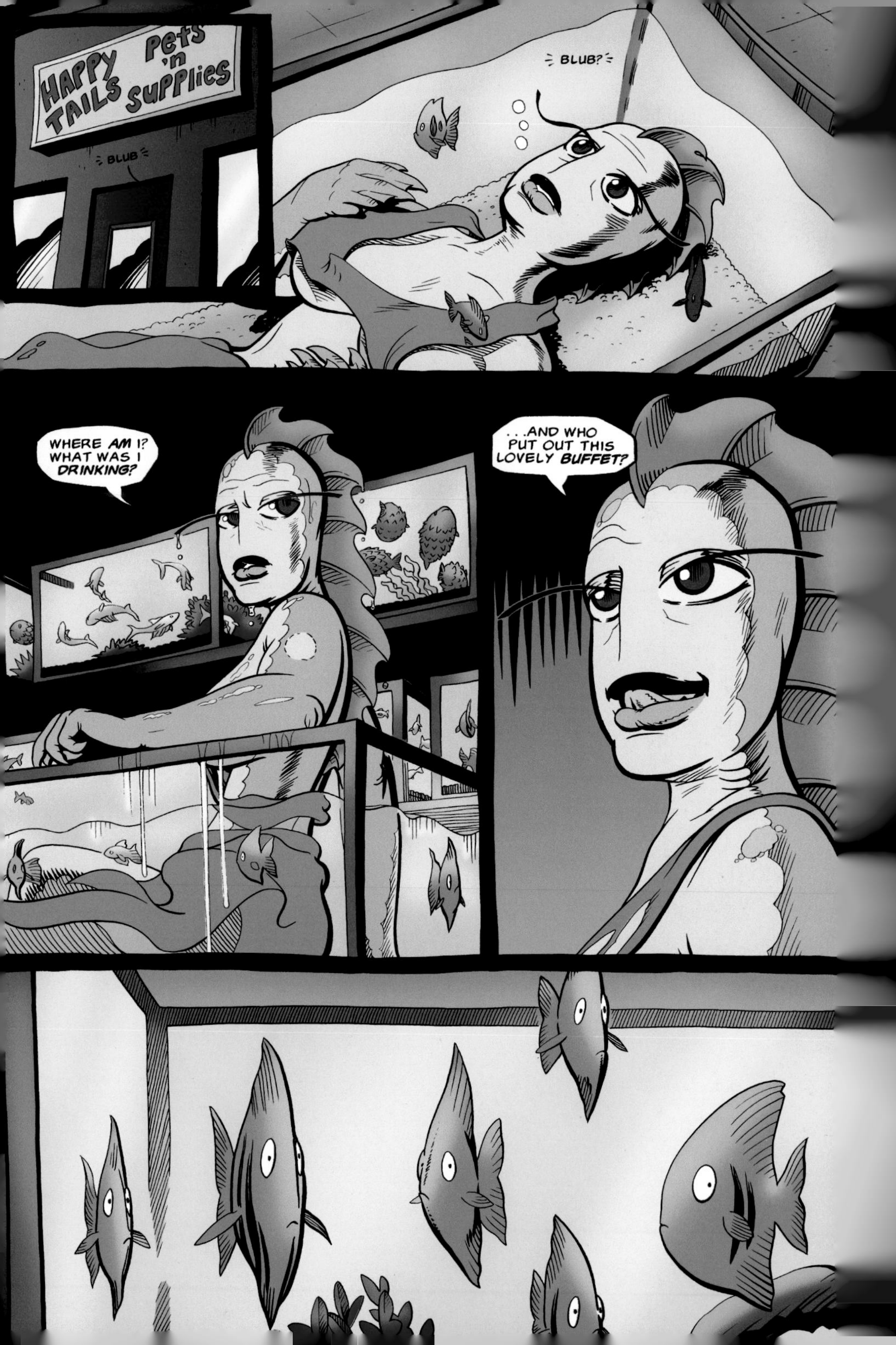
HAPPY TAILS Pets 'n Supplies
BLUB
BLUB?
WHERE AM I? WHAT WAS I DRINKING?
. . .AND WHO PUT OUT THIS LOVELY BUFFET?

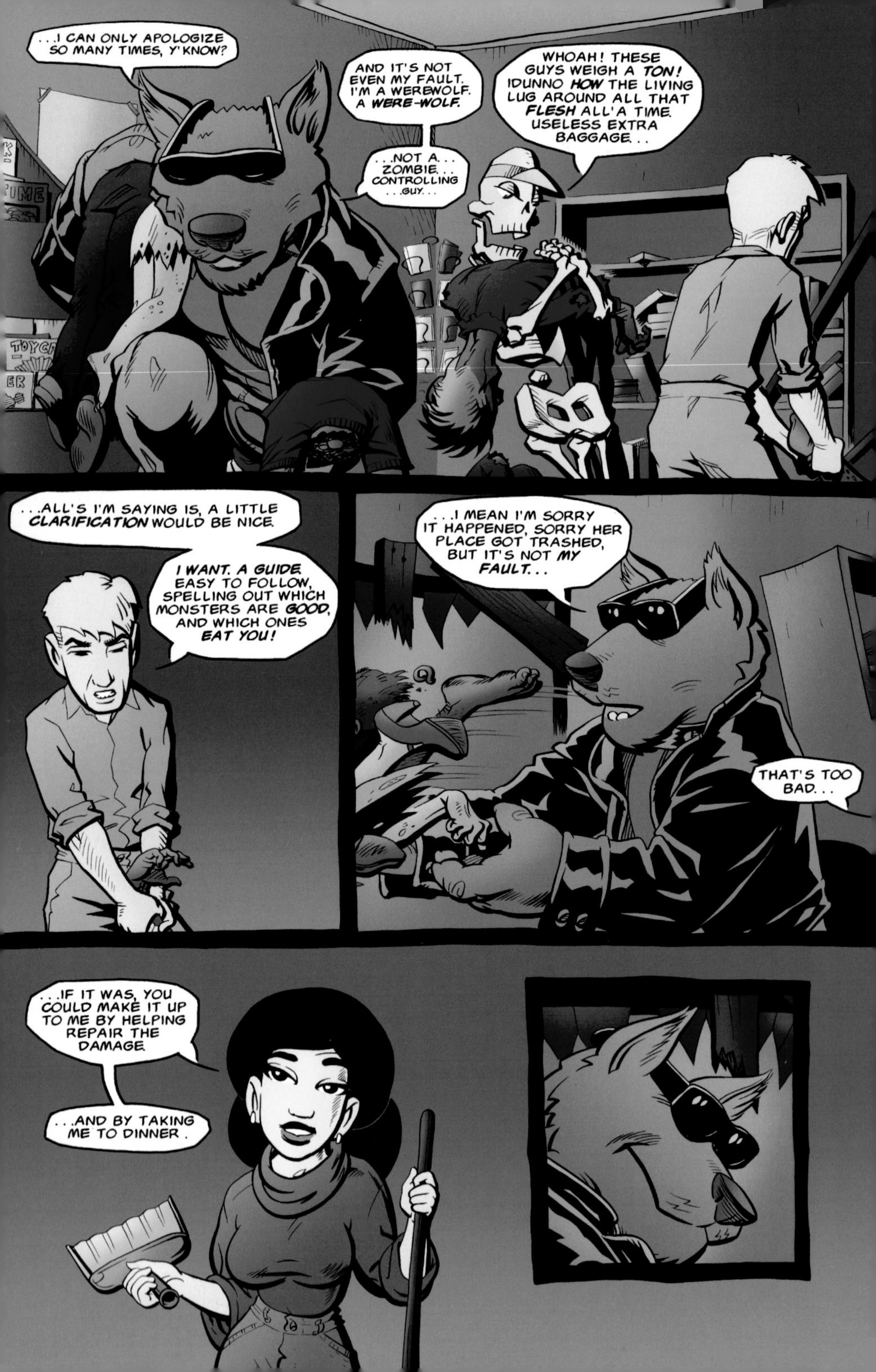
...I CAN ONLY APOLOGIZE SO MANY TIMES, Y'KNOW?
AND IT'S NOT EVEN MY FAULT. I'M A WEREWOLF. A WERE-WOLF.
...NOT A... ZOMBIE... CONTROLLING ...GUY...
WHOAH! THESE GUYS WEIGH A TON! IDUNNO HOW THE LIVING LUG AROUND ALL THAT FLESH ALL'A TIME. USELESS EXTRA BAGGAGE...
...ALL'S I'M SAYING IS, A LITTLE CLARIFICATION WOULD BE NICE.
I WANT. A GUIDE. EASY TO FOLLOW, SPELLING OUT WHICH MONSTERS ARE GOOD, AND WHICH ONES EAT YOU!
...I MEAN I'M SORRY IT HAPPENED, SORRY HER PLACE GOT TRASHED, BUT IT'S NOT MY FAULT...
THAT'S TOO BAD...
...IF IT WAS, YOU COULD MAKE IT UP TO ME BY HELPING REPAIR THE DAMAGE.
...AND BY TAKING ME TO DINNER.

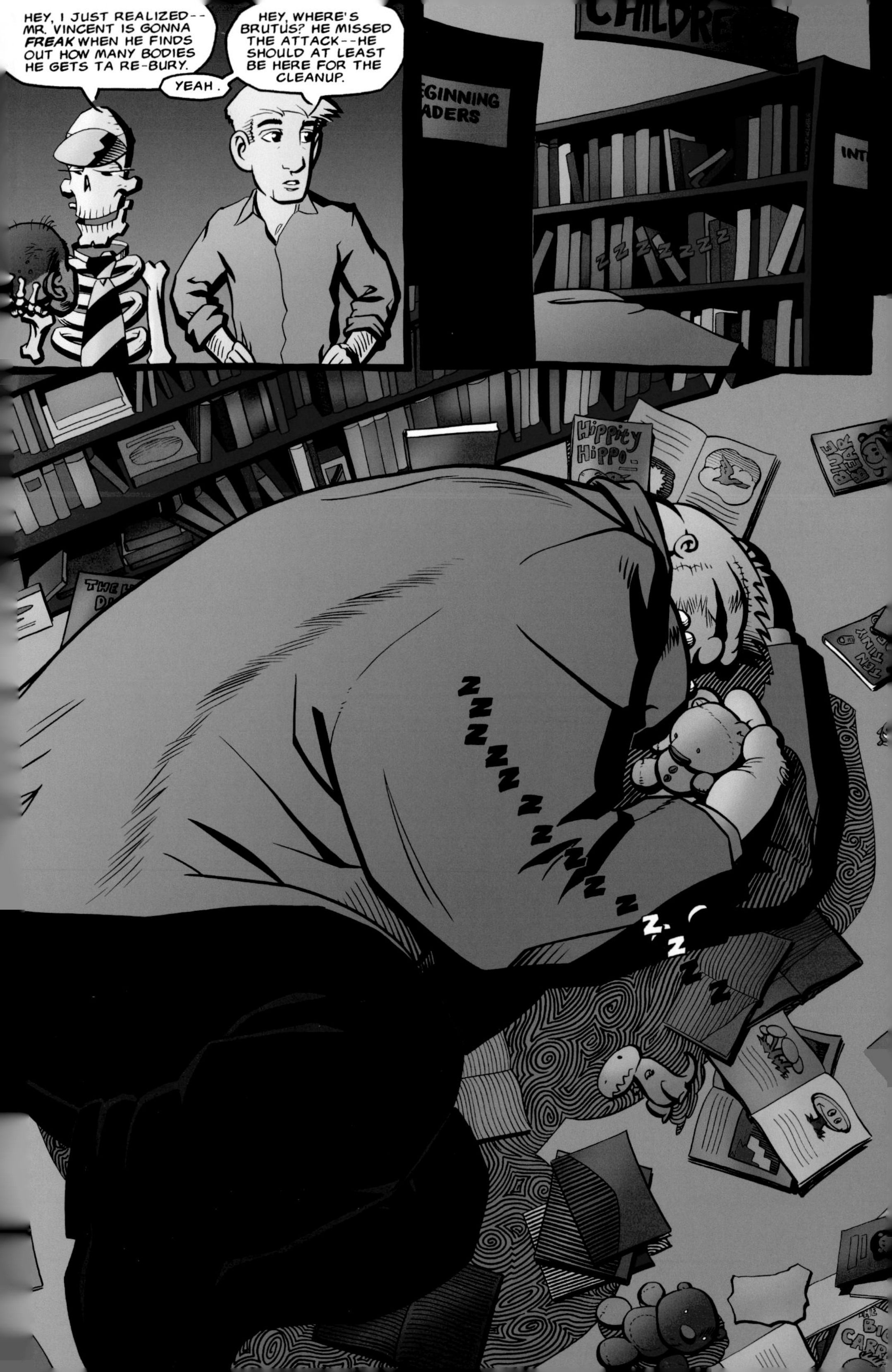
HEY, I JUST REALIZED--
MR. VINCENT IS GONNA
FREAK WHEN HE FINDS
OUT HOW MANY BODIES
HE GETS TA RE-BURY.
YEAH.
HEY, WHERE'S BRUTUS? HE MISSED THE ATTACK--HE SHOULD AT LEAST BE HERE FOR THE CLEANUP.
Hippity Hippo
BLUE BEAR
TEN TINY
ZZZZZZZZZZZZ

**Also by Richard Moore:**
Boneyard in color:
Vol. 1, $10.95
Vol. 2, $11.95
Vol. 3, $12.95
in black & white:
Vols. 5-6, $9.95 each

P&H: $3 1st item, $1 each addt'l.

We have over 200 titles,
write for our color catalog:
NBM
40 Exchange Pl., Suite 1308
New York, NY 10005
www.nbmpublishing.com

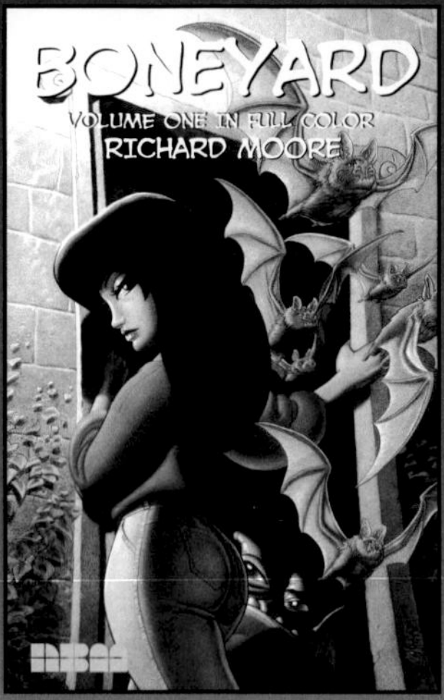
BONEYARD
VOLUME ONE IN FULL COLOR
RICHARD MOORE

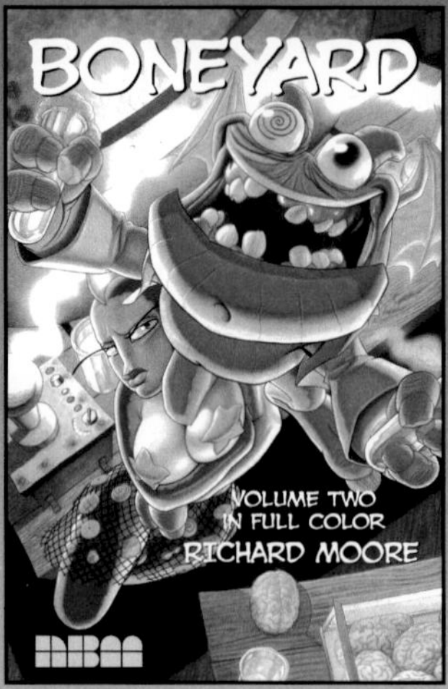
BONEYARD
VOLUME TWO
IN FULL COLOR
RICHARD MOORE

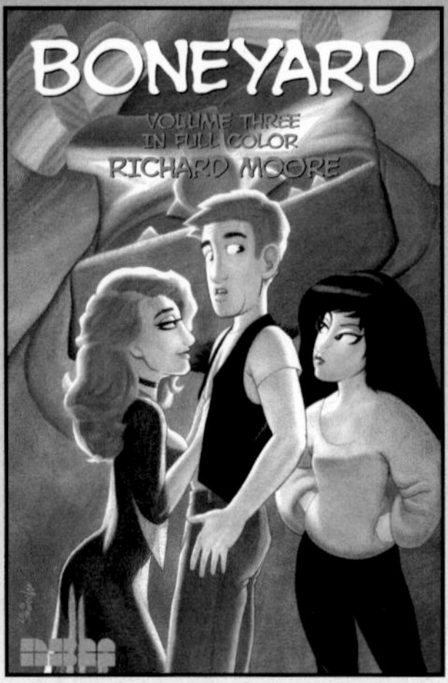
BONEYARD
VOLUME THREE
IN FULL COLOR
RICHARD MOORE

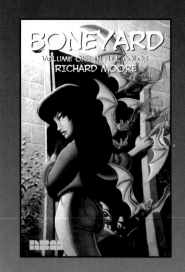